The Jharro Grove Saga: Book Five

Priestess of War

Book Ten of The Bowl of Souls

By Trevor H. Cooley

Books by Trevor H. Cooley

Noose Jumpers:
Book One: Noose Jumpers

The Bowl of Souls Series:
The Moonrat Saga
Book One: EYE of the MOONRAT
Book 1.5: HILT'S PRIDE
Book Two: MESSENGER of the DARK PROPHET
Book Three: HUNT of the BANDHAM
Book Four: THE WAR of STARDEON
Book Five: MOTHER of the MOONRAT
The Jharro Grove Saga
Book One: TARAH WOODBLADE
Book Two: PROTECTOR of the GROVE
Book Three: THE OGRE APPRENTICE
Book Four: THE TROLL KING
Book Five: PRIESTESS of WAR
Book Six: BEHEMOTH
The Dark Prophet Saga
Book One: Sir Edge
Book Two: Halfbreeds (2021)

The Wizard of Mysteries
Book One: Tallow Jones Wizard Detective
Book Two: Tallow Jones, Blood Trail
Book Three:(Upcoming)

Dedication

For Justin: My brother. My friend. In many ways you grew up with the characters in my books as much as I did. They were always a part of our games and I'm certain I bored you to death describing my story ideas. In many ways I patterned a lot of Fist's attitudes off of you. Like him, I can count on you to make the right and big-hearted decision in every situation. I love you, man.

Table of Contents

Chapter One

A few hundred yards away from Talon, two enormous armies faced each other in a wide valley. A meeting was being held in the center that would determine the future of those armies and all of Malaroo. None of them knew that an act of betrayal was planned. Not yet.

Talon clung to the tree she was hiding in and looked down on the clearing below. Durza knelt in the grass meekly, her arms folded while two Roo-Tan scouts with their magic wooden weapons watched her closely. One of them had the point of his gray sword pointed at her chest, while the other had an arrow drawn and ready to fire.

"Don't ya get pointy please," Durza said, smiling at the two men. The gorc's head was topped with a filthy blond wig and she wore a ragged blue dress. Like most gorcs, her skin was a leathery mottled green, but her cheeks were covered in an obscene amount of rouge and her lips had been painted pink. "I waits nicely."

"Silence, filthy thing!" the man with the sword spat with distaste. "Be grateful we did not gut you on sight."

Talon did not move, but a low hiss escaped her lips. If her master's instructions had not been explicit, Talon would have leapt down and slaughtered both men. Nevertheless, it was a struggle. She opened herself up to the calming magic of the black robe she wore, letting it soothe her anger.

On one level, she understood the men's repulsion. Talon herself thought Durza's insistence on attempting the human form of beauty ridiculous. Still, that was for her to think. These Roo-Tan men had no right. She hoped they did not give her further reason to attack them.

"I will be quiet. I is a quiet lady. I . . ." Durza's voice trailed off and her back straightened. She pointed excitedly into the trees with one dirty finger and declared, "They come! That man and Deathclaws. They come! Uh, and a monster and a lady and another man!"

Talon shifted her position in the trees and glanced in the direction Durza indicated. Moments later, Sir Edge and his party came into view, led by a young man with blond hair. The named warrior was accompanied by his rogue horse and an unfamiliar woman wearing leather armor, but Talon barely spared them a glance. Her eyes were on her brother.

Talon hadn't seen Deathclaw in many months. Not since the day she had attacked the Sampo refugees at the beginning of Ewwie's war. The darkness within her surged towards the surface of her mind. She wanted to launch herself at him, caress him, claw him, bite him, taste his blood, and revel in the pain as he bit her back. Talon fought the compulsion down and stayed still. To reveal herself now would seem an attack and she needed them to listen to her master's warning.

Deathclaw looked different in so many ways. He was broader at the shoulders and walked more upright than before and, in addition to the sword strapped across his back, he now wore a bandoleer of throwing knives across his chest. But perhaps strangest of all, the raptoid had somehow grown a pair of lips that pulled back from his teeth in a snarl as he saw Durza.

Talon's brother darted forward, rushing past the two Roo-Tan men. He gripped Durza's throat in one powerful hand. His voice was a familiar rasp. "Where is Talon, gorc?"

Durza's eyes bulged with surprise. "Ack! Death . . . Claws! Don't hurt . . . Durza!" She clutched at his wrist. "I'm . . . friend. 'Member me?"

"Don't hurt her, Deathclaw," said Sir Edge. "We don't know that she's done anything wrong."

There was a casual tone of command in his voice. He was used to issuing orders and even more, he was used to them being obeyed. Talon blinked. Surely Deathclaw would not obey such a lazily given command. She was going to have to announce her presence and distract him before he killed Durza. To her surprise, the raptoid released the gorc as ordered.

Deathclaw hissed and flinched as he sniffed at the hand that had clutched the gorc. "She stinks!"

"That's my perfoom!" Durza said with a frown, clutching at her throat and feeling for punctures. "Wanted to smell nice. Why you scratchedes me?" she complained. "Don't wanna talk to you no ways. I comes to talk to Sir Edge."

"We will take charge of her," said Sir Edge to the two Roo-Tan scouts. "You can go back to your work. You too, Aldie."

The two scouts accepted his command as readily as Deathclaw. They stepped back and lowered their weapons, then nodded and headed off into the trees, the blond-headed man trotting reluctantly after them. Sir Edge focused on Durza.

"I'm Sir Edge," he said, a tone of reassurance in his voice. He walked towards her but stopped before coming within arm's reach.

The rogue horse began prowling the perimeter of the clearing and Deathclaw turned his head, scanning the trees. Talon wondered if they suspected she was nearby. The pheromones she had emitted would keep them from sniffing her out, but it was still possible she could be seen. She held perfectly still, grateful when her brother's eyes slid past her place of concealment.

"You are Sir Edge?" Durza said, her tone hopeful, though she already knew this to be true. She had sensed his spirit when he had visited their master's house and Durza's bewitching magic never failed her. The gorc stood, adjusting her wig and brushing off the skirts of her dress. "I am Durza. I'm a good friend. My Master tells me to find you."

"Why?" Sir Edge said. "Who is your master?"

"My Master is the Stranger Man," she replied.

The man frowned.

"The Stranger is in the meeting with the Protector right now," said the tall woman with the bent nose. She wore armor made of runed leather and carried a gray quarterstaff strapped across her back along with a bow and quiver. "He seems to be on Aloysius' side."

"No!" said Durza. "He taked him!"

"I will find out the truth here." The woman approached the gorc, reaching out her hand.

"It might not be wise to touch her," Sir Edge warned. "We don't know-."

The woman gripped the gorc's shoulder. Talon tensed as she saw a flash of spirit magic pass from Durza into the woman. The woman gasped, her eyes wide.

"Whatchoo doin'? That's my brains!" Durza said in alarm, pulling her shoulder from the woman's grasp.

The woman stepped back, letting out a slow breath. She swallowed. "She's telling the truth. She and Deathclaw's sister have been living with the Stranger for months. Talon came here with her. She's around here somewhere."

Talon's eyes widened. How had the woman known?

"It's over here!" said a child-like voice.

Talon glanced down and saw that a little dark skinned elf girl stood below the tree and was pointing up at her. Another surprise. Talon had no time to figure out where the child had come from because Deathclaw was there in a rush.

Talon's brother shot up the tree towards her. Her breath caught in her throat and she barely had the presence of mind to suck in her gut and avoid being raked by his slashing claws. He grasped a handful of her robe instead.

"Deathclaw!" she hissed and launched herself at him.

She wrapped her arms around him and barely avoided his biting teeth as her weight pulled him away from the trunk. The two of them fell towards the earth below, breaking branches as they went. They hit the ground in a tangle, Deathclaw hissing in frustration that she was able to squirm away from his ripping claws.

Talon managed to get one foot up between them and shoved herself out of his grasp. She rolled to her feet and let out a plaintive chirp in the old language of the raptoids, a plea for mercy. She held out both hands, her claws spread wide. "Sstop! My masster ssends me!"

Deathclaw was unmoved by her gesture. He leapt to his feet and drew his sword in one smooth motion. Talon knew the burning pain that sword could inflict. "You will not get away this time!"

"No!" cried Durza. "Don't hurts her!"

Deathclaw lunged at her and lashed out with his sword. She ducked under the blow and rolled to the side, narrowly avoiding the follow-up slash of his tail barb. From the corner of her eyes, she saw that Sir Edge had drawn his own swords and was keeping pace with them, looking for an opening.

"I am not here to kill!" Talon said insistently. She stepped backward, avoiding another slash of Deathclaw's sword.

She never had understood his determination to kill her. In the past Talon had seen it as sort of a grand game, a game of pain she had been eager to play. But since the work of the Prophet and the Stranger to help her keep her madness at bay, Talon's confusion had grown. What had she done to deserve the anger and determination that burned so brightly in his eyes?

Deathclaw maneuvered around Talon, forcing her to stay between him and the bonding wizard, Sir Edge. That other beast, the rogue horse that Sir Edge rode, growled ready to leap.

"She's telling the truth," said the tall woman with the bent nose unexpectedly. "At least Durza thinks so."

The woman had drawn her bow and had an arrow fitted to the string. Though she didn't look eager to shoot, something about her smelled dangerous.

"If that's true, Talon, then stand still!" commanded Sir Edge. Now that his voice was directed at her, she sensed the authority that he radiated. He was an imposing man, tall and powerfully muscled, but that wasn't what made a stab of fear strike her gut. This man had magic. She had felt it before and it hadn't been pleasant.

Nevertheless, Talon slowed to a stop. He was right. There was no need to fight back and no need to hide. She threw back her hood boldly and turned her back on her brother to stare Sir Edge in the face. The look of revulsion that passed through the human's eyes caused her to wince. His look was not that of a man who

11

wished to listen. Her fear spiked again. Talon's lips drew back from her razor-like teeth and she hissed hesitantly.

"Hold out your tail!" Sir Edge snarled.

Talon understood his intention immediately. This man knew of the potent venom that her old master Ewwie had placed in her tail. She lifted the base of her robe and slid her tail into view. Talon heard Deathclaw's sword split the air behind her as he lopped the spiked barb off the end of her tail.

Any other creature would have cried out with the pain that shot up her spine. The bite of his sword felt like fire. Talon suppressed a gurgle of pleasure. To her this pain was as familiar as an old friend. Her tail barb would grow back. It always did. In the meantime, she hoped this gesture would cool the human's anger long enough for her to deliver her master's message. She forced a reassuring smile to curl the corners of her mouth.

As usual, Durza overreacted.

"Noo!" wailed the gorc at seeing her friend maimed. Durza unleashed a wave of bewitching magic that swept over the clearing, demanding that everyone drop their weapons.

The magic was overwhelming in its intensity. The humans faltered. The woman fell to her knees, her bow dropping from her fingers. Sir Edge's hands loosened on his swords, his arms drooping. Even Deathclaw hissed, twitching as he resisted the spell. But the rogue horse was unmoved.

The enormous beast, a patchwork mix of scales and fur, leapt at Durza. It pinned her to the ground under its weight, its sharp claws ready to rip the life out of her. Durza cried out, desperately turning her magic on the beast.

"Sstop, Durza!" Talon demanded, pointing a long clawed finger at her friend. Durza whimpered, but dropped the attack. The wave of compulsion ceased.

Sir Edge shook his head, shrugging off the vestiges of the magic. "Don't hurt her, Gwyrtha," he said and his rogue horse backed off of the gorc, growling. He lifted his sword towards Talon once more.

Durza sobbed and looked at Talon with pleading eyes. Talon knew that her friend wanted nothing more than to flee.

Unfortunately, that could not be. They had a message to deliver. If she died after that, perhaps it would be a blessing.

Talon pulled off her black robe and dropped it to the ground, no longer allowing its emotionally dampening powers to affect her. Her old instincts surged to the surface, but she ignored them and stood before Sir Edge and her brother boldly.

"Leave her be. Killss me if you need. Masster ssays not to let you killss me. But do it if you musst! I am broken. He triess to fix me. The Prophet triess to fix me. I try! But it iss hard. To die iss best! Durza can tellss you the message."

"I think she's being honest," said the woman with the bent nose. She had been slower to recover from Durza's magic than the others. She breathed heavily as she picked up her bow and rose back to her feet. "In Durza's memories, Talon is trying to change. She struggles, but she tries."

Sir Edge shook his head. "I'm sorry, but after all she's done, I can't just take your word for it."

With that, the man darted forward, thrusting out with his left sword. Talon smiled, accepting her fate. The magical blade plunged into her belly.

Talon felt the steel of the sword part her skin, but there was no pain. It was sucked away by the sword. Her emotions left her along with the gibbering madness of the broken part of her mind. The urges were gone, nothing but empty voices.

This was the moment she had feared. This had happened to her the last time her flesh had tasted his blade. Talon was a creature who thrived on sensations and to have them taken away was something that went against everything she was.

Dispassionately, she felt the steel part her abdominal wall, severing loops of intestine and piercing a kidney on its way to protrude from her back. It would have been a dire injury for most, but Talon had survived worse. It was only the beginning, though.

She felt another familiar, but unwanted sensation as Sir Edge's presence appeared in her mind. It was as though Edge's thoughts had entered her through the sword. Talon's mind had been violated this way once before by her old mistress, the Moonrat Mother.

Her thoughts were laid bare before him. He saw her daily struggle. Her indecision. Her desire for life and death. That wasn't enough for him, however. He sent his magic further into her mind. He pulled her deepest memories to the surface, memories she had been forced to abandon, and as he did so Talon experienced them again.

She was a simple raptoid once more, a creature driven by instinct as she followed Deathclaw and the rest of her pack through the arid desert dunes seeking food. Once again, she lived through being paralyzed by magic and having her body deformed by Ewwie's magic. She was taken back to his dungeons and subjected to experiments that had taken her beyond the limits of pain.

Only this time she saw the events subjectively, unable to feel the agony. She saw how the things Ewzad Vriil did to her should have killed her. But the innate adaptive and regenerative blood magic of her dragon heritage kept her body alive while her own indomitable desire to survive chose insanity over complete loss of reason. She had chosen to love him and the pain he gave her. She also began to enjoy dispersing that pain to others. Then the Moonrat Mother had come and broken her once again.

Experiencing it all again without emotion, it was more evident to her than ever how broken she had been. The things she had done were twisted and nonsensical. It was all so confusing. Even worse, it was hopeless. The Prophet and the Stranger had tried to fix her, but the old urges still existed.

"He takess!" Talon howled. "He takess!"

Even devoid of emotion, she disliked having the shattered mess of her mind seen by another. It was shameful. Her one relief was the fact that after seeing all this he would surely kill her. Then the madness would end.

Sir Edge stopped pulling on her memories. He paused for a moment, his sword protruding from her back, and Talon caught a glimpse of his thoughts. It wasn't as she expected. There was no revulsion or horror over what she had been. Instead there was another emotion, one that she was unfamiliar with; compassion.

"Now I give," Sir Edge promised.

With that, he returned her pain. Her feeling of self-loathing and disgust flooded her mind with such intensity she didn't even manage to enjoy the pain of her sword wound. Then her sensations were flooded again as he poured new memories into her mind.

She saw from Sir Edge's-no, *Justan's* perspective. She felt foreign emotions as she experienced his childhood. She felt his human pains and pleasures as well as the strange feelings of love and sadness. As he grew up, she experienced the joy that came from the companionship of his loved ones. She experienced the pain of human guilt and grief as he made mistakes and lost friends.

The thoughts and feelings came so quickly, she had no way to analyze them. There was no room in her mind for her own opinions, she could only accept what she saw as real and true. For a time it was as if she was Justan.

Then the human's memories skipped forward and she began to experience the pain caused by her own actions, starting with his horror back in Ewwie's keep as he had watched Talon slaughter the prisoners in the hallway. Then she felt the sorrow and fear she had caused the woman Nala and her family when she had killed all their animals.

She felt the pain and loss caused by her murder of his mentor, Master Coal, starting with Justan's own sorrow and continuing with the pain felt by his family and bonded. Finally, he shared with her the pain and mourning Deathclaw had felt when he had seen the suffering she had caused and been unable to stop it. Then, his determination to kill her and end it.

The memories ceased. Talon stood numbly, disoriented as Justan slowly removed his sword. The wound tingled as his magic healed her from within.

He stumbled backwards. Exhausted by the intensity of the magic he had used. His rogue horse that Talon now knew was named Gwyrtha moved behind him, giving him something to hold onto. He clutched her saddle and breathed deeply as he recovered.

Talon blinked as her mind tried to cope with all she had experienced. Then as connections between her own experiences and his came together, a tide of raw emotion overcame her and she collapsed to the ground, sobbing. For the first time in her life, she felt her own guilt.

Deathclaw, who only understood a small part of what Justan had done, crouched next to her. He let out a questioning chirp.

"Talon!" Durza cried. She scrambled up off the ground and ran to her side. "Talon, is you okay?"

The gorc placed her hand on Talon's arm and Talon looked up into her overly rouged face. Without completely understanding why Talon lunged at her, throwing her arms around her friend. "I'm ssorry, Durza! I'm ssorry."

"What did you do to her?" the woman named Tarah asked.

"Did you . . . fix her?" asked Talon's brother.

"No," Justan said. "I forgave her."

Hearing those last words was too much. Talon's mind fled. She clung to Durza and shook with an uncontrollable stream of tears. She knew nothing but sorrow for the things she had done.

Talon did not hear the remainder of the conversation or even register the fact that Sir Edge had seen her master's message while searching her thoughts. He left with his friends and she remained with Durza, unresponsive to the gorc's plaintive questions.

It wasn't long after that when talks between the two armies broke down. While Talon experienced her own internal horror, true unspeakable terrors went on just a few hundred yards away. The ground shook under the raptoid and the gorc as the Troll Mother feasted. Thousands upon thousands of Roo-Tan, Roo-Dan, kobolds, imps, and merpeople were devoured alive and digested, their souls taken into the trollkin's god to eventually be reformed and reborn anew.

Durza heard the screams and cries, but was unable to get her friend to move. She extended her magic and gained a meager understanding of what was happening. She was aware of the great troll behemoth that lived beneath the swamps. Her master had taught her how to use her witchy-witch magic to keep it at bay. But she had never seen it like this. It seemed so hungry. She didn't know if the tricks he had taught her would still work.

She tried to use her magic to calm Talon, but the raptoid was too far gone to respond. With desperation, Durza ignored the

16

way Talon's unthinking claws tore her dress and skin as she forced herself free of her friend's grasp. Then, standing next to Talon, the gorc focused her magic into a single sharp command and sent it into the raptoid's mind. "*Nothing*," Durza said. "*You feels nothing.*"

Talon stopped sobbing and fell limply. Her eyes stared back at the gorc with unthinking stupor. Durza frowned.

"Not that much nothing. Stand up, Talon! Stand uuuup," Durza urged as the ground continued to shake around them.

She retrieved Talon's magic robe and draped it over the raptoid. To her relief, Talon let Durza lift her arms and put them through the sleeves. When Durza pulled her to her feet, the raptoid complied. Then, as quickly as she dared with Talon's thoughtless stumbling steps, Durza pulled her friend away from the valley.

For hours they travelled, continuing long after the ground stopped its shaking and the danger was past. Durza kept Talon going, using her magic to keep dangerous wildlife and curious humans away. Finally, as darkness came, Durza laid Talon down and curled up next to her, cradling her friend's head in her lap and crooning tunelessly until they were both asleep.

The next morning, Durza awoke with a gasp. Talon was still asleep next to her. She shook the raptoid. "Talon! Wakee-wake! It's up time!"

Talon let out a confused hiss and sat up, turning to face her with irritation. "What, Durza? You . . ." the raptoid's eyes widened and her lips trembled as emotions began to flood her again. "I'm sssorry-."

Durza stopped her with a ringing slap. Talon raised a shocked hand to her face. "Now, you-you stop it, Talon. No more cryings right now, okay? The Master talked to me. He talked in my dreams. He told me where to find him!"

Chapter Two

Fist let out a sigh of contentment and placed his large hands behind his head, his eyes closed. He was lying on his back on a comfortable bed. No, it wasn't a bed. It was softer than that. The ogre felt lighter than air. It was as if he was lying on a cloud. He could feel the warmth of the sun upon his body.

At that thought, a slight frown crossed his features. He had experienced this before. Many times. He grew certain that if he opened his eyes the peaceful feeling would be gone, replaced by some kind of horrible vision. He clenched his eyes closed, willing that softness and warmth to linger.

A rumble reached his ears and the warmth of the sun was diminished by a cool breeze thick with the smell of rain. A storm was coming. Fist groaned. It was happening again. He tried to ignore it.

"Let the dream stay nice," he pleaded.

A sudden weight settled on his lower body, pushing him deeper into the cloud. A thin hand smacked his face and an insistent female voice said, "Hey! What are you groaning about, Big Guy?"

Fist cracked an eye open and saw Maryanne's amused eyes looking down at him. She was leaning over him, the tips of her hair dangling down to tickle the sides of his face. The sun behind the gnome's head lit her auburn hair, turning it the color of fire. Fist smiled up at her, his cheeks flushing as he realized she was straddling his hips.

"What?" she asked, sitting up. Her skin-tight leather armor creaked as she folded her arms. "Don't just lay there grinning stupidly. We've got things to do."

"No we don't," he said and reached up one arm to grasp the back of her neck. He pulled her back towards him. Her eyes narrowed in playful protest but she allowed him to bring her in for a deep kiss.

It lasted only a few moments before she pulled out of his embrace and sat up again. "I mean it, Fist," she said reproachfully and pointed off to the right. "That storm's coming on quick and it ain't made of clouds."

The cool breeze picked up again, turning into a gust that blew her hair to the side, exposing her floppy ears. The smell of approaching rain was thicker now, but beneath it was a putrid undertone. There was a rumble of thunder and, despite his determination to ignore it, Fist looked in the direction she was pointing.

Lightning flickered in the menacing, oncoming clouds. Only Fist knew that it wasn't truly lightning. The clouds were made up of swarms of flies and winged moonrats and the flashes of light were caused by the flickering glow of their eyes. As if on cue, Fist heard the stomp of oncoming feet and saw his father running towards them, his heavy feet obliterating the clouds beneath him.

"This is my dream!" Fist growled.

Mistress Sarine had taught him that his recurring dreams were part of his spirit magic. She said that they were the Creator's way of speaking to him and that if he could hold onto his awareness that it was a dream, he could control certain aspects of it. In this case, he wanted to go back to his interesting encounter with Maryanne. He willed everything else to go away.

Evidently, that was not an aspect of the dream he could control, because the storm only grew darker. Crag's face was bloodied and bruised as he shouted out at him. "Fight!"

Maryanne stood and held his mace out to him, her gaze firm. "C'mon, Fist. He's right. Stand up and fight!"

Grumbling, Fist rolled to his knees and climbed to his feet. If this was how the dream had to be, he would face it as a warrior. He snatched his mace from the gnome's hand and he was suddenly outfitted for war. His iron breastplate shimmered with earth magic and his shield was heavy on his left arm. Fist gritted his teeth and sent out threads of earth and air magic. Lightning crackled over the surface of his skin.

"We will fight this evil together," he promised.

Yes! Fight! Kill! cried Squirrel enthusiastically, appearing on Fist's shoulder. The furry animal was wearing a vest made of chainmail and a tiny sword was clenched in one of his small hands. Fist lifted one thick brow. Squirrel certainly had grown bloodthirsty since arriving in the mountains.

The wind picked up, buffeting Fist as the smell of rot increased. His father ran towards them as fast as his legs would carry him over the fluffy clouds. Crag arrived just in front of the storm, a look of frustration on his battered face. "I said fight!"

"I am ready," Fist said, his eyes fixed on the oncoming horde. He was able to make out individual beasts in the cloud now and between the snarling moonrats and specks of flies were larger winged creatures, some of them as large as Fist himself.

"Not them, Toompa!" Crag shouted and swung a heavy fist.

Fist had known this was coming. This dream usually began with Crag punching him off of the clouds. He raised his shield to catch his father's blow. There was a meaty thud and the ogre chieftain grimaced, shaking his hand.

"We will fight together this time," Fist declared and reached out with his magic, sending a bolt of lightning into the enemy ranks. There were pained screeches as moonrat eyes burst and blackened bodies fell from the air.

Maryanne fired rapidly, her arrows taking out moonrats one-by-one. Fist saw a large beast break free from the others and hurtle towards her. It was dark and menacing, a tangle of clawed appendages attached to wings. Maryanne's next arrow struck at the heart of it. The creature continued towards her as the light died from its eyes.

"Maryanne!" Fist cried out as the beast's heavy body slammed into the gnome warrior, bowling her off the edge of the cloud.

Fist didn't hesitate. He ran and dove off the edge after her. Squirrel wisely leapt from his shoulder and landed on Crag. Crag and Squirrel continued to fight, Squirrel valiantly skewering flies on his tiny sword as Fist fell from view.

As Fist plummeted after her, he saw Maryanne push her way free from the dead beast's limp limbs. The spry gnome spread her arms and legs wide, somewhat slowing her descent. Fist plowed into her back.

"I got you!" he declared, wrapping his massive arms around her.

"What the hell're you doing?" Maryanne shouted back at him in surprise. "Did you jump after me on purpose? Now we're both falling, ya goblin brain!"

"I know that," Fist replied. He wasn't afraid for himself. He always fell in his dream and the landing never hurt him. Of course, landing in the Black Lake led to its own unpleasantries, but he had learned how to will himself not to fall into the Black Lake.

Maryanne, on the other hand, might not be under that same protection. Despite the fact that he knew this was a dream, he couldn't bear the idea of seeing her die. Besides, he knew from experience that some aspects of the dream tended to come true.

"This is my dream," he said, holding her tightly as the wind whipped past them and the distant ground closed in. "I choose."

"Then choose to let go of me!" she snapped and struggled in his arms.

Fist ignored her, willing their descent to slow down. He tried to change the reality of the dream, envisioning both of them standing safe on the shores of the lake below. But as he looked at the approaching mountain range, he realized he wasn't falling towards the Black lake this time. He was headed somewhere between the lake and the Thunder People Territory.

"Let go," Maryanne repeated, still trying to pull free. "You're gonna land on top of me!"

"We're not gonna hit the ground," Fist promised her, but his normal tactic wasn't working. They were still hurtling towards the rocky ground below. As the earth rushed up towards him, Fist could make out the forms of a large group of people rushing away from the Thunder People's home. *It's my dream*, he thought again and tried to picture himself and Maryanne joining the group of people below.

"I said, let GO!" Maryanne snapped her head back, smashing his nose. To his horror, she managed to push free from him just as the ground came up to meet them.

The gnome warrior spun in the air and landed deftly, somehow absorbing the momentum of the fall in a roll on the ground before rising to her feet.

Fist, on the other hand, landed with a splat, face down in the mud. The air was blasted from his lungs and he laid there for a moment unmoving, humiliated. Of course she would land fine without his help. She was a gnome warrior after all.

He could hear the rattle of armor and stomp of footsteps as people marched all around him. A powerful hand gripped his shoulder and pulled him free from the muck, bringing him to his knees. "Dag-gum it, Fist! Get yer sorry hide up. We got a garl-friggin' war goin' on!"

"Lenny?" Fist said, wiping mud from his eyes.

The dwarf's familiar red handlebar mustache was askew and he looked battered and bruised from the fighting, but he just grinned his gap-toothed grin and charged ahead with the others, waving Buster in the air. Fist stood, watching as Academy warriors and brawny ogres rushed past him, intermixed with Mage School wizards. He tried to make out faces to see who else had come with Lenny, but they were all ablur.

"C'mon!" said Maryanne, standing beside him without a spatter of mud on her.

The gnome warrior ran on ahead of him, pulling an arrow from the magical quiver at her waist. Fist tried to run after her but his movements were slow. His arms felt heavy and he grew lethargic and weak. People continued to rush by him, heading towards what he was certain was a massive battle at the Black Lake. Fist tried to take charge, tried to will himself forward, but for some reason this was yet another aspect of the dream he couldn't control.

"Oo-ooh! Ride?" Rufus asked.

The ape-like rogue horse ran up beside him, his enormous mouth stretched with a wide grin, exposing plate-sized teeth.

Squirrel was standing on Rufus' shoulder and Fist's eyes widened at the small animal's appearance. His chainmail vest had been replaced with a bandoleer of tiny throwing knives and his wide fluffy tail was gone. In its place was an arching reptilian tail with a pointed barb on the end.

"What happened to you, Squirrel?" Fist asked slowly, curious despite his sluggish state.

I am Deathclaw, Squirrel replied and opened his mouth to expose razor sharp teeth.

Fist would have recoiled but, somehow in the logic of the dream, it made sense. "Thank you, Rufus," Fist said and tried to raise his heavy leg.

No! said Squirrel, shaking his head. *You can't come up. Not with all those snakes.*

"Snakes?" Fist looked down and discovered that his arms and legs were weighed down by dozens of mud-covered brown snakes, each of them latched to him with their teeth.

Fist wasn't a squeamish sort. He fought giant spiders and ravening trolls without fear. But there was something about snakes that he found unnatural. There was the sinuous way they moved and the fact that even the smallest ones could kill an ogre if they were poisonous enough. He had killed many before, but always with a shiver. This was too much.

He screamed. It was a deep and sluggish sound. It had to be the venom of the snakes that was affecting him.

Fist . . , came the familiar sound of Justan's thoughts.

Fist didn't listen. He frantically tried to wave his arms and stomp his legs to shake the snakes off, but all he managed was an odd sort of slow shuffle. His scream continued, panicked in his mind, but aloud it sounded as if he were simply trying to hold a low note.

Fist, I need to talk to you, said Justan's thoughts again and Fist realized that Justan was there, standing in front of him. There was a tired look on his face.

"Snaaakess," Fist said in slow motion, pleading to Justan. "Heeellp!"

This is just a dream, Fist, Justan said patiently, his arms folded. *Sorry, but I need you to wake up. Something horrible has happened.*

The sorrowful feeling coming from Justan's thoughts jolted through to Fist and he realized that he had let the dream take over. The sluggishness disappeared. "Justan, is that really you and not part of my dream?"

It is, Justan replied. He held out his hand.

Fist reached out to him and the snakes weren't there anymore. The moment their hands touched, the dream faded from his mind. Fist became aware of the hard ground beneath the thin layer of his bedroll. He could hear Maryanne's soft snore nearby and could feel the weight of Rufus' heavy arm over him.

Fist muted those sensations and focused on his connection with Justan through the bond. *I am sorry, Justan. I was trying to reach you a while ago and while I was waiting I must have fallen asleep.*

It was a long day. We just now stopped for a few hours of sleep ourselves, Justan said. *I couldn't wait for tomorrow, though. I needed to talk to you.*

Once again, Fist was overwhelmed by the weary sadness that filled Justan's thoughts. The ogre was afraid to learn what he had to say. *I have a lot to tell you, too, but what happened? Did someone . . .* He hesitated to say the word *die*, but that was definitely the feeling he was getting.

I-I . . . Justan hesitated, unable to form his thoughts into words and Fist's heart sank. *I'll just show you.*

Justan's memories flowed into Fist's mind. He saw the two massive armies facing each other. He saw the small platform in the middle of the small marsh at the center of the valley where Jhonate's father was meeting with the Gnome Warlord to decide whether there would be peace or war.

Aldie led Justan away from the valley and Fist's heart leapt as Talon came into view. *She's back?* Fist feared that Deathclaw's sister had killed someone close to them. *What was she doing in Malaroo?*

Just watch, Justan replied and the memory continued.

Fist watched with awe as Justan used his sword to try and heal Talon's insanity. Then Justan's focus shifted to the treachery occurring at the armies' center. Chaos erupted as the ancient troll behemoth rose from the ground beneath the armies and men were swallowed right and left. Thousands of lives were lost right before Justan's eyes.

When it was over, Fist's mind was just as numb as Justan's had been. So many gone. Fist didn't know most of the people personally. Justan had spent more time with the victims of the massacre. But he had known Djeri the Looker. Fist had spent several nights on guard duty with Lenny's nephew and had liked him.

And Aldie, Justan said. I didn't see it myself, but I heard. He was helping evacuate the valley and was pulled underground.

Fist winced. Sir Lance's son had been so brave during the war. For him and Djeri to die in a foreign land in a war that wasn't theirs? *Horrible.*

There were so many lost that the remainder of the army has been in confusion. Since we stopped, Xedrion has had his officers put together a list of those missing. The number keeps growing, Justan sent and his sorrow turned to rage as he added, *and it's all because that gnome was in league with Mellinda.*

That last thought pierced through the haze in Fist's mind. *But that can't be true.*

And yet, it is. Somehow she survived our attack in the Dark Forest and found a new body, Justan said, sending the images he had pulled from Talon's mind. *Fist, she has the Rings of Stardeon. She must be more powerful than ever.*

But, Justan, Mellinda is here, Fist said. *Locksher saw it. That's what I was going to tell you tonight.*

It was Justan's turn to be stunned. *How is that possible?*

Fist sent his memories through the bond and told Justan about their mission to the Black Lake and how it had grown in size and the number of infested monsters had increased. He showed Justan how Locksher had allowed himself to become infested so that he could follow the evil magic to its source.

He discovered that it was Mellinda's power, Fist explained and repeated what Locksher had said, telling Justan that when Jhonate had hewn Mellinda's soul in two, her power had found a way to escape into two orange moonrat eyes that had been left behind in the mountains. *Her evil is what created the larvae. It worked a lot like the way she made the moonrats.*

Justan digested all that Fist had shown him. *Then what you're facing is her power only? None of her old intelligence is behind it?*

That is what Locksher sensed when he was communicating with it, Fist replied. The way the wizard had explained it, this was just the abscess that had grown from Mellinda's soul as she had accumulated more and more evil power over the centuries. Her intelligence was gone.

And Locksher thinks that the Dark Prophet has taken control of this power? Justan asked.

He said that this is the part of Mellinda that was connected to the Dark Bowl. It was running wild and the Dark Prophet sent one of his servants to take charge. This had made the evil more dangerous than before. Now the larvae had more of a purpose than to mindlessly breed and control the living. *This servant is using some kind of red spirit magic to make Mellinda's power do his will.*

Red spirit magic? Justan hadn't heard of that before. Every spirit magic he had seen had been white, black, or gray.

Dark red, Fist replied. He hadn't seen it himself but that was how Locksher had described it.

Justan considered it for a moment. *I'll have to ask Beth or Tolynn if they know what that color means.*

Locksher thinks that this person is probably one of the Dark Prophet's old soldiers or priestesses, Fist added. *She was really powerful. We barely escaped.*

It had been the storm that saved them. It had been a harrowing ride away from the lake for the four of them clinging to Rufus' broad back. The thickly falling snow had obscured their escape, but the mysterious woman had come after them, blindly lashing out with air magic in a vicious attack. Wind whipped at them with the fury of winter's last gasp.

Rufus' climbing skill had been sorely tested. The rogue horse nearly fell several times. The ice and slush that clung to the mountainside was treacherous and that was before their enemy sent out vibrating strands of earth magic. Tremors shook the cliff face. Rocks loosened from beneath his hands and he had been forced to make several ill-advised leaps.

For his passengers, the experience had been terrifying. If Locksher hadn't used air magic to lash everyone to Rufus' back, surely some of them would have fallen to their deaths. As it was, all of them had been battered and bruised by the constant jerking about. Rufus himself had fractured a wrist after one particularly long fall and Fist had needed to repair it through the bond before they continued on.

Did Maryanne ask my great grandmother if she recognized the woman? Justan asked.

She was going to, but I fell asleep before she had time to tell me what she found out, Fist replied. Mistress Sarine's bonds had given her an extraordinary lifespan. She had been one of the Prophet's companions during the war two hundred years ago. If their new enemy was one of the Dark Prophet's priestesses she should recognize her.

Okay, let me know what you find out tomorrow night, Justan replied and Fist felt the bonding wizard's weariness overtake the bond again.

I will, Fist said. A feeling of guilt surged within him. The evil he faced in the mountains seemed small compared to the importance of the events Justan faced. *Justan . . . I am sorry that I was not able to be there with you.*

Don't be, Justan assured him. *I can see now that we are both where we need to be. Your mission is every bit as important as . . .* His thoughts brightened as an idea occurred to him. *Fist, maybe more help is coming than you know. Before he left, the Prophet told Tarah Woodblade he had somewhere else important to be. Somewhere where major players needed his help. Maybe he's coming to you.*

Really? Fist replied, hope stirring in his chest. If the Prophet came surely everything would all end up alright.

I don't know it for sure, but it makes sense now that we know the Dark Prophet has taken control of the Black Lake, Justan pointed out. *And even if the Prophet isn't coming, the news of what Locksher learned today should force the Mage School and Academy to get moving up there.*

I hope so, Fist said somewhat doubtfully. They certainly had been dragging their feet so far. It was mainly the Mage School Council that was slowing things down. The Academy wasn't prepared to move on their own.

I should go now, Justan said and Fist felt him yawn through the bond. *Xedrion will want to continue our march soon and I should sleep as much as I can.*

Okay. Justan . . . Tell Jhonate I am sorry about her siblings.

I will, Fist. We'll talk again tomorrow.

As always, Fist replied. It was their common goodbye at the end of the night, yet Fist felt a twinge of sadness every time Justan's presence faded.

Fist's awareness of the world around him increased as his thoughts retreated from the bond. He could hear the distant sound of ogres at campfires, but everyone in their own camp seemed to be asleep. His body was still tired and sore and he tried to drift back to sleep himself, but his mind was too active after all that Justan had shown him.

Fist carefully lifted Rufus' heavy arm off of his chest. Fist hoped not to wake him, but rogue horses were notoriously light sleepers. The intense core of energy that powered them meant that they needed very little rest, but Rufus had used an immense amount of power the day before. To his relief, the ape-like beast simply rolled to his back with a grunt and kept sleeping.

Fist turned to his other side and reached out to gently nudge the gnome sleeping next to him. "Maryanne," he whispered.

Her snore stopped mid-breath and she cracked an irritated eye at him. "Huh?"

"I just finished talking to Justan," he replied, feeling a bit guilty for waking her.

She let out a soft groan and rolled to face him. "And?"

"And . . ." He grimaced. "I wanted to know what Sarine told you."

She sighed. "Sorry. It's just that I feel like I was tied up in a sack and beaten by a dozen orcs."

"Sorry," Fist said, well aware of the beating they had all taken earlier that day. "Do you want me to heal you?"

"You do know how to make me tingle in all the right places." Maryanne gave him a tired smile. "But no. I'll be fine. What did your bonding wizard have to say?"

Fist briefly told her about the disastrous events in Malaroo. "He says that the woman leading those troll people was Mellinda."

She frowned. "Impossible."

"That's what I told him," Fist said. "But the people that saw her swore it was true."

"Sure is something strange going on there," Maryanne said.

"Did you ask Mistress Sarine about that red spirit magic Locksher saw?" Fist asked.

"Yeah. That concerned her. She said she was going to look into it," Maryanne replied. "Sarine was pretty distracted, though. She said the Prophet showed up at the Mage School today raising holy hell."

"Really?" Fist said with a grin. "Justan said John might be coming up here to help us!"

"I don't think so," she said regretfully. "He was mainly mad at them because they hadn't done the ceremony to call a new head wizard. He told them to get off their butts and start making decisions and then he left."

Chapter Three

Darlan stopped in the middle of the Grand Hallway, her eyes drawn to the wall where the portal to the Academy stood. The portal was currently closed. An incredibly detailed mural depicting an open portal was painted in its place. The painter who had created it had used magic to create phosphorescent pigments that gave it a quite realistic glow. Too realistic in Darlan's mind.

The mural had been painted just after the War of the Dark Prophet, not many years after the portal had first been created. The story was that one of the council members felt that the inactive lodestones looked ugly sitting on the bare wall when the portal was not open. They decided to employ a mage from the Alberri Mage School who was well renowned for his talents. He got carried away.

She wondered if any of the wizards who had authorized the mural all those years ago had understood how bad of an idea it ended up being. Perhaps they found it humorous. During the decades when the portal had originally been open, it had been embarrassingly common occurrence for people to walk right into the wall not realizing the portal was closed. From the grumbles Darlan had heard since the portal's recent reopening, it had become an issue again.

Darlan shook her head and turned away. Rolling her eyes at the mural wasn't why she had come down this hallway. The Prophet had left instructions.

John's visit to the Mage School's High Council had not been a pleasant one for any of the Council members. He had scolded them as a parent might scold children. For a group of respected and established wizards, that was a hard thing to swallow.

Darlan in particular had taken his anger quite personally. When he had started in on the others, she had folded her arms and nodded in agreement. Then he had turned his gaze on her and she had realized that she was being lumped in with the rest of them. Darlan was used to dealing out scoldings, not receiving them. It had been several hours since he left and her skin still tingled from the tension that had been in the room.

She strode down the hallways of the Rune Tower, the frown on her lips startling silent the few students that crossed her path. It had been strange to see a look of fury on John's face. Whenever she had seen the Prophet in the past he had been so calm and in control. Even during the war he hadn't acted this much under stress. It was as if he had barely been able to keep himself in check.

Briefly, she wondered what would happen if he ever did lose control. With his raw power would he have been able to strip them of their magic? Strike them dead with a look? She rubbed away the goosebumps that raised on her arms at the thought of it.

At any rate, John had been well within his rights to bring up the issues he had. The Prophet had orchestrated the founding of the Mage School thousands of years ago himself, directing the wizards of the time in building a place of learning that could house the Bowl of Souls. He was not an active member on the council, and technically they didn't have to obey his demands, but they had to listen. It was written in the school's bylaws. He had their ears whenever he wished it.

Sighing, Darlan walked towards the far side of the wide hall, her eyes focused on the door that led up to the Hall of Majesty. That was her destination. At that moment it was the last place she wanted to go. She frowned at the anxiety that rose within her chest at the thought of going up there.

Darlan threw open the door and started inside. She was one of the most powerful wizardesses of her time. She had spent nearly a century of her life at this school and had stood near the Bowl of Souls many times. There was no reason for her to feel anxious about approaching it now. Nevertheless, by the time Darlan started up the curving staircase, her stomach was a roiling sea of nerves.

She hadn't climbed five steps before the door opened behind her and a matronly voice called out, "Wait, Dear! I need to speak with you on the way."

Darlan winced and paused so that her grandmother could catch up to her. She had chosen this route specifically because it was less often taken. Sarine was on the short list of people she had most wanted to avoid along the way.

Darlan glanced back at the woman and gave her a polite smile. "Mistress Sarine."

Sarine climbed the stairs quickly, deceptively spry for her age. Darlan was unsure exactly how old she was. Her hair was gray and simply coiffed, tied in a long braid behind her head, and she had a pleasantly plump face. In fact, if not for the vibrant energy in her eyes, she looked like a woman that would be more at home rocking by the fire than traipsing up and down the staircases of the Mage School.

Sarine shot Darlan a brief frown as she arrived on the step below her. "I thought we were past that, Dear."

"Grandmother, then," Darlan said, then nodded at Sarine's bonded elf who was trailing behind her. "Sir Kyrkon."

Kyrkon nodded back at Darlan, an amused expression on his narrow face. Amusement seemed to be the elf's default expression whenever Darlan was conversing with her grandmother. She often wondered if she should be offended by that. He had no business looking amused at the moment. Not when his bonding wizardess was using him as a pack animal.

The named elf warrior was following behind Sarine carrying a large bag full of colorful yarn and knitted goods. The woman was always knitting. Darlan understood the appeal somewhat. She had become somewhat of a seamstress in her years away from the school. But there was a time and a place for that sort of thing and the setting didn't seem to matter to Sarine. Even at council meetings, she would sit a bit back from the table, a ball of yarn in her lap, her needles clicking away. Darlan wouldn't have been surprised if she had been knitting while climbing the stairs.

No sooner had the thought passed through her mind, then

Kyrkon held out a pair of needles, a length of knitted fabric already hanging from them. Sarine reached back and took them from him, only glancing down at the needles briefly to remember where she was in the pattern.

Repressing a snort, Darlan turned away from her and continued slowly up the staircase, the sound of her grandmother's needles ticking away behind her.

"Don't roll your eyes at me, Dear. Knitting helps me keep my thoughts in order," Sarine said, following a couple steps behind her.

"I wasn't-."

"Don't deny it. I could practically hear your eyes rolling in their sockets," Sarine claimed. "You always do that when I knit in meetings."

Darlan opened her mouth to give Sarine her real opinion on the matter, but stopped herself. No sense starting an argument in the stairwell. She changed what she was going to say. "So . . . last night after the meeting. You ran after John. Did you catch up to him?"

Perhaps Sarine had gotten some sense out of him. After all, she had been one of the Prophet's companions during the war two hundred years ago. She had fought with him all the way to the Dark Prophet's Palace. Darlan wasn't aware of anyone alive closer to John than her.

"Briefly," Sarine replied.

"In the time that you did get to speak with him did you get anything more out of him than what he told the rest of us?" Darlan asked.

Sarine hesitated before saying, "Not a great deal. He was in a foul temper, Dear."

Darlan was certain there was more. "Go on."

Sighing slightly, Sarine added, "He took time to chastise me again for not making things happen sooner. He reiterated that dark times would be coming and he wanted me to see that his motions were carried out."

"You mean his instructions about easing the naming

restrictions?" Darlan asked.

During the war, John had made a remark that restrictions for warriors should be relaxed. In the past, they had only been allowed to stand before the Bowl once in their lifetime. The result was that very few were brave enough to try for fear that they would lose their one chance and the number of named warriors in the lands had dwindled.

"Among other things," Sarine replied. "But our conversation was cut short. He wouldn't let me follow him any further than the outer gates. He flat-out commanded me to stay inside the grounds." With a suspicious tone, the old wizardess added, "I think he was travelling with someone he didn't want me to see."

Kyrkon snorted from the stairs behind her. "Now-now, Begazzi. He was in as big a rush as I've ever seen him. If John was hiding someone it was probably just because he didn't want to take the time for introductions."

"Maybe," Sarine conceded, but from the way the clicking of her needles paused, Darlan could tell she wasn't convinced. "I think he had a rogue horse waiting in the trees. You know he rides them to get from place to place quickly."

"No reason to go down that road, Begazzi," Kyrkon said, using her former name. "You'll just get yourself worked up."

"Why do you think the Prophet would hide a rogue horse from you?" Darlan wondered.

"Because he knows I would bond to it and he's afraid he'll run out! There are only a handful of them left and he hoards them like the rarest of gemstones," Sarine declared with an irritated grunt. "As if he were the only one that needed a swift ride."

Darlan knew there was more to it than that. From what Justan had explained to her, a rogue horse was the ultimate bonded. Their bond gave their wizards long life, speed and agility, along with an enormous source of energy. Sarine had been quite irritated when she'd learned that Fist received a rogue horse of his own after being a bonding wizard for so short a time. She felt it an insult that John hadn't given her one after two centuries of service.

In Darlan's opinion, the Prophet probably figured that

Sarine's existing bonds already give her what she needed. After all, she received her long life from Kyrkon, her toughness from the dwarf, Bill, and her agility from Maryanne. Surely, anything else was just a luxury. But Darlan didn't say so. Instead, she pressed on, hoping that Sarine's desire to converse with her had been sated.

Sarine sped up, her needles clicking again. "Wait just a moment, Dear. I still haven't mentioned the reason I wanted to speak with you in the first place."

"No?" Darlan said. "Then what did you wish to speak to me about?"

"To be blunt, Dear, I was wondering why you haven't been named yet," Sarine replied.

Darlan's foot caught on a step and she nearly stumbled forward. After a brief pause, she continued on as if nothing had happened. "That is a strange question. The Bowl names whom it will."

"Don't be disingenuous, Dear," Sarine chastised, her needles clicking away. "The Bowl can't name those who don't approach it. I've seen the way you avoid going up to the Hall of Majesty. You don't attend when students you know are being raised. From what I hear, you had Fist raised to apprentice without even taking him to the Bowl."

"You know I don't believe in using the Bowl for such ceremonies," Darlan replied.

Having students dip their weapons into the Bowl of Souls while becoming apprentices or mages was a relatively recent addition to the Mage School's practices. Darlan felt it neared sacrilege to include that holy relic in such an unintended way. She had said as much to the rest of the council on multiple occasions.

"You are trying to avoid the question," Sarine pressed.

"That is nonsense. I've been at this school most of my life," Darlan said, keeping her tone even despite the fact that her nerves were set on edge. "I have stood at the Bowl many times."

"And when was the last time you placed your dagger in its waters?" Sarine pressed.

Darlan's fists clenched. Nearly 100 years ago, but that was none of Sarine's business. They came to a short landing and she turned to face her grandmother.

"Enough. Hundreds of wizards try every year and only a handful are named. Many powerful and experienced wizards fail. What makes you think I would be chosen? I . . . oh. I see," Darlan said in sudden understanding. Her brow tightened. "That's what John talked to you about before he left you at the front gate. He wanted you to convince me to stand before the Bowl again."

Sarine didn't bother to deny it. She glanced down at her knitting briefly as she picked up a thread from a different color of yarn before continuing her pattern. She cocked her head as she met Darlan's eyes once again. "Why are you afraid of being named?"

"Afraid . . ?" Darlan's jaw tightened. "This isn't about fear. It's practicality. Tell me, Sarine. How would being named benefit me? To gain a bond to a ritual dagger I rarely use? To receive a rune on my left palm? Not very useful. Sure, it would assure that my hand can never be lopped off, but I've yet to come across a situation where I've needed that particular protection," she pointed out. "Why would I want it?"

Sarine's droll look did nothing to soothe Darlan's irritation. The old woman's voice was positively condescending as she replied, "I refuse to believe that you are so naive as to think those things are what naming is about."

Darlan scowled. "I have yet to see any other benefits that come from it. I have no need for the additional fame and title. That's for certain." She swallowed back the surge of guilt that rose within her chest. "Besides, I have no desire to change my name once again. I am perfectly happy with my names as they are, thank you!" She cleared her throat. "Now, I believe we have wasted enough time with this conversation. It is time we hurried along. No doubt they are waiting for us."

With that, she turned around and began climbing the steps once more.

"We are not finished with this conversation, Darlan!" Sarine snapped.

Darlan ignored her and continued up the winding staircase, increasing her speed once again. She felt a slight sense of relief when her grandmother didn't immediately rush after her. That relief soured when she heard Sarine's voice echoing up from behind her.

"Do you believe that display of childishness?" Sarine asked Kyrkon. "As if I would accept that she really thinks the importance of being named is about how it will benefit her!"

Darlan winced, glad that she couldn't make out Kyrkon's amused reply. Of course she knew better. If that's what she believed, she would have been back to the Bowl long ago. Sarine had been right when she said that it was fear that kept Darlan away.

She let out a sigh of relief when she finally reached the door at the top of the staircase. It opened into a familiar extravagant hallway lined with the paintings of named warriors and wizards from the past. She walked past their sternly painted countenances, feeling their lifeless yet somehow accusing eyes on her as she entered the room at the end of the hall.

Sitting in the opulently decorated waiting room were the rest of the council, each of them wearing formal robes that best suited their position on the council.

"Good morning, Sherl," said Wizard Beehn cheerfully. The wizard's yellow robe looked far too large on his body. Ever since bonding to Alfred it seemed he got slimmer every day.

"Good morning," she replied and nodded to the rest of them. "Mistress Sarine is not far behind me."

"And what delayed you?" asked Wizard Spence, the council's Earth Wizard. He was a spindly middle-aged man with red hair and a prominent widow's peak. He was also a traditionalist and often on the opposing side of Darlan's arguments. "Did you stop to help her ball some string?"

"Yarn, Spence," said Wizard Windle, the council's Air Wizard. He was a soft spoken but opinionated gentleman who looked uncomfortable without a pipe clenched in his teeth. "This morning is not the time to start a tiff."

"I second that. Especially after last night," said Master Barthas, the Fire Wizard. He had joined the High Council not long before Sarine, having come from the Mage School in Alberri. He was an old frail-looking man and the deep red of his robes made his face seem all the paler, but that did nothing to dull the confidence that blazed from his eyes. "I say we get this over with quickly."

"I agree," said Beehn. He was likely eager to get back to his experimental projects. Even without Wizard Locksher around, he was constantly coming up with ideas. "Shall we go inside, then?"

"We must wait for Mistress Sarine," said Windle. "According to tradition, we must all enter the Hall of Majesty together."

"I don't know what's keeping her," Darlan said, looking over her shoulder towards the empty hallway. "She was right behind me."

"Tell me, Darlan," said Wizard Valtrek, who had been silent up until now. He had chosen not to wear the blue robes of his office as Water Wizard, but instead had gone with white ambassadorial attire. He was eying her with a calculating gaze. "Which of us do you think the Bowl will choose?"

Darlan blinked at him. She fully expected the job to go to either Master Barthas or Sarine. They were level-headed and already named. But she didn't want to say that where either of them would hear. Instead, she said, "I do not wish to speculate. The Bowl will choose who it will."

"It usually chooses the wizard with the most experience," Windle offered mildly.

"If that's the case, Mistress Sarine would be the obvious choice," Beehn replied.

There were noncommittal shrugs from Master Barthas and Wizard Spence.

Valtrek smiled at their responses. "I beg to differ. The Bowl has many more factors to consider than age alone. Mistress Sarine has been away from the School for two hundred years. Spirit magic is new to most of us. Is the Mage School ready to be led by someone without elemental magic? Wizardess Sherl, on the other hand, is more qualified in many ways. Who among us could dispute her experience and power? Besides, she has spent more time at the school than any of us including her grandmother."

Technically, it was true. Darlan had been a resident wizardess at the school for most of her long life. It was only in the last twenty years that she had finally gotten away.

Wizard Spence snorted. "There hasn't been a female Head Wizard in over five hundred years."

"Head Wizardess," Darlan corrected, though her frown was directed at Valtrek. What was he playing at? "But it's not happening. The only reason I accepted a position on the Council was because you needed an Academy Representative." She couldn't be Head Wizardess and live at the Academy with her husband.

"The Bowl will choose who it will," Valtrek replied, his grin widening.

At that moment, the door to the stairwell opened and Sarine walked down the hallway towards them. She was alone, no knitting in her hands, and had a look of frustration on her face. "I'm sorry I'm late. I was having a . . . discussion with Sir Kyrkon."

Valtrek stood. "Well, now that we're all here . . ."

He beckoned towards the door and the Council prepared themselves. Moments later, they entered the Hall of Majesty single file and in order of seniority.

Darlan felt a chill as she looked up at the multiple tiers of chandeliers hanging from the domed ceiling high above her head. She always felt such a feeling of awe in this place. It seemed silly to her that she had avoided returning for so long. Then her eyes rested on the Bowl of Souls and she remembered why.

The Bowl was large and golden and sat atop a marble pedestal. It looked rather plain from a distance, but up close she knew that the underside of it was covered in a multitude of tiny runic carvings. It pulled at her. Beckoning.

Darlan first stood before the Bowl at age nineteen when she was raised to the position of apprentice, then again at 27 and 33 as she was raised to mage and wizardess respectively. Each time, she had felt an electric thrill as she plunged her dagger into its waters, secretly hoping that the Bowl would find her worthy and name her on the spot.

For years after that, she would return every six months and

try again, eager for it to find her worthy. She wanted to prove to herself and everyone else that she was one of the greatest of her time. But each time the Bowl stood in silent rejection.

Darlan became the School's most feared and respected Dark Wizard hunter. At first, she loved the job, but over time her feelings changed. Often times she was hunting down people she knew; students she had trained. A few of them had even turned to darkness while seeking a way to surpass her.

She grew weary of it all. As the decades went by, she felt more and more chained by her position. She considered retiring. A life away from the responsibilities placed on her by the school had sounded so wonderful, but the Council didn't want to let her go. She was too valuable. Besides, her "auntie's" olives were keeping her young and able to continue.

It was around this time that she learned the truth of the Bowl. Becoming named wasn't just a validation of one's prowess or a method to increase one's power. It was a declaration of fealty to the Bowl and the Prophet, which meant it came with an accompanying set of responsibilities.

The next time she entered the Hall of Elements, the Bowl had called out to her. It urged her to plunge her dagger within its depths. Darlan knew that if she did so, she would be named. If that happened Darlan also knew that she would obey the requirements placed upon her. She would do so because if the Bowl requested something of her, it would be the right thing to do. She would have no choice but obey.

Darlan had run. She had never approached the Bowl again. Until now.

The High Council members surrounded the Bowl, spacing themselves evenly apart. Sarine raised her arms towards the Bowl and the rest of the Council did the same.

Darlan could instantly feel its pull. The Bowl wanted to name her.

"We approach the Bowl of Souls today as members of the High Council of the Mage School," Sarine intoned. "We request that the next Head Wizard be chosen."

The eight of them reached out with their magic, letting their powers rest on the rim of the bowl. A ring of soft white light rose from the Bowl in response. Whether the light was made up of elemental or spirit magic was unclear, but it did not have a color to their mage sight.

The ring of light settled on the threads of their magic as the Bowl searched them to make its decision. Darlan felt a strange sensation inside her mind as if her thoughts and desires were being read. No, it was more than that. It was as if her very being was being examined.

At that moment, a sudden certainty entered her mind. She was the best choice for the job. All she had to do was step forward. If she did so, the magic of the Bowl would take over. She would be named and become Head Wizardess. A quiet voice began a chant somewhere in the center of her mind.

Darlan's fear spiked. She took a step back. The voice stopped.

The circle of light rose from the lip of the Bowl, becoming so bright that for a moment it was all Darlan could see. Then the moment passed. The circle of light dimmed as it settled on the Bowl's choice.

Darlan's jaw dropped as the light landed on Wizard Valtrek's head and faded slowly into his body. His eyes were wide, his hands trembling until the glow faded. Valtrek had been chosen, but not named. The Council looked upon their new leader and Darlan knew that if this ended badly it would be her fault.

"I saw . . . I have been given instructions. I know what to do," Valtrek said numbly. "It's so clear to me now."

"What is it?" asked Wizard Beehn,

Valtrek blinked and shook his head. He looked at them as if momentarily unsure why they were there. Then a smile appeared on his face. "We must contact the Academy Council. It's time we went after that evil in the mountains."

Chapter Four

Lenui Firegobbler paced back and forth outside of the newly-built Battle Academy Smithery, his face fixed with a scowl of anxiety and frustration. A low, but continuous, stream of curses tumbled from his lips. "Dag-gum bug-farmin', dirt-sniffin', tar-eatin' . . !"

The streets around him echoed with the roar of the forges and the clang of hammers on metal within the building. This combination of sounds usually had the effect of calming Lenui; helping him put his thoughts in order. But this afternoon was an exception. He had trouble on his mind.

The workers and students that passed by kept their distance, greetings withering on their lips as the massive dwarf, five-feet-tall and nearly just as wide at the shoulders, stomped through the dust of the street, continuing his bitter stream of curses.

" . . . Flea-ridden, brain-bitin', corn jiggin', log rippin', nose-farmin'. . !"

Lenui should have gone inside and gotten his hands dirty. Crafting something would help him work out his frustrations. Thing was, Bettie was inside and she wasn't going to like what he had to say. Lenui wasn't quite ready to face his wife yet. Only other thing that helped this kind of mental state was fighting, but since there weren't any monsters nearby to slay, he settled for pacing.

" . . . Frog kissin', hoop skirtin', corpse raisin', troll hum-!"

The door to the smithery banged open. Bettie's stern face poked out of the open doorway. "Would you stop your yappin' and get your arse inside already?" she barked, interrupting his tirade. "I been waitin' for you half the day."

Lenui's mouth hung open mid-curse. How had the dag-blamed woman heard him over the roaring of the forges? "I'll come in when I durn well feel like it!"

"Yeah?" she said, her brow rising. "Well I'd say you're feelin' like it now!"

Lenui scowled. "I'd say yer wrong!"

A grin parted her lips exposing slightly pointed teeth. "Just get in here," she said with a snort and ducked back inside.

"Dag-blast it!" Lenui said, stomping one foot, before following her into the smithery.

When work on rebuilding the Academy began, the smithery had been one of the first new buildings raised. Metal parts were a necessity with any build and with an undertaking this large they were needed in huge quantities. The smiths were given huge orders for tools and brackets and nails and sconces and anything else needed by the workers.

It hadn't gone well at first. The Academy's regular crew of smiths, brought back after the war, had rarely been pressed to make basic tools and parts before. Most of them had been brought into the Academy forges at a young age and taught by Forgemaster Stanley who tended to buy such simple things from the smiths in Reneul. Their previous work had almost exclusively been weapons and armor and, though they were capable craftsmen, they didn't know how to make anything else efficiently.

Orders piled up and work on the Academy rebuild slowed as projects were held back by lack of parts. The builders were forced to wait on orders to come in from other cities. That was, until Bettie arrived.

The Academy's new forgemaster refused to put up with the excuses of less experienced smiths. At six-foot-three and with more muscles than any of the men, the half-orc was an imposing force. Bettie saw where their skills were lacking and brought in a handful of experienced Wobble dwarves to work as her assistants. Under the lash of her iron tongue, the Academy smiths were given a swift course on tricks of the basic smithing trade. After just a few short weeks, the smithery was now swiftly and efficiently meeting the needs of the builders.

The heat of the forge rolled over Lenui as he walked inside. Despite the multiple vents and built-in chimneys installed in the building, the interior of the smithery was more than ten degrees hotter than the spring afternoon outside. This made some people uncomfortable. It was right pleasant as far as he was concerned.

Lenui slammed the door shut behind him.

Bettie said nothing but turned and led him past the forges. Sweating humans looked up as he walked by. A few of them smiled at him, but quickly looked away when they saw the expression on his face. From the dwarf's demeanor, it seemed a larger than usual storm was brewing between the volatile couple and that was never a comfortable thing for the other smiths.

Lenui ignored them, mentally preparing himself for the battle he knew was coming. Problem was, it was hard to keep his mood focused. While they walked, his son, Jack, stared down at him with a wet gap-toothed smile, his hands gripping his mother's black ponytail. When Bettie was in the smithery, she lugged the child around in a pouch, strapped to her back like he was a sword in a scabbard. The child was most calm around the sounds of metalwork, something that Lenui found gall-durned adorable.

"Whatchoo grinnin' at, Jack?" Lenui grumped.

The baby giggled in response. Half his teeth were in and a curly fuzz of red hair capped his scalp. He cooed at Lenui, his slightly green-tinted skin glowing in the firelight as he let go of his mama's hair and reached for his daddy, his chubby hands grasping.

Lenui wasn't exactly sure what aspects of his heritage Jack was going to lean towards. At six months, the boy was already the size of most one-year-old dwarves. He seemed to have the wide frame of his father's heritage and the long legs of his mothers. But that didn't matter. He was a Firegobbler either way.

Betty opened the door at the back of the forge and led Lenui into the house attached at the back that was their home and private workspace. Unlike the metallic tang of the smithery, these rooms smelled of oiled leather and cooking spices. She took three paces into their great room and swung around to face him.

"What the hell's your problem?" Bettie asked, her eyes fierce, her hands on her hips. "Stumblin' around outside? Growlin'

44

and scarin' folks?"

"I wasn't stumblin'!" Lenui objected. "And I wasn't scarin' nobody."

"'Course you were! I was standin' next to Jimmy who was hammerin' away, and I could still hear you lettin' out a string of swears that'd curdle milk." Her expression turned wary. "What're you so pissed at?"

Lenui frowned. Surely he hadn't been that blasted loud. "I'm just steamed that that rat-milkin', mud-licker of a witch won't stay dead."

They had both been in the combined council meeting that day. The wizards had come through the portal to let them in on many surprises, one of them being the fact that Valtrek was the School's newly selected Head Wizard. But the most disturbing revelation was that Wizard Locksher had discovered that the evil that had been festering in the mountains was powered by Mellinda's magic.

Her glower lessened slightly. "Guess I can't blame you for bein' mad about that. But you do realize she ain't alive. Not really. That stuff in the mountain? That's just her magic and stuff. That's how Valtrek put it."

"Don't care how that moon-sniffer put it," Lenui declared. "It might be maggots instead of moonrats and it might be in the mountains instead of the dag-blamed forest, but it's still that witch we're dealin' with."

Bettie sighed. "Fine. Still don't explain where you been all day. I've been waitin' to talk to you for hours."

Little Jack, frustrated that he couldn't see his daddy from his angle, let out a screech of complaint and gave his momma's hair a hard pull. Grunting at the interruption, Bettie reached back and grasped the child. "Hold on, Jacky boy. I'll set you down."

"You never done like it when I called him Jacky," Lenui pointed out. Whenever he did it, he got barked at.

"Well, it's been growin' on me," the half-orc replied. She pulled the baby out of his harness and got him half way over her head before stopping with a wince. "Ack! Blast it, Lenui! Gimme a hand here. He ain't lettin' go."

"Naughty Jack, pullin' Momma's hair," Lenui said reproachfully.

Bettie bent down and Lenui reached up to help extract his son's pudgy fingers from his momma's curls. It wasn't exactly easy. His little fists were clenched hard and his fingers were sticky. He also seemed to think this game of tug of war was funny. He giggled as his daddy pried and when Lenui finally pulled the baby's hand free, he pulled several hairs out with it.

"Sorry 'bout that, Darlin'," Lenui said.

"Darlin'?" she asked suspiciously. "You butterin' me up or somethin'?"

"I can say that. Yer my dag-gum wife, ain't you?" he said, then changed the subject, planting a big smooch on the boy's face. "Our Jack here's got strong hands, just like his daddy. Don't you, bo- ack!"

One of those strong hands had just grasped a fistful of Lenui's mustache. It wasn't in a nice spot, either, but just at the base of the nose where it was most sensitive. Half 'stache hair and half nose hair. Jack laughed at his daddy's pained expression.

"That's right. You get him," Bettie said approvingly, then attempted to assist Lenui.

While the three of them struggled, a distinct squirting sound was heard. Jack chose that moment to let go. Bettie held the boy out at arm's length, her nose wrinkled.

"Ugh, he done soiled his drawers again." She carried Jack over to the table and grabbed a clean cloth diaper. She placed Jack down to clean him up and glanced back at Lenui. "Well? I asked you a dag-gum question! Where you been since the meetin'?"

"Oh, uh. Faldon called me into another meetin'," Lenui explained. "You know. About the plan."

Now that the Mage School was onboard, the army of warriors and wizards the schools were sending to combat Mellinda's power was finally being assembled. The Academy rebuild was to be put on hold and every graduate not on a crucial post was being called in. In just a few short days, they were marching to battle.

"I heard the plan," she said with a nod. "It's about blasted time we got our arses in gear. But what'd they need you for? Wobble ain't part of this."

As the Wobble Representative, Lenui's responsibilities on the Council were to coordinate the execution of the contract between the dwarves and the Academy. The Wobble smiths had their hands full meeting all the orders made by both schools. They couldn't spare a force of their own and Lenui had already said so.

"Well, it's a different part of the plan." He swallowed. This was the part he had been avoiding speaking to her about. "See, we're needin' to send a small group up separate from the army in secret. While the rest of the army heads straight fer that black lake, we're bringin' a secret weapon up to Fist and them ogres."

"Huh." Bettie finished changing Jack and carried him over to his play area. She set him down in the area that was surrounded by a wrought iron fence two feet tall. To Bettie's pride and consternation, the boy was an ambitious crawler. She was afraid he would wander over to the workbenches and pull something down on his head. Bettie handed him a hammer to chew on and turned back to face Lenui. "What kind of secret weapon?"

"I don't rightly know. That nose-picker Valtrek wouldn't say. All's I know is it's comin' from the Mage School and they can't bring it through the blasted portal. Wizard Beehn is drivin' it up here with that con-founded Wind Wagon of his."

"And?" she said expectantly, folding her arms. "They needed you at this meeting because . . ?"

It was like she already knew what was coming. He reached up to rub the back of his neck. "Uh, well, I know the area. Been up there lots of times. And since I know Fist real good, they was-uh . . . hopin' that I'd go up there with 'em." He waited for her to yell, but she just looked back at him. "Course, I told 'em you'd be madder'n hell if I, uh . . . ."

He licked his lips

"If you 'uh' what?" she asked expectantly.

"You know. You wouldn't want me to . . . ." Bettie was acting so calm. She knew where he was going with this. Why was she being so quiet about it? Surely she was about to bust out in anger any minute. Lenui frowned. He'd be horn-swaggled if he was gonna just sit back and take it. "Listen, woman! I don't care what yer gonna-!"

"You're goin'!" Bettie barked, thrusting a heavy finger in his direction. "And don't you think you're gonna get out of it, neither! Can't have my husband bein' a dag-gum layabout when Fist needs our help!"

Lenui blinked, his jaw hanging open.

"That ogre's been away from Sir Edge for months. I can tell you from experience that bein' away from your bondin' wizard ain't easy! He could use a friend," she said. "And that's just the small stuff! He's basically up there tryin' to be king ogre and deal with all that evil with nothin' but a thug of a giant, a crazy gnome warrior, and an even crazier wizard to help him!

"Anyway, it'll do you good to get out," she continued with a dismissive gesture. "You're no good stayin' still in one place too long. You'll start drivin' me crazy!"

" . . . right," Lenui said numbly. "So don't you try and stop me or nothin'."

"What're you talkin' about?" the half-orc said. She pointed over to one of her workbenches at a pile of finished leather. "Grab that armor and bring it over to me."

Flabbergasted, Lenui walked over and picked up the bulky pile. He turned to face her. "But . . . Now, just a gall-durn minute. What do you mean, I'll 'start drivin' you crazy'?"

"I've heard it from every dwarf I've ever met. 'Lenui Firegobbler's the best at everything a dwarf can be'," she complained. "And they're right. You're the meanest. You're the toughest. You're the best fighter. You're the best drinker." She shrugged. "A passable lover."

"Passable!" Lenui protested.

"You may even be the best blasted blacksmith in the friggin' known lands!" Bettie continued. "But one thing you ain't is a settler. Hell, truth be told, you're only half blacksmith."

Lenui sputtered in confusion and outrage. He would have gesticulated wildly if his arms hadn't been full of blasted leather goods. "That ain't true!"

"'Course it is!" she declared. "Sure, your papa is a Firegobbler; true smithin' blood if there ever was one. But you're momma's the dag-gum queen of rogues."

Lenny threw the armor on the ground. "I ain't like her!"

"'Course you ain't," she said with a sigh. "But you gotta admit you do got that same wanderlust in your blood. You can't be satisfied with a life settled down. You never have been."

Lenui couldn't argue with the past. No matter how many times he'd tried over the years to set up shop and stay at the forge, he hadn't been able to sit still long. As much as he loved smithing he eventually had to go adventuring. He shook his head.

"Maybe it was that way before. But life with you, Bettie girl . . . It ain't ever too settled." Lenui grinned his gap-toothed grin. "Yer always an adventure."

The half-orc snorted. "Don't you try comin' at me with a mouthful of roses, Lenui Firegobbler! You know I ain't happy about this!" She gave him a pouty look. "I'd always rather you stay than be goin'."

Lenui sighed. "I understand that, Bettie. I know I just got this new job here. The Wobble folks're dependin' on me." He reached up and rubbed the back of his neck again. Now that he wasn't so worked up it was harder to ignore the many good points arguing that he shouldn't go. "'Sides, we just barely got married. And I got me a son now. I know you don't want me runnin' off and leavin' you stuck with Jack all on yer own."

"You think I can't handle bein' alone with my own son?" she scoffed, startling him. "Like I said. You ain't gettin' out of this!"

"What's yer miff?" he said. "I'm just sayin' the same durn things you said to me when I wanted to go and help Djeri save that rogue horse."

"That was different! We're here now and this is part of your job. 'Sides, if you had gone with 'em you could've been the one that was-." Her mouth clamped shut.

"That was what?" Lenny asked. So she was bringing that up again. Really? When it was an argument she'd never win? "Blast it, if Id've been there with 'em, maybe I would've made a difference! Maybe the dag-blamed rogue would've lived."

Bettie blinked at him, then said softly, "We don't know that." She squared her shoulders. "Point is, now's different."

Lenny scratched his head. This was making no sense to him. "So you really want me to go?"

"No," she said with a frustrated laugh. "But you're goin' anyway! That's what I've been sayin'!"

"Well, okay, then. We agree. I . . ." Lenui's voice trailed off, confused. Things never went this way. Sometimes it ended in fierce kissing, but never quiet agreement. His bushy brows rose in sudden understanding. "Just a gad-burned minute!"

"What?" she snapped.

"Yer tryin' to turn this around on me, ain't you? You think if you yell at me to leave, I'll argue back and stay!"

Bettie's massive shoulders shook as she let out a belly roar of laughter. "Ah gods! My husband's a dag-gum idiot!"

Lenui frowned. "Smart enough to catch on to you."

"Dag-blast it, Lenui! I knew you was goin' before you came in here. Faldon came by earlier and told me about the plan already." She pointed at the floor. "Take a look at that leather you threw down, stupid."

"What're you talkin' 'bout? It's just one of those new suits of armor you've been workin' on." He looked down at the detailed leather breastplate and his eyes widened as he noticed the red letter 'F' sewn onto the center. He looked up at her in surprise. "For me?"

"You hated your old set," Bettie said, her eyes gauging his reaction. "And since its gone . . . I mean, since you gave it to your nephew. I thought, why not make you one that you might actually wear?"

"Me?" he said, raising one bushy eyebrow. "In leather armor?"

He'd never considered it before. Armor of any type was too constrictive. Besides, he had beaten down plenty of leather armor wearers in his day. As far as he was concerned, it wasn't much better than cloth.

"And why not?" she asked. "Does it have to be a crab suit or nothin' with you? 'Sides, this ain't just any leather armor."

He picked it up again, paying attention this time. Except for the red 'F' in the center of the chest piece, the armor was a nondescript brown. It consisted of a cuirass along with a set of thigh plates and greaves. The plated sections were thick, but not too weighty and seemed surprisingly flexible. He examined the runes worked into the leather and nodded appreciatively. It was ambitious work. "How long you been workin' on this?"

"Just got it magicked a few days ago, but I've been workin' on it for weeks," she added. "Ever since that Woodblade girl left us back at Coal's Keep."

He cocked his head. "This is made with that stuff she gave you? I thought you said it wouldn't work."

"Yeah, well I started makin' this set before I found that out," Bettie said with a scowl.

Woodblade's grampa's formula, though effective, depended on Jharro Tree sap. Bettie's grand plans for mass manufacturing of the recipe were ruined when she discovered the stuff was sacred to the elves in the grove. That had been a particularly bitter revelation. She'd had Tolivar talk to Willum about it, but he'd refused to even ask the Roo-Tan for it.

"Blasted woman!" Bettie griped. "Sellin' me an impossible dream. The sap she gave me was more than enough to finish this set, though. Try it on."

"I dunno. I'm perty hard to fit," he said dubiously.

"You think I don't know every inch of your body by now? I said, try it on!"

Frowning, he loosened the ties at the sides of the armor. As he pulled the cuirass over his head, he could smell Woodblade's formula. It had a distinctly minty aroma.

"Well?" she asked.

He rotated his arms and arched his back, then nodded appreciatively. Bettie had been smart about the construction, keeping his particular likes in mind. It was sleeveless and the flexibility of the leather added a nice freedom of movement. "I'd say my wife's the best dag-gum leatherworker I ever seen."

"And you'd be right," she agreed. "Now the best thing about that formula is it's durn hard to pierce. Almost as good at stopping arrows as plate. Also, with the runing I added, it'll repel water and fire."

"And if I get hit by a hammer?" he asked with a knowing smile.

Bettie chuckled. "So you noticed those runes too, did you?"

"That's some clever work. If'n it works, the stuff actually could be better than plate." According to the runes he had seen in the leather, the armor had an effect of repelling force that came against it. The harder it was hit, the harder it pushed back. "Does it work?"

Bettie shrugged. "It has its limits. After all, leather don't hold magic as well as metal does. But I gotta tell you, there's somethin' about that sap. It's like it makes the magic stronger."

"Bah!" said a small voice and there was the sound of metal hitting the floor.

Lenui looked towards Jacky's pen and grinned. "That little booger."

The six-month-old had used the bars of his pen to pull himself to a standing position. He wobbled there on unsteady legs, his hands gripping the bars, a serious look on his face. The sound they had heard was him throwing his hammer out of the pen.

Lenui placed his arm around his wife's waist and pulled her in close. "Least I didn't miss his first time standin' on his own."

"That you didn't," Bettie said and draping her own arm across her husband's broad shoulders. "Good boy, Jacky!"

Though she was smiling along with him, Bettie was knotted with worry inside. Lenui would possibly be away for months. He was gonna miss a lot of Jacky's firsts.

She hated that he was going up there to fight this evil and hated even more that she couldn't go along with him. But she had to let him go and quick, before he found out what had happened to his nephew Djeri. If Lenny heard about that, there would be no stopping him. He'd be off to Malaroo.

Just the thought brought back the horrific memories

Willum had shared through the bond the night before; the nightmarish landscape of that behemoth swallowing people up by the hundreds. She swallowed. There was no way she was letting her husband go up against that.

Chapter Five

Deathclaw darted forward, keeping his body low to avoid a sweeping attack. His senses were heightened, his mind in complete focus, slowing the world down around him as he found a narrow opening for his blade. He thrust Star out in a fierce stab.

"Whoop!" cried Cletus, jumping backwards and sucking in his narrow gut to avoid being skewered. "Almost!"

Deathclaw's attack had left him exposed and the raptoid knew it. In his mind's awakened state, he could see Cletus' chain weapon circling back around, the ball on the end aimed at his head. It was coming too fast for him to avoid completely. He arched his back and twisted his head, allowing the weapon to skip off of his cheek instead of making a direct hit.

"Got you!" the lanky gnome said gleefully as he brought the weapon back in and spun it in a tight loop at his side, readying himself for another attack.

Had it been one of the heavy steel balls that Cletus usually used, this glancing blow would have shattered Deathclaw's cheekbone. That result was something the raptoid would have found uncomfortable, but it would have been an acceptable result. Instead, the small weighted bag on the end of the chain delivered a stinging slap, connecting with a puff of blue powder.

This left him unharmed but marked, a blue spot on his cheek joining several other blue marks on his body. Cletus, on the other hand, was unmarked. This meant that he had so far proved the superior fighter. That was not an acceptable result.

And yet, if your sword strike had landed, Cletus would have been badly injured and we don't have a way to heal him out here, Justan reminded him calmly through the bond.

Justan watched the two warriors battle from his perch on the rear porch of Beth's house. He kept his hand gripping the handle of Peace. The weapon's magic pulled away his emotion, allowing him to focus on their movements. The sparring match was occurring in Sir Hilt's training circle, a wide area that had been cleared of vegetation. Its only decoration was a ragged wooden training dummy, which both warriors had used to their advantage during the fight.

I know how to avoid a death blow, Deathclaw replied angrily.

Don't hurt him, though, Gwyrtha added from her position just outside the training circle where she lay, sunning herself on the open ground. She yawned widely, exposing her impressive mouthful of sharp teeth. *He's a nice gnome.*

"Ready?" Cletus asked, his body balanced on the tips of the toes of his left foot as he pirouetted, his chain swinging in wider and wider loops. Suddenly, he lurched towards the raptoid, his long arm sweeping forward, sending the weighted blue end at his opponent in a straight line as if it were a spear thrust.

Letting out a chirp of defiance, Deathclaw tossed his sword into the air and spun, letting the chain pass narrowly by. Mid-spin, he pulled a throwing knife from the bandoleer that was slung across his chest. As he came back around to face Cletus, he caught the hilt of his sword with his off hand and threw the knife.

The thrown blade darted for Cletus' chest.

Justan watched with time-slowed eyes as the gnome turned, sliding his body to the side. As the blade reached the spot where his heart would have been, Cletus's head shot forward and he caught the knife's handle in his teeth. At the same time, he jerked the chain back towards him.

Deathclaw snarled in frustration at the gnome's ridiculous dexterity. He didn't notice the gnome's retraction of the chain until too late. The blue bag hit him on the back of the knee with a puff of blue powder. Had it been one of the gnome's bladed attachments, it might have severed a hamstring.

Cletus laughed in a child-like manner, balancing the tip of the throwing knife on one finger. "This is fun! I like fighting you,

Death-guy. Most people can't slow the world like you!"

"My name is Deathclaw!" Deathclaw hissed.

Though his emotions were sucked away by his sword, Justan was awed by the gnome's performance. This wasn't the first time Deathclaw has sparred with Cletus, but it was the first time Justan had watched them do it and it was a dazzling display. "So you can slow the world too?"

Cletus blinked and said matter-of-factly, "For me, the world is always slow."

Coming from anyone else that statement would have felt like a boastful exaggeration. But from what Justan had seen of Cletus, the gnome didn't know how to embellish the truth. That meant that somehow, Cletus lived his life in a constant state of high sensory focus.

"Amazing," Justan said. Not even Deathclaw could do that. He wondered what it would take to defeat him. With Cletus' combination of dexterity and skill with his weapon, it would be near impossible for a swordsman to do so alone.

"You give him too much credit," the raptoid complained, his eyes narrowed at the gnome. "He leaves openings. I just have not managed to pierce them yet."

"Cletus, when was the last time you lost a fight?" Justan asked.

"When I was little, I got beat lots," Cletus replied. He blinked for a moment and his face momentarily took on a blank expression. It passed quickly. "But one day I won. No one ever hit me since."

"No one has even hit you?" Justan asked.

"Nope," said the gnome, pausing to rub his nose.

Just how long ago was that? Justan wondered.

Gnomes live a long time, Gwyrtha volunteered. The rogue horse was still lying on the ground, but her head was up and she was watching them intently.

"Can we fight now?" Cletus' asked, his eyes bounced curiously between Justan and his bonded. A sudden smile broadened the gnome warrior's face. "Come on, Mister Sir Edge.

You fight me too! I like fighting two scary guys."

Justan stood, rotating his shoulders. "Why not? This could be fun."

"I do not need your help!" Deathclaw hissed.

"This will be good practice," Justan replied. "I doubt he has faced two bonded warriors."

"Only once. They were real mad." Cletus said with a shake of his head. "But maybe you two will be better?"

The gnome sent the throwing knife back at Deathclaw with an effortless toss. The raptoid snatched it out of the air and placed it back in his bandoleer, his lip curled in anger.

"No, Justan. I must defeat him alone," Deathclaw said, then added through the bond, *Do you not believe I can?*

Justan understood the frustration in his thoughts. Deathclaw was unused to accepting defeat and yet it was all he had received at the hands of this gnome. His pride had been bruised. Unfortunately, from what Justan had seen, the likelihood of the raptoid defeating Cletus was slim. At least with the parameters of the fight set as they were now.

Justan grunted and put Peace away in its sheath, allowing his emotions to flow back over his mind. Clinical detachment was not what Deathclaw needed from him at the moment.

"Cletus, I believe that Deathclaw can hit you," he said confidently. "And he can do it without me moving from this spot."

"He can?" Cletus said with an eager smile.

Deathclaw cocked his head at Justan. "What do you have in mind?"

Justan addressed Cletus. "But if he is to fight his best, you must put away your sparring bags. Use your regular weapons."

Cletus gathered the ends of his chain in his hand, but hesitated. "If I do this, I will hurt him."

"Does that bother you, Deathclaw?" Justan asked.

The raptoid's eyes narrowed. "I do not fear pain."

"Okay," Cletus said with a shrug. "I will try not to kill him."

He removed the two practice bags from the chain and

reached into his vest to withdraw shiny metal implements. On one end of the chain he clipped a curved blade. On the other, a steel ball. Both items were engraved with tiny runes.

Justan switched quickly to mage sight to see if he could determine their uses. Their glow was dull, a mix of black and blue, likely just reinforcing magic so that the implements couldn't be damaged. He didn't see any spirit magic on the implements but he noted that there was a soft white glow to the chain.

"Deathclaw, give me your sword," Justan said.

The raptoid narrowed his eyes, confusion flooding the bond. "Why should I do this?"

"It only slows you down," Justan replied. He glanced over at Cletus, who was polishing the curved blade implement with the edge of his vest, humming tunelessly to himself. "Your sword work is not your strength."

Deathclaw frowned. He had put a great deal of effort in his training and his skill with the weapon had grown greatly from what it was at the end of the war. He had even modified the fingers on his right hand to improve his grip.

Don't let that bother you. You are good, Justan explained through the bond. In fact, he figured that Deathclaw was as good as most Academy trained swordsmen. *But Cletus is different than other opponents. From what Willum has told me, he is a special talent even among gnome warriors. You won't defeat him with Star. You will win because you are a raptoid.*

Begrudgingly, Deathclaw held his sword out to Justan. *Very well. What would you have me do?*

This is no longer a regular sparring match. Your goal in this fight isn't to defeat Cletus. It is only to mark him, Justan sent, reminding Deathclaw of his old raptoid tradition of stalking dangerous prey.

If a raptoid pack knew they couldn't defeat an enemy, they would follow the beast around and harry it for weeks, getting in just close enough to slash it with their claws. Over time, the beast would tire. Sick from infection and lack of sleep, it would become easy to defeat.

Just cut him? Deathclaw said, looking down at the long

claws of his left hand.

That's all? Gwyrtha asked with a snort, laying her head back down on the ground. She rolled to her back, letting the sun warm her belly.

Justan ignored her, keeping his thoughts directed to Deathclaw. *He has not been wounded in battle since he was a child. You will be the first warrior in decades, perhaps centuries to do so.*

This is a worthy goal, Deathclaw decided with a nod. He pointed to Cletus. "This fight does not stop until I cut you, Gnome."

Cletus blinked and looked up from his polishing. He grinned and nodded. "You think so?"

Deathclaw pulled the sword sheath off of his back and tossed it to Justan. He grew more eager as he thought about it. "Do not hold yourself back. Your weapon will not kill me."

Cletus' smile widened at the confidence in the raptoid's voice. "Okay!"

Justan slid Star into its sheath and watched with interest as Deathclaw went into a crouch, his arms raised at his side as he stalked the gnome. Cletus twirled his weapon. As the two warriors circled each other, Gwyrtha began to softly snore.

Deathclaw made the first move. He ran towards the gnome and ducked down low, his chest close to the ground to avoid the slashing end of Cletus' weapon. The blade missed him by inches and Deathclaw leapt towards the gnome.

Cletus slid to the right, letting Deathclaw slip past him and into the arcing path of the weighted ball. The raptoid arched his back, bending over backwards to avoid the attack. He then was forced to drop to the ground and roll to the side as the slashing end swung down from above to scrape the dirt where he had been.

Justan nodded in approval. Deathclaw's mind and senses were in complete focus, enabling him a complete awareness and control over his body that only he could achieve. He contorted, avoiding the slashing and bashing attacks of the gnome's weapon while somehow managing attacks of his own. He struck at Cletus with his wicked claws and slashes of his barbed tail.

Cletus, however, was every bit as agile and seemed to have an almost unnatural sense of what Deathclaw's every move would be before he made it. The gnome spun and hopped and ducked, acrobatically dodging each strike. The only way that Justan knew he was having difficulty with Deathclaw was the fact that Cletus had stopped making comments and odd exclamations.

It was truly an impressive display. Several minutes went by without either of them managing to land a blow. Then the tone of the battle shifted. Cletus had taken control of the fight, leading Deathclaw around the circle, keeping him at bay with frequent sweeping attacks. Finally, tired of taking only the openings that Cletus gave him, Deathclaw let himself be hit.

He waited for the bladed end of the weapon to sweep towards him and darted forward, twisting his torso slightly to lessen the severity of the wound. The blade was sharp. Its edge cut through the tiny scales of his skin starting at his right shoulder and continuing at an angle across his back, just skipping across the bone of one rib. Deathclaw lunged at the gnome, his claws stretched out before him.

Cletus, his eyes wide with surprise, rolled backwards onto the ground and kicked upwards with both feet, sending the raptoid up and over him. Deathclaw arced over him and hit the ground in a roll.

"Close!" Cletus gasped as he came to his feet, more wary of the raptoid who was already coming back at him.

Hot blood poured down Deathclaw's back. Justan watched with slowed vision while sending tendrils of thought through the bond to probe the raptoid's injury. Several layers of muscle had been cut, something that would have hampered Deathclaw's movement had his body not been so adaptive to injury. Other muscle groups were already taking up the strain while his regenerative powers kicked into gear.

The two fighters were now outside of the training circle. Deathclaw lurched after Cletus, who was backing into the space between Beth's home and the guest house behind it. The gnome spun the two ends of his chains in front of him defensively as he considered the best form of attack.

Gwyrtha's eyes opened suddenly and her mind perked up from sleep. *Beth is coming. I smell her and the baby.*

Alright, Justan replied absently, his mind bent on the fight. It was difficult to aid Deathclaw's healing while the raptoid was moving so fiercely.

Gwyrtha rolled over and came to her feet, looking into the trees in the direction of the Grove. *And that Tarah woman is with her.*

"Hi, Gwyrtha," said a young disembodied voice and out of thin air, a small elf child appeared. She looked to be one of the Jharro Grove elves, with dark skin and black hair, but she wore clothing in the Roo-Tan style and white ribbons were woven into the intricate braids that framed her face.

Gwyrtha snorted. *Hi, Esmine.*

Esmine's insubstantial form patted Gwyrtha's nose and turned her eyes onto the two warriors. She disappeared and reappeared next to Justan. "What're they fighting for?"

"Sparring," Justan corrected briefly, completely absorbed with the battle.

Esmine folded her small arms. "Oh. Boring," she said and disappeared again.

Beth and Tarah soon appeared on the trail, approaching the house. Beth carried Sherl-Ann in her arms and walked at a brisk pace. She was wearing her usual garb, a brown blouse and a pair of baggy pants that were gathered at the ankles.

Tarah followed behind her, wearing the green and brown leather armor that she had gotten from Bettie, her gray staff held loosely in one hand. The woman was drenched with sweat, having just finished an intense training session with Tolynn. Nevertheless, her exhaustion didn't explain the blank expression on her face.

Justan didn't even turn to look at them. The battle between Deathclaw and Cletus had reached a ridiculous speed. The two gifted fighters danced around each other, rushing across the yard. If Justan hadn't slowed the world, he wouldn't have been able to keep track of it.

Deathclaw leapt to avoid a low spear-like thrust of the steel ball and Cletus' weapon struck the side of a large rain-collecting pot that stood near the porch. Half of the pot broke into large shards and water spilled out over the ground.

"Hey!" Beth said at the sound of the broken pottery. "Settle down!"

The two of them weren't listening. There was no room for anything else in their minds, but each other, both warriors looking for the next possible opening.

Deathclaw finally decided it wasn't worth dodging attacks anymore. He dove right into Cletus' wall of whirring chain. His left side took a rib-cracking hit from the heavy ball. The curved blade cut deeply into his thigh. The raptoid ignored the blows and continued forward, but Cletus juked to the side and Deathclaw's outstretched claws met only air.

Expecting that he would likely miss, Deathclaw twisted and lashed out with his tail as he looked for the next incoming strike of the gnome's chain. The ball came in quicker than he expected, striking his left side in nearly the same place as the time before, turning one of his cracked ribs into a broken one.

Deathclaw noted the injury, but there was no time to worry about it. He tightened his control over his senses and, slowing the world as much as possible, focused on grabbing that chain. He felt it gliding across his palm. The slivery metal slid through his fingers, but at the last moment his hand clenched, grasping it just above the ball.

Exulting, he yanked back on the chain, expecting to pull the gnome into striking range. However, there was no resistance. Cletus stood still, holding loosely to the far end of the chain, a look of shock on his face.

"You got me," Cletus said in a stunned voice, his expression wooden. A wide gash crossed his cheek not far under his eye. Deathclaw realized that his tail barb must have caught the gnome across the face when he had spun around.

Cletus reached up to his cheek and touched it, then looked at his bloody fingers. The sudden smile that followed caused the wound to gape. "Death-guy, you got me!"

Breathing heavily, his body aching and tingling as it tried to repair his various wounds, Deathclaw lurched in surprise and pain as the gnome caught him up in an excited hug.

"You did it!" Cletus said with a laugh. He let go quickly and turned to face the others. He pointed at the gash. "Look you guys! Tarah! Look what he did!"

Tarah, who was standing on the porch, her blank stare resting on the broken rain pot, turned her head and looked at him. Her eyes widened, her mouth dropping open ever so slightly as she noticed the gnome's injury for the first time. "Oh."

"I can feel it hurt! Look, I think it's a deep one!" Cletus added, spreading the wound open with his fingers so that they could see.

Beth winced. "We see it, honey. Now stop messing with it and come here."

"Okay," Cletus said and leaned in close so that she could see it up close. "Will it need to be stitched up? I can do it. I know how."

"That won't be necessary," Beth replied firmly, reaching for a pouch tied at her hip. "I will do it, but first let's put something on it so it doesn't get infected."

"Ooh! Will it leave a scar? A mean one?" Cletus asked excitedly. "So I can look scary?"

"Hopefully I'm a better seamstress than that," Beth replied. While she tugged at the pouch strings with her free hand, Sherl-Ann squealed and reached for the gnome's wound. Beth pulled her away and held her out to Tarah. "Take her for a moment. Would you, Tarah dear?"

Tarah was still staring in surprise at Cletus' wound. Blinking as if suddenly waking from a trance, she accepted Sherl-Ann from her mother. "Uh, they broke your pot," she said, pointing towards the broken rain pot and the muddy ground around it.

"I'm sorry, Pretty Beth! So sorry! I can fix it!" Cletus darted over to the broken pot and picked up the shards, trying to put them back in place.

"Don't bother, Honey," Beth said with a sigh.

He managed to put the pot more or less together. He smiled

at his success, but when he let go it collapsed instantly. His shoulders slumped. "No, I can't."

"I don't care about the pot, Cletus! Now come back over here." Beth said.

Justan had closed his eyes and sent his thoughts through the bond to inspect Deathclaw's injuries. As usual, the raptoid's regenerative magic was already at work. His bleeding had already slowed. Justan focused on fixing the broken rib. *I knew you would do it.*

All I did was gash him, Deathclaw replied, but he could not keep the satisfaction out of his thoughts.

Justan smiled. Finished with the rib, he helped to close the gashes in his back and thigh. He then left the raptoid's body to finish its work.

He opened his eyes to see Beth uncork a small ceramic jar that she had taken out of her pouch and dipped her finger inside. When Cletus returned to her side, she pulled out a dollop of pink waxy substance and reached up to rub it over the gnome's wound. Justan smelled the unmistakable minty aroma of Jharro Sap.

"Stings a little," Cletus said with a wince. His nose wrinkled. "Stinks like elf magic and tree blood."

"Cletus," Justan said curiously. "When you were fighting with Deathclaw I noticed spirit magic in your chain. Do you have a spirit bound to it?"

"In Chainy?" The gnome thought about it for a moment and nodded. "Yep." He kissed the weapon. "Good Chainy."

"Can I touch your, uh, Chainy?" Beth asked, her curiosity piqued. Hesitantly, Cletus nodded and held it out towards her. She ran the fine chain through her fingers, her eyes closed in concentration. Her brow rose in surprise. "It's . . . a kitten. Or at least it was a kitten when it was bound. The binding spell is very old."

His chain . . . is a kitty? Gwyrtha sent.

"An odd choice for a weapon's spirit," Deathclaw agreed.

"Good Chainy," Cletus repeated, pulling the weapon out of Beth's fingers and caressing it gently.

To Justan it made all too much sense. He shook his head in sad disbelief. "So it's true. I was hoping that was just a story."

"What story?" Beth asked, frowning at the expression on his face.

Justan folded his arms. "The last time I was in the Mage School library I saw a book about gnome warriors. It was one of the books recently unsealed now that the ban on teaching spirit magic has been lifted."

It had been a thick volume with an elaborately engraved cover entitled: *Deadliest Fighters; The Rearing and Training of Gnome Warriors in Alberri*. He had picked it up out of curiosity and had been leafing through the volume when a chapter title had caught his attention. '*The Barbaric Practice of Bound Weapon Imprinting*'.

"It had a section that discussed the way gnome warrior children were raised," Justan continued. "From the time they are small, the stewards encourage them to interact with different weapons. Once they have grown to a certain age and show a propensity for a particular weapon type, the stewards take the other weapons away. Sometimes, this doesn't go too well."

"Why take the other weapons away?" Deathclaw asked. "Is it not good for warriors to know many types?"

"Not for us," Cletus said, still caressing his chain.

"Right. The way their minds work, finding a focus is very important," Justan explained. "The narrower the focus, the better their chance to excel. For gnome scholars this means finding a favorite field of study. For warriors, this means specializing in a particular weapon type. Some of the human stewards believe that in order to get the most out of the warrior's skills it is best if they get the child to focus on one particular weapon."

Justan sighed. "But, like I was saying, the children didn't always cooperate. Some of them grew bored when left with only one choice. According to this book, the stewards came up with a way to make sure that the children became attached to their weapon."

"They gave them a pet," Tarah replied sadly. Sherl-Ann patted her face in response.

"Yeah," Justan said. "Then once the child was attached to the pet, the stewards would kill it and bind its soul to the weapon."

"How horrible!" Beth said, reaching out to pat the gnome's shoulder. "But how would that work? The requirements for binding-."

"They left the kitten with him for several days. Until they were sure that he loved it," Tarah said. "Then they told him that if he did not defeat his teacher, the kitten would die."

Beth looked to Tarah. "Did you see this last night? Is that what affected you so badly?"

It had only been three days since Tarah had returned from the treaty massacre. The poor thing had been a sobbing mess mourning Djeri's loss. Tolynn had spent her time with Tarah training her vigorously, trying to shake her from her grief while Beth had tried to convince Tarah that there was still a chance that Djeri could be able to return to her. After all, they knew that he was still alive, even if he was inside the belly of the behemoth.

The combination of Tolynn's exhaustive training and Beth's mothering had seemed to be working. She had even made progress in her ability to control her magic. Just the day before, Tarah had been determined to find a way to rescue the dwarf. Then Beth had told her to try her powers on Cletus. That had caused another collapse. One she was just now seeming to wake up from.

"Of course, defeating his teacher was an impossible task," Tarah said, but she wasn't speaking to Beth. Her mind was still on what she had seen in Cletus' memories. "But they had him convinced. He fought hard and when he failed, the kitten died. This fulfilled the requirement that he be the one responsible for its death. Then they did something with the chain. I think it must have been prepared in advance, like my staff was, to absorb the kitten's blood."

Justan grimaced, "They made him eat it?"

"No!" said Cletus. "I wouldn't eat Chainy!"

"The stewards must have tricked him into it somehow," Tarah replied. She ran a hand through her hair and sighed, realizing that it was an oily mess. She really needed a bath. "Anyway, they told him that the cat could live in his chain. All he had to do was call out to it and, well, it worked. It's the only weapon he's cared about since."

"How long ago was that?" Justan wondered.

"It is hard to tell with him," Tarah said. "He doesn't think of time like the rest of us."

"Sometimes I think this world is a horrible place." Beth said with a shake of her head. She pulled a needle and some thread out of her pouch and beckoned at Cletus to come closer. "Alright, Honey, now bend down so I can do this at eye level."

"Like this?" Cletus said, bending his narrow seven foot frame and leaning in close to her.

She grabbed the gnome's floppy ear and moved him where she wanted him. "Now stand still while I do this. It might sting, but the sap will keep it from hurting too much."

Hilt comes, Gwyrtha sent.

Esmine reappeared suddenly, the elf child sitting on Gwyrtha's back. "Hilt's coming," she said, pointing to the trees beyond the guest house.

Moments later, Hilt walked around the edge of the building carrying a bulging bag over his shoulder. He frowned. "Hey! Who broke the rain pot?"

"Sorry!" Cletus said.

"I told you to hold still!" Beth snapped, tweaking the gnome's ear. She raised her voice. "Cletus and Deathclaw were fighting, Dear!"

Sir Hilt came up to the porch. The named warrior's eyebrows shot up when he saw what Beth was doing. He glanced at Deathclaw. "You hit him?"

"I did," the raptoid said.

"No need to be so proud about it, Scaley," Beth grumped.

"But he should be," Hilt said, grinning approvingly as he set the bag down gently on the porch. "I've sparred with Cletus many times and I never managed it."

"Da!" cried Sherl-Ann, twisting in Tarah's arms and reaching for her adoptive father.

"Sherl-Girl!" Hilt replied, taking the baby in his arms. He

planted a kiss on her cheek and looked back at Justan. "Didn't know you'd be down here. Saw Jhonate leaving her mother's rooms back at the Palace. I figured you would be with her."

"Oh," said Justan. Beth's house was just far enough from the palace that he couldn't make out Jhonate's emotions through the Jharro ring on his finger, but he knew she was probably irritated that he wasn't there. "Actually, the reason we are here is that I wanted to talk to you. I thought you would be back from that last meeting a while ago."

Ever since the army had returned from the treaty disaster, Xedrion had been in constant meetings. There was so much to decide with the dual threats of the Troll Mother and the Mer-Dan Collective to worry about. Justan and Hilt had been taking shifts as the Protector's "Outsider Representative" in these meetings and in Justan's mind they were just wasting too much time. Action was needed and the Roo-Tan were nowhere near ready to act.

"I stopped at the market on the way home," Hilt explained, gesturing to the bag. "What did you want to talk to me about?"

"It's about my swords," Justan said. "Ever since we returned to Roo-Tan'lan, I can't get them to work right."

Chapter Six

"Your swords don't . . . work right?" Hilt said, one eyebrow raised. Sherl-Ann, focused on her father's face, tried to duplicate his expression but just ended up blinking weirdly.

"Okay, that didn't quite come out right," Justan said, chuckling at himself. "What I mean to say is that, when we were back at the valley, I was able to do things with the magic of my swords that I haven't been able to replicate since we came back."

"Ow-ow-ow!" complained Cletus, jerking back from Beth and pulling the needle and thread out of her hand, leaving them to dangle from the gash on his cheek. She had only been partway finished with the second stitch. "You said 'sting', Pretty Beth. That's an ouch!"

"Shush and be still!" Beth reprimanded. She smacked the top of his head and grasped his ear, pulling the tall gnome's face back in close again. "If you keep moving, there will be many more ouches." She picked up the needle and went back to work, mumbling under her breath, "Blasted warriors become babies when a wound needs tended to!"

Sherl-Ann yawned and Hilt shifted the baby in his arms. "What haven't you been able to do, Edge? I'll see if I can help you work it out."

Justan hesitated. "It's complicated. Look, I think the thing that would help me the most is if you could tell me how you are able to control the magic in your swords."

"That's a bit of an odd question coming from you," Hilt said. "Your magic is much more complicated than mine."

"But maybe it isn't," Justan replied. "The thing I am trying to understand is this. You don't have any magical talent of your own, right?"

"Correct," said Hilt, wondering where Justan was going with this.

"Then how do you make your swords work the way you do? Lenny told me that there are limits when making magical weapons. He said that once he set the magic in the runes, it couldn't be changed. For instance, Lenny runed Fist's mace to speed up the movement of whoever is holding it. The downside is it's tiring and he can't turn that magic off. He has to wear a glove when holding the mace if he doesn't want to be sped up."

Hilt nodded. "I think I understand what you mean. Lenui explained the same thing to me the day I asked him to make my swords. But I would think the answer would be obvious to you." He turned to Tarah. "Could you take Sherl-Ann, please?"

"Sure," Tarah replied, but when she reached for the baby, Sherl-Ann complained, crying out and reaching for Hilt as he placed her in Tarah's arms. Tarah stuck out her bottom lip. "Hey, what's wrong? It's me. 'Rah-Rah', remember?"

Sherl-Ann's cries only increased as she stepped away from Hilt. Beth rolled her eyes, knowing how this would go. "Sherl-Ann. Shh, baby girl! Listen. Do you want to go to Deathclaw?"

The child's bawling ceased suddenly. "Caw-Caw?" She said, looking around with red-rimmed eyes.

Giving Beth an irritated hiss, the raptoid trudged over to Tarah and held out his hands. "Very well. Come, Sherl-Ann."

"Caw-Caw!"

Much to Tarah's chagrin, the baby went to him happily. "Fine," Tarah said. "See if I share my food with you later."

Ignoring her, Sherl-Ann placed a sloppy kiss on the side of Deathclaw's scaly face before laying her head contentedly on his shoulder.

Babies, Deathclaw grumbled through the bond.

Smiling at his daughter's attachment to the raptoid, Hilt returned his attention to Justan. "Lenui made Northwind and Southwind with the same limitations any other magical weapons have."

The named warrior drew his swords from the sheaths at his hips and spun them with his wrists. To the casual eye, it would have seemed that he had regained full mobility of the hand that had been severed, but Justan noticed that the movement of the left sword was slightly behind that of the right. He also knew that Hilt still struggled with his grip. It was possible that he would never regain full strength with that hand again.

"When I first received them, they had but one ability. You should be able to see it using your, uh, mage sight. Watch," he said and spun the swords again, slowly.

As they moved through the air, Justan's mage sight showed him a yellow blade of air magic extending from the tips of the swords about two inches past the metal.

"The way Lenui designed them, the air blades get longer the harder the swords are swung." Hilt raised his right sword and swiped downwards sharply. This time the air magic extended further. "If I swing as hard as I can, I can get the air blade to extend a full foot from the tip."

"Deadly for an enemy who does not know it is coming," Deathclaw observed.

Hilt smiled. "Quite handy in battle, yes? But also a nuisance. When I first began to train with them, there was quite a frightening learning period. I gave myself several nasty cuts before I got used to the magic."

"I imagine it was dangerous to your fellow soldiers too," Justan observed.

"Indeed! In the press of battle, an otherwise safe move could wound an ally," the named warrior replied. "Not to mention training battles. For a long time, I had to carry two sets of swords. Since I couldn't safely spar with Northwind and Southwind, I needed a pair for practice."

"Were they the two swords that you gave me?" Justan asked.

"Right," Hilt said with a smile and a nod. "Those were the first swords Lenui made me, long before I had gained any notoriety. Whatever happened to those anyway?"

Justan blinked, realizing, strangely enough, that Hilt hadn't broached that subject before. "Oh. Well about that-."

"He broke them," Deathclaw said, softly patting Sherl-Ann's back. The baby had nearly fallen to sleep, her clear blue eyes drooping shut.

Justan shot the raptoid a mental glare. "Well, technically, I only broke one of them. It happened while I was fighting one of Ewzad Vriil's armored orcs. The other one was stolen from me when his men captured me back in Dremald. I'm not quite sure what happened to it."

"Oh," said Hilt, sounding a bit disappointed. "That's a pity."

"I felt terrible about it," Justan said. "That was a few months before Lenny made Peace and Rage for me."

Sir Hilt waved away Justan's apologetic look. "Such things happen. Anyway, once I felt confident with the blades, I took them to the Bowl of Souls. I dipped them in the water and, well, you know what happened there."

Justan nodded. "So it's as I suspected. Your ability to control the swords came from the bond the Bowl gave you."

"That is likely the way in which I am able to communicate my desires to them, yes, but there is more to it than that," Hilt said, giving Justan a strange look. He flipped the swords over and held them out so that the naming runes on the hilts of the swords were showing. They were identical to the one on the back of his hand. "When the Bowl placed these runes into the swords, their magic changed. More than that, they themselves changed. Before, they were just swords; tools for battle. Afterwards, they had desires. Feelings. It was as if they had gained souls of some kind."

Justan rubbed his chin. He didn't think of his swords as having souls, but there was a kind of personality behind them. Master Coal had mentioned the same thing about his dagger, but Justan had never heard it anywhere else and he had read every book he could find on the subject.

"Like Chainy?" Cletus asked hopefully, turning his head to look at them.

"No," said Beth, jerking the gnomes head back where she

wanted it. Her stitch work was intricate; tiny stitches in a long row. "I've certainly never felt any kind of spirit bound to Hilt's swords and I've touched them many times." She let out a snort and spared her husband a questioning look. "Are you funning us? There's no kind of soul in there."

Hilt sighed. "Yntri said much the same thing the first time I told him about it. This is why I don't mention it. But it's true. It's not like they have specific thoughts to convey. They are just feelings, but-. Oh, how do I explain it?" He licked his lips, then lifted his right sword. "I always refer to Northwind as a she because she feels like a female to me. Her motivations seem a bit mysterious, while Southwind is always more straight forward. You know, like a man."

"Why does being mysterious make it a girl?" Tarah asked with a frown.

"These are just the impressions I get from them," Hilt replied. "It's difficult to explain it."

"Girls are strange," Cletus said helpfully.

"I said, 'no moving'," Beth growled at the gnome.

Hilt looked to Justan for help. "Surely, you know what I'm talking about."

"I understand what you mean. Peace usually feels hungry, while Rage seems eager. But I always figured that was just because of the type of magic that is in them. I didn't feel any kind of emotion at all from my rune dagger after I was named."

"Rune dagger?" Beth asked.

"That's how I thought of it back then," Justan explained. "It was a ceremonial dagger Lenny gave me. It had two blades on it and that's what I dipped into the Bowl when I was named. Afterwards a rune appeared on each blade. One to match each hand." He shrugged. "I didn't associate any kind of magic to the dagger then. It wasn't until later that I came up with the idea to ask Lenny to put the blades into the magicked swords he was making me. When he did so, the blades just sort of blended into the swords seamlessly."

"And that's when you felt their personalities start to come out?" Hilt asked.

"I guess so," Justan replied. He remembered that the swords had seemed to call out to him when Lenny had finished them. "Maybe it has to do with the fact that the original dagger they were in wasn't magic, but the new swords were."

"Ah! That could be it!" Hilt said. "Maybe it only happens when your naming weapon already has its own magic. Most named warriors and wizards don't have magic weapons when they first come to the Bowl. That could be why everyone doesn't know about it."

"Or both of you men are just a little bit too into your swords," Beth observed. Tarah snorted in agreement.

"I think we are getting a bit off track here," Justan said to the women and returned his attention to Hilt. "The point is that I need your help figuring out how to control the magic."

Hilt slid his swords back into their sheaths with a flourish. "Perhaps it would help if you tell me what it is your swords normally do. I know that one pulls away emotion and the other can create explosions, but we haven't discussed it further than that."

Justan nodded, realizing that Hilt was right. Even with all the sparring they had done on the road from the Academy to Malaroo, the subject had never come up. "Well, you're partially right. Peace drains emotions and pain from whomever it touches and Rage stores those emotions, converting them into energy. The explosions it makes comes from the release of that energy. But that's just a very basic explanation. They do more than that."

"Such as?" Hilt asked.

"Well, while I am touching someone with Peace, I can hear their thoughts," Justan said.

"Really?" interrupted Tarah Woodblade, eying him with interest. "Do you see just what they are thinking at the moment, or glimpses of their past?"

"Well, for the most part, it's just what they happen to be thinking at the time," he replied.

"That sounds somewhat like my power," Tarah said. "When I touch a creature's track, I catch a brief glimpse of what was in their mind when they made the track."

Justan nodded thoughtfully. "For me, it mainly happens in

battle when my mind has the world slowed down. When I am cutting someone with Peace I gain an understanding of them."

"Mainly in battle?" Beth asked. She was very nearly finished and didn't take her eyes off of her work while she spoke. "So it happens when you're not cutting people with them?"

"Well . . . I don't often touch people with my sword unless I'm fighting them," Justan replied.

The only other times he could think of were when he had been using the sword to take away someone's pain. The first time had been when Qyxal was dying, then later when Aldie had been gravely injured by a basilisk. He didn't recall knowing their thoughts at the time, but in both of those situations, he had placed the sword in their hands and let go.

"What of your battle with the Protector?" Deathclaw reminded him.

"Right," Justan said. Maybe it only worked if he was holding the sword at the time. "I just placed the blade against his cheek to calm him, but while Peace touched him I knew his thoughts."

Tarah smiled slightly and shook her head. "So your sword's magic makes you a listener. I went a long time thinking my staff did that for me."

"I guess I hadn't thought of it that way," Justan said thoughtfully. He supposed that he could use Peace in that manner, touching people with it to hear their thoughts. "It seems like a pretty aggressive way to listen to someone, though. I can't come at somebody with my sword and expect them not to see a threat."

"Listeners are always seen as a threat, Dear. Even if we just come at you with our ears," Beth observed. Finished with her stitching, she let go of the gnome and took a step back. "There, Cletus. How does that feel?"

"Tight!" Cletus said proudly, smiling as he rose to his full height. "It hurts when I smile!"

Beth sighed. "Just don't mess with it, Honey. Okay?"

"I won't!" he said as he reached up to gingerly probe the stitched wound.

75

"Perhaps you should chain him up until he is healed," Deathclaw mused.

"So, Edge, I don't understand," said Hilt. "What part of your sword's magic isn't working?"

Justan looked back at Hilt. "Sorry. We got a little off topic. Do you remember in the meeting the other day when I explained how I knew Mellinda was actually alive?"

"That you learned it from Deathclaw's sister?" Hilt asked.

There had been quite the debate when they had brought that particular bit of news to the assembled house leaders. No one wanted to believe that the Troll Queen herself was the one responsible for the behemoth's attack. Even after Xedrion had declared that he believed Justan's story there was still disagreement.

"Yes, but one thing that I didn't tell the assembly was how I learned this information," Justan said. "I stabbed her with Peace and read it from her mind."

Hilt gave him a quizzical look. "Why didn't you tell them that? The Roo-Tan understand spirit magic. They might have found your story more believable."

Justan let out a frustrated chuckle. "That's the problem. I can't replicate it! I didn't learn the information because it was on her mind at the time I was stabbing her. I went back through her lifetime of memories. Mellinda's involvement was just one thing that I learned along the way."

"Then you have magic like mine!" Tarah said, excited that someone else shared her talent. "You can read the past."

Justan raised a cautious hand. "Not normally and not since. And that's just one of the things I haven't been able to do since. There are actually multiple things I did that day that were new to me!"

"Alright," said Hilt. "Let's talk through them, then. Maybe we can puzzle it out."

"Alright," Justan said. He had been going over it in his mind repeatedly the last few days. "First of all, when I saw Talon come out of that tree, I was able to keep Peace's calming magic from working on me. I was able to hold on to my anger."

"You usually can't do that?" Beth asked.

"No," Justan replied. "Any time I touch the sword, my emotions are sucked away. I don't know how I did it."

Hilt raised a finger. "Okay then. Think back on that. What was going through your mind at the time?"

Justan sighed and thought back to that moment. "I drew my swords. Peace started pulling at my emotions, but I pushed back. I wanted to hold on to my anger. The sword just . . . obeyed."

"Then that proves it was listening," Hilt said. "Perhaps you just need to talk to it. Tell it what you want."

"Hilt loves talking to his swords," Beth said with a wry smile.

Hilt gave her a wounded look, "I meant through his connection with them. Not aloud."

"That's right, Dear. You only speak aloud to them when you're polishing them," she said, then glanced at Tarah. "He murmurs to them. It's cute. Like he's grooming a horse."

"I've tried communicating with it," Justan interrupted. "I send my intentions through the bond. It hasn't worked."

"That may not be enough. Try using words, as if you were talking to one of your bonded. Beth teases, but sometimes that works," Hilt said, glancing at his wife. He looked back to Justan. "Now what other things where you able to do that day that you can't reproduce?"

"Well, like I was saying earlier, I stabbed Talon. Then when my sword was inside her, I-I used it to enter her mind and read through her memories. I . . . wanted to understand her. I wanted to know why she was so evil."

"And?" Tarah asked. She had been there that day and had seen what Justan had done. She hadn't understood it though. "What did you discover?"

"I understood her," he said, his voice thick. "Her past was so horrible. The things she went through . . . she had been broken by Ewzad Vriil." Justan swallowed. "Then I sort of reversed the process. I sent my memories into her mind. I showed her what it was to be human. I think I might have broken her again."

Trevor H. Cooley

There was a moment of silence while everyone digested this information. Finally, Beth spoke up.

"That goes beyond listening," she said. "I can't do that. I can only see a general picture of who a person is. I sometimes catch a glimpse of someone's future, but I only see someone's memories if they decide to share them with me and I can't communicate with them on the level that you did."

"It is beyond what I can do as well," Tarah added. "I can see someone's past, but I can't share anything with them. I can't even speak in their minds."

Beth patted her shoulder. "You will learn. It is early yet."

"But I have done this before," Justan said, his brow furrowed. "With my own bonded. For the time my sword was in her body, it was as if our bond was every bit as strong as my bond with Deathclaw. I was even able to bring my magic through the connection and heal her as I withdrew my sword, and that is something I have never been able to do with anyone else. I can't use anything but defensive magic unless it's through the bond."

Hilt's back straightened. "I may know what this is. Beth, remember what Jhandra warned us about Roo-Dan witches?"

Beth blinked. "Oh! Edge, would you show me your swords?"

Justan drew his swords, encouraged by the excitement in her voice. The moment he touched Peace's handle, his emotion was sucked away, but his interest remained. He held them out. "What are you looking for?"

She stepped close to him, looking over the surface of the weapons. "Can you turn them so that I may see the runes?" Justan flipped the blades so that the runes showed and she nodded. "Hmm, interesting."

She reached out and touched the surface of Peace's rune and for a brief moment, he saw into her soul. He saw a strong, confident woman, whose actions were propelled by painful memories of the past and fears of what she had seen in the possible future. Beth was both fascinated and afraid by what she was learning from his runes. Then she lifted her fingers from the sword and the connection ceased.

78

Beth narrowed her eyes at him. "You were peeking."

"It was the sword," Justan replied. "And don't try acting offended. You do it to people all the time."

"Hmm," she said and touched the sword again. "Try now."

"I . . . see nothing," he said.

"So it is like listening. Just touching someone with your sword won't work if someone has their defenses up." Beth nodded. "May I see the runes on your hands?"

Justan stabbed the tips of his swords into the ground and left them standing there. His emotions returned as he held out his hands; left palm up, right palm down. Beth bent down and touched his naming runes. She bit her lip and grunted.

"I believe I just learned several things about your abilities," Beth declared.

Ooh. Really? said Gwyrtha. The rogue horse padded over to them and pushed her head between Beth and Justan, looking at his hands as if she would suddenly come to conclusions of her own. Esmine's child-like form was sitting in her saddle, watching the scene with interest.

"What did you learn?" Justan asked.

Beth scratched the patch of fur behind Gwyrtha's ears as she explained, "First of all your naming runes are interesting. Your wizard rune is matched with Peace and your warrior rune is matched with Rage."

"Right," Justan said. He had known that from the beginning.

She pointed at Peace. "The other runes etched into Peace's blade are spirit magic runes. Specifically, bonding magic runes with a little blessing magic sprinkled in."

"Oh," he said, his eyes widening. "I recognized the elemental runes on Rage's blade."

"A smattering of all the elements, yes," Beth said. "But don't feel bad about not knowing spirit magic runes. They aren't taught in the Mage School. Well, they might be now, but not when I was an apprentice. Yntri Yni taught me to recognize them."

"Do you know what those spirit magic runes are supposed

to do?" Justan asked.

"Not exactly. The elemental runes on Rage speak of the storage and release of power, but spirit magic runes are a bit awkward to read," she explained, her voice taking an almost lecturing tone. "The nature of spirit magic isn't precise like elemental magic. Elemental spells are exact formulas designed to work the same way every time based on the basic laws of nature. Spirit magic spells are different for every individual, powered more by feelings than by critical thought."

Deathclaw cocked his head and looked to Hilt. "Does she usually talk like this?"

Hilt chuckled. "Rarely."

"She does it when she's teaching," Tarah said. "I call it her 'Mage School voice'."

"Shush, you two," Beth said, but kept her eyes on Justan. "The result is that the use of spirit magic runes is different from person to person. What they are feeling when making the rune is the most important thing. It's as if each spirit magic user develops their own language."

"So, you know what types of magic the sword uses, but not exactly how it's done," Justan said, disappointed.

"From the runes alone, yes," Beth said. "But what Hilt reminded me of earlier makes it all come together."

"Something about Roo-Dan witches?" Justan said.

"Right," she said. "The elves teach the Roo-Tan people at a young age how to defend themselves from spirit magic attack. If they are on their guard, it is difficult for the witches of the Roo-Dan to affect them. To counter this defense, the witches employ enchanters."

Justan nodded. While witches were bewitching specialists and listeners were bonding magic specialists, enchanters were binding magic specialists.

"They bind the spirits of small creatures into piercing weapons, often tiny darts that the witches can blow from a pipe. These darts act like a connection between the witch and their target. If the dart pierces their skin-."

"It pierces their soul," Justan finished in sudden understanding. It all began to make sense. Fist had learned this when researching the maggots used by the evil in the Black Lake. "If your soul is pierced, they are already past your defenses."

"Right," Beth said in approval. "My bow works on the same principal. When I fire an arrow, the spirit of the viper in my bow attaches itself to the arrow and strikes the target, piercing their spirit and paralyzing them."

"And that's what I was doing when I stabbed Talon," Justan said. "I pierced her soul and used Peace as a conduit for the bond. That's how I was able to use my magic from within her."

Oh! said Gwyrtha.

Deathclaw hissed softly as he mulled the possibilities of this new form of attack Justan could employ. There was something disturbing about him thinking such thoughts with a sleeping baby on his shoulder.

"I have no idea what you are talking about!" Cletus said, employing a half grin so as not to stretch his stitches.

Justan's excitement drooped a bit. "I don't know how I feel about using the bond in an attack, though. The idea feels . . . dangerous."

Hilt nodded. "Very smart of you, Edge."

"Right," Beth agreed. "There is a danger inherent to using bonding magic in an attack. A bond goes both ways. If someone pierces you to enter your mind, whether by using a bound spirit or direct bonding magic, they leave a portal to their own mind open. The Roo-Tan are taught how to launch a counter attack in such situations."

That wasn't exactly what Justan meant by the attack being dangerous, but he filed away the advice. "I see. I doubt people would be expecting it, but I would need to be careful for that."

"Maybe they wouldn't expect it now," Hilt said. "But if word got around that the famous, Sir Edge could see into your very soul with his blade, certain people would know to get prepared."

"I suppose," Justan said, thinking specifically of the nightbeast Vahn and the possibility that the Dark Prophet could send another servant after him.

"There's also a very basic danger to consider," Beth said. "If you send your thoughts into someone's body and that connection is suddenly cut off . . ."

Justan grimaced at the thought of having the bond severed while his spirit was partially inside. "Would part of me be . . . trapped behind?"

"I don't know about that," Beth said. "But it could be damaging. It would be very disorienting to say the least."

"If you were stunned on the battlefield, you would be helpless," Hilt added.

Justan ran his hand through his hair. "Yeah."

Justan! came a distant and irritated thought. *What are you doing down there?*

"Uh, Jhonate has found me. I'd bet she's on her way down here." Justan said and replied through the Jharro ring on his finger, *I was speaking with Hilt and Beth.*

We have training to do, she reminded him, her anger only lessening slightly.

"I probably should go and meet her," Justan said.

Hilt gave him a knowing smile. "Ah! Well I hope we were helpful. We didn't exactly solve your problem."

"Actually, you helped a lot," he assured him. "I have a much better idea of what I'm dealing with now. I'm sure I'll figure out how to get my sword's magic under control."

"Sure. All you've gotta do is go around looking for volunteers to stab so that you can practice," Tarah said.

"Yeah, there is that," Justan agreed.

I'd let you! Gwyrtha declared.

"I appreciate that, Gwyrtha, but that wouldn't prove anything. I can already read your mind."

"I already got cut today," Cletus said regretfully.

Justan chuckled. "I'll look for someone else then."

Chapter Seven

Hello, Peace, Justan sent through his bond with the weapon. The only response he received was the familiar hungry serenity that he usually felt from the sword. *Uh, this is Justan speaking.*

He winced, feeling incredibly silly trying Hilt's suggested method. It wasn't that he didn't believe that there was some sort of intelligence there. After all, Master Coal had suggested something similar. But even if there had been a sort of intelligence given to his swords by the Bowl of Souls, it was very basic. In the past, when attempting to commune with the swords, he had simply sent them his intentions. Why should they respond to something as complex as the common tongue? Nevertheless, he tried again.

I need you to listen. There are times when I don't want my emotions sucked away. Justan waited for a moment and thought he might have felt a sort of questioning emotion. Encouraged, he continued, *I am going to touch your handle. And when I do, please don't use your magic on me.*

He reached up with his left hand and touched the leather-wrapped handle. His heart surged as, for a moment, he felt no change in his emotions. Then he felt a stinging whack across his buttocks.

"You are slowing down!" Jhonate declared, shifting her staff back to her other hand where she held it loosely at her side, her legs pumping. "Don't let your mind wander. Focus on the trail."

"I doubt I slowed much," he replied, breathing heavily. After all, they were heading through the forest at a break-neck speed. Despite the stamina and reflexes given by his bonds, he was still uncomfortable with the pace.

Jhonate was really pushing her limits. From the moment he had joined her on his way back from Beth's house, there had been an intensity to her emotion. Perhaps this was the way she was handling her grief over her lost family members.

I was communing with my swords, he explained through the Jharro ring.

"Talk and run," she reminded him. "Mental communication is cheating."

Justan smiled at Yntri Yni's old training tips coming from her lips. It reminded him of the days when he had first met her, when she was the mysterious taskmaster and he was just a stubborn teenager. How things had changed between them. Then again, she was still a taskmaster. Perhaps he was the only one who had changed.

"Hilt suggested I try speaking to my swords," he said aloud, focusing on keeping his breathing steady. "He thinks that the Bowl of Souls gave them a sort of intelligence and that talking to them could coax them to do what I want."

"Why would that not be the case?" Jhonate asked, jumping over a log that had fallen over the trail. She made a mental note to send someone to clear that obstruction later. "Many magical things have thoughts. You had to commune with your bow, did you not?"

"It's not exactly . . . the same thing," Justan replied, wincing as a low hanging branch gave him a face full of leaves.

"No?" she asked, having ducked low to avoid that same branch. "Your bow was given you by our Jharro tree. Your runes were given you by the Bowl of Souls, both ancient and intelligent beings."

"I guess you have a point," he admitted and as he thought about it, her point triggered a memory. "You know, when I first came to the Mage School, Master Latva taught me that there is intelligence in all things. He used his magic to show me tiny sparks of intelligence in the basic elements that make our world."

Jhonate grunted. "This is why my people have long distrusted wizards. The reason why your magic works on the elements is because your powers subjugate that intelligence. You bend it to your will and force it to do that which is against its nature."

Justan's eyebrows rose at the intensity in her tone. "Is that what you believe?"

She frowned. "Not I. That is the old Roo way. Back then, my people worshiped the elements as gods. This is no longer so, but . . ." She hesitated a moment, then made a decision, taking off down a narrow side trail. "This way."

Justan was caught off guard by the change of course and it took him a moment to catch back up. This new trail was too narrow to run side-by-side so he stayed right behind her. "But what?"

"We no longer worship the elements. Instead of gods, we have the Grove," she replied. "Yet another reason to distrust wizards."

"And yet your father seems to be considering letting them into the country," Justan said. "What do you think?"

"Most of them would not be a problem. Many that I have met are good people," Jhonate replied. "But they would all be interested in our country. Especially in our use of spirit magic. They would want to visit the Grove and if we allowed it, there are those who would be tempted by its power. It has happened in the past."

Justan couldn't argue that point. Wizards were greedy by nature. Even the best of them could be dangerously curious. He thought of Wizard Locksher and his experiments with trolls. Justan shook his head. Perhaps the Roo-Tan had been smart to keep wizards out.

The narrow trail came to an end at a clearing. The trees opened up in front of them and Justan saw that that they had come to the edge of a cliff.

Jhonate stopped at the edge and stood there, looking into the distance, her shoulders rising and falling as she breathed heavily. He listened through the Jharro ring and, though she was trying to keep her thoughts reined in, Justan caught a glimpse of a confusing tide of emotions warring within her.

He stepped up next to her and looked out over the valley

below. It was a grand view. A landscape of lush green treetops covered the valley floor, edged on the left side by the leaves of the Jharro trees that flickered green and blue. At the bottom, he could see a section that had been cleared by the elves; the newest section of the Jharro Grove. The year-old Jharro saplings were the size of fully grown oaks, but the elves had planted them quite far apart and from this distance, it just looked like a very sparse orchard.

"A beautiful sight," Justan said, then examined the clearing around them. A fire pit had been dug nearby and he could see several grass mats next to it. "So-?"

"Where are Deathclaw and Gwyrtha?" Jhonate interrupted, her eyes fixed on the trees below.

"Not far back on the trail," he replied. They often roamed the forest while Jhonate took Justan on his runs. Deathclaw liked to hunt and Gwyrtha liked to pester him along the way.

"Tell them to keep their distance," she said. "And to let you know if anyone comes this way."

"Okaayy," he said slowly. The feelings she was letting leak through the ring were starting to make sense. His heart beat faster. "What is this place?"

Jhonate turned towards him but did not meet his eyes. "There are those among my people who come here when they do not wish to be disturbed."

Justan swallowed. "And you don't wish to?"

She lunged towards him and threw her arms around his shoulders, pulling him in for a deep kiss. No longer able to hold her mind in check, the connection between them overflowed with the intensity of her emotions; a mix of fear, grief, love, and overall, passion.

Justan kissed her back, letting his feelings join with hers. He lived for times like this. With all the tension in Malaroo, combined with the stress of keeping proprieties, they came far too seldom. The kiss was a long one and with every moment that passed, their ardor grew. Finally, he pulled back, a wide smile on his face. "I love you."

"And I you," Jhonate said, her green eyes burning. She fell backwards, pulling him to the ground on top of her and kissed him harder, her hands gripping the back of his head, her lips crushing his.

Justan pulled back, laughing. "Slow down. One of us is going to lose a tooth."

"I do not care!" she said, a snarl curling her lips. "I do not care about any of it! Not customs. Not propriety! Nothing matters but right now."

She shoved her hands up under his shirt and ran her fingertips across the muscles of his chest. She traced the Scralag's frost-encrusted scar. Justan's breath caught as Jhonate ran her nails down his sides. She grasped the waistband of his pants.

"Wait!" Justan gasped. He grabbed her hands. "We are heading towards dangerous ground, here."

"I am tired of waiting," she growled.

He looked into her hungry eyes and pleaded. "Stop it! You are forcing me to be the good one and I don't want to be the good one!"

"There is no bad here. Just us," Jhonate said. She tried to pull her hands out of his grip.

Justan held tight. "Yes there is. We have waited a whole year. If we give in now, it would be wonderful, but you would regret it later. I can't do that to you." He forced a smile. "Also, I promised your father and I have no wish to fight him again."

Her eyes narrowed. "When did you discuss this with him?"

"He has mentioned it a few times," Justan said. On three separate occasions, actually. They hadn't been comfortable talks. "He says that you are too much like him and that I needed to be prepared to defend myself." He gave her a firm look. "We should wait until the wedding."

Jhonate groaned and all fight left her. She lay limply, tears welling in her eyes. "The wedding may never happen."

Justan laid on his side next to her. He kissed her gently on the cheek. "Why not?"

"Father wants to wait until this 'situation' is over!" she said bitterly. "But this is no longer just a 'situation'. A war started in that valley. Wars can last years, Justan, and anything could happen to us in that time." She looked at him pleadingly. "What if we never have the chance?"

"Nothing is going to happen to either of us. I won't allow it!" he promised. "And we aren't going to wait that long. There is still hope for us to end this war quickly. If not, we'll still make it happen. Even if we have to do it behind your father's back." Justan hesitated. "Surely there is someone nearby who will marry us without his permission. We could ask Tolynn?"

Jhonate smiled at the thought. "Oh, that would rankle him! And she might do it. But no." Her smile faded. "That would not work. If we did that, your parents would not be here either."

Justan bit his lip. "They would understand. Mother would bluster, but she would forgive us."

She sat part way up, leaning on her elbows. "And Fist? He is in the middle of a war of his own. How would you feel about having the marriage without him there?"

Justan frowned thoughtfully.

Jhonate let out a sigh. "I thought as much." She rolled to her feet.

"Hold on," Justan said, sitting up. "The Academy's army should be joining Fist in three weeks. With the wizards' help, they should have that cleared up. Then Fist can come down to join us. My parents, too. That's a couple months at most. Then we can marry."

She folded her arms and gave him a dull look. "You are certain of this?"

Justan wanted to be able to assure her, but that would just be a lie. Even with the might of the Academy and Mage School, the power in the Black Lake had the Dark Prophet behind it. That made it too dangerous to be discounted. He fell back to the ground.

"Never mind. I've changed my mind." He reached one arm up to her. "I give in. Take me now."

Jhonate gave him a playful scowl and smacked his hand away. "That moment has passed. Now get up. We have a run to finish."

Justan moped. "Can we walk?"

"No," Jhonate said and reached for his hand. She pulled him to his feet and kissed him again. She looked deep into his eyes. "Thank you for stopping me, Justan. I love you."

"And I you," he replied.

That night there was another long meeting. Again, nothing was decided about the course of action against the Mer-Dan Collective or Mellinda and her budding army of trollkin. Instead, the house heads were worried about funeral arrangements.

Justan understood why they felt it necessary to decide these things. With nearly 10,000 lost, the Roo-Tan people needed to be able to mourn. Families were still being notified. Yet there were no bodies to bury. No Jharro weapons to be returned to their trees. Technically, he wasn't sure that those swallowed up should actually be considered dead. Everything considered, wasting time on funeral plans made little sense.

In the end, Xedrion said much the same. Though he had lost two sons and his first wife on that day, it was not time to sit still with their hearts in their hands. There would be time for wakes and memorials later. He ended the meeting with the declaration Justan had been wanting to hear. Now was the time to act.

Knowing that the next day would be a long one, Justan had decided to retire early. He ate a quick meal with Jhonate, thankfully one with a small banana quotient, and retired to his rooms in the palace. He sat on his bed and drew Peace. A calculated calm settled over him.

Changing his mind, he set the sword onto the bed next to him. He couldn't go into this with his mind already calmed. He would speak to the sword first, then test to see if it had worked.

Gwyrtha laid on the floor next to his bed and yawned. *Talking to swords again?*

It is something he must do, Deathclaw told her. The raptoid was sitting on the roof of the building, looking over the palace grounds as he rolled the blades of his throwing knives across the backs of his long fingers. *As leader of our pack, he must learn to use all of his talents.*

But this is a boring one, she complained.

Not so, Deathclaw replied. *It would be a great advantage to us if Justan could pierce an enemy and pore through his knowledge.*

A sense of disquiet rose within Justan at that remark. He tuned out the rest of their conversation and dove deep into the bond. He came to the point where the connections of his two swords converged. Though these bonds were just as real as any of his other bonds, they felt different. Smaller somehow.

As he did when speaking with Artemus, he visualized the two bonds in his mind as if he were standing in front of them. Whereas the connection to the old specter was large enough for him to walk through, these bonds were barely large enough for him to fit an arm through.

Testing that theory. He reached an imaginary arm, really a tendril of thought, through the hole in the bond that led to his left sword. *Peace? Do you understand me?*

He felt a pulse. A slight change in the sword's usual calm, yet thirsty demeanor. His mental fingers touched something hard and unyielding.

Sir Hilt says that I should try and speak to you directly. He says I should explain what it is I need from you. He paused and thought he felt his connection with the sword become wider. Encouraged, he pushed his arm further inside. The hard surface inside was smooth and cylindrical. *What I need is for you to listen to my thoughts. There are times that I will not want you to take my emotions and I need to be able to depend on you to obey.*

The hole opened wider and Justan was able to push even more of his thoughts inside. He was able to reach his fingers around the object and he realized what it was. A sword grip. An idea occurred to him. He sent a command through that mental representation of his hand. *This is how it feels when I want you to stop taking my emotions. Do you understand?*

The sword grip dissolved from within his fingers. Justan frowned, unsure if the sword had understood.

I think you are on the right track, said a cold whisper.

Artemus? He hadn't been able to contact his great

grandfather since convincing him to freeze the ground during the Troll Mother's attack. Justan withdrew from his connection to the sword and turned to face the sound of the voice.

To his surprise, the old man was standing right behind him. Usually, he was only able to communicate through a peep hole in the barrier that walled off the Scralag from the rest of the bond. The most Justan saw was a flash of eyes or frosted hair but now Artemus looked much like he had the day Justan had first met him.

Justan's great grandfather looked to be middle-aged, with thick brown hair only lightly streaked with gray and a short beard that was thick across his chin, but left his lips bare. He wore a blue and gold striped robe and his eyes were the color of ice.

The old specter glanced around, reaching out to touch the cloudy walls of the bond. *So this is what you see when you imagine yourself navigating the bond. It's quite bare of decoration, but still, the detail. I must say, to build a mental construct of this complexity while maintaining so many bonds is an impressive feat. Quite an act of mental dexterity.*

I am glad to see you awake and active, Justan said. *Things had been so quiet on your side of the bond, I was growing worried.*

Yes. After I used my power, the Scralag and I had a bit of a tussle. It wore us both out, I'm afraid, Artemus said apologetically. The old wizard's thoughts seemed remarkably clear.

But it seems you came out on top, Justan said, pleased. *I knew you could do it.*

Hello, cold wizard! came Gwyrtha's cheerful thoughts.

Greetings, Gwyrtha, Artemus replied. *I assume Deathclaw is listening in as well?*

I am, wizard, Deathclaw said warily.

In the beginning, most of Justan's communications with his great grandfather had been just between the two of them. But as Artemus' periods of lucidity had grown, he had begun to converse with the other bonded. Fist was the only one he had not spoken to directly. The moment had never been right. Perhaps that would change tonight.

Artemus, I will be contacting Fist soon. Would you like to try joining in? Justan asked.

Indeed. I would enjoy that. I haven't known many ogres in my time and those that I did most often had to be dispatched, the old wizard said.

Artemus' thoughts very much reminded Justan of some of the other older wizards he had known. Master Latva in particular. He even had a dry sense of humor that came out sometimes.

What woke you? Justan asked, wondering if there was something he could replicate.

I was alerted earlier when some . . . interesting emotions flooded the bond. You are lucky, my boy, to have a love that fierce, Artemus replied. *I must say, I feel more awake than I have in a long time.*

Oh, Justan replied, his cheeks coloring.

It brought back memories, the old wizard said with a dusty chuckle. *Begazzi and I had quite the wild courtship.*

Is that so? Justan said.

Oh yes, Artemus said. *She was quite a bit older than me and had never been in a relationship before. What a wildfire she was. She was already a bonding wizard at the time and her thoughts when we were together used to drive old Bill crazy. For the longest time, he'd never look me in the eye.*

Justan let out an embarrassed chuckle. *I . . . see.*

What kind of thoughts were these, that would make a dwarf avoid you? Deathclaw wondered.

Like the ones in Justan's dreams, Gwyrtha suggested.

Yes. I imagine they were, said Artemus with a laugh. *Though I imagine Justan would prefer us to block those sorts of feelings out. Old Bill learned to do so.*

Well, I'm glad to have you awake and with us, Justan said. He tried to change the subject. *Uh, when I was trying to speak with Peace you said you thought I was on the right track?*

Yes! Artemus said. *It seemed to me that you were making good progress.*

How could you tell? Justan asked,

I had a naming dagger of my own. Her name was Whisper. She had no magic of her own before the Bowl runed her, but she was much more than a simple tool all the same. She was a conduit for my magic. A great means of defense and attack as well. I had several spells I used her for. Artemus frowned, stroking his chin thoughtfully. *Though my memory slips a bit when I try to recall them.*

Did you have to go through something similarly humiliating when you first tried to communicate with this weapon? Deathclaw asked.

Uh, no, Artemus said. *But from what I understand, each one has a temperament of their own. Some of my colleagues had a devil of a time. Don't worry, my boy. The bond was reacting to you and that means you were making progress.*

At least he wasn't the only one with difficulty. Justan cocked his head. *Whatever happened to Whisper? When Locksher found your . . . remains under that boulder, he didn't find a dagger. Just your book and spectacles.*

I'm afraid that is because my killer stole her, Artemus said and a frosty breeze rippled through the bond, ruffling the old wizard's hair. *I can sense her even now. The connection is weak, but she is someplace north and west of here.*

Do you know who it was that did this? Deathclaw asked.

Justan's curiosity rose. From the way Artemus' body had been crushed under that cluster of boulders, he had always assumed that his great grandfather's death was the result of a battle with another wizard or perhaps an attack from a giant.

Artemus closed his eyes and the chill breeze blew a moment longer before he responded. *The events of that day are blurry in my mind.*

What if we could find your dagger and retrieve it? Perhaps having your naming dagger nearby would help you regain your memories, Justan suggested.

The specter gave a doubtful grunt. *That is . . . possible, I suppose. However, my link to her is weak, corroded over centuries. The fact that there is a link at all is a mystery to me. It is likely the blade cracked upon my death. That is the fate of any weapon runed by the bowl when its owner dies.*

But you did not pass on, Deathclaw reminded him. *Your*

spirit lingered.

Artemus chuckled. *True. So stubborn was I. So foolishly determined to live up to my part in John's prophecy.*

Then there is still hope, Justan said. *I promise you. After this is all over, we will go and search for it.*

Artemus patted his arm. *That is a kind gesture, my boy. But it is an irresponsible promise. I made those in my youth myself and I will not hold you to it. Too much is unknown for you to guarantee future plans.*

I still intend to do so, Justan insisted.

Justan keeps his promises, Gwyrtha said in agreement.

We shall see what the future brings, Artemus allowed with a smile. *Perhaps if I am able to regain my presence of mind, I will be able to see Begazzi again. That would be enough.*

Bringing you to see my great grandmother is something I can absolutely guarantee, Justan said.

The old specter seemed pleased by that. The breeze blowing through the bond warmed, becoming merely cool. *Very well. That is a promise I'll accept. Now. Let us cease this dilly dallying. The elemental has been quiet so far, but I cannot guarantee how much longer that shall last.*

Justan nodded. Depending on how his day had gone; more specifically, if and when the evil in the mountains had attacked, the ogre could already be settling down for the night. *But before I reach out to him, you should know what occurred while you were sleeping.*

Justan sent the wizard a long string of memories, catching him up on the events that had occurred in the mountains and the revelation of the dark power behind the evil. The transfer of information took only moments.

Oh my, the wizard said, frowning. *Something about the situation seems so familiar.*

Is there anything you can think of that could help Fist understand what he's up against? Justan asked hopefully.

I must think on it, Artemus said, stroking his beard.

I'll reach out to Fist, then.

Usually Justan moved through the bond to find his connection with Fist. This time he reached out and used his thoughts to pull the connection to him. A hole opened up in the cloudy wall before him and he poured his thoughts into it. His surroundings disappeared and he saw only the milky whiteness of the bond.

The distance between them, an obstacle in the beginning, was merely a nuisance now. Though there were still obstacles; things like the transfer of energy or healing at this distance wasn't practical, but as long as they both concentrated on it the connection came easy to them now.

He sensed that the ogre was lying down on his side conversing with someone. Or actually, Justan realized, kissing someone. Maryanne. It had to be. Briefly, Justan considered waiting to talk to him until later. But there was no telling how long Artemus would be this awake.

Fist, Justan sent.

The ogre jerked. *Oh! Uh, a minute!*

He said something to Maryanne, before rolling to his back. The ogre pushed his thoughts through the bond. *Sorry.*

I could see you were busy, Justan replied with a smile. *Push your thoughts through a little further. I want to show you something.*

Justan pulled most of his thoughts back through the bond, leaving just enough of his presence inside to keep his connection with Fist active. He reappeared in the section of the bond where Artemus stood, then focused on the wall. The cloudy substance that made up the bond formed into a likeness of the ogre's head. It was as if Fist's face were made of cotton.

Fist, can you see me? Justan asked.

The cloudy face blinked. *Justan? This is new. I didn't know we could do this.*

I'm learning many things today, Justan replied. *Fist, Artemus is with us today.*

Hello, Ogre, the wizard replied.

Hello! Fist said excitedly. *I am glad you are awake enough*

95

to talk.

I'm here too! Gwyrtha said. *And Deathclaw*!

The raptoid grunted.

Hello, everyone! Fist said.

So tell me, Fist, Justan said. *Did you have an eventful day*?

No attacks, Fist replied.

Things had been quiet since the night Wizard Locksher had invaded the mind of the evil. Locksher was worried that the lack of attacks meant that the Dark Prophet's servant was planning something big.

We spent the day building up our defenses, Fist said. *It was hard work, but nice. It has been good for everyone to have time to heal. Have you learned anything that could help?*

Justan looked to the wizard. *Artemus*?

I am not certain. Something Justan mentioned keeps sticking in my mind. It's this red spirit magic that your friend Locksher saw. It does not make any sense to me. Spirit magic is always in shades of gray depending on the intent of the user. The only red magic I know is fire and there is no way that this servant of the Dark Prophet could be using elemental magic to control the mind of that evil menace.

Yes. Sarine was puzzled by it too, Fist said.

Was she? The wizard said, his eyebrows rising. *Oh, right. You are there with that young gnome she is bonded to. Tell me, does Begazzi know of my existence yet*?

Fist's cloudy face grimaced. *I don't think Darlan has told her yet. So I haven't told Maryanne.*

Oh, Artemus replied, disappointed.

Tell her, Justan decided suddenly. *My mother does not have a right to keep this a secret. Sarine should know that Artemus is here.*

I'll get in trouble, Fist worried.

I'll take the blame, Justan said.

Fist sighed. *Okay. I'll tell Maryanne when we are done here.*

How exciting! Artemus said. *And a bit disconcerting. How shall she react? What shall she expect. Oh my. What do I expect?*

I don't know the answer to that, Justan said truthfully. He could understand the wizard's trepidation. It wasn't as if they could renew their old relationship. He was just a spirit now. Right? He didn't envy either of them. *Have you changed your mind? Do you want us to continue keeping it a secret?*

No? No. Tell away. It is for the best. Tell away, Fist. I shall await Begazzi's response eagerly.

Fist nodded. *So, Justan, is there anything else I need to know?*

Well, I have learned some interesting things about my swords. He sent Fist everything that had happened that day, leaving out only the small details of his encounter with Jhonate that afternoon. *I am still having difficulty getting Peace to do what I want, though.*

But you are learning and that is good! Fist said. *Soon you can heal other people besides us.*

Deathclaw hissed a laugh. *Fist! Only you would think of stabbing people to heal them.*

Like I did with Talon, Justan said. It was an angle he had not thought too much on. A way around the restrictions that the Scralag placed on his magic. The possibilities were intriguing. *You know, being able to heal someone from within the bond gives me a distinct advantage. I can see and manipulate wounds and ailments in a way that would be much more difficult for other wizards, no matter how skilled.*

I think it's a great idea, Fist said.

Me too! Gwyrtha agreed.

But you are missing some of the possible applications, Deathclaw argued. *If you can enter someone's body to heal, you can also enter it to kill. Pick them apart. Render your enemies to fluids*!

Justan recoiled at the idea. *No!*

That's quite the reaction, Artemus observed. *Why does the thought unsettle you so? Deathclaw is merely being practical.*

Justan didn't reply right away, struggling to find the words to explain.

I understand, Justan, said Fist. *You think it feels too much like what Mellinda and Stardeon did.*

Justan sighed. That was it. *Thank you, Fist. You have a way of seeing right to the truth of things. That's what it is. Mellinda and Stardeon spent years trying to find a way past the rules of the bond. Why should I be eager to do so?*

I see, said Artemus, nodding sagely. *It seems like cheating to you.*

Justan shook his head. *No. It's more than that. The idea of it seems evil. Creating a bond with Peace to force my way into someone's mind? Steal their knowledge? That's how Mellinda used her powers. Using the bond to forcibly change people's bodies? That's how Stardeon's rings work.*

Deathclaw snorted. *Human morality! I still do not understand it.*

What would you have me do, Deathclaw? Explode people from within like Ewzad Vriil? Maybe while I'm at it I should find some dragons and change their bodies so that I can use them as assassins!

The raptoid hissed in affront.

But you're Justan, Gwyrtha said. *You wouldn't be like them.*

She is right, Justan. You would never, Fist said.

Wouldn't I? Justan growled. *I did it to Talon! I hated her too much to accept that she was a messenger. I enjoyed stabbing her. I went into her mind, expecting to find that she was hiding her motives, but even after I knew the truth I could not stop. I peeled her mind open. Against her will, I took every memory she had, no matter how horrible, no matter how much she wanted it hidden!*

He swallowed, his thoughts thick with emotion as he continued, *It was only after I understood why she had become the way she was that I realized what I had done. I tried to do my best to fix her after that, but for all I know she is even more broken now.*

There was silence in the bond for several moments. Finally, a cool hand fell on Justan's shoulder. Artemus' ice blue eyes looked directly into his.

You are right to fear becoming like them, my boy. After all, both Stardeon and Mellinda started with good intentions. She wanted to end a bad relationship with one of her bonded and he wanted to help her. If they, some of the most intelligent and powerful wizards of their time, could go bad, why not you?

I'm no better than them, Justan said.

Yes you are! Gwyrtha insisted.

Justan shook his head. The Prophet had shown him what they used to be like. They had been good people before they gained power they shouldn't have had.

But I believe you underestimate yourself, my boy! Artemus said, smiling as he patted Justan's shoulder. *Now I am aware that, of all your bonded, I probably know you the least well. And I would understand if you found it hard to trust my judgement, considering that I spend much of my time as a bloodthirsty icicle with teeth. However, I hope you will give this some thought. There is one aspect of this power that you have not considered. Something that makes you completely different from Stardeon and Mellinda.*

Yeah? What is that? Justan said sourly.

It's source, Artemus replied. *Stardeon and Mellinda begged the Prophet repeatedly to give them a way around the restrictions of the bond, but he denied them. Why? Because what they wanted was a way around the Creator's will. They rebelled. Out of evil acts was their evil born.*

You, however, did not ask for such a thing. Nor would you. The very thought of abusing this power repulses you and that is the correct reaction. No doubt the Bowl of Souls saw this in you when you were named. Otherwise, your swords wouldn't have been given this ability.

Justan frowned. *But I didn't have these swords when I stood before the Bowl. Lenny was the one who gave these swords their power.*

Actually, that's not true, Fist said. *Remember what Lenny told you when he gave them to you? When he put the blades of your knife into the swords, they runed themselves. He wasn't even sure how they worked.*

Artemus smiled. *There you are, my boy. Do you really need further proof? The power of your swords came from your naming runes. Those runes came from the Bowl of Souls, and you know who the Bowl's ultimate master is. The mere fact that you have this power proves that it is the Creator's will you have it. This means He trusts you to make the right decision with it.*

See, Justan? Gwyrtha said, sending him a toothy mental grin of her own.

Justan couldn't find the strength to smile back. Now he understood that this newly realized power had come with a weighty responsibility. Somehow, the confidence his bonded had in his ability to handle it made it feel all the heavier.

Chapter Eight

"It is dangerouss for you!" Talon said. "They would fear uss and attack!"

"The Master says go. So we goes," Durza reasoned. "They is not so many as you said."

"Thousandss sstill," Talon replied. "We are two."

The Mer-Dan army camp was a shadow of its former self. The Roo-Dan warriors and spirit magic users had been the hardest hit with two thirds of their numbers dead or swallowed by the Troll Mother. The large mass of tents and campfires still stretched across the grassy plain, but more than half of the tents were empty and the fire sites cold. The survivors were superstitious about going through the belongings of the recently deceased and had left them where they stood.

Only one section of the camp was fully manned and this was a new group of perhaps two thousand Roo-Dan warriors that had arrived after the treaty disaster. They were camped on the outskirts of the army and were waiting while their leaders met in the command tent.

The imps and kobalds had taken heavy losses as well. Despite their wily use of magic, a full third of their combined army was gone. Far more practical than their human allies, they had dismantled and removed the tents and dirt mounds of the fallen. The result was that a much wider gap had opened up between their side of the camp and the human side.

Durza noted the gap. "We go in the middle and run. If they catches us, we will tells them of the Master."

The gorc adjusted the blond wig on her head and began to

stand up from the bushes that concealed them, but Talon pulled her back down.

"No, Durza! Do not letss them ssee you!" the raptoid pleaded. "I have been here before. Masster is prissoner here. We musst wait for dark. I will go in firsst, then come back if it iss ssafe."

Durza doubted that would work. Talon wasn't herself. The raptoid's cat-like eyes were red-rimmed and her voice hoarse from the constant weeping she had indulged in since Sir Edge's attack. Durza, though a constant weeper herself, was growing quite tired of it. The gorc gave Talon an uncharacteristic scowl.

"No more waiting, Talon," the gorc replied. "We is already late!"

The journey to the Mer-Dan encampment should have taken no more than two days at the most. Talon's moaning and dragging her feet mixed with bouts of hysteria had turned those two days into an agonizingly long week. Durza was unaccustomed to being the assertive one. She was a hider and a sneak. Not a leader. She was eager to get back to her master so that he could take over again.

"These peopless could hurt you!" Talon said worriedly.

Durza grasped the hood of Talon's black robe and pulled it over the raptoid's head. She wasn't sure how much it would help but there was magic within the robe that was supposed to calm Talon down. "Master says to come. So we come! We tells them we is here for the Stranger Man. They will listen."

"I don't like it," Talon whispered, but this time when Durza stood the raptoid didn't stop her.

Durza grasped Talon's hand and strode for the gap in the encampment between the human and kobald lines. The army was truly in a state of disarray, but they were still soldiers. Talon and Durza didn't make if half way before they were surrounded by short stocky warriors whose skin was covered with stony scales. Swords and pickaxes were pointed at them.

"Stop, intruders!" one of the soldiers barked. She was a bulky female brute with a gold circle painted on her forehead, denoting that she was a kobald captain. Her lip curled in distaste.

"What is a gorc doing here?"

Durza straightened. "We is servants of the-."

"She wears a human wig!" one of the kobalds chortled.

"I am Durza. I is a proper lady," Durza declared.

Another kobald spat. "Disgusting. I say we kill it!"

The kobald lunged forward, swinging a pickaxe. Talon darted forward and lifted her arm. The weapon speared through her forearm. She hissed in the soldier's surprised face. "Touch Durza and I sspill your innardss!"

His eyes widened at the horrific visage under the hood. The rest of the soldiers growled, readying themselves for attack.

"Stop it!" Durza shouted, sending out a command with the weight of her considerable power behind it.

The force of the bewitching magic caused the mighty kobalds to cringe. The one who had attacked let go of his pickaxe and stumbled backwards.

Durza used that stunned moment to turn back to the female kobald captain. "We is servants of the Stranger Man. We was told to come here!"

The human side of the army had felt that pulse of bewitching. Some were stunned stiff by the command. Others were approaching. There were shouts of "Witch!"

Talon tore the weapon from her arm and tossed it to the ground. "Take us to our masster, sstony one!"

The kobalds took another wary step back.

"Hold your ground!" the captain growled to her soldiers before replying to Durza. "If your master really is the Stranger, then you may be our enemy. Wait here while I send a messenger." She jerked her head towards Talon. "If the Warlord wills it, your friend will be healed of her injury."

"I care not of thiss wound," Talon said, raising her arm. The kobalds were shocked to see that, though there was still a gaping hole in her flesh, the bleeding had already stopped. The raptoid's voice took on a pleading tone and tears welled up in her eyes once more. "I musst ssee him!"

"Do you have any weapons?" the kobald captain asked.

"Only my eating knife," Durza said and held out her small belt knife.

The kobald took it from her and glanced at Talon, "And you?"

"I am a weapon," Talon said and opened her robe, letting it fall to the ground.

The sight of her wicked claws and barbed tail had almost as great an effect as Durza's magic. The kobalds took one look at her fearsome appearance and brandished their weapons again.

The kobald captain tilted her head. "What are you?"

"An evil thing." Tears ran down Talon's scaly cheeks and she collapsed slowly to her knees. "A monster that killss. Perhapss you sshould kill me."

"Do not listens to her," Durza said, forcing a nervous laugh. "She just misses the master." She tuned her voice down to a harsh whisper. "Now is not a good time for this, Talon. Stand. Be brave for Master, yes?"

The kobalds kept a close eye on them while a messenger was sent. By the time he returned, the number of soldiers surrounding the pair had grown, including crossbowmen and four Roo-Dan witches prepared to counter any spell the gorc might cast.

"You are to bring them to the command tent, Captain," the kobald messenger said, a sour expression on his face. "The Warlord says he has been expecting them. Bring only one witch with you."

The captain gave the messenger a dubious look, but nodded to the two prisoners and started towards the command tents at the center of the encampment. Durza pulled Talon to her feet and picked up her black robe before following. One of the human witches broke off from the others and followed, a scowl and a spear at the ready.

In front of the command tent were stationed two heavily muscled guards with wary expressions. The captain nodded to them as she approached. "I have two servants of the Stranger here. Warlord Aloysius has summoned them."

A man exited the tent at the sound of her voice. He was a rather mild-faced man with a shock of brown hair atop his head.

He wore a white robe with a red sash.

"You can go, Captain," the man said, then pointed at the witch who stood behind them. "You. Follow behind."

The massive command tent was sectioned into multiple rooms by canvas walls that had been runed with sound deadening spells. The spells were effective. Outside, not a sound was heard of the dealings going on. When Durza and Talon entered the main hall, they were surprised by the sound of loud voices in disagreement.

The bulk of the wide rectangular room was taken up by a long table. Sitting at the table were representatives of different factions within the Mer-Dan collective along with the imp and kobald generals of the warlord's demon army. Inkwells and quills and stacks of paper cluttered the table before them. One of the Roo-Dan chieftains was currently arguing with a merman councilman.

At the head of the table, on a high-backed and intricately carved chair, was Warlord Aloysius. The gnome had a full head of hair and a regal bearing. He was wearing a suit of black chain armor and a silver circlet sat on his brow. He was listening to the ensuing argument with a bland, but patient expression. Behind him, standing against the rear wall was a line of stewards wearing green and black sashes, waiting in case the warlord needed them. The chair to his right was empty, belonging to the red-sashed steward that had ushered the visitors in. Sitting to his left was the Stranger.

Matthew looked quite different than he had the last time Talon had seen him. He was cleanly shaven and no longer looked sickly. The robe he wore was still brown and plain, but clean. The hilt of the sword still protruded above his left shoulder. A lit pipe hung from the corner of his mouth and his eyes brightened when he saw Talon and Durza enter the tent.

One of the stewards at the rear of the tent rang a gong and the two arguing parties quieted. The red-sashed steward cleared his throat. All eyes in the room turned towards the new visitors. Faces twitched at the appearance of a garishly make-upped gorc in a wig and dress accompanied by a reptilian creature out of nightmares.

"Ah, they are here," the gnome warlord said and rose from his chair. The rest of the assembly rose with him. He gestured to Talon and Durza. "I would speak with you privately. Stranger, attend us."

"Yes, Warlord Aloysius," Matthew said obediently, inclining his head. He stepped away from his chair.

The warlord then nodded to two of the black-sashed stewards who stood at the back of the tent. "Jessica. Andred. Continue the discussions until I return."

The two accomplished negotiators bowed and came to the table, sitting in the chairs at either side of the warlord's throne.

The Merman ambassador, a plump and sweaty individual wearing a gaudy silk robe, cleared his throat. He was missing an ear and three fingers from his left hand. The scars looked pink as if the wounds were freshly healed. "Warlord Aloysius, we did not gather here to speak with representatives! Our fledgling nation teeters on ruin. These discussions need your presence here."

A few of the other representatives harumphed in agreement. Others looked down at the papers in front of them, too cowed to speak.

Aloysius' expression hardened. "Elder Qelvyn, I would think that your remarkable survival of the behemoth's attack would have taught you some humility." He waved a casual hand. "These talks have gone on for hours longer than necessary. You already know my instructions on each pertinent matter. But perhaps if you gather your minds while I am gone, you will have something new to say when I return."

Qelvyn's plump face reddened, and he gave a short bow. "Yes, Warlord. I apologize for my outburst."

Aloysius gave him a perfunctory nod and turned to enter a flap at the rear of the chamber. Matthew followed close behind, careful not to let the sword hilt snag on the canvas. Durza and Talon hurried after him, excited to see their master alive and well. Behind them walked the red-sashed steward and the human witch who had accompanied them from the camp.

The room they entered was a familiar one for Talon. It was the room where she had found her master imprisoned the last time she had infiltrated the camp. The decorations were bare, but for two plush chairs that faced each other.

As soon as the flap fell shut behind the red-sashed steward, Aloysius addressed the witch. "You. What is your name?"

The human blinked and fell to his knees, his hands clasped before him. "Uh, Eldris, Warlord. Eldris of Baeve."

"You are an experienced witch?" the gnome asked.

"So it has been said, Warlord."

"I understand that this gorc demonstrated bewitching power of her own upon entering the camp," Aloysius said. "Did you witness this?"

The man's face wrinkled. "Demonstra- . . . uh, she made an attack, yes, Warlord. A big one. Every witch 'cross the camp felt it."

"How powerful would you say this gorc's power is?" prodded the red stashed steward, following his master's line of questioning. "We did not notice it behind the spells on this tent."

"Right mighty, Sir," the man said. "Made our ears pop. Maybe only four or five witches I know of could top it. Maybe the high shamans too. Maybe."

The steward's expression turned to anger. "And yet you saw fit to accompany it into the tent with the leadership of this nation alone?"

The witch groveled. "There was four of us watchin' it, Sir. But I was the only one told to come along!"

"Dismissed," Aloysius interrupted with an off-hand gesture.

The steward glared at the witch. "Leave us! If I hear of another slip like this I shall slit your throat!"

The witch scampered out of the room.

"Masster!" Talon stumbled towards Matthew and clutched his robes. Her body trembled as she looked at him with pleading eyes and sobbed. "Please . . . I am hurt. I hurt sso manyyy. Can I die now?"

"My, my. What did that boy do to you?" Matthew reached out and cupped her face, "Oh. I see. He gave you the understanding I could not. John chooses his champions well. Unfortunately, I do not have the time to discuss it with you at present. Sleep now."

Talon's eyes rolled up in her head and she slid silently to the floor. Durza crouched next to the raptoid and draped her black robe over her. She patted her friend gently. "See, Talon? It'll be okay."

"Seems your assassin is broken, Stranger," the red-sashed steward observed.

"No. Just recently pieced together, Shade," Matthew responded. "Talon will recover eventually. I doubt the same can be said for you."

Aloysius watched the interchange with passing interest, then spoke to Matthew as if Talon and Durza weren't even there. "Your opinion on the talks, Stranger?"

"The merman wasn't wrong," Matthew said with a puff from his pipe. "This nation you stitched so cleverly together is fraying at the seams. Despite the assurances some of these chieftains are giving you, it is obvious they hesitate to speak the truth in your presence. They are hiding things from you."

"They wouldn't dare," Shade said.

Matthew ignored him. "I fear that away from your ears, these leaders speak of you as a tyrant leading them to destruction. Frankly, your responses in the meeting so far likely reinforce that judgement."

"When I agreed to listen to your advisements, I did not ask for impertinence," Aloysius warned.

"As you wish, Warlord," Matthew said obediently. "Though may I point out that you did command me to tell you openly of my opinions when we were alone."

The gnome took a deep breath. Unexpectedly, he nodded. "So I did. Continue, then."

Shade scoffed. "There is no need to listen to him, Warlord! I could advise you just as well as he can."

"You, Oliver?" Aloysius said with an arched brow. "Pray tell."

"Yes, Shade," Matthew agreed. "Tell him why those leaders don't tell him the truth of the situation."

"If they lie it is because they are hiding something," Shade replied. "Not because of anything he did wrong. The Warlord is infallible. So it was foretold."

"Is that what was foretold?" Matthew said in mock surprise. "I don't recall that, which is awkward since I was the one who foretold of his coming in the first place. What say you, Warlord Aloysius? Have you never made a mistake?"

Aloysius stood very still. "I do not like being questioned."

Shade nodded. "Then let me strap him back to that chair, Warlord. He will no-!"

"Oliver!" the gnome commanded. "You have been my most trusted servant. Still yourself before my opinion of you changes."

The red-sashed steward's face reddened and he went down to one knee. "I apologize, Warlord."

Aloysius returned his gaze to Matthew, his expression hard. "I do not like being questioned. However, I would be foolish to let my dislike rule me. All rulers, no matter how great, benefit from being questioned from time-to-time. I will hear you. What I will not stand for is being insulted."

Matthew took one deep draw from his pipe and smiled. Smoke poured from his mouth as he replied. "Then our relationship needs to change, Warlord. You see, as your advisor, I will need to tell you hard truths. Things that you will not like to hear. Depending on your willingness to accept them, you may take these hard truths as an insult. I cannot control your feelings." He paused to rethink that comment. "Well, I could, but I never would. The thing I can promise you is that I will never attack you personally. But I cannot promise you won't be insulted."

Shade trembled in anger at his audacity, but the steward stayed his tongue.

Aloysius cocked his head. "I am beginning to wonder if I have any control over you left at all. Tell me truthfully, Stranger. Is the magic of my sword still affecting you in any way?"

"In a sense it is," Matthew said. "The magic compels me to

answer you truthfully, as you just requested. It also keeps your previous commands in force. For instance, the blood magic and demon races are still far more fertile than I would ever recommend."

"And yet, you did not fully answer my question," the gnome observed. "Ever since that debacle at the treaty, your pallor has changed. Your attitude has changed. You even seem to have some of your master's approval back. What else has changed? In what ways can you disobey me that you could not before?"

"I do not look for ways to disobey you. I look for ways to help you." Matthew removed the pipe from his lips. "In answer to your question, I do believe that if you asked me to stab myself again I would refuse to do so. I also believe that if you threatened to kill another in order to force my hand, I could find a way to thwart you. However, I am not able to deny any reasonable request."

Aloysius blinked. "And what have you done, that makes the Creator willing to forgive you so quickly."

"I have suffered," Matthew said. "You do not know the depths of the pain I felt as I was forced to face the results of my many failures. Still, suffering is not what my Master demands. He has seen what only He can see. He knows how much my heart has changed."

The gnome chuckled in disbelief. "Tell me, Stranger. Could you remove that sword from your back?"

"I could," he said. "If my Master willed it."

"Then do it," Aloysius said. This was a key test of the magic. Those who were pierced by the sword were forever unable to remove it by themselves. Even if commanded by the sword's owner.

"I will not," Matthew said. "The sword is not mine to remove. You will be the one to remove it once you are ready to accept me as your equal."

"Equal?" Aloysius said, astonished at the Stranger's audacity.

Matthew shrugged. "Also, if you must know, I have always been plagued with an itch in the center of my back. I can never quite reach it on my own. Talon could attest to you that I am always needing it scratched. Right now? No itch."

"And your humor has returned as well." Aloysius shook his head. "Stranger, you are truly an indomitable foe. Do not think, however, that I will fall prey to your tricks. I will not withdraw that sword. To do so would be to show weakness to all of my subordinates. If the proof of my control over you is gone, my alliance with the demons is gone."

"You believe I am tricking you?" Matthew said.

"You attempt to. Otherwise you would have removed that sword," the gnome observed. "I know you, Stranger. Your tendencies are well documented. Your pride would not allow you to be subservient to anyone if you could help it."

Matthew returned the pipe to the corner of his mouth and took a short puff. "I don't doubt that you have likely studied every word you could find about me. Likely every published word. But not every word was written."

"Truly?" said Aloysius and his tone wasn't one of disbelief, but of curiosity. "Tell me something I don't know."

"Very well," the Stranger replied. He pursed his lips thoughtfully "May we sit? This is a very old tale and these two chairs are going to waste."

The gnome warlord smiled. "Please do."

They sat in the plush chairs and Matthew steepled his fingers before him. "The beginning of this civilization was not the true beginning."

"Many scholars have suggested that this was the case. Strange artifacts have been found that seem to predate any written era," Aloysius said. "Kobalds find uncounted mysteries in their tunneling."

"When the Creator called his prophets, this world was in ruins; a burnt husk of its former self."

"Tell me a story of the previous world," Aloysius said, his visage eager.

"Ever a scholar. What a stir you could make in your community with information like that," Matthew said. "I'm surprised you didn't ask me when I was most under your sword's sway. Unfortunately, I am not allowed to speak of that time. Besides, the story I have to tell is more pertinent to the information you need to know.

"Now, as I was saying, the Creator pulled us from untold horrors. Out of all the crumbled world's poor survivors, why He picked us, He will never say. But each of us had a particular talent that shone brightly. David was the sly one. John, the compassionate one. I-."

"What of the fourth?" Aloysius interrupted. "Tell me of her."

Matthew sighed. "You truly do know everything written on us. Even, it seems, things I had thought eradicated. The fourth is, again, something I am not allowed to speak of. Particularly to you. To do so would be disastrous."

The gnome leaned back in his chair, his mind examining every word. "I had to ask. Go ahead with your tale."

"Well, while the world recovered and the races were formed, we were taught much at our Master's knee. It was during this time that our bonds with him were given and our powers gained. When He deemed the world ready, we were given our responsibilities. Each of us were placed over the races that could most use our particular talents.

"David was assigned the goblinoids because of their devious nature and tendency for violence. His cunning would be needed to gain their trust. John was assigned to the humans. They, with their short lives and talents in areas good and evil, needed someone with his depth of compassion. It was evident early on that they could be the most easily destroyed, or perhaps, be the greatest menace of all.

"As for me," Matthew hesitated. "I never did tell you my talent. Do you know what it was?"

"You were the smart one," Aloysius said.

"And I was confident in my intelligence," Matthew agreed. "He gave me perhaps the hardest task, The Blood Magic and Demon Races, and it took me to my limits. My charges were the most dangerous but the least numerous."

"I know all this," Aloysius said. "You tried many ways to keep us in check. You tried ruling over us like David did with his goblinoids. You tried gently guiding us like John. In the end, you chose to harry us from a distance. This was perhaps your most successful attempt, but in the end, also a failure."

"There is truth in what you say," Matthew admitted. "However, that's not the part of the tale that is pertinent at the moment. You see, early on I knew that I needed to focus more on particular races than others. The elves and merpeople were hardy, but withdrawn. The dwarves and kobalds were industrious but not inclined to conquer.

"The dragons and bandhams were capable of intelligence, but rarely used it. They had enmity with each other from the beginning, which kept their numbers in check. In fact, the balance this relationship created is what gave me the idea for the plan I have been enacting for the last thousand years. But I am getting ahead of myself again.

"My biggest problems came from the imps and the gnomes. The imps were wily and vicious, smarter and more dangerous than David's goblinoids. The gnomes, on the other hand, were a strange dichotomy, either the smartest of all the races or the dumbest. Either the most physically inept or the most physically talented."

"I am aware of our proclivities," Aloysius said wearily.

Matthew continued anyway, "In both cases, they were unable to fend for themselves. I tried many things. I begged my Master for help on the issue. For a time I even wondered if a race this inept deserved to be saved. This is when I received the prophecy that Shade so clumsily tried to refer to earlier," he said, glancing at the still-kneeling steward.

"It was at this time that I learned why the gnome race was so crucial. I saw into the future, just glimpses of the bits He needed me to know. Once in every era, a gnome warlord would be born, someone with the skill of the scholar and warrior, and even more importantly, someone who had the ability to focus on many things at once.

"Now each gnome warlord would be born with a special intended task and each one was talented in some ways more than others. The first loved battle above all and his leadership was crucial to quell the Great Imp Uprising. The second had talents split straight down the middle. She came at the Time of the Warlords. You know how crucial she was to the world. In both these cases, I was at their sides. I was their guide."

"You were their instructor," Aloysius corrected, leaning forward, bitterness in his voice. "You raised them. You directed them. You commanded them. And you wish to do the same to me. I know."

"That was perhaps true for the first. I was trying David's way at the time. But it is not true of the second. I held back. I advised her only," Matthew insisted. He looked Aloysius directly in the eye. "I saw your coming on the same day I saw the others. And like the others, your talents are unique. You have the skill for battle, but that just gave you the thirst to learn about it. Your greatest asset is your mind. I knew something about you way back then. Something that I found hard to believe at the time. You are smarter than me."

There was perhaps nothing he could have said that would have startled Aloysius more. The gnome's jaw dropped. "You admit this?"

"I know it to be true. When it comes to application of knowledge, you are my superior. The fact is proved by how you have come all this way without my help. With mere research alone, you recognized your worth, devised a plan, and set about making sure that you would be able to enact your part when you would be needed."

Aloysius regained his composure quickly. "You claim to know all this and yet you ask me to see you as an equal? I think you believe that you are better than me."

"No. I do not like some of the decisions you have made. There are aspects of what you have become that I believe are terrible. But I cannot blame you for being this way. Again, you got here alone. I neglected my duty. I should have been there at your birth. I should have taught you a moral center, but I had already distanced myself from my own. You acted intellectually based on your knowledge and experience and your only support was stewards who thought you could do no wrong. No, Warlord Aloysius, there is only one way in which I am your superior and that is experience. I offer it to you."

Aloysius' face tensed up. "You praise me with one hand and slap me with the other. Yet, you expect me to do your will?"

"No, Warlord. I would advise you only. As I did with the second. The fight that comes is one that you must undertake. I can help you to prepare, but you must command."

Aloysius leaned back in his chair once again. He said nothing for quite some time, but simply looked at the Stranger and thought. Matthew let him. He eased into his chair as much as he could with the sword in his back and smoked in silence. Durza tugged on his leg, but he waved her silent.

The chamber's flap opened and Steward Jessica's calm face poked in. "The representatives wish to break for dinner, Warlord. May we dismiss?"

"No," Aloysius said. "Tell them I will address them shortly."

"Yes, Warlord," she said and bowed her way back out.

The gnome rubbed his proud chin. "Very well, Stranger. I will allow you to continue as my advisor. I will try to heed your words even if they chafe my pride. However, I will not remove that sword from your back. As I said before, it is one thing that proves to your races that I am in charge. Their fear of you is deep. I will make commands of you from time to time that you must obey in front of them. I cannot be seen to be under your influence."

Matthew gave him a short bow. "Your terms are understandable given the circumstances. I have but one concession to ask for. Please, when we are alone, call me Matthew. I hope that one day, I can overcome that 'Stranger' moniker."

"I will think on that," the warlord said. He seemed suddenly uneasy with the deal he had just made, but he didn't let that distract him. "Before Oliver interrupted, you were attempting to give me council regarding my talks with the local leaders. Continue."

Matthew smiled. "What I was saying before is that the leaders fear you. They worry that they have put a tyrant over them.

In every meeting since they put you in charge, you have browbeat them and cast their objections aside without appearing to hear them. If things continue, they will abandon you. The Roo-Dan will scatter back to their villages and the merpeople are too small in number to be much help to your army."

"And you are here to save the day?" Aloysius asked, though this time there was no bitterness in his voice.

Matthew shook his head. "Do not misunderstand me. I do believe that you can keep this collective held together. Choice words here and there should do it, something you excel at. What they need from you now is encouragement rather than harshness. If you treat them as comrades instead of vassals, they will rally back behind you. More importantly, what they need now is a victory and soon."

"May I speak, Warlord?" Shade asked, unable to continue his obedient silence.

Aloysius nodded. "Indeed, Oliver. Stand and speak."

Shade did so and Matthew found it a remarkable feat that he did not wobble after kneeling so long. "He says they need a victory. A victory against what? We have two enemies now, each one more formidable than we should attack with our current numbers."

"Go on," the gnome prodded.

"In my opinion, this situation is not worth mending. Sure, we could stay down here and, with your intellectual might, we could defeat both of them, but for what gain? We would likely be left with an army so depleted it's not worth bringing back with us!"

"He speaks wisdom," Matthew agreed, "if coming back to Alberri with a conquering army was your lone goal in your endeavor here. But you never think so simply. That was just one facet of your plan, was it not?"

"You think you know my mind?" the gnome said.

"You wouldn't come this way if that was your only goal. You could buy an army if that was the case, but you know that you can't build your empire by conquering alone. You need to be seen as legitimate to the rest of the known lands. A united Malaroo does that for you. Otherwise there is only a series of pointless wars in your future. Endless lives lost just to build your power and put down the eventual rebellions that will come. What will you have left when the battle you were born to fight arrives?"

Shade snorted. "Those words sound grand, but they don't match with what you said before. A fight here means lives lost. I suggest we leave."

"When I said the people needed a victory I wasn't speaking of a victory in battle," Matthew said. "And leaving Malaroo now is not possible. If you do that you could lose everything."

"How?" Shade demanded.

"He is right, Oliver," Aloysius said. "Abandoning our effort here is not an option. I made an error in my calculation with Mellinda. I suspect that her goal now is the same as it ever was. She wishes to destroy the Jharro Grove and her small trollkin army is about to swell by 30,000 troops. The Roo-Tan will lose if they fight alone."

Matthew nodded. "And then you won't have a world worth protecting on your prophesied day. Your only hope is to somehow get the Roo-Tan back to the treaty table. That is the kind of victory that will keep your Mer-Dan collective together. Then, with Malaroo's combined armies at your disposal, you can set your mind to destroying Mellinda and the Troll Mother."

"Rebuilding that treaty will be impossible," Shade said. "The Roo-Tan think we betrayed them."

"And in a way, they are right," Aloysius admitted. "But there is hope. Xedrion is proud, but he is a reasonable man. He will likely ask for concessions in the treaty, though."

"But will he even agree to meet?" Shade asked.

"You will need to surprise him," Matthew said. He gestured to Durza and the sleeping Talon. "That is why I asked you to let my servants join us here."

Chapter Nine

Fist fell.

His stomach rose in his chest. The wind whipped past his plummeting body as the ground far below rose up to meet him. He felt a momentary panic and disorientation before he remembered.

"This dream again," he said.

How strange. This was the first time that the dream had begun with him falling instead of up in the clouds with his father approaching. Fist rolled over to face upwards. The sky above him was dark and full of heavy clouds. But he knew they were not clouds. A storm of enemies was ready to rain onto the earth, bringing destruction to the world below.

"You idiot!" Maryanne snapped, her voice raised so that it could be heard over the rushing wind.

He turned his head to see that the gnome was falling next to him. She was spread-eagled. Her auburn hair was streaming upwards, the long tops of her ears flapping in the wind. Squirrel stood on her back, raising a tiny sword in his hand. Electricity vibrated along the length of the blade.

"Idiot?" Fist tried to flip back over, but began tumbling end over end. His stomach lurched.

The gnome warrior cursed and tilted her body, gliding close enough to grab his arm and help him level out. She swung herself around so that she was facing him. Now both of them were hurtling towards the earth belly-first.

"Yes! You're an idiot!" A scowl was on her pretty face. "Don't you know a fall from this height could kill you?"

"Yes," Fist said. "But I've had this dream before. So I

know it won't."

"Don't talk crazy at me, Fist," Maryanne replied. "Falls are a serious thing."

I like your dreams, Squirrel said from his perch on Maryanne's back, swiping his electrified sword through the air. *I want one of these.* He grinned, exposing a mouthful of fangs. *My teeth are sharp here.*

"Did you come into my dream this time?" Fist asked. Squirrel had monitored his dreams before. Was it possible that Squirrel could enter his dream through the bond?

Maryanne lashed out with her hand, smacking the ogre across the cheek. "Pay attention, Big Guy! When you're falling, you've gotta know how to land."

Puzzled, he glanced down at the mountainscape rising towards him. "If I was really falling from this high I don't think how I landed would matter."

"The important thing is to land feet first, but don't take all the shock on your ankles or knees," Maryanne continued. "Roll with the impact!"

"Does that even work if you're falling straight down?" Fist wondered.

Better you just don't fall at all, Squirrel advised.

That wasn't an option in this dream. The ground was rushing up quickly. Just like the last time he had dreamt it, he wasn't falling towards the Black Lake. Instead, it seemed as though he would land at a point somewhere between the lake and the Thunder People Territory. He could see the small forms of wizards and Academy warriors intermixed with ogres, running down a wide muddy trail.

"Remember!" Maryanne said, rotating her body so that her feet faced downwards. "Roll with the impact!"

Fist bent his knees, but his body didn't rotate like hers. He was still face down, but with his knees jutting out. He reminded himself that this was his dream. He willed his descent to slow.

Fist hit the mud with a splat. He lifted his head from the muck slowly, his thoughts filled with consternation. He bet that

Maryanne had landed just fine.

We did! Squirrel agreed.

A strong hand grasped Fist's shoulder.

"Dag-blast it, Ogre! Get yer arse out the mud!" Lenny barked. "We got us a witch to burn!"

Fist blinked the mud out of his eyes, noticing that the dwarf was wearing an unfamiliar suit of armor. It was leather, but with an enormous metal plate in the center with a red letter 'F' embossed in it. The dwarf turned away and shouted, his hammer held high in the air.

"Wait! Lenny . . ." Fist said weakly as he watched the dwarf storm ahead with the others.

People streamed by him on either side. Fist tried to stand, but was moving so slowly. Why was he moving so slow? Then he remembered why.

Snakes, Rufus said.

Lots of snakes, Squirrel agreed. The animal was perching nearby on top of Rufus' head. The rogue horse was standing there with a bland expression, one large finger in his nose. Maryanne was nowhere to be seen.

Fist looked down. Dozens of mud-covered brown snakes hung from his torso and legs, latched onto him with needle-like fangs. Panic welled within him. A scream built within his chest.

Lots of snakes in your dream, Fist, Squirrel said, shaking his head. He reached into his cheek pocket, but instead of a nut, he pulled out a tiny roast chicken leg. He tore into it with his razor teeth. *Shock them.*

Fist's panic faded at Squirrel's comment. The snakes weren't real. They were part of the dream. He sent vibrating strands of earth and air magic across his skin and the snakes fell from his body, writhing and convulsing.

Fist cocked his head at Squirrel. "Hoooowww diiii-." Whatever was in the snakes' venom had caused his body to slow. He continued in the bond instead. *How did you come into my dream, Squirrel?*

I wanted to see, Squirrel said with a shrug. As he did so, the fur on his shoulders fell out, revealing skin covered in tiny scales. He shivered and a chain reaction started down his back, his dense fur falling out in clumps.

Squirrel, your hair, Fist said. He attempted to raise his arm to point and it rose slowly.

Huh? Squirrel lifted his own arm and the fur fell away to expose a reptilian arm tipped in long black claws. *Ooh*! He turned around and looked at his tail just as the fur fell off in one long section. He now sported a long reptilian tail with a barbed tip. Squirrel began to laugh.

Fist slowly frowned. He did not like the way this dream was going. It was time for it to end. Without knowing exactly how he was doing it, he closed his eyes and stepped out of the dreaming world.

Fist's eyes opened again to a sky full of fading stars. It was early yet. The morning sun was just approaching the horizon. He was laying in his bedroll, a cold mountain breeze blowing past his face. He sat up. Maryanne was laying in her own bedroll on his right, still sleeping. Rufus, however, was nowhere to be seen.

The Big and Little People campsite was at the rear of the Thunder People camp close to the base of the cliff face, not far from the prison caves. On the far side of the fire site, he could see the still forms of Locksher and Qenzic. Lyramoor was already up, likely patrolling the defenses. A short probe of the bond told him that Rufus had accompanied the elf.

Charz was gone as well, though it was likely he had never returned to camp the night before. The giant often spent nights in the women's caves enjoying the attention of the Ogre females. Charz enjoyed this lifestyle. There were plenty of fights to be had and the ogres fawned over him. He was likely the only one of Fist's tribe that would be sad when this was all over.

Squirrel? Fist sent, knowing he was somewhere close by. *How did you get in my dream*?

The little creature scampered out from inside Maryanne's bedroll where he had been sleeping. A spike of consternation stabbed through the bond. *Why did you wake up? I was almost Deathclaw again.*

I don't want you to be Deathclaw, Fist said. His little friend was too obsessed with becoming like the raptoid assassin. Fist feared it would get him hurt. *I like you as Squirrel.*

Squirrel is weak, Squirrel said, folding his arms defiantly. *Squirrel hides and watches when the fight comes. You need a Deathclaw like Justan has.*

Our tribe does not need you to fight. Fist reached out and Squirrel climbed onto his forearm. Fist brought the small beast close to his face.

The ogre reminded himself that Squirrel was actually quite big for one of his kind. Their bond had allowed him to grow larger than others of his race. He was more the size of a house cat than a squirrel. Still, in Fist's hand he seemed so tiny.

The ogre stroked Squirrel's head with one finger. *You are my friend. I do not want you to get hurt.*

Squirrel pushed his finger away. A memory flooded Fist's mind. It was one he had seen before. Squirrel frantically trying to stop ogres as they attacked an ogre female, one of them smashing Fist's head with a boulder. *Squirrel could not save Puj. Squirrel could not save you. Deathclaw could.*

You trapped Glug. You killed Beard, Fist said. *Not Deathclaw. You. And you found a Squirrel way to do it. But that is over. We have Maryanne with us now. And Charz.*

They were there before, Squirrel reminded him.

And Rufus, Fist added. *He can fight so you don't need to.*

Squirrel sat quietly, thinking on it a little longer. Finally, he shook his head. *I will find a way. I will find a Squirrel way to do it.* With that, he jumped down from Fist's arm and skittered off towards the cliff face.

"Squirrel problems?" asked Maryanne with a yawn. She frowned sleepily and reached into her bedroll to pull out a handful of tiny seeds. "Blast it! Got seeds down my smallclothes."

"At least that means he likes you. Otherwise it'd be poop," Fist said. He sighed and rubbed his face with his hands. "I'm worried about him. He constantly thinks about fighting."

Maryanne pushed her blankets aside and sat up, shivering

in the morning air. Fist tried not to notice the way her undershirt gaped open at the neck. She leaned against his arm. "Don't worry too hard, Big Guy. He's a resourceful critter."

"I know, but . . . I liked it better when he preferred to hide in the trees." Fist said.

"I get it. But people grow. They change. Especially ones that started out without much smarts. I should know." She rolled to her knees and leaned in to kiss him. "Don't worry too hard. Also don't think I didn't notice you look down my shirt."

Fist blushed. "I didn- . . . I tried not to."

"I know you did," she said with a chuckle. The gnome warrior turned away and started pulling on her leather armor. "That's one of the things that makes you so cute."

Rufus' voice sounded loudly through the bond. *Attack coming*!

Fist stood out of his blankets. "They're coming!"

"Finally," Maryanne said, lacing herself up quickly. "How close are they?"

Fist reached to Rufus through the bond. "Lyramoor sighted dead ones coming up the east pass. Rufus smells more coming from the south fork as well!"

A horn sounded from the top of the cliff wall, as a scout alerted the rest of the camp. The horn was one of the innovations brought to the Thunder People by the ogres who had once been of the Sound People tribe, their other contribution being large sets of drums spaced throughout the territory that soon beat rhythmically, joining the horn in rousing the ogres to action.

"Augh! I had hoped for another day," Locksher complained, dragging himself out of his bedroll as Qenzic the Heir trotted by. Sabre Vlad's son was already dressed and armed for battle with his small shield strapped to his left arm.

The Academy graduate made a habit of sleeping fully dressed and Fist had tried to emulate him. The ogre had slept in his long pants and a shirt, so all he had to do was pull on his boots and strap on his breastplate. Maryanne was still dressed faster than him. She appeared at his side to help him attach his shield harness.

"You should be quicker to rise, Wizard!" she said with a yawn. "Maybe don't keep such late nights."

Locksher had set up a makeshift lab in one of the smaller nearby caves and spent every spare moment in there working on various tests. He was determined to figure out the mystery of the woman that the Dark Prophet had put in charge of the Black Lake. Unfortunately, his only major clue was that red spirit magic that no one could quite figure out.

"You seem tired yourself, Maryanne," Locksher noted, using fire magic to heat a cup of potion he had poured from a flask. "Dark circles under the eyes. Constant yawns. What excuse do you have?"

She set Fist's shield on his back. "Sarine again. Come along, they'll be needing you soon."

The wizard waved them away, taking a sip from his now steaming cup. Fist and Maryanne jogged towards the territory entrance, passing ogres in various states of readiness. Four days without an attack had made them lax.

"So did you tell her?" Fist asked.

Maryanne had been uneasy about the idea of telling Mistress Sarine about the fact that her long dead husband whom she had mourned almost two centuries ago still existed in some bizarre form, his soul trapped inside a scar in her great grandson's chest.

Maryanne's nose wrinkled. "Yes. Which is why I didn't get much sleep. The old lady talked up a damn storm."

"Then she was happy about it?" Fist asked.

"Kind of. Kind of not," she replied.

They passed the big cave where ogres were milling about carrying supplies. Fist caught a brief sight of Mog standing at the entrance. He hoped that Charz would be able to coax him to fight today. The netherhulk was eleven-feet-tall and powerful, with acidic saliva and a thick skin resistant to the Black Lake's maggots, but he was notoriously lazy. They could only get him to come out and help half the time.

"What do you mean, 'Kind of not'?" Fist asked

The gnome shrugged. "At first, she was thrilled. The thought of seeing old Artemus again had her feeling like she was a girl of fifty. Then she got mad that Sherl had been keeping it a secret." She punched Fist in the arm. "I'm still kinda mad at you about that by the way."

"I didn't want to keep it secret," Fist said, echoing the defense he had made the night before. "Mistress Sherl told me to wait and . . . well, she's my Mistress."

She rolled her eyes. "Yeah, yeah. Anyway, after spending an hour grumbling, she starts to get worried 'cause the last time he saw her, she was young and now she's old and wrinkly and saggy."

Fist frowned. "I don't understand how that matters. He doesn't have a body at all."

"And there's that. It's weird," she said, reaching up to rub her eyes. "She's probably yelling at Sherl about it now and I'll get to hear about it tonight. I'm just glad I'm not in Kyrkon's place, hauling her knitting around while she agonizes about the whole situation all day."

"Instead, you'll spend your day fighting stinking dead things," he said regretfully, wishing that he was the one back at the Mage School worrying about less death-defying pursuits.

Maryanne smiled. "Thanks, Fist. You're right. I should be looking at the positive side of things."

Ooh! They are at the first trap, Rufus sent excitedly.

The long days since the last battle had given the defenders plenty of time to rig surprises. In the east pass where Lyramoor had seen the army approaching, several spiked pits had been dug and carefully concealed. While such inconveniences wouldn't destroy the infested dead, it would immobilize many of them and slow down the army's approach.

Rufus watched from a clifftop far away as the first group of dead stepped on what appeared to be sandy earth and fell into the trap. The dead at the front lines were clumsy goblinoids, their movements controlled by the magic of larvae crawling within their flesh. Perhaps a dozen fell inside before the army's movement stopped. Then something surprising happened.

The larger of the goblinoids, a pair of orcs, began reaching down into the pit to haul up those not too badly damaged to continue. While they worked, the dead forces parted, allowing a pair of strange creatures to come forward.

These were narrow long-limbed creatures with small whiskered heads. Thick brown shells rested on their backs and forearms. When most of the fallen dead had been retrieved, these new creatures began clumsily tearing into the cliff wall on either side of the pit with thick claws. Clumsy or not, their digging was effective. Dirt and rocks began pouring inside.

Rufus relayed what he had seen through the bond.

"Something's different with the evil this time," Fist said, his brow furrowed with concern. "The dead are acting smarter."

"Like how?" Maryanne asked. As they ran, she spied a familiar ogre that was still asleep by his fire despite the alarm. She paused to boot him upside the head. "Up, Rub!"

"Up!" Rub shouted, then rubbed at the side of his head. "Ow . . ."

"They're working together," Fist told her, still receiving Rufus' view of the scene. It was a bit disorienting, like seeing from his eyes and the rogue horse's at the same time. He had to stop jogging and close his eyes. "They were helping each other out of one of our pit traps. Now they've got some diggers filling them back in."

As Rufus watched, another creature came into view, pushing its way to the edge of the pit. It looked like a lupold; oddly-shaped beasts with the torso and head of a wolf, but long limbs with claw-tipped humanoid hands. However, this was one covered with reddish fur and was much larger than the lupolds that had climbed the cliff face to attack Fist's companions high above the Black Lake.

The creature walked on all fours, but stood shoulders above the infested goblinoids and the other beasts that worked to fill in the pit. This one did not move with the clumsy movements of the controlled dead. It was agile and actively sniffed out the area. When it stopped at the pit's edge and stood on its back legs, it was as tall as any ogre.

It took a few steps back, then ran and leapt across the pit, landing easily on the far side. The creature paused and sniffed the air. It crept forward, testing the ground in front of it until it found the edge of the next pit. Growling, it upended the latticework of sticks and skins that kept the trap disguised.

"And now they have some kind of big lupold thing out there tripping our traps," Fist added. "I don't think it's infested."

"A big one? I've heard of those. It's called a lupero. That's not the best news," Maryanne said. She saw his discomfort and smacked his back. "Try walking with one eye open. I find that it helps sometimes when Sarine is showing me something and I'm on the move."

Fist cracked open his right eye and was happy to discover that she was right. He still saw both sources of vision at once, but it wasn't quite as disorienting. "I wonder why that works."

"You got something in your eye, Big Fist?" Rub asked. The ogre was still sitting there, one hand rubbing his head while he squinted up at them.

"Just get moving, Rub. We got a fight coming," Maryanne said. She grasped Fist's hand and pulled him on towards the defenses. "Can Rufus do anything from where he's watching? Throw a rock down at it or something?"

"Not from where he is. Even if he could get close enough I don't want him to. He's alone right now and there could be more surprises. But he's not far from a boulder trap Lyramoor set up. If he waits until the creature gets to that spot, he can push it down the slope and . . . Oh." Fist slowed back down to a walk again.

Maryanne frowned. "What do you mean, 'oh'?"

"He's just gonna throw that boulder."

Rufus ran for the boulder trap, growing in size as he went. He sensed Fist's doubt, but ignored it. Throwing rocks was something he had done for centuries, after all. There wasn't all that much to do in the valley where the Prophet had secreted the rogue horses away and the handful of them with arms had made a game of it.

The boulder was three feet in diameter and dense, bigger than he would usually attempt. Lyramoor had directed a pair of ogres to roll it to the cliff's edge and wedge it in place so that it could be pushed at the right moment. The idea was that it would fall and hit the steep slope at the cliff's base, setting off a rock slide that would pummel and bury anyone at that narrow point of the pass.

When Rufus reached the boulder, he had become large enough to pick it up and cradle it in the crook of his massive arm. The rock was still back-strainingly heavy, but Rufus was a rogue horse that had developed an instinctive ability to change the nature of his body's malleable chemistry on demand.

The muscles of his wide ape-like torso grew denser, his ligaments stronger, until carrying the rock was less of a burden. He stood up straight on his cat-like rear legs and focused in on the lupero in the distance far below. It had destroyed a third pit trap and, while he watched, leapt over it to approach the final one.

Rufus hefted the boulder experimentally, his tongue poking out of the side of his wide mouth. He nodded thoughtfully and increased the size of his body a bit more, until he felt he had a good grip. Then he lifted the boulder and rested it on his shoulder as he began to spin.

"He thinks he can do it, but there's no way he can aim from that distance," Fist said. To Maryanne's consternation, the ogre stopped walking and closed both eyes again.

Rufus launched the boulder through the air. His back twinged.

Fist winced. "He hurt himself a little, but . . . whoa."

The rogue horse ignored the pain in his back and watched excitedly as the rock hurtled through the air towards his target.

The lupero reached the edge of the last pit trap and looked up just in time for the rounded rock to strike him square in the muzzle. Its skull instantly shattered, its neck and spine compacted. The rock splattered the beast against the ground before rebounding and crashing into the pit behind it.

"He squished it!" Fist said, pumping his arm into the air.

"Good for him," Maryanne said and tugged on his arm. "Now come on! I want to be there before the fighting starts!"

Good aim, Rufus! Fist sent.

Ooh! Ooh! See! Rufus replied excitedly. *I can do it*!

There was a stirring in the ranks of the infested army. Another lupero pushed its way to the front, this one slightly bigger than the first and with a black stripe across the top of its head. It leapt over the first three pits to sniff at the smashed remains of the dead lupero. A growl rumbled in its throat and it looked up at Rufus on the distant clifftop.

It reared back and howled, then began to climb up the sheer walls of the pass.

A series of angry barks echoed from further in the army's ranks. Four more luperos climbed up out of the pass to join it. A dozen of the smaller gray lupolds came with them. Together, they streaked towards the base of the cliff where Rufus stood.

The rogue horse looked down on them in surprise. He shifted to spirit sight. Each of these creatures were connected to the far distance by a dark red thread of spirit magic.

Chapter Ten

Fist opened his eyes. "We gotta run!"

He grabbed the handle of his mace. Its magic immediately took hold of his body. His reflexes sped up and he ran through the outskirts of the camp towards the paths leading to the cliffs where Rufus stood. Ogres heading to man the territory's defenses grunted in surprise as he rushed past them, pushing some aside as he went.

Maryanne had to sprint to keep up with him. She sounded quite cross with him as she yelled, "Where are you going? What happened?"

"A bunch more of those lupold things climbed out of the pass and they are going after Rufus!" Fist said.

"How many?" she asked, leaping over a smoldering campfire in her way.

"Over a dozen," he replied between breaths. "And five more of the bigger ones!"

Maryanne swore. "Does he have anyone else with him?"

"Lyramoor is up there somewhere, but I did not see him!"

"Tell Rufus to grab Lyramoor and head our way!" the gnome said. "We'll need more help to fight that many off." She stopped to grab a few more ogres to help, but Fist ran on.

Rufus! Get Lyramoor and come to me! We'll fight them together.

The rogue horse watched the lupolds streaking across the mountainside towards his position for a moment longer, then nodded. *Okay.*

Fist reached the territory's edge and bolted past the line of ogres bunching up in readiness for the coming attack. He saw

Qenzic at the front lines giving instructions, but did not bother him. It was good to have the Academy graduate in charge down there. The ogres had resisted the idea of listening to people of the smaller races, but they had soon learned to trust in the intelligence and skill of the experienced human and elf.

Fist sent a feeler through the bond to check on Squirrel and tell him what was happening, only to find that Squirrel was already watching him through the bond.

I am staying back like a good squirrel, the animal said petulantly. He was somewhere inside a dark cave. *I will watch from here.*

There was something suspicious about his little thoughts, but Fist didn't have the luxury of figuring out what Squirrel was up to. He headed up one of the steep pathways that lead to Rufus' location. The magic of his mace took a heavy toll on him, but today it seemed to be affecting him more quickly than usual. He was already breathing heavy.

Rufus, I need some energy, he sent.

Okay, said the rogue horse, shrinking to a more manageable size as he followed Lyramoor's scent.

Fist tapped into the rogue horse's deep stores. The energy filled his body and, though he did not go any faster, his breathing became less ragged. Linked to Rufus' energy he could run with his mace all day, though his body would likely pay for it.

I got the elf, Rufus reported, but no sooner had Lyramoor mounted Rufus' back, than the lupero leader climbed to the top of the cliff face. His companions soon joined him, along with their snarling smaller cousins. *They're coming*!

Rufus bolted towards Fist's position, chased by the ravenous barking beasts. If this had been a race on flat terrain, there would have been no contest. Rogue horses were the fastest beasts afoot, especially over long distance. But the mountain clifftops were ragged and uneven and lupolds are natural sprinters and climbers. They fanned out behind him, each one taking a slightly different path. Rufus was unable to gain any ground.

Lyramoor held tightly to the mane that ran down the center of Rufus' wide back with one hand, while reaching into his weapon sash with the other. He pulled out throwing knives and, using his uncommon agility, was able to turn and hurl them behind him with precision.

One struck a snarling lupold in the open mouth, causing it to stumble and tumble down a steep rocky incline. Another pierced the shoulder of a lupero. The large beast slowed, but did not stop, driven by whatever was behind that red magic.

Fist arrived at the top of the path and saw Rufus in the distance, heading towards him, the lead lupero at his heels. He ran to an open flat area of rock and stood at the ready, sending strands of earth and water magic into the ground at his feet.

Though the rock looked solid, it actually wasn't. Deep cracks and striations ran through it, with multiple layers of different types of strata. He went to work, widening some cracks, strengthening some layers, liquefying dirt and filling in spaces between the layers with water magic. It was complicated work, but the days of constant battle had given Fist a lot of practical experience. Many of the things Darlan had struggled to teach him before now made perfect sense.

Get behind me! he sent, showing the rogue horse what path to take.

As Rufus ran, columns of rock erupted from the mountainside around him. Fist's aim wasn't perfect, many of the beasts just ran around the obstacles, but several ran face first into them, while others found themselves launched into the air as the columns rose under their feet. The lead lupero took a glancing blow that sent him tumbling across the ground.

Good one! Squirrel said from within Fist's mind. It was as if little beast was sitting inside his skull, chewing a nut and watching from behind his eyes.

Fist doubted that he had killed any of the creatures. His main goal had been to slow them. Though it was likely that bones had been broken. He took pride in that. His next attack would be more deadly.

He reached into his magical stores, only to find that they were more depleted than he expected. Fist cursed his power level, knowing that he would never be as strong as most wizards. He was forced to pull more energy from Rufus.

Fist forced the water and dirt up to the surface, causing pits to open up in the earth and flooding the area in front of him creating a wide pool of water and mud. Then he pulled up strands of air and earth magic and waited for the right moment. He could feel Squirrel behind his eyes, watching his every movement eagerly.

Rufus hit the watery stretch of ground and followed the shallow pathway Fist had sent him through the bond. The lupolds weren't as lucky. Some of them were slowed by water two feet deep. Others became stuck in muddy quagmire, while others were forced to swim through deep pools. Rufus made good ground on his pursuers and soon joined Fist on dry ground. Fist waited for the right moment, wanting as many of the beasts in range as possible before he released his spell.

The lead lupero, having recovered from his tumble, stopped at the edge of the water. He let out a growl and his companions stopped next to him. The lupolds in the water turned around and headed back towards him.

Fist couldn't wait any longer. He sent vibrating strands of gold and black magic into the center of the water-soaked earth. At the same time he sent a similar set of strands into the sky above.

A bolt of lightning blasted down out of the clear sky, accompanied by a peal of thunder.

Good! Squirrel enthused.

Every beast still in the water slumped, steam rising from their bodies. The beasts outside the area of effect cringed, but did not flee. The lead lupero with the black stripe growled and the two other luperos that had been outside the water came to his side, one of them limping slightly with a throwing knife still protruding from its shoulder.

"We gonna stay and fight or run some more?" Lyramoor asked.

"We fight," Fist said. "I got most of them."

The scarred elf hopped down from Rufus' back and unsheathed his dual falchions. "No you didn't. That was an impressive strike, but those are wizard hunters."

The lead lupero let out a sharp bark. Some of the beasts in the water began to stir. Those at the center of the strike remained still, but the others began dragging themselves back to their leader. All in all, it seemed four of the luperos still survived, along with half of the lupolds. Yet another of the smaller beasts tried to join the others, but struggled, unable to move its rear legs.

"Wizard hunters?" Fist asked.

The elf nodded. "Lupolds are resistant to magic, one reason why the orcs in Khalpany like to keep 'em as pets. Luperos, though." He shook his head. "Those nasty things are even better at shaking off magic. Dark wizards train 'em and keep 'em as watchdogs in case the Mage School sends someone after them. Never heard of a group this large, though."

"Wish I knew that before," Fist said. Darlan was training him to be a war wizard like she was. She had hunted dark wizards for decades. Surely she had run into such things before.

Lyramoor laughed. "Yeah. Sometimes I forget you're still just an apprentice." He elbowed Fist on the arm. "You do pretty good, though. You get the job done."

"Thanks. I think," Fist said. It was uncharacteristic for the elf to try to be nice. Maybe Qenzic had been talking to him.

The surviving pack of wolf-like beasts parted down the middle and prowled along the outside of the wet ground, taking the long way around, still intending to fight. Fist noticed something else strange about them.

"What's that around their necks?" the ogre asked.

The elf rotated his swords in his hands, readying himself for the fight that was about to come. "Yeah, I noticed that too. I don't know. Collars of some kind, I guess."

Fist switched to spirit sight. "That red magic is linked to those collars. They are probably being controlled. Maybe we should try and cut them off?"

The creatures reached the far edges of the wet stretch of rock and sprinted towards them, the lupolds barking, the luperos slavering.

"Let's just kill 'em," Lyramoor suggested, facing the beasts approaching from Fist's right. "Magic may be weak against those things, but they still die on the end of a sword just like anything else."

Nodding, Fist pulled his shield off his back and pulled more energy through the bond. "Ready, Rufus?"

"Ooh-ooh! Yes!" the rogue horse huffed, rearing up on his back legs and pounding his chest with one enormous fist. He turned to face the beasts coming from the left side.

Fist now had to decide which group to face. He sent a question to Rufus through the bond, *Can you stop the ones coming at you so that I can help Lyramoor?*

They will bite, the rogue horse suggested. He didn't look forward to that inevitability, but he wasn't afraid of it either. *You will heal me.*

Fist nodded and stood next to the elf as the creatures grew near.

Make your mace shock! Squirrel suggested eagerly from behind Fist's eyes.

I was going to, Fist said. The beasts were resistant to magic, but what could it hurt? Considering how outnumbered he was, he even went a step further. Blue arcs of electricity crackled across his whole body.

Rufus waited until the beasts were almost on him before running towards them, increasing in size with each step. The beasts worked in concert, the two large luperos lunging for his neck while the three smaller lupolds ran around him to attack from his rear.

The rogue horse, now twice as tall as their height on all fours, reached out with both hands and grasped the luperos by their torsos. Their jaws snapped at empty air. Their clawed hands tore at his thickly furred arms.

He twisted his body and threw one of them into the muddy expanse at his right. It rolled and stood, ready to come back at him. Rufus' back twinged again, but he ignored it.

The rogue horse swung the other lupero around, using its long body to knock aside the smaller lupolds that were lunging for the tendons at the backs of his legs. He then lifted the large beast into the air with both hands and threw it at its muddy companion. The two creatures yelped as they collided, but were quick to come back to their feet.

Lyramoor rolled to the side to dodge the snapping jaws of one lupero, then spun to his feet, whipping both swords out in a vicious circle. One lupold was slashed across the muzzle. Another received a long gash along its ribs.

The elf didn't pause. Continuing his spin, he stabbed into the side of another beast and swung his other sword around, gashing the muzzle of the first lupold again. The creatures backed slowly away and circled Lyramoor, wary of the dual sword wielder.

The lead lupero ran straight for Fist. The ogre swung his shield out and connected with a glancing blow to its striped head, knocking it to the side and sending volts of electricity through its body. He followed up with a backhand swing of his mace that narrowly missed the head of a lupold who was lunging for his legs.

The lupero shuddered and snarled. Fist snarled back at it, building the electric charge around his body back up again. He could feel Squirrel's approval within his mind.

Rufus grabbed the rear leg of a lupold that was running by and swung it through the air, bashing it savagely against the rocky ground. While he was distracted, a muddy lupero reared up and bit into his shoulder. The beast whipped its head back and forth, tearing at his flesh.

Roaring, Rufus opened his wide mouth and bit the head of the beast that was biting him. He tore it free of his shoulder and thrashed his own head back and forth, clamping down with his teeth until he felt a satisfying crunch. He spat out the convulsing creature and grimaced at the taste it had left behind in his mouth.

Fist's mace bashed in the side of a snarling lupold, one of its spikes bursting all the way through the side of the creature. He swung back around, lifting his shield to block the incoming attack of the lead lupero, but the beast didn't come at him. It took a few steps backwards, growling as it saw the other members of its pack being destroyed.

"Come on!" Fist shouted and when he lifted his mace back up it was surprisingly heavy. The body of the now dead lupold was stuck to the spikes. Straining, Fist pointed the mace at the striped headed lupero. "You're next."

It bared its teeth at him and made as if to lunge, but an arrow streaked in, piercing its right eye with a zap of electricity. The lupero dropped to the ground, then rose shakily back to its feet. It stumbled to the side and let out a bark, then ran away on unsteady legs.

It was followed by one lupold and another lupero, both wounded, but still able to run. Another arrow streaked in, hitting the leader in the hindquarters, but it merely stumbled before continuing.

"You jerk!" shouted Maryanne from the top of the trail. She stormed towards him with a scowl, her hands clenched into white-knuckled fists. "Running on like that!"

Fist turned away from her approach, watching as Lyramoor pierced the heart of a dying lupero with a thrust of a falchion. The rocky shelf was littered with the bodies of the wolf-like beasts. Rufus was pounding a few of them just to make sure they stayed dead.

Fist could sense that the rogue horse had several wounds that needed to be tended to. He walked towards Rufus, dragging his lupold-laden mace on the ground beside him.

"Rufus, are you al-." Fist stumbled to the side, nearly falling as Maryanne kicked the back of his knee. "Ow! Why did yo-?"

She punched him in the arm. "I lost sight of you! Didn't know which trail you'd taken! I've been running all over the mountainside dragging ogres with me to find you!"

"Hey, Big Fist! Did I miss the fight?" asked a disappointed sounding ogre who was breathing heavy as he reached the top of the trail. There were two more behind him, each looking equally winded.

"I couldn't stop! Rufus and Lyramoor needed my help!" Fist said. He lifted his mace and shook the lupold's body at her. "I got here just in time."

"It's true," said Lyramoor, pointing at the landscape that Fist had rearranged with his magic. "With those numbers, they might've taken the rogue horse down before I could kill 'em all."

"Yeah? Well . . ." She bared her teeth at the elf, then turned her glare on Fist. "Just don't do it again."

Fist sighed and turned back to the rogue horse.

Rufus was bent over the body of the lupero he had bitten to death. He spat blood and dirt out of his mouth, then sniffed at it as he switched to spirit sight. The dark red magic was gone.

Fist came to the rogue horse's side and patted his flank. "You notice something?"

Its blood tastes funny, Rufus said with a grimace. He smacked his lips.

Fist reached through the bond and probed the rogue horse's injuries. The shoulder wound was ragged and deep, but no major blood vessels had been damaged. Fist worked on closing the wound, then healed the gashes in his arms where the luperos had clawed them. Finally, he looked at Rufus' back. There were a few partially torn ligaments that he was able to repair.

"You're like me," he told the rogue horse.

"Me?" Rufus smiled. "Like you?"

"Just too big for our own good," Fist said with a nod. "Justan had to fix my back a few times. I had to learn to walk different so I didn't hurt it so much."

"Hey! You three come here," Maryanne called to the ogres who were still standing at the top of the path. She pointed at the dead creatures. "I want you to take some of these down to the camp so that Wizard Locksher can look at them later."

The ogres walked closer, frowning. One of them spoke up. "Womens don't tell us what to do."

"Do it," Fist said. He agreed with Maryanne's idea. The wizard would want to examine the beasts. "And don't take off those collars around their necks."

"But . . ." said another. "You not think we should burn them?"

"No," said Fist. "They don't have any of the evil in them."

"Oh." The ogres looked relieved.

"Just take two of the small ones and two of the big ones," Maryanne said.

They looked at Fist and he nodded back at them. He planted his mace on the ground and began using his foot to pry the lupold carcass off of it. "Should've used the blunt side," he mumbled.

Maryanne trotted up to him and rubbed his shoulder where she had punched him. "Fist, sorry I got mad at you. I-."

"Don't worry about it, Maryanne," Fist said, grabbing her hand. "You are part of my tribe, so you can get mad at me if you want. I don't like that, but if I have to choose between the safety of my bonded and you being mad, I'm choosing them."

Her mouth closed and she nodded slowly. "I see. That makes sense."

She turned away and Fist frowned. He sensed that had somehow hurt her feelings by what he had said, but he couldn't understand why. It seemed perfectly reasonable to him.

"We should get back down there!" shouted Lyramoor. The elf had run back to the cliff's edge to check on the progress of the approaching army at the eastern pass. "They've gotten past the pit traps."

I look at other side! Rufus ran to the other side of the rocky shelf and looked down at the south fork. This series of trails that led to the south fork entrance of the Thunder People Territory were long and winding, but had fewer choke points for simple traps like in the eastern pass.

There was one good spot for a trap at the joining point of the trails and Locksher had set that one up himself. The wizard had imbued a series of rocks with elemental magic and had placed them at key points along the trail, ready to be ignited at the right moment.

"Ooh! They come!" the rogue horse announced.

Fist ran over to join him, arriving in time to see several columns of shambling dead creatures coming down the trails to meet at the joining of the fork. The lead beast, a sweating and grunting giant who was not yet dead, but fully under the sway of the evil, stepped over the magical wards the wizard had set.

The rocks the wizard had planted erupted in an expansive burst of fire and air. The series of explosions ripped through the morning air. Fist felt the concussive force of the blasts even from his vantage point high above.

Maryanne reached his side, wide-eyed as she saw the plumes of smoke and fire rising from the trails. Chunks of the infested bodies began to litter the slopes with a wet patter and she laughed out loud. "How many did we get?"

"I don't know," Fist said, shocked at the extent of the damage. As the smoke cleared, he saw deep craters pitting the trails where the magic-infused rocks had been left. "But it was a lot."

Not all of them were destroyed, however. Many of the bodies began to move. Even those that were horribly mangled were still controlled by the larvae inside of them. Some even stood. On top of that, more dead and infested were still streaming in from further up the trails.

Suddenly, there was a loud crack. A large slab of the slope above the trails shifted and broke free. It slid down the mountainside, causing a rumble that Fist could feel in his feet. The trails disappeared from view, covered by an enormous sheet of rock.

"*Oooh*," said Rufus and Squirrel simultaneously.

"That wasn't supposed to happen," Maryanne said.

"Guess we don't gotta worry about enemies from that side anymore!" Lyramoor said with a laugh, having run up just in time to see the slide.

"They might find another way around," said Fist numbly.

"Naw," replied the elf. "At least not today."

"I guess so," the ogre said, feeling a bit sick to his stomach.

He couldn't count the number of times he had hunted those trails in his youth. Now they were gone forever. It didn't necessarily matter that their disappearance was to his advantage. This war had already changed his people in more ways than he could count and evidently it wasn't finished.

"Your people will make new trails," Maryanne commented, seeing the look on his face. She then leaned in close to Fist's ear and whispered, "They'll have to be quick about it, too. How is our 'secret weapon' supposed to arrive with all the paths closed?"

Fist blinked, having forgotten about Lenny's side mission. He and Maryanne were the only ones who knew about it. Valtrek's instructions had been very specific on that point.

"We'll have to worry about that later." Fist turned away from the destruction. It could wait until the fight was over. "Let's go help with the east pass."

Chapter Eleven

The evil army marched on.

The pit traps had been filled in by the digging beasts and the other traps set by the academy graduates had proven ineffective. A rock slide trap, triggered by an ogre atop a hill overseeing the pass, had fizzled out before reaching the enemy, merely pelting a few of them with gravel. The other trap, designed to collapse the sheer walls at the pass' exit, never triggered at all, letting the invaders pass by unharmed.

Upon exiting the pass, the enemy stumbled into the Thunder People's first line of defense. The large amount of rock and earth that had been removed from the pass to create the pit traps had been repurposed into building a series of earthen walls that kept the shambling dead confined to a circular area.

Standing above the area on the surrounding slopes were Qenzic's Throwers. The Academy graduate had selected them from amongst the best rock hurlers the ogres had. Not surprisingly, most of them had formerly been of the Rock People tribe.

The ogres hurled rocks and boulders at the enemy, their purpose being to break bones and disable the enemy. Broken bones did not actually kill the dead, but an immobile corpse was useless to the evil. The throwers were an effective group.

Fist and Maryanne climbed onto a ledge overseeing the attack and watched as dozens of dead and infested creatures collapsed under the deadly assault. Corpses and rocks began to pile up. Fist noted that the majority of this first group of invaders were goblinoids or humans.

"Whoever is in charge of the evil is testing us," he suspected.

Maryanne nodded, firing an electric arrow into the neck of a heavily tattooed orc. It fell silently, the larvae controlling it bursting with the magic's discharge. "We're wasting our defenses on the rabble."

She was right. Qenzic's throwers began to run out of ready ammunition. As the hail of rocks slowed down, more dangerous beasts began to exit the pass. Among them were infested, but living, ogres who picked up the thrown rocks and began hurling them back. They were joined by a trio of giants and the pair of armored digger beasts that had filled in the pits so effectively.

The throwers that were standing on the open slopes were easy targets. Several of them fell, downed by their own method of attack. Others were forced to abandon their positions.

"Our turn!" shouted a loud voice and Charz came to stand upon the wall, his trident thrust high into the air.

Behind him was the next group of defenders. They were called "Crag's Clubbers", and consisted of the strongest and most adept fighters in the tribe. Crag and Fist's brother Burl were with them and, to Fist's relief, Mog. The netherhulk carried a long stalagmite across his shoulder and, despite a wide yawn, seemed ready to fight.

"I should go down there with them," Fist said, itching to put his mace to further use.

"Not a good idea," Maryanne said, firing the last of her shock arrows. One of the infested ogres collapsed. She lowered her bow as she waited for the magical quiver at her waist to bring the arrows back. "You've already had a fight today and we may need your magic for healing later."

The clubbers descended upon the enemy and worked with efficiency, bashing the limbs of dead and infested alike. The key was to avoid being bitten or getting enemy blood on you. That way you avoided a larvae infestation yourself.

Rufus joined them on the ledge, having shrunk his body down until he stood at their height and he could stand on the narrow outcropping comfortably. He looked down at the battle below and pounded his fist on the ground while looking around for something to throw. "Ooh! Ooh!"

Fist realized that his desire to fight was partially because of the excitement of his bonded. Especially Squirrel. The little beast was still watching through Fist's eyes and living vicariously through him at the moment. Squirrel really wanted the ogre to get down there and zap some enemies with his magic. "I'm feeling fine. I'll just pull more energy from Rufus."

Rufus nodded happily, eager to help.

The gnome snorted. "And what happens when you do too much of that?"

Fist frowned. The last time he had fought all day using borrowed energy he had awoken to a debilitating headache. Locksher had told him that it was the result of mental exhaustion. "I can handle a headache."

"Is that what you call it?" Maryanne said, reaching to her quiver as she felt the first electric arrow return.

The gnome drew and fired, striking a giant in the lower back. The electric shock wasn't enough to destroy all the larvae in its body, but the giant lost all strength in its legs. Convulsing, it collapsed to its knees. Crag saw the opening and wasted no time descending on the giant with bone-cracking blows.

"It wouldn't be as bad as that time. Locksher said I just needed to get used to using that much magic." The wizard had likened it to the soreness that comes when overworking one's muscles. Eventually, one's body gets used to it. "He said that students used to get those kinds of headaches all the time when he was an apprentice."

"Don't be selfish, Fist. A headache that leaves you unable to move for half the day is a liability," she pointed out. "Our tribe can't have our leader down when a fight is going on."

Fist looked down at the battle below regretfully. He didn't like it, but he knew she was right. Besides, his magic had been feeling strange all morning. The spells he had used when fighting the lupolds had taken more energy to enact than they should have.

Now that he thought about it, just watching the battle was draining him slightly. He wondered if he might be taking ill. He would have to ask Locksher to look at him later. Meanwhile, he would watch and stay ready to assist. He could be needed to fight or heal at any time. At the moment it didn't look like he was needed down there anyway.

Charz was in his element. His rocky skin impervious to the burrowing of larvae, he didn't have to worry about getting bloody. This allowed him to get in close to the infested. Part way through the battle, he tossed his trident to the side and waded in with bare fists. The rock giant laughed as he used his centuries of gladiatorial experience to disable the infested in a variety of ways.

The battle went on into the afternoon, members of the clubbers replaced as they grew tired. The narrowness of the pass had made their job simple. Only a few enemies could exit at a time. Fist noted that it was more like chopping down trees than fighting a war.

The biggest problem became clearing away the disabled enemies so that there would be room to continue fighting at the choke point. Mog was the most effective at this aspect of the battle. The netherhulk's acidic saliva dissolved larvae on contact, so he would simply lick his hand before grasping the bodies and pulling them out of the way so that the ogre burners could get to them.

The burners, a long line of ogres with their hands wrapped in thick hides, would drag the disabled corpses to the burn piles to be safely incinerated. The ogres in this group were the most likely to become infested. The ogress healers stayed close by the burn piles, ready to bind the hands and feet of anyone who showed the symptoms until either Locksher or Fist could electrify them.

The fighting wound down as the sun began its long decent. Horns sounded and drums pounded, signaling that the enemy was turning around and leaving the pass to head back towards the Black Lake. The clubbers were able to return to the camp to celebrate their victory.

For the rest of the tribe, the work wasn't over. Lyramoor, seemingly tireless, oversaw the clearing of the defenses. Body disposal would continue into the night as would the details assigned to setting up new traps.

The dead had never attacked at night. Locksher theorized that this was because the larvae used the eyes of the host bodies to direct them. Nevertheless, guards were kept on watch at all hours in case the evil decided to try something new.

Fist left the battlefield and went to the healers' camp. He had hoped to join Locksher there, but to his consternation the wizard was nowhere to be seen. The ogresses said that he had left them hours ago. Fist stayed to heal the few wounded and to electrify the infested, then went looking for his master.

He found Locksher in the small cave he had appropriated as his laboratory. The wizard was hunched over the slab of rock he was using for his workbench, a pipe in his mouth and a pair of spectacles perched on his nose. The body of one of the gray lupolds was draped across one end of it. A greenish smoke wafted from the cave entrance and a glowing orb lit the area with a soft glow.

"I was looking for you at the healers camp," Fist said, standing just outside to avoid the acrid smoke. "There were people hurt over there."

The wizard looked up. "Ah, there you are, Fist! Come. Look what I've discovered."

"Did you hear what I said?" Fist asked in frustration. "People were hurt."

Locksher set down his pipe and cocked his head at the ogre. "I am sure there were, Apprentice. There was a battle going on after all. I assume you saw to them?"

"Yes, Master. But-," Fist chose his words carefully. "We need your magic at the battlefield if we are going to survive until the Academy army can reach us."

The wizard gave him a patient look. "Fist, have you ever known me to be lackadaisical?"

Fist frowned, trying to remember what that word meant. It hadn't been one of his words of the day, but he was pretty certain he had read it before and had asked Darlan what it meant . . . "Oh! Uh, I guess not."

Locksher gave him a short nod and returned to looking over his bench. The wizard was picking through some kind of chunky slurry on a steel tray. "Efficiency, Fist. As I don't have a rogue horse to drain, I put my magic where it will go to the best use. Hence, the explosions this morning."

Fist couldn't argue the effectiveness of that. "Yes, Master. But-."

"I stayed in the company of those female ogres long enough to determine that my help was not needed. In addition, I told them to send for me if a severe injury happened." The wizard reached into the pocket of his robes and pulled out a pair of spectacles identical to the ones he was wearing. He held it out. "Now come in here and see what I have been doing."

"Okay," Fist said, still not pleased. The ogresses hadn't known where to find the wizard. It was likely that he had told them, but they had forgotten.

He ducked into the smoke-filled cave and put the spectacles on. "Ugh! What is that smell?"

The wizard gestured to the tray in front of him. "This is the stomach contents of one of those lupids you killed earlier today." He smiled. "Marvelous creatures, lupids. Resistant to magic, as I'm sure you discovered."

"Lupids?" Fist said with a cough. "I thought they were called lupolds."

"Yes, well that is one of the breeds." He gestured to the corpse of the beast on the bench and others that were lying on the floor in the rear of the cave. "Lupolds, luperos, lupins. All of them are part of the lupid family, bred by dark wizards mostly."

"That's what Lyramoor said." Fist pinched his nose and breathed through his mouth. That seemed to help a great deal. "So why are you looking in their stomachs?"

"You can tell a great deal from what an animal eats," Locksher replied. He gestured to the tray again. "What do you see in here?"

"Uh," Fist bent closer to look at the gray goop.

"Hey! What're you two smokin' in here?" said the loud voice of Charz, startling Fist so much that he banged his head on the ceiling of the cave. The giant rested his forearm above the cave opening and peered in, his nose wrinkling.

Fist ignored the giant and, rubbing the top of his head, said, "Master, I can't tell what that stuff is."

Locksher sighed. "What you are seeing is partially digested meat. A mix of goblinoid, human, and a trace of ogre."

"You can tell that?" Charz asked. "Looks like soup."

"From the putrid state of it," the wizard continued. "I'd say these lupids have been eating the bodies of the dead that were too badly rotted to be useful as infested carriers. The stomach contents were also free of larvae or even eggs, so that means that their mistress had the bodies drained of their parasites before letting her pets feast."

"That reminds me. I'm really hungry. How 'bout you two?" Charz said suggestively, rubbing his belly.

"Okay, but does that actually tell us anything useful?" Fist said.

"It just verifies that these beasts are domesticated and being cared for by whomever it is that the Dark Prophet sent to supervise Mellinda's power," Locksher replied. "In other words, they are her pets. Clean of any contamination from the Black Lake."

"But . . . couldn't you already tell that by the collars they were wearing?" Fist asked.

Locksher pursed his lips. He cleared his throat. "Always be thorough, Fist. There are surprising developments in any investigation." He reached into his pocket and pulled out one of the collars. "Speaking of the collars they were wearing. What do you see?"

"You seriously are just gonna ignore me?" Charz asked with a scowl.

The wizard lifted the collar up in front of Fist's face. It looked to be made of leather with a metal clasp that had a red stone in the center of it. Fist switched to spirit sight and saw that it shimmered a faint white.

"I see a little spirit magic in it," Fist said. "But it's not like before. When we were fighting them earlier, a red line of spirit magic was linked to them."

Locksher raised an eyebrow and looked closer at the collar himself. "More of that red spirit magic, eh? How fascinating. Do you know what this collar is?"

148

Fist shrugged. "My guess was that they were a way for her to control them since they aren't infested."

"Ah!" the wizard said with an approving nod. "Good deductive reasoning. You are quite close. These collars serve two purposes. The first one is, as you suspected, as receivers for spirit magic. You see, an accomplished witch can control animals within the range of their power, but once the beast is out of their range, control is lost. These allowed her to add a great distance to her range. The collar's secondary purpose is as a sort of receptor. This red stone allowing her to see what it is the animals are seeing. She couldn't give them accurate instruction otherwise. "

"Then . . . she was using them as scouts." Fist said.

Locksher nodded. "I would assume so."

"But that doesn't explain why they attacked Rufus," Fist pointed out.

"Hey!" interrupted Charz with a scowl. "Time to listen to the giant! I've been trying to tell you big brains that supper's on! The lady ogres have got food just sitting there waiting for us!"

Meat! Rufus agreed through the bond and Fist realized that the rogue horse was elsewhere in the camp with Qenzic standing next to a huge sizzling roast. The smell of it set Fist's mouth watering.

He swallowed. "Sorry, Master Locksher. Can we continue this later? I haven't eaten all day."

"Indeed!" said the wizard and to Fist's surprise added, "I am quite famished myself. This has been very hungry work! First, let me dispose of this bile."

The wizard took a moment to incinerate the contents of the metal tray and Charz led them across camp to a fireside next to the Big Cave. There, on a spit being rotated by Marg the Gutter, was an entire leg of mammoth, steaming and dripping with grease. The leg was huge, easily as long as Charz was tall and nearly as thick.

Qenzic sighed. "Thank goodness you're here. She wouldn't let us eat until you came."

Meat! Rufus agreed saliva dripping from one corner of his wide mouth.

"Dear me!" said Locksher apprehensively. "What an enormous . . . meal."

"It's a ceremonial roast," Lyramoor explained. "Thanks to our work in today's battle. Crag said they would've given us one sooner, but none of the hunting parties killed a mammoth until yesterday."

That was good news. The presence of the Black Lake's army had cut off most of the tribe's regular hunting grounds and the ogres had been forced to send hunters southward down the slopes. Having hunted mammoths himself, Fist imagined that dragging a beast this large up the slopes must have been quite a pain.

"This meat is for whole Big and Little People Tribe!" Marg, the tribe's resident butcher, barked, looking very put out at having this duty. "Crag told me to cook it, but it not my job!"

Fist understood her irritation. A roast like this took a very long time to cook. She must have been at it for hours already. He wondered if Crag had ordered her to cook it as a punishment.

Fist looked around. "Has anyone seen Maryanne?" He hadn't seen her since the fight had ended.

"You no need wait for you skinny women," Marg said dismissively. "She not eat much."

Fist frowned, wondering what the gnome warrior was up to. Since arriving at the Thunder People Territory, Maryanne hadn't left his side for more than an hour at a time. What if she was mad at him?

"Didn't want to wait for her anyway! Let's eat!" Charz said, grabbing a steaming hunk of meat and pulling it off the roast in one strip.

Lyramoor dug in as well, cutting a piece free.

Locksher stepped closer, staring at the deep red meat exposed by the giant's eager pull. "This doesn't seem to be an efficient cooking method for a roast this size. It looks raw in the middle."

"So? What's wrong with leaving it bloody?" the giant asked, lifting the dripping meat and taking a large bite out of it.

"That's what you have to do," Fist explained. "When ogres have a roast this big, we eat on it all night, pulling off strips and turning it to keep cooking as we go."

"That how you eat," Marg said, looking at the wizard like he was stupid.

"Marg," said Fist. "You don't have to stay here while we eat. Rufus will turn the spit."

"I not?" Marg blinked a half smile appearing on her face. "The gwatch do it?"

"Not a gotch," Rufus reminded her, but nodded, happy to help. "I turn."

Marg grunted and patted Rufus' arm. She placed his hand on the handle of the spit. "You good gwatch. I go."

"Not Gotch!" Rufus protested louder, but she just smiled before walking away. The rogue horse began turning the roast, trying to do it slowly like she had done.

"Somehow she seems less bright than most ogres," Qenzic observed.

"Brain like a brick," Lyramoor agreed.

"She doesn't talk well, but she's smarter than you think," Fist said with a frown. He had never liked the way people treated Marg. She was good at her job. "Still, I thought I should get her to leave before Locksher offended her by cooking the roast with his magic."

The wizard pushed back the sleeves of his robes. "It really must be helped along. I do not have all night to wait. " He raised his hands and paused, glancing at Fist. "I have likely not eaten this particular type of beast. Is it gamy? I have a spell that can take out odd flavors."

"Tastes like cow to me," Charz replied.

"I dunno," Lyramoor disagreed. "Kind of like a mix between venison and wild yak."

Qenzic used a knife to cut off a piece. He chewed it. "It's pretty good. Could use some salt I guess."

"A useful observation," Locksher said with a nod. The wizard reached into a pocket deep within his robes and pulled out a white rock. He looked at it sadly. "I'll probably have to use the whole thing."

He blew and the rock disintegrated into a fine powder that flowed through the air on streams of golden magic before disappearing into the roast. Locksher then sent threads of fire throughout the meat, cooking it completely through.

"There! It should be edible now." He excised a steaming piece with his ceremonial knife and took a bite, chewing with a satisfied nod.

Fist tore a strip free, hissing through his teeth as he burnt the tips of his fingers. He juggled the meat from hand to hand until it cooled enough to handle. He took a bite and groaned. Not only had he been starving, but the complex flavor of the mammoth meat brought back memories of his childhood. Being part of eating a celebratory roast was one of the few happy memories he had from those days.

"Go ahead, Rufus. Eat," Fist said. "You don't have to keep turning it."

The rogue horse smiled and pulled off a hunk, heedless of the way it sizzled in his hand. He stuffed it in his mouth. *Meat*!

The Big and Little People tribe ate on for several minutes in silence, pulling apart their meal a piece at a time.

Fist began to worry about Maryanne again. The more he thought about it, the more likely it seemed that she was still angry with him about their conversation earlier in the day. Surely she knew what he had meant when he said that his bonded were more important than her feelings being hurt.

He bit his lip. Then again, he could also see how she could take offense. Women were so complicated!

"You know what I figure?" Charz said, breaking the silence as he tore another large hunk of meat off of the roast. "Today's fight was an experiment."

"What do you mean?" Qenzic asked.

"That lady you guys saw at the Lake. The one the Dark Prophet sent." Charz said. "I don't think she was trying all that hard to beat us today. No, I figure she was feeling us out. Seeing what we were capable of."

152

"Maybe," Qenzic agreed, cutting another slice of meat as he talked. "It did seem like she was testing our traps and defenses. From what we saw at the lake, I know she had more dangerous beasts she could have thrown our way."

"Uh huh!" Rufus agreed, nodding heartily, his mouth full.

Fist dragged his thoughts away from Maryanne and back to the current conversation. "But shouldn't she know that already? She has sent the dead here many times before."

"Yeah, but," Charz paused to swallow. "I figure she wasn't so worried about us. She's got conquering Dremaldria to worry about. Why bother focusing on one big ogre tribe just trying to survive?" He shook his head and took another bite. "She was content to keep us at bay. 'Least she was 'till you all went up to the lake and poked her in the tush."

Locksher nodded, frowning thoughtfully. "You make a sound point, Charz. While we were trying to discover information about the evil, we inadvertently let her know that she had more potent enemies at her flank."

Lyramoor snorted. "We let her know? You mean you. Of course she's mad! A wizard poking around in your brain'll put your back up."

"Not to mention the arrow Maryanne shot at her," Qenzic added. "And the lupolds we killed."

"And the gwatch Rufus fought," Fist said. "We caught her attention and suddenly, the Thunder People are a threat worth paying attention to."

Locksher did not like the blame being placed his way. "Now, now. While I will admit that there were some unforeseen consequences, that foray into enemy territory was necessary. We would not have discovered the origination of the evil or the identity of the person controlling it otherwise."

"Oh?" said Lyramoor. "Did you actually figure out who it is?"

Locksher's mouth opened and closed a few times before the words came out. "I have narrowed the possibilities down to a short list. Most of them are ancient. Some long assumed dead. But to be an associate of the Dark Prophet and have resources and power like this it really can't be someone new."

"You make it sound like that list isn't so short," Lyramoor scoffed. "Come on. We're looking for some old priestess that's come out of hiding. Are there really that many?"

"The Dark Prophet has been around from the beginning of recorded history. In that long time he has always preferred priestesses to priests," the wizard said, scratching his head. "There are quite literally a hundred possibilities considering the many ways that the Dark Prophet has used to extend his servants' lives over the years. That being said, I've narrowed it down to priestesses within the last thousand years. No matter the method, a longer lifespan would be quite unlikely since his priestesses are always human."

"Always?" said Fist. "But isn't he mostly worshipped by the goblinoids?"

Locksher gave him an appreciative nod. "Good question, Fist. Yes. That is true. However, the Dark Prophet has always been jealous of the Prophet's stewardship over the Human Race. It gives him particular pleasure to surround himself with fawning members of his enemy's flock."

Charz laughed as an idea came to him. "Hey, what do you wanna bet those wizard hunter dogs she sent today were supposed to be coming after Locksher?"

"Ohh. Right!" said Lyramoor. "She sends in a pack of lupolds expecting to get back at the wizard that bit her, only one of 'em gets killed by Rufus!"

"Me!" Rufus agreed happily, banging one fist against his chest.

Charz laughed again. "Oh. Oh! And since she's an ancient wizardess she's got to know about rogue horses. So she saw Rufus beat that gwatch thing back at the lake and recognized what he was, so-." He smacked his hands together. "She assumed that Locksher is Rufus' bonding wizard!"

"Why on earth would she think that?" Locksher asked.

"Because she never saw me with him," Fist said, his brow raised. "You were the only one of us to use magic. Even if she had been watching from the eyes of the creatures that attacked, I was staying by you in that cave while everyone else fought the lupolds that day. Then Rufus defeated the gwatch without my help and we left."

Charz nodded gleefully. "So today, the wolf things see Rufus kill their friend and she sends them after him, thinking they'd find Locksher up there too."

"And Fist surprised them," Lyramoor said. He leaned back and took another bite of meat. "An ogre mage wipes out most of her pack. Ho, that must've roasted her!"

Fist swallowed. If Locksher was right, then those lupids were her pets. "So the next time her army comes, it shouldn't be so easy."

"Nope!" said the giant with an eager grin. "She learned a lot from us today. Next time she'll be taking us seriously."

"What're you greasy-faced monsters talking about?" Maryanne asked, walking into the firelight.

"We figure the lady at the Black Lake was just testing us today," Lyramoor replied.

She walked up to the surprisingly diminished roast and cut herself a healthy slice. "I'd have to agree with you there. After those lupolds died, the rest of the fight seemed pretty tame." She tore into the meat and nodded appreciatively. "What kind of animal is this?"

"Mammoth," Charz said.

"Huh," she said and shoved the rest of it into her mouth.

Fist eyed her suspiciously. Maryanne didn't look angry, but he couldn't always tell by how she looked. "Where have you been?"

The gnome held up a finger, her cheeks bulging as she chewed. She cut off another piece as she swallowed. "I had an errand. Actually, Fist. I could use your help. Could you come with me for a minute?"

"Uh, okay," he replied. "You sure you don't want to eat a bit more first?"

"Naw, I already had a bite. Not as good as this, though," she said and shoved the piece into her mouth before grabbing his hand and pulling him away from the fire.

"I guess I'm going now, then," Fist said.

"Too bad! We're not gonna save you any!" Charz shouted after them.

Maryanne led him past multiple campfires of celebrating ogres. Several of them called out to Fist and he waved back, but she didn't stop for him to talk. Fist became concerned she was taking him somewhere away from the others where she could yell at him properly.

He cleared his throat. "Maryanne . . . I'm sorry about what I said earlier."

"Huh? When?" she asked, frowning at him.

"When you were mad that I didn't wait for you," he said. "You know. About my priorities?"

"Oh that," she said, shaking her head. "Well, I understand. I am bonded too, remember?"

The way she was responding was even more puzzling. "But . . . I want you to know that I think of you as more than just another member of my tribe."

She smiled. "Is that so?"

"And if it was you that was in trouble, I would have run to you even if everyone else didn't know where I was going," he said.

"How sweet," she said, coming to a stop near the cliff face. "But you might want to think that through a little better. If someone's in trouble, it's best to tell people where you're running off to."

"Yes. But what I'm trying to say is-."

She placed a finger on his lips. "I know exactly what you are trying to say."

Fist looked around. The sounds of celebration were even louder here. Laughing ogres walked in and out of a series of well-lit caves in the cliff face. "These are the women's caves."

"I know," Maryanne replied, still smiling. "I had to set this up with Momma Zung. That's why I was gone so long." She shook her head. "That ogress is not a good cook."

She led Fist up a short trail to one of the larger caves.

Fist balked. "Wait. Why did you have to talk to Momma Zung?"

Momma Zung was the ogress in charge of all the females in the tribe. She decided which one of them could mate and when. She was probably the second most influential person in the tribe after Crag himself.

"You'll see," she said and tugged him towards the cave.

He pulled his hand out of hers. "I don't want any of the Thunder People females."

Maryanne blinked at him for a moment, then laughed. "I'm not bringing you here to mate with some ogress, you goblin brain!" She frowned briefly and slapped him on the arm. "Why would I want you to do that? Just follow me."

Confused, Fist let her pull him inside. She led him through a dark tunnel and into an open chamber. Two light orbs that she had borrowed from Wizard Locksher lit the chamber with a soft glow. He could hear the sound of water trickling and saw that a rivulet of water entered the chamber from a hole in the wall and ran across the floor into a pool that had been carved out of the floor of the cave.

"Surprise!" Maryanne said with a smile. "I thought you could use a bath. There's nothing quite as good after a long battle."

Fist scratched his head. He had come to the women's caves many times before and had never seen this place before. Ogre women didn't bathe very often. "What is this place?"

"Mother Zung told me about it," Maryanne said, reaching into a pouch at her side and pulling out two small rocks carved with tiny fire runes. She tossed them into the pool and when they hit the water, they began to glow. "She says the Water People brought the idea with them when they joined the tribe. They've been digging channels for water throughout the caves."

"A bath," he said, a smile spreading across his face.

She shrugged as the pool began to bubble and steam. "It's not the same as a nice tub, but heating the water helps."

Fist leaned in to kiss her quickly on the lips. "Thanks so much! I haven't had a bath in so long!" He set his shield and mace aside and unbuckled his breastplate, then sat down to pull off his boots.

He had gained an appreciation for bathing during his stay at Coal's Keep and had learned to enjoy it even more at the Mage School. This was going to be so wonderful. He began to pull off his shirt, but stopped and turned to face her.

"Oh. I'll wait for you to leave before I . . ." His voice trailed off as he saw her set her leather armor to the side. "But you . . ."

Maryanne stripped off her underclothes and stepped into the steaming water, easing back with a satisfied sigh. She raised an eyebrow at the gape-mouthed ogre. "Well? Get in here."

Chapter Twelve

Lenui Firegobbler heard the riders approaching before they appeared. He handed the wagon's reins to Old Bill, who was sitting on the bench next to him. Lenui placed his hand on the handle of his throwing hammer. It was probably just the scouts returning, but it didn't hurt to be cautious. This trip had gone too smoothly so far. He was certain something had to go wrong sooner or later.

"Someone's comin', Swen!" he barked, glancing back to see that the wooden-faced archer already had an arrow nocked and ready.

"I heard." Swen was sitting on the bench atop the second wagon. They had chosen the tall Academy graduate for the duty because he had the blank look of a caravan driver. No one would see the man and think he was dangerous. They'd be wrong, though. He was a dead-eye shot with either of his bows.

Lenui relaxed when the riders came into view. It was just Wild Dinnis and Helmet Jan. "Well? You find anything?"

"No," said Dinnis boredly. Tolivar's old sword seemed to be working its magic. The young swordsman had gained a taste for battle since the last time Lenui had seen him. Unfortunately, the goal of this journey was to avoid battle. At least until they could get up to the Thunder People territory.

"We just saw animal tracks. Nothin' to fret about," added Helmet Jan. The harsh-voiced pikewoman wore a cloak with a long cowl to cover the shiny helmet she always wore. The helmet was an odd thing. It was polished and shiny, tight to her head, covering everything but her mouth and chin. The woman never took it off, not even to sleep.

Lenui was certain that helmet was magical. It only had narrow slits for her eyes to see out of, but the woman saw remarkably well. In fact, she was an excellent scout. Lenui figured that the inside was covered in runes, allowing her to see in ways the rest of them couldn't. He ached to take a peek at the thing but the blasted woman wouldn't take it off to let him look inside.

The three Academy-trained humans had been picked as escorts for this mission because they were a small and relatively unknown trio that had already worked together on a long travel assignment. Also, since they had just recently returned to the Academy, Wizard Valtrek had figured it was less likely that any of them could be a spy for whoever was controlling the evil in the mountains.

A five person crew was pretty small for a mission this important, but that was the point. Even if the enemy somehow got wind of their approach, a group this small wouldn't be seen as a threat. As far as anyone would be able to tell, they were just a small merchant caravan with two guards.

"Did you see that wagon trail I told you about?" Old Bill asked the two scouts. Sarine's bonded dwarf had a clean-shaven upper lip, but a long gray beard that hung past his belt. He was dressed in merchants' finery. "It should fork off of the road not far from here."

Jan shrugged. "Maybe. I saw somethin', but it's pretty overgrown. Wouldn't have noticed it if you hadn't told me to be lookin' for it."

The old dwarf nodded. "Can't say I'm surprised. That's how he'd want it."

Old Bill was something of a legend in the dwarf community. He was just over six hundred years old and had been one of the Prophet's companions in the big war. However, not many folks knew what he looked like. He had been in hiding with his bonding wizardess for the last 200 years and even the people that once knew him figured he was long dead. He was even less recognizable wearing fancy red and gold embroidered robes and a floppy merchants' hat.

The old dwarf had multiple reasons for being on this

mission. One of them was that as one of Mistress Sarine's bonded, he was able to stay in contact with the Mage School High Council and let them know of the mission's progress. Another one had something to do with this surprise side mission that the dwarf had sprung on them earlier that morning.

Lenui frowned. There was too much secrecy on this trip. The three Academy students knew nothing except that they were to escort these two wooden merchant's wagons to the mountains.

Lenui was the mission leader and the only thing he knew was that one of these wagons contained the secret weapon they were bringing to help Fist and the ogres in their fight. He didn't even know what the weapon was. He didn't like not knowing things.

Old Bill called back out to the Academy warriors. "Head back up to that trail if you would. See if it's clear enough that we can take these wagons down it. We may have to clear a path."

"Really? Path clearing?" Dinnis complained. "That's what our Academy training gets us? At least with Tarah, we occasionally got to stab things."

"Stop your whinin'," Helmet Jan replied. "We don't get to choose our jobs. Just be glad you're not stuck guardin' some noble's old auntie. At least you'll get to wave your sword around while you're clearin' brush."

The two of them turned their horses around and headed back up the road.

Lenui took the reins back from Old Bill. "So, you willin' to tell me why we're makin' this side trip yet?"

The old dwarf sighed. "You know I can't tell you anything more until we get there. All I can tell you is that it shouldn't delay us very long. We've been making very good time. The Academy army is still over a day behind our progress."

While their caravan was taking a westerly route up to the Thunder People Territory, the Academy army was making a direct northerly approach to the Black Lake. It was a large force, a thousand Academy troops, joined by two thousand Dremald Garrison and cavalry, along with a couple hundred wizards and mages. They were going at a slower pace, however. Largely, because so many of them were on foot.

"Yeah, we got the cushy job compared to them. An easy ride up mountain trails," Lenui said with a scowl. "Why do I feel like I got the dag-gum turkey detail?"

"I'd say it's because you don't trust Head Wizard Valtrek," said Old Bill.

Lenui's eyes narrowed. "Could you not call him that?"

The old dwarf shrugged. "Like it or not, that's his position. The Bowl chose him. If the Bowl trusted him, we should too."

"Maybe it did," Lenui admitted. "But it didn't name him, did it? That there tells me that it knows there's somethin' off about that dag-blasted cotton-chewer."

"Mind your tongue, Lenui," Old Bill said. "You should be above that kind of talk."

Lenui's scowl deepened and he had to force down the long string of curses he wanted to direct Old Bill's way. In the beginning, he had been excited about the prospect of journeying with the old dwarf. After all a legend like Old Bill was sure to be an excellent companion, full of old stories. Unfortunately, folks hardly ever lived up to their legends. Old Bill was mild-mannered, prudish, and a bit of a bore. Even worse, he disliked two of Lenui's favorite things; swearing and spicy food.

It had surprised him. He had met Old Bill briefly when he was young and he had seemed so different back then. The dwarf was two full inches shorter than Lenui, but he had seemed vibrant. Manly. The kind of dwarf you'd follow into any battle. Now he just seemed . . . soft.

Bill even spent his nights sleeping in the bed in the first wagon. He said it was to keep up the ruse that he was the wealthy merchant. Yeah, right. What had happened to the dwarf in the last two hundred years? Had he spent the whole time in an elf vineyard, holding the old lady's yarn?

They came upon Bill's "wagon trail" about a mile up the road. Calling the trail overgrown was an understatement. It looked like it hadn't been used in years. It took them an hour to clear enough tree-limbs out of the way that the high-sided wagons could pass down it. Even then, going was slow. The trail had been washed out in several places and at one point they had to get out and remove an entire tree that had grown in the center of the road.

Finally, they came to an obstacle too great for them to take those wagons through. An enormous boulder was standing in the path, dense greenery on either side of it.

"Where'd that come from?" Helmet Jan asked.

"It must have rolled down the mountainside," Swen suggested.

The woman frowned. "From where? This is a flat stretch of ground. Even if it'd somehow rolled down from that far ridge, it would've had to crash all the way through the forest on its way here. You see any downed trees?"

"Well, however it got here, it's got us stuck," Dinnis said. He looked back at Lenui. "Is your hammer strong enough to break this apart?"

Lenui snorted. The thing was ten feet tall and easily just as wide. "Maybe if I had a few days to whack at it."

"That's alright," Bill said. "Our goal is only another couple miles ahead. We'll hitch the horses up to the back of the wagons and pull them back to that clearing we just passed. We can camp for the night and Lenui and I will continue on foot in the morning."

"Just the two of you?" Swen said.

"You think we can't handle a gall-durn two mile hike?" Lenui asked, shaking his head. "He's right. It's more important that you three stay and guard the wagons."

As the Academy soldiers went to move the horses, he looked back at the dwarf. "And once we get on that walk, yer gonna tell me where the hell it is we're goin'."

"There is no need for you to be disrespectful," Bill replied. "I'll tell you our goal when the time is right."

"What does it matter?" Lenui said. "You could tell me now. No one's listenin'!"

The old dwarf folded his arms. "Head Wizard Valtrek's instructions were very specific. The fewer of us that know the mission, the less chance there is that someone could tell the enemy if captured."

"That's piddle-talk!" Lenui said. "Whatever that evil thing is, it ain't gonna bother holdin' us fer questionin'!"

Shaking his head, Bill walked to his wagon and went inside, closing the door behind him. Lenui watched him leave with open mouthed wonderment. What kind of dwarf walked away just because he was being questioned?

Old Bill didn't come back out until the rest of them had set up camp and Lenui had a pot of pepperbean stew boiling. He had made sure to pick the reddest pepperbeans just to spite the dwarf. They were just about soft enough and he was just adding dried pork flakes to thicken it up when the old dwarf approached him, a lit pipe hanging from his mouth.

"I refuse to eat that," Bill said, his voice even-toned, though the glare in his eyes meant business.

Lenui frowned. "Tough rocks. It's my night to cook. You sayin' you don't like the way my stew tastes?"

"I'm not saying it to insult you. It tastes great for the half second before my tongue runs screaming," Bill replied.

"Nonsense!" Lenui barked. "I am the best trail cooky there's ever been. That heat's important. Warms up yer insides. Cures colds. Kills gut bugs. Gives you energy the next day."

"I was cooking for hundreds of years before you were born. A good trail cooky takes his companions' wants in mind," Bill replied. "I've asked you time and again to make something else or at least tone it down. You continue to make it hotter than any normal person, I don't care if they're dwarf or bandham, could tolerate!"

Lenui snorted. "Ain't my fault you don't know good food when you taste it."

"I'm not the only one who feels this way." The old dwarf looked around the campsite. Jan was on first watch and was patrolling the perimeter, but the other two pretended not to be paying attention. "Well? Tell him."

Dinnis was laying in his bedroll. "Don't drag me into this. I just want to sleep."

"I have grown used to it," said Swen, who was sitting by the fire, whittling an arrow.

"They feel the same way I do. They are just reluctant to speak up," Bill said.

"Yer friggin' crazy," Lenui said. "What happened to you? Yer a dag-gum legend. When did you become a wet-willow?"

"And then there's that foul mouth of yours. I demand an apology," Bill said firmly. His tone was still even, but he was puffing on that pipe so fast it was as if his head was steaming.

Lenui blinked, taken aback. "Fer what? Questionin' that piece-of-dirt Valtrek?"

"For continuing to curse at me even though I have told you I don't want to hear it!" the old dwarf said. "Just because you're a young dwarf doesn't mean it's okay for you to disrespect your elders!"

Lenui took his stew off of the coals and set it next to the fire to thicken. Then he turned to face the dwarf. "I may be half yer age, but I ain't no 'young dwarf'. And as long as you keep whinin' 'bout it, I'm gonna say all the dag-blasted swears I can garl-friggin' think of!"

The old dwarf looked at the others exasperatedly. "Do you see where my frustration is coming from? He's supposed to be a legend himself. 'Lenui Firegobbler, the greatest leader of this generation!' Still, he throws tantrums like a toddler."

"I never said I was no great leader," Lenui harrumphed. "And don't act all high and mighty to me, dag-blast it! Yer supposed to be a dwarf. Cursin' is a proud part of our heritage!"

"I'm not saying that cursing doesn't have its place in our tradition," the old dwarf allowed. "But only during holidays! And the cursing competition was done as a joke! Your generation is the one that started bringing that muddy language into every day speech!"

"That's blasted bunk! My grandpappy used to curse me to sleep at night!" Lenui declared.

Old Bill rolled his eyes. "That's right. You're from Corntown where coarseness is second nature. But the rest of us weren't ever that way. It's your generation that spread it around to the rest of the dwarves. Now it's become so common place nobody can speak the common language proper anymore!" He pointed his pipe at Lenui. "It's one of the great travesties of our age. Two hundred years of young dwarfs so empty headed, they can't spit out a coherent sentence!"

"That's tiddle-pucky!" Lenui snapped. "Yer just against it 'cause you ain't quick witted enough to keep up with me."

"I'll have you know that back in my younger days I was the champeen curser of my town!" Bill claimed. "I just knew the proper time and place for it."

Lenui let out a belly rumbling guffaw. "Bull-apples!"

Old Bill's face twisted into a deep scowl. "You challenging me, boy?"

"I been challengin' you since we left the dag-blamed Academy," Lenui growled.

"So be it!" The old dwarf pointed at Swen. "You're one of the judges."

Swen's brows moved slightly closer together in his version of a frown. "I don't know that I would be the best judge."

"What're you talkin' 'bout?" Lenui said. "Yer so impartial, yer practically a tree."

"He means you're perfect," Bill said. "Dinnis!"

The swordsman, who had just fallen asleep, groaned. "What do you want?"

"You're the second judge," Bill said. "There has to be two and Jan's out on patrol."

"But it's been a long day and I got early morning watch," Dinnis complained.

"That don't matter," Lenui declared. "Whichever one of us dwarfs loses has to do the rest of the night's watch on his own."

Dinnis sat up in his bedroll, his arms folded. "Fine by me. I'll judge."

Old Bill laughed. "Is that all you want to wager, Lenui?"

"It's a start," Lenui said, licking his lips as he tried to think up a good proper punishment. "Also, when I win, you can't complain 'bout my cursin' fer the rest of the trip!"

Bill snorted. "Fine. But if I win, you can't cook dinner for the rest of the trip."

166

"Ha! Done!" Lenui said.

"You better win, Bill!" said Jan from the trees. "I'm tired of crappin' out live coals!"

"Yer supposed to be on watch!" Lenui barked. "If you got eyes under that helmet, keep 'em open!" Lenui pointed a finger at Dinnis. "And you gotta be impartial! No pickin' him just 'cause he's old!"

"He's older than you? I thought you were about the same age," Dinnis said.

Lenui's jaw clenched until he was close to cracking a tooth. "Just judge it fair!"

"I shall judge it fairly as well," Swen announced in his monotone voice.

The two dwarves gave the wooden-faced man a dull look, then focused back at each other.

"You know the traditional rules for a cursing competition?" Bill asked.

"Who the hell needs rules?" Lenui replied. "Just let her rip 'till one of us throws a punch. The one with the weakest skin loses!"

"Corntown boys." The old dwarf shook his head. "Traditionally, there are three rounds. First two, we fire off at a judge. The third round, we go at each other."

"Fair 'nough," Lenui said with a brusque nod. "We go at Dinnis first."

"Very well," Bill said. The old dwarf faced the Academy graduate and took a draw of his pipe as he thought about it. "You, son, are an out-of-control, caterwauling bed-wetter!"

Dinnis blinked. "I-I don't wet the-."

"Just judge!" Lenui barked. "And yer also a lily-livered corn-swillin' rooster-nugget!"

"And a self-flagellating whimplepuss!" Bill added.

"A baby-faced, arse-sniffin' corn-shucker!"

Bill pursed his lips. "A limp-wristed, turkey giblet with road apple gravy."

Lenui chuckled despite himself. "That was a good one. Oh.

My turn. Dinnis, yer a toe-chewin', corn-grindin' tickle-fairy!"

Dinnis frowned, red faced. "These sound more like insults than curses."

Bill patted his shoulder. "That's part of it, son. Now you judge. Who won?"

"I don't like either of you much right now," the swordsman replied. "But I'd say Lenny won."

"Ha! I tell you it was over before it started," Lenui bragged.

"I was just warming up. Round two," said Bill calmly.

Lenui walked around the fire to face Swen. "Yer a horse-faced, stank-fingered, lackawilly!"

Old Bill strolled to Lenui's side and removed the pipe from his mouth. "You are a bow-licking, flibberty-wicket with a loose goiter."

"Pfft! He's a stone-faced, apple-grindin', puffle-wagon!"

Bill inclined his head. "Went way back for that one, didn't you?" He sniffed at the bowman. "I declare you to be a blank-eyed, moon-gazing, willy-whittler."

"I already used willy!" Lenui declared. "And he's a weed-chewin', squint-eyed, rock-wiper!"

"I used it better," Bill reasoned. "And he's a straight-backed, pissle-puncher with an arrow fetish!"

They could hear Helmet Jan's cackle from the trees at that one.

"Alright. Round over. Who won?" Lenui asked.

A single tear rolled down Swen's cheek.

Old Bill paused. "Swen, son. You know we don't really feel that way about you. It's just a competition."

"He's fine!" Lenui said.

Swen sniffed, but his voice sounded no different than usual. "It is not what you said. You were just reminding me of my grandmother." The tall man wiped the wetness from his cheek with the back of his hand. "I declare Bill the winner of this round."

Lenui scowled at the archer and faced Old Bill. "Round three then! Yer a doe-eyed, baby-lipped, purple-nosed, crack-pickin', dangle-sack!"

"You, sir, are an ankle-biting, bare-chinned, pickle-brained, tackle-smacker," Bill replied.

So he was going for age, eh? Lenui fired back. "Droop-nippled, jiggle-handed, saggy-britches!"

The old dwarf blinked. "You are a finger-burning, lack-whit, who uses a fork for a spoon."

Lenui's lips twisted at the slam on his cooking and went for a low blow of his own. "Yer a prune-dippin', half-squatin', soup-gummer in line fer a coffin!"

The old dwarf's eyes narrowed. "You are a no-talent, numb-tongued, over-spicing, hammer-bender!"

Lenui bared his teeth. "Limp-noodled, brittle-boned, dirt-farmer who fights with a tiny hatchet!"

Bill spat at Lenui's feet. "Empty-headed, anvil-dropping, sword-cracker!"

Lenui sputtered and kicked dirt over the old dwarf's spittle. "Gray-haired, double-caner who needs help combin' his beard!"

The old dwarf went for the throat. "Cotton-eared, cold-forging, over-priced, tin merchant!"

"Why you-." As Lenui delivered his last volley, he stepped in closer with each taunt, enunciating every syllable until the two dwarves' foreheads were only an inch apart. "Half-blind. Candy-arsed. Droopy-diapered. Granny-sniffin'. Wrinkle-taster!"

Old Bill' reared back and head-butted Lenui right in the nose. Lenui's head was rocked back, sparks floating in his vision. He stumbled to the side. "Ha! You lose!"

"Are you alright, Lenny?" Swen asked. "You seem about to fall over."

"I never fall over, dag-blast it!" Lenui declared and stood still, forcing away the darkness that was trying to invade the edges of his vision. He pointed a steady finger at Old Bill. "I won."

"You're bleeding," said Dinnis in surprise.

"I don't bleed," Lenui said and reached up to touch his nose. He felt a stab of pain and his finger came away bloody. He felt his nose again, this time more tenderly. "You broke my dag-gum nose . . ."

"I-I'm sorry for that," Bill said, his face red. "You won. You beat me soundly."

Lenui laughed out loud. "Holy hell, you broke my dag-blasted nose!"

"That was wrong of me," Bill said.

"No!" Lenui said, still laughing. "You don't get it. I never broke a single bone in my gad-flamed life. My friends and I used to punch each other in the face fer fun. No one could ever break my nose."

Bill blinked. "I don't quite understand what you're trying to say."

"So you got my gall-durn respect is what I'm sayin'!" He clapped the old dwarf on the shoulder. "Old Bill, the legend! Hoo-wee! It's good to see the dwarf comin' back out of you!"

A smile spread across Bill's lips. "I suppose that curse fight did bring me back to my younger days. I haven't head-butted anyone in decades."

"What happened to you, Bill?" Lenui asked. "Too much time spent with Khalpan elves?"

The old dwarf sighed. "Being bonded changes a person I suppose. And being away from my people this long . . . maybe I've become too sensitive to things that didn't used to bother me so much back in the day."

"Uh, guys!" said Helmet Jan. She backed into the firelight, her pike held out in front of her. "I don't get it, but I think we have a fight on our hands."

Swen and Dinnis stood, raising their weapons in their hands. Lenui and Bill soon followed suit, hammer and hatchet at the ready.

Following her, but stopping at the edge of the firelight, were two wolves, a bear, three trolls, and perhaps most strangely of all, a goblin. It wore long pants and a ruffled white shirt under a dark overcoat.

The goblin pointed a clawed finger and spoke in a shrill voice. "Leave this place or die. The great evil has come!"

Chapter Thirteen

"A dressed up goblin?" said Lenui in disbelief as everyone readied their weapons. "Swen, shoot one of 'em. Scare 'em off."

Swen nocked an arrow on his smaller recurve bow.

"Don't fire quite yet!" said Old Bill. "Not unless they attack!"

"But those are trolls," Dinnis said. The swordsman had already grabbed a dry branch and plunged it into the fire.

He was right. There were definitely three trolls standing just outside the firelight, but they weren't attacking. Even more strangely, they were standing next to a bear and two wolves that were also not moving. Trolls didn't care what their prey was as long as it was living. They should have pounced on the other creatures first thing.

"That goblin talked 'bout a great evil," Lenui pointed out. "Maybe it's talkin' 'bout-."

"Leave or die!" the goblin insisted, his yellow eyes wide and sinister. "The evil will have you!"

The wolves growled. The bear roared. The trolls hissed.

Lenui pulled one of his throwing hammers from a loop at his belt. He had two of them. They were a new weapon he had designed and he was eager to try them out.

He asked Old Bill, "You think these things are controlled by that evil in the mountains?"

"I would say there's definitely magic involved." Bill replied. "But I think they're just trying to scare us off. This close to-."

"Then die!" the goblin cried and the animals attacked.

The wolves darted for Helmet Jan. They were large gray creatures, with thick pelts and snarling muzzles. She leveled her pike and speared one of them down the gullet. The other one kept coming and she swung her foot up, booting it under the chin.

This only delayed it momentary. The wolf shook its head and lunged just as Swen's bow twanged. His arrow entered between two ribs, piercing its heart, and it fell dead at her feet.

The bear barreled towards Lenui and Old Bill. It was a grizzly, a terrible shaggy old beast. Its gaping mouth showed enormous teeth. Old Bill pulled out his hatchet, unafraid to face it. But before it could reach him, Lenui threw his new hammer.

The moment it left his fingers, the weapon's magic kicked in, the air runes in the handle propelling it forward at increased speed. When the hammerhead connected with the bear's skull, the mix of air and earth runes in the hammer's head doubled the force of the impact.

Lenui had never been a thrown weapon specialist, and it was only a glancing blow to the bear's temple, but the beast stumbled. Lenui's grin broadened. It was like Buster had birthed a speedy baby.

Unfortunately, the blow hadn't been enough to take the beast down. Lenui hurriedly pulled his old hammer as it continued forward and swung a heavy clawed paw at Bill.

The old dwarf jumped back, barely avoiding the claws, then jumped forward, swinging his hatchet with both hands. He may have been living a cushy life the last two hundred years, but he still knew how to swing an axe.

The hatchet slashed into the bear's neck and the magic in the weapon lashed out, creating three more long gashes just as deep. It was as if the hatchet's blade was but one of a great cat's many claws. Blood spurted from the wounds, but the bear did not stop its attack. It turned its head, attempting to bite him. Bill jumped back again and its jaws caught nothing but air. It swiped its heavy arm again just as Lenui arrived.

Lenui swung Buster with all of his might. The hammer's head struck the bear's forehead dead center and its skull caved in with a crunch. The bear collapsed with a sighing groan.

The trolls screeched and ran for the horses. Dinnis charged after them, Tolivar's old sword Meredith drawn. The four draft horses and the two Academy-trained mares had been tied not far from the wagons. Upon hearing the screech of the trolls, the draft horses strained at their ropes.

The magic of the sword filled Dinnis' veins with a burning drive. With a shout he swung at the left leg of the closest troll, lopping it off at the knee. The tall creature, ignorant of pain, swung around at him and fell. Dinnis' back swing took off the upper third of its skull, leaving the thing to flop senselessly while he went after the next one.

One of the trolls reached the horses. Three of the draft horses snapped their tethers and ran into the trees, while the fourth screamed and tried to back away, held back by the stubborn rope. The Academy trained horses were more assertive. They reared and kicked, knocking the beast back. It lunged at the trapped draft horse.

Dinnis reached the next troll and slashed the back of its knees, causing it to collapse. He then hacked apart a reaching arm and cleaved its head from its body. Snarling, he went for the third troll only to find it twitching on the ground, an arrow through its skull.

It all happened quickly, the trained fighters dismantling the attackers with efficiency. None of them was injured, though the one trapped draft horse had received a nasty gash across its chest. Now there was just the aftermath to deal with.

"Swen and Dinnis, go get them horses that run off!" Lenui commanded. The two soldiers nodded and went after them.

Lenui bent and picked up the hammer. "I think I'm gonna call you Buster Junior."

He put it away. Now to deal with cleaning up. The wolves and bear they could just leave to rot. The problem was the trolls. "Bill and Jan, help me drag them blasted screechers into the fire afore they get back up."

"Wait," said Bill. "I'll help you with that, but Jan, I need you to go after that fancily dressed goblin." The creature had run off as soon as the fighting started. "But don't kill it! Bind it and bring it back here."

Jan glanced at Lenui and he gave her a nod. Jan headed off into the trees. She was well suited for this job. The magic in her helmet gave her excellent night vision as well as letting her see the heat left behind by the goblin's tracks.

"You think we can get anythin' out of that stupid thing?" Lenui asked the old dwarf.

Bill shrugged and walked over to grab the twitching leg that Dinnis had lopped off of the first troll. "I can only hope so. As you know, goblin's aren't much for conversation, but this one seemed smarter than most."

Lenui frowned at being left with the big piece, then winced at the shooting pain that went through his nose because of the frown. With all the excitement, he had forgotten about his broken nose. He grabbed the troll's other leg, and repressed a grimace as his fingers gushed into the slime that covered its skin.

The dwarf pulled its body, convulsing as it tried to heal its brain, over to the fireside. It wasn't all that difficult. Trolls were tall and gangly, but not all that heavy.

The campfire flared as Bill tossed the leg into it.

"Hey, watch my pot! Don't want no troll slime gettin' in our dinner!" Lenui snapped and as Old Bill reluctantly carried the pot to the side, Lenui rolled his troll into the fire. The flames rose even higher and the slime covering his hand was set ablaze. He cursed and wiped his hand in the dirt, putting out the flames. "Dag-blasted frog-humper!"

"You wanna give me a hand with this one?" Bill asked, having walked to the second troll Dinnis had dispatched.

"Don't pretend you ain't strong enough to bring it on yer own," Lenui said. He walked over to find the missing top part of that first troll's skull. If left alone long enough, even that small piece would eventually grow into a full-sized troll on its own. "I think yer just tryin' to keep me distracted so's I don't ask you more questions."

"About what?" Bill asked, dragging the troll that was missing its head.

"You know quite well what," Lenui replied and felt a

squelch as the heel of his boot smooshed into the open top of the skull he had been looking for. "Blast it!"

He had to pull his foot out of his boot and lift it up with the piece of skull to carry over to the fire. He didn't know if a little troll brain matter on his heel would become a problem, but when it came to trolls, you always chose the side of caution.

"You know more than yer lettin' on about this thing, Bill," Lenui said, tossing the skull cap into the fire and picking up a stick to clean out the grooves in his boot heel. "We both know that there was magic controlling them things and I'm pretty dag-gum sure it weren't the same evil we're chasin' after."

"What makes you say that?" Bill wondered, wincing as the second troll burst into flames.

"'Cause that gall-durn goblin warned us first! Then those trolls scattered the horses . . . them animals was attackin' together," Lenui replied. He had scraped off all the brain matter that he easily could. Shrugging, he dipped his boot heel into the fire, then quickly rubbed it out in the dirt before putting his foot back in. "Well? You gonna say somethin'? Cause it's got to be somethin' to do with why we came out this way."

Bill sighed. "I'll tell you soon enough. I just want to get that goblin back here and make sure you're right before I say anything. In a way, what we're here for is just as important as our other mission."

They retrieved the troll's head and together grabbed the troll with Swen's arrow still stuck through its skull. With its brain pierced, the thing couldn't properly heal the wound, so they were able to drag it over and toss it in with the others.

Lenui didn't like how high the fire blazed. It was basically a beacon for anyone to see and that wasn't good. Hopefully, the tree cover around them hid it somewhat.

Jan came back to the camp a short time later with the fancy goblin draped over her shoulder. They could hear it's muffled complaints despite the gag she had shoved in its mouth. It wasn't looking quite as proper as it had when they had first seen it. Its arms were tied behind its back and its clothes were dirty and disheveled from being dragged through the forest. It had a large goose egg protruding from the top of its skull.

"I hope this is worth it," Jan said, as she tossed it onto the ground in front of them. She gestured at the wet front of her scalemail, her lips twisted in a scowl. "Damn thing peed on me. I'll be smelling it for days."

Bill gave her an apologetic grimace. "Don't worry. I've got something in the wagon that should help with that." He crouched beside the goblin and pulled off its gag. "Let's see what it has to say."

"Run!" it said. "Flee from this place!"

"Enough of that, you dag-blasted orc turd!" Lenui barked.

Old Bill raised a hand, giving Lenui a calming look. He smiled at the goblin. "Tell me, son. What is your name?"

"I'm no orc turd! Not your son neither," the goblin snarled, his language surprisingly complex for one of his race. "You should run for the evil is coming!"

"You still haven't told me your name," Bill replied.

The goblin eyed him suspiciously. "Name's Chi-Chi."

Both Jan and Lenui snorted.

"Very well, Chi-Chi," said Bill. "I am here as a friend of Master Porthos. Did he send you to chase us away?"

The goblin blinked, unsure how to respond. "Y-you . . . Porthos says big evil comes. You should go." He nodded, gaining confidence as he cried. "Flee or die!"

"I see. So he's still alive as we hoped," said Bill, smiling. "Listen, Chi-Chi. My name is Bill and I'm an old friend of Master Porthos'. It's urgent that you bring me to see him. I must speak to him about this big evil that's coming."

The goblin frowned.

"Who is this Master Porthos?" Jan wondered.

"If this works out, you'll find out soon enough," Bill said. "Well, Chi-Chi. Will you take me to him?"

"I . . . don't think I'm supposed to do that," Chi-Chi said.

"Well," said Lenui, giving the goblin his widest gap-toothed grin. "We could kill you instead. And just walk up the trail to find him our own selves."

"Oh," said the goblin, thinking hard. "I will take you. I guess he can kill you if he needs to."

"Fine," said Bill, standing up. "We'll go now. Untie his arms."

"You're not following this goblin into the dark alone," Jan said.

"Dear, I am 637 years old. I fought the Dark Prophet himself. I can handle a nighttime stroll with a goblin," Bill replied.

"'Sides, I'm goin' with him," Lenui said. "You go and see to that horse the troll scratched. Don't need it gettin' infected. When Swen and Dinnis get back, y'all get the wagons turned 'round. Don't come lookin' fer us unless we ain't back by mornin'."

"Are you certain this is how you want to handle this?" Bill asked.

Lenui untied the goblin's arms. "Now you better not try runnin' away. And no more pissin' on folks. I'll cave yer little skull in."

The goblin narrowed its eyes at him. "You just follow close. Lots of holes you could fall into."

Bill quickly ducked into his wagon. He returned with a small pack on his back and was carrying a walking staff that had a small light orb attached to the end. He tapped the orb to activate it and gave Lenui a nod. The two dwarves followed the goblin into the woods, their way illuminated by soft light.

The foliage was thick between the trees. They had to push their way past bushes and duck under branches as the goblin followed a path that they never would have found otherwise.

Lenui waited until they were out of earshot of the camp before speaking. "Alright, Old Bill. Now that we're on the way, tell me who this Master Porthos is. At this point, I'm figgerin' he's a named wizard, but why go out of our way to meet him when there's lots of wizards at the Mage School who could help?"

"Very well," Old Bill said with a sigh. "Master Porthos is a very powerful witch."

Lenui frowned. "I thought lady named wizards was called

'Mistress'."

"The term for a bewitching specialist is witch, whether male or female," Bill said. Pushing a branch out of the way so that he could slip by. "Actually, I'm surprised you don't recognize the name. He was there at the Battle of Thunder Gap with the rest of us. If not for him, you may not have been able to save the day."

"Blasted . . !" Lenui swore as the branch swung back and caught him across the nose. The goblin laughed and if he had been close enough, he would have booted the nasty thing. He held his hand in front of his face protectively as they continued. "Yeah, well I was way too busy struttin' 'round back then to notice the names of wizards. 'Sides, I try not to think of that battle very often. Too many bad memories."

"I see," said Bill. "Well after the Prophet ordered the ban on spirit magic Porthos, like Sarine, was one of those spirit magic wizards who had no elemental magic to fall back on. He had to go into hiding and this little piece of land is where he went to ground."

"So . . . he a bondin' wizard too?" Lenui asked.

"Careful, dwarves," Chi-Chi interrupted, peering back at them with amused eyes. "There is pits all around us. Stay on the track if you don't want to be dead."

Though it was hard to see how a pit could be hiding among all this brush, Bill took care to step right behind the goblin. Lenui made sure to copy the old dwarf's movements.

Bill cleared his throat. "No, Lenui. That would be horrible if we had just slaughtered a bunch of bonded animals. I imagine Porthos used his bewitching magic to control those beasts we fought. This is why he wouldn't have been able to see who we were. I hope he isn't too upset we slaughtered the creatures, though. We didn't have much choice."

"I figgered that much," Lenui replied. "I was askin' 'cause of how old he's got to be. Hell, he'd have to be a lot older than two hundred years if he was named before the war. Human wizards don't last that long 'less they're bonded to somethin' long-lived."

"Oh. Well as for that . . ." Bill scratched his head before replying. "Porthos was Sarine's second husband. After the war, he joined us in Khalpany for a few years before they-. Or he . . . well, they divorced. Sarine remained fond of him, though. Even after he moved out here, she sent him a regular box of Kyrkon's goodies."

"Elf magic," Lenui said with a nod. That explained the wizard's long life. "Fine. But if that's the case, why weren't you sure he was still alive?"

"Ah, that. About thirty years ago, they had a bit of a long distance tiff. Porthos stopped replying to letters and we stopped sending his packages," Bill said. "To be honest, I am hoping he's not still terribly miffed."

Lenui let out a snort, ignoring the way it stung his broken nose. "Humans! Runnin' off after a fight? Why a good fight's just a precursor to a long night of lovin'!"

"Not far now!" said the goblin, glancing back at them.

Lenui leaned in towards Bill's ear and said with his best attempt at a whisper. "Is it okay that we've been sayin' all this stuff in front of him?"

"I heard that, too," Chi-Chi replied.

"If he's Porthos' assistant, we haven't discussed anything the old wizard doesn't already know," Bill replied. "You should be ready for anything when we get there, by the way. Porthos is a bit of an eccentric. Who knows what we'll find?"

The goblin stepped out of the dense foliage and into an open area where the trees were spread much farther apart. A field of manicured brown grass stretched between the trees and in the distance, up a short incline, they could see the glow of a lamp burning behind a frosted window.

Standing between the dwarves and the wizard's residence was a meadow full of forest creatures. There were more wolves and trolls, foxes and badgers, and perched in the limbs of the trees above them, various birds of prey looked down, their eyes eerily reflecting the light of Bill's staff.

"What are you doing, bringing strangers here, Chi-Chi?" asked a perturbed voice.

A figure walked past the assembled animals and stepped into the light. He was a man of average build, with long pale hair. He wore a thick overcoat and deerskin pants and carried a nocked bow.

"They said they're friends of Porthos," the goblin said defensively. "They would've killed me if I didn't bring them."

The man looked at the goblin's disheveled appearance and glanced back at them. "You didn't have to be that rough with him. If you really are friends of Porthos, you should have known what he was."

"To be honest, I wasn't yet certain if Porthos was still alive," Bill replied. "We had to capture Chi-Chi here to make sure."

"And you killed old Mister Claw," the man pointed out. "I liked that bear! Sure, if Porthos hadn't been controlling him, he would've had me for breakfast, but you grow fond of the things!"

"Sorry, son," Lenui said with a shrug. "You gotta kill a bear that attacks you."

"I'm gonna go and change," Chi-Chi said.

"Yeah, go clean up," the man replied grumpily and the goblin slinked away.

Bill cleared his throat. "Let us make proper introductions. My name is Bill. I am an old friend of the master, and I'm here to ask for his help."

The man cocked his head. "Yeah, Porthos just told me he knows you. He wants to know if Sarine is somewhere around."

Bill gave the man an apologetic smile. "Sorry, but no. It's just me. For now, anyway."

The man nodded his head at Lenui. "And who's this dwarf?"

"Name's Lenui Firegobbler," Lenui replied. "Most humans call me Lenny, though."

"Porthos may remember him better as the 'Hero of Thunder Gap'," Bill added.

The man shrugged and shouldered his bow, putting the arrow away in its quiver. "He says you're okay, then." He held out his hand. "Name's Bryon. I'm Porthos' apprentice."

"Really?" said Bill, shaking the man's hand. "It's good to know that he's passing on his knowledge. How is he

180

communicating with you right now?"

"Oh." He gestured to the dagger he was carrying at his belt. It had a beautiful handle, silver with gold inlay. At the center of the hilt was Porthos' naming rune. "He has me carry this around with me. The old wizard likes to watch things through my eyes. He doesn't get around much anymore."

"Why's that?" Lenui asked, shaking Bryon's hand. The man had a firm grip, but there was something just a little off about him. Lenui wasn't quite sure what it was just yet. Something about his face.

"He's old," Bryon said. He squinted at Lenui in the dim light. "Did you know you have a bloody nose?"

"Oh," said Lenui wiping his wet upper lip on the back of his sleeve. Being smacked in the face by that branch had caused it to bleed again. "It's broke."

The man leaned in close. "Yeah, it's pretty bent. You want me to set it? I'm good at that sort of thing."

"Well, my goal ain't to be pretty," Lenui said. Then he thought of Bettie's reaction. "But go ahead."

Bill brought the staff in closer so that the man could get a better look.

"This'll hurt," Bryon said, and reached out with both hands. He placed his thumbs on either side of Lenui's nose and pressed in. Hard.

There was a crunch and Lenui saw sparks in his vision again. It took all of his willpower not to punch the man in his blasted gut. "Gah! Son of a friggin' . . . turtle-faced, mustard-weaver!"

"Yeah, sorry about that. If I'd been born with elemental magic I could've healed it right up," Bryon said with a slight shrug. "But I wasn't. That's why I'm here instead of the Mage School. The nose is straight, though. I used some blessing magic to reinforce it. Just don't let it get hit again and it should stay straight."

Bill glanced at him and chuckled. "It might even be straighter than it was before I broke it."

Lenui blinked the sparks away. It still hurt, but it was easier to breathe now. "Uh, thanks, son."

Bryon shrugged. "No problem. Come on. I'll take you up to see the old man. He doesn't want me to, but I think it'll do him good to visit with friends."

Bryon turned and walked up towards the house. Lenui gave Bill a questioning look, but the old dwarf just shrugged and followed the man. They walked between the unsettling stares of the bewitched wildlife.

Lenui's skin itched at those cold eyes watching him. These kinds of animals weren't supposed to sit so still when a dwarf walked by. It just wasn't natural.

They reached the steps of the modest cottage and Lenui could tell that it was well cared for. The porch was clean and straight, not a crack in the wood, and there were pots of planted herbs covered with a thin mesh to keep them from freezing in the night.

The man opened the door and they entered a warm sitting room with padded chairs and a stoked fireplace. A deer was standing in front of the fireplace. A doe. It watched them with calm curiosity.

Bryon patted the doe's head and picked up a lighted lantern off of a side table. He motioned them to follow him and walked through a doorway into the back. Lenui stared at the deer. Hesitantly, he reached out and petted the top of its head. It cocked its head and looked at him without fear.

"I'm dag-gum hungry," Lenui told the thing, thinking of the pot of pepperbean stew he'd left back at the camp. "I could eat you whole right now. Don't that worry you?"

The doe sniffed his leather armor and the red letter 'F' at the center of his chest. It certainly didn't seem worried. He wondered if it knew what kind of beast this leather came from.

"Could be yer uncle fer all you know, dumb animal." Shaking his head, Lenui petted it again, then followed after Bill and Bryon. They had gone down a short hallway. Bryon had opened a door and gone inside, carrying the lantern in with him. Lenui could hear them talking.

"Here they are, Master," Bryon said. "And don't you gripe at me. I told you I wasn't gonna let you just hide behind my eyes."

"Porthos," said Bill, sounding genuinely surprised. "It's . . . good to see you alive."

Lenui walked into the room behind the old dwarf and stopped, speechless. Master Porthos was ancient. No, beyond ancient. He was lying in bed with his skeletal hands folded across his chest, withered and frail with pale, nearly translucent skin. A wisp of hair laid flat across his sagging scalp. His cadaverous face was fixed in a determined scowl focused on his young apprentice.

Bryon shook his head, refusing to pity his master. "No. Talk to these friends of yours yourself. I'm not speaking for you this time."

Porthos' thin lips pulled back from yellowed teeth. His voice was soft and papery. "There was a time when a wizard's apprentice showed him respect."

"If you want respect, change your own chamber pot," Bryon replied. He noted Bill's glance. "Sorry about that. When I became his apprentice nearly forty years ago, I didn't know it was going to last this long."

"Forty years?" Lenui asked, raising a bushy eyebrow. "You don't look that old."

"Oh. I'm a half-elf," Bryon replied. He fingered his rounded ear and Lenui understood what he had found strange about the man. He had slightly elven features. "I just took after my mother's side so you can't tell it by the ears." He sighed and gestured at his master. "But don't waste time talking to me. He's the one you're here for."

"Porthos," said Bill again. "Sarine sent me to find you."

"She did?" the old wizard said with a smile that somehow made his face seem more cadaverous. "Did she send you to deliver an apology before I died?"

Bill let out a regretful sigh. "No, but she did want me to tell you that she has forgiven you."

The ancient man rolled his dull eyes. "Of course. Damn me, but I do still miss her. Even after all these years. There. Tell her I said that. Tell her . . . I forgive her too."

"I will," Bill said with a kind smile. "But, Porthos, I'm afraid that is not why I came either. I'm here about that evil in the mountains."

"That." Porthos shook his head slowly. "I sent Chi-Chi to warn off your little group. If I would have been able to see who you were, I would have had him use different language."

"That weren't no warning," Lenui said. "They flat out attacked!"

The old eyes settled on him. "Lenui Firegobbler. Two hundred years older and still just as impetuous. He first warned you. Then, when you didn't budge, my animals attempted to drive you off, scatter your horses. The purpose was to save your lives and keep anyone from bothering me. You were the ones who felt the need to kill."

"This is great," said Bryon with a smile. The half-elf was leaning back against the wall, his arms folded. "More words than I've heard him speak in months."

"Oh, quiet, you," the ancient master said with a weak wave of one hand.

"Back to that evil we came to speak with you about," Bill said.

"Yes. Nasty business. A wraith, I believe," Porthos said. "How it became so powerful, I have no idea."

Bill frowned. "You have felt it even down here?"

"For several weeks now. It's using flies and larvae to spread its control. I'm able to keep its little minions from this area and so far, I've been able to keep it from discovering me. Don't worry. You are safe enough where you are."

"Then it's as we feared," Bill said, looking at Lenui. "Its influence has already broken out of the mountain passes. At this pace, it could spread all over Dremaldria by the end of summer."

"Yeah, but we're gonna stop the blasted thing first," Lenui said confidently. "What did he mean by calling it a wraith, though?"

"It's a rare phenomenon," Bryon explained. "If a powerful spirit magic wizard dies, sometimes their magic refuses to go on with them. It can wander around causing havoc. Especially, with bewitching magic. It can cause the local animals to go crazy."

"So like an elemental," Lenui said, thinking back to Justan and the Scralag in his chest. "But fer spirit magic."

"Precisely," said Porthos. "So you can calm yourselves. These things happen from time to time. It's difficult to deal with, but wraiths use up their power fairly quickly. A few more weeks and it will die out on its own."

"Porthos," said Bill. "This isn't some small time wizard's spirit we're dealing with. Remember the tales of Mellinda. The Dark Goddess?"

The ancient master frowned. "You mean the Troll Queen? She was destroyed centuries ago."

"Not destroyed," said Lenui. "Just imprisoned. She got loose and we tried to kill her last summer, but . . . seems it didn't quite work. Her magic done high-tailed it up to the mountains."

"Do you see?" said Bill. "This is a far greater problem than you have imagined. To make things worse, the Dark Prophet is trying to find a way to return."

"But how is that possible?" Porthos said. He tried to sit up, but couldn't quite manage it. "You saw him destroyed. John did it himself!"

"Yes," said Bill, a mournful expression on his face. "I was there. I saw his body twisted and burned. But he found some way to cling to existence. During that kerfuffle last summer that Lenui was referring to, the Academy and the Mage School managed to stop his plans for receiving a new body.

"But now this new evil has appeared. A black lake full of those larvae you have been sensing. Porthos, I'm telling you, the Dark Prophet is somehow behind it. Up until the end of winter, the evil was just building, preying on the goblinoids in the peaks. But the Dark Prophet sent a servant of his own to take control of it. Probably one of his priestesses. We haven't been able to discover who, but whoever they are, they are looking to conquer! Even now, an army assembled by the Academy and Mage School are advancing on its location."

"Is that so? I shall get to the truth of the matter," the master said. He leaned back into his pillow, closing his eyes. "I can feel the power of the wraith even now. Its flies buzz at the edges of my land. Hold on while I grasp one."

Lenui edged over to Bryon. "Just how far can his gall-durn magic reach, anyway?"

The half-elf shrugged. "A few miles in any direction when he's really concentrating. It lessens when he tries to control things. The bigger the mind a creature has, the more power it takes to control."

"So that goblin of yers?" Lenui asked.

"Chi-Chi? He can get pretty mean if Porthos isn't calming him, but he isn't fully being controlled. He just showed up on the land one day and he's kind of become a servant of sorts," Bryon replied.

Porthos breathed in suddenly, frowning in discomfort. His eyes stayed closed. "I see it now. You're right. This is big, far larger than anything I expected. It is very difficult not to be noticed . . ."

His voice trailed off and the room fell silent. No one dared speak for several moments, all of them waiting on the master's next words. There was a thumping sound from within the house.

"What's he doing?" Lenui whispered.

Bryon shook his head, his hand gripping the master's naming dagger. "I'm not sure, but I think he's used that fly as a gateway. He's sent part of his mind through to get a better look at the wraith. It's taking a lot of his power to do so. He's lost hold on some of the animals around the house."

Porthos' lips moved again. "Ohh . . . Why, I can tell right away, now that I know to look for it. The style of her bewitching. The flavor of her thoughts on the magic. She hasn't changed."

"Who?" Bill asked. "Who is she?"

The master didn't answer, his corpselike face pinched in concentration. "And that red tint . . . I've only seen that once before, but she's bolstered her spirit power with blood magic. Of course, that vile creature! She'd have to do that to control so immense a power. I shall try to learn more."

186

Bryon pushed away from the wall. "His heart's beating way too fast. I'm afraid his body can't handle this."

"We have to let him try," Bill said.

Porthos gasped again. "She is on alert. I must flee before I'm seen." Seconds later, his eyes opened, a look of fear on his face. He looked around the room as if unsure where he was. A smile reached his thin lips. "I escaped unseen."

"Then she don't know you was lookin'?" Lenui asked.

"She knows someone was poking around," Porthos said, "But she doesn't know who they were or what exactly they learned."

"Who is she?" Bill asked again.

The master blinked at him. "It is not good news I'm afraid. She is Cassandra. David's Priestess of War."

"Oh hell," Bill said, his shoulders slumping.

"The Priestess of War?" Lenui said in disbelief. His thoughts were haunted as he thought back to that day two hundred years before. "I thought I'd killed her."

"So did we all," Bill said.

The ancient man grimaced as he tried to sit up. "Bryon, pack us for a journey. If they are going to fight Cassandra, they will need my help."

"No, they won't." Bryon gave Lenui a pointed look. "No, you won't. He's not going to survive a journey to the top of the mountains. I'd be surprised if he could handle a horse ride across the lawn. Look at him! It's been six months since I've been able to get him to climb out of bed."

Bill sighed. "He's right. Porthos, I'll admit, when we came here, I was hoping you would be able to join us, but I can see that it isn't possible now."

"Bryon," said the old master, managing to get up on one elbow. "I know that I am feeble and I know that you haven't seen me at my peak. But I was named at the Bowl of Souls. That means I have responsibilities."

Porthos held out his left hand palm up, displaying his naming rune. It was wide and flat and firm on his palm. As shriveled as the rest of his body was, that was the palm of a man in his prime. "The journey will be difficult, but they will need me if they are to reach their goal undetected. Cassandra will not be expecting me." He smiled. "Besides, I have you. Use your blessing magic to bolster my withered bones. I'll make it."

Bryon glared. "Even if I was able to keep you alive long enough for you to get close enough to help them in this fight, facing this thing would kill you. All you did was take a peek and it nearly gave you a heart attack!"

"Then I'll die," Porthos said. "I'm not looking forward to the experience, but if I were to die that way? Fighting for the principles of the Bowl? That would be nice. Much better than falling asleep one day and not waking up."

Grumbling, Bryon walked to the side of the bed and helped the old man sit up. He sat behind him and pressed his knee into the old man's back while pulling on his shoulder. There was a series of pops and Porthos groaned with a mix of pain and relief. Lenui couldn't see the flows of the blessing magic Byron had used, but he could see the results. The ancient man's back straightened and a bit of color came back into his face.

Bryon grasped Porthos' arm and lifted it up, forcing his shoulder into full rotation. The half-elf shook his head. "This is a long shot. I could reinforce your joints and blood vessels. Straighten your back every morning. Still, I doubt you'd survive a journey. A horse ride would break you to pieces!"

"That's okay. He won't need to ride," said Bill, nodding as he gained confidence in his plan. "He can lay on my bed in the wagon."

"So you'll be joinin' the rest of us beggars on the ground, then?" Lenui asked, folding his arms in surprise.

"I'll be fine," Bill said. He took the pack off of his back and pulled out a jar in some kind of knitted cozy. "And I believe this should help even more. Olives from Kyrkon's own vineyard."

"That could do it," Bryon said, scratching his head. "Pure elf magic."

The old man smiled and held the jar close. His eyes welled with tears. "She has forgiven me then. Bryon, open them for me."

Lenui smiled as the man placed one of the ripe brown fruits into his mouth, tears dripping down his wrinkled cheeks. Then his smile faded. "Somethin's been ticklin' my brain. Somethin' you said earlier. You said that the Priestess of War's been usin' blood magic. How? She was human last I heard."

The old man swallowed and pulled another plump olive from the jar with trembling finger. "Yes, well that will be a problem we'll need to face. Her spirit magic has been tainted red and that can only mean one thing. Cassandra has been drinking the blood of elves."

Chapter Fourteen

The Black Lake didn't act like water. It didn't ripple with the breeze. The edges of the cliff face surrounding it weren't reflected on its surface. The lake was, in fact, not truly a liquid at all, but a flowing mass of larvae and decaying organic matter with the consistency of hot tar.

The blackness absorbed the light that shone on it and, instead of rippling in the breeze, it shuddered slightly like the skin of a pudding. Every once in a while, the stillness of the lake was disturbed, its surface swelling and shifting as some monstrous form contorted within its depths.

The air above the lake was filled with shifting swarms of flies that weaved with the currents produced by the lake's heat. The shoreline was covered with hundreds of corpses, lying in an unmoving state. The dead came from many races, most of them goblinoid, but there were also a mix of humans and members of the blood magic and demon races, along with more strange and exotic beasts whose lives had been taken by the lake's evil.

Normally, the heat and flies would equal a quick deterioration of the dead, but the corpses rotted very slowly. The larvae that infested them retarded the decay of the bodies and kept the connective tissues firm, keeping them useful to the evil power that dwelled at the lake's bottom.

The Black Lake's surface bulged again not far from the shoreline as a rounded shape emerged. A glistening sludge-covered thing, looking as if it were made from the essence of the lake itself, stepped up onto the shore. It was about the height of a man, but bulky, the details of its form obscured by the blackness that weighed it down.

The corpses lying on the shore stirred, some of them lifting their heads to watch as it moved up the slope past them with heavy ponderous steps. The thing moved up the one clear pathway between the dead, headed towards the large rock building that protruded from the side of the cliff wall.

The building was tall and square with smooth walls that looked as if they were formed from a single sheet of rock. It's door was a flat sided boulder and the building was topped with a slanted roof that pointed towards the lake. A steady stream of smoke belched from the single chimney that protruded from the roof's highest point.

The lake thing stepped onto the flat rocky porch and waved a dripping arm. The heavy boulder rolled back from the building's entrance and the thing made its ponderous way inside. As soon as it passed through the doorway, the boulder rolled shut behind it.

Inside was a stark entryway. Lit with glow orbs, its only decoration was a box full of ash. The thing made to move towards the open doorway beyond, but stopped in the center of the room.

Slowly, the sludge rolled off of the creature in great clumps. Emerging from the blackness was the Priestess of War, hooded and covered by a red cloak. She stepped over the pile of putrid blackness on the floor around her and called out with a firm voice.

"Vastyr. I return."

Cassandra threw back her cloak to reveal a woman clad in armor. Her breastplate was polished, but glowed a dull black with earth magic. Her waistline and thighs were girded with studded leather. Plates of runed steel covered her shoulders, but her muscular arms were bare, revealing pale skin covered with scars and protective tattoos. Her boots were made of an exotic type of avian leather, the toes of which were tipped with curved talons.

The priestess wore an open-faced helmet that clung tightly to her head, a round jade stone resting across the center of her forehead. Her skin was pale, her lips black. She had a youthful face that would have been beautiful if not for the many scars that marred her brow, nose and jawline. Most prominent was a horrific scar that curved down her right cheek, pulling down her lower eyelid. This was the result of a wound that had blinded her right eye, leaving it pupilless and white.

The Priestess of War was proud of her scars. Each one was proof of an escape from death. Early on, David had prophesied that she would not be killed by a mortal warrior, but only by a wizard. Therefore, in her centuries of life, she had never allowed a wizard to heal her. She had relied on surgeons and the life magic of elves to heal her wounds.

"Vastyr!" she repeated irritably. He usually did not make her call twice.

"I am sorry, Priestess. I was indisposed," said a soft male voice.

Vastyr was an elf. Tall, lithe, and fair, his head was topped in a tumble of blond curls, he was dressed in the robes of a Khalpan servant. His garments were gray and simple, but made of elegant materials, a sign that she doted on him. He glanced at the pile of sludge on the floor and wrinkled his nose in distaste. He gave her a hopeful look.

The elf hated the stench of the black lake and the evil that inhabited it. Since their arrival, he had rarely left the house. Not that she blamed him. This sort of evil was the antithesis of the life magic of his race. Still, he was a servant. Servants shouldn't be so squeamish.

"You forget your place," Cassandra said reproachfully. "One day I shall make you clean it with your bare hands, maggots or no."

Grunting, she sent out a surge of air magic, causing the sludge to roll into a neat ball. She then sent threads of fire into the core of it, burning the ball to ash. Cassandra let the ash fall to the floor. "There. Tidy up."

"Yes, Priestess," the elf said with a deep bow. He pulled a broom out from behind the doorway and began to sweep the ash.

Vastyr was the only servant she kept at her side and truly the only one she needed. The orcs that were her laborers were fully under her power and slept in the various caves around the mountainside along with any other creatures that she thought were more useful alive than fed to the lake.

The priestess unpinned her cloak and draped it over her arm, then walked through the doorway. The great room beyond took up the bulk of the building. Light orbs lit the expanse and the walls were covered in elaborate sculpture work she had done with her magic while bored. Its rock floor was covered with animal skins and a great fireplace sat at one end.

She walked to the front of the fireplace where her favorite hound was sleeping in front of the fire. He was lying on a rug made from an unfortunate member of his kind that had tried to bite her. Raj, an alpha lupero with a stripe of black fur down the center of his forehead, looked up at her approach and wagged his tail. She scratched his head.

"Are you recovered, Raj? Ready to serve me again?"

Raj had come back to her from this last battle sorely wounded, many of his pack dead. She had underestimated the threat posed by that large ogre tribe and the odd combination of leaders that defended it. That wouldn't happen again. She approached her throne.

This was where Cassandra did most of her work. Her throne was carved from the wood of a Valaeh tree and studded with stones that amplified the range of her spirit magic. Standing next to the throne was a large chest made of magically reinforced wood and bound with iron.

Cassandra threw her cloak over the back of the throne and removed the key to the chest from a necklace around her neck. She went to one knee and opened the lid. Inside were her greatest treasures. Some of them were powerful magical items, but most were trophies. Souvenirs plucked from the hands of dead enemies.

Resting atop a tidy pile of broken naming daggers was a long box covered with bewitching runes. She took it out and sighed regretfully before opening it. Inside was a long curved dagger made of black iron and stained with the blood of centuries of sacrifices. In its pommel was a cluster of jade stones, each one a spirit magic transmitter of great power.

This was Celos the Jade Dagger, one of six daggers forged by the Dark Prophet himself and tied to his soul. It was a powerful artifact and rightfully hers as one of his high priestesses. The moment the box was opened she could feel its power assaulting her mind.

The dagger had not always affected her this way. At one time, her dedication to the Dark Prophet and naming at the Dark Bowl had made her immune to its powers. But the deadly injury that had destroyed her right eye and removed her from the great war had changed that. The part of her soul bound to the Dark Prophet had been damaged. Ever since that day the presence of the dagger tugged at her memories, making her forgetful, even losing her sense of self.

Cassandra shut the box and let out a slow breath. The jade stone in her helmet had once been strong enough to protect her mind, but the effect of the dagger's magic had only increased as each of its sister daggers were destroyed. The Prophet had found and destroyed the last of them recently and ever since then, even her helmet was unable to stop the effects completely.

Gritting her teeth in determination, she closed the chest and stood, the runed box gripped tightly in her hands. Cassandra sat in her throne, feeling the magic of the jewels boosting her strength. Then she removed her helmet, exposing tightly cropped ebony hair marred only by one wide streak of gray.

Vastyr rushed to her side, taking her cloak from the arm of the throne where she had tossed it earlier. "Cassandra, must you?"

She narrowed her eyes at him. The elf really shouldn't have called her by name, but over the years she had come to allow him some slip of decorum, at least when they were alone. "I have no choice in the matter. Without the dagger I cannot reach the Master."

That had been another side effect of the soul-damaging wound. The only time she could hear the Dark Voice was when the dagger was clutched in her hands. While she was connected to her master, the dagger could not harm her, but there was always a time just before and just after, that she was vulnerable.

Vastyr hung her cloak in its proper place, then came up behind her. The elf placed his hands on either side of her head and began rubbing her temples. "But must you speak with Him again so soon? I don't like what the dagger does to you."

The strength of his fingers created a marvelous pressure, easing a slight headache she hadn't even known she'd had. She enjoyed it for a few brief moments before slapping his hands away. "You forget your place! I am His Priestess of War. I speak with him when I must! Now go. I shall call for you when I need your presence."

Vastyr bowed, his face unreadable. "Yes, Priestess."

Cassandra watched as he retreated to the kitchen, then looked at the palm of her right hand. She switched to spirit sight and watched her dark naming rune swirl into existence. Taking a deep breath, she opened the box.

The dagger attacked at once. Rage and the desire to kill filled her mind. Her eyes fell on Raj, who was still reclining in front of the fire. The lupero was watching her eagerly. It knew these emotions intimately and waited for instruction. She reached into the box with her right hand and grasped the dagger, fully intending to rush over to the beast and kill it.

"Calm yourself, Cassandra," said the Dark Voice.

The urge to kill left her and her sense of self returned. She closed her eyes and gave herself over to her connection with her Master. *I am calm, David.*

Cassandra always received a sort of thrill when calling her god by his true name. Only his high priestesses were allowed to do so. It was a sign of his respect for her that made her zeal to please him all the stronger.

"Good. Report."

There was another attempt at intrusion last night. I chased the wizard away before he was able to discover anything, she replied. The fact that the wizard had come as close as he had was a frustration for her.

"This was the same wizard as last time?"

I was not able to see into his mind, but I believe so. That bonding wizard. Her lupids had been so close to finding and killing him. That rogue horse would have led them right to its master. If only that ogre mage had not intervened.

She was still disgusted by that fact. An ogre mage of all things. And how had such a simplistic beast been so powerful?

Had the bonding wizard been teaching him? Well, it wouldn't matter. The ogre would die and for the crime of killing so many of her pets, she would make its death especially painful.

"This must not happen again. Everything is progressing as I wish. John has been distracted, his resources spread thin. If this bonding wizard sees into your mind, sees my true plans, all may come unraveled."

He shall not, she assured him. *I have just returned from placing some very nasty surprises within the wraith should he try a third time.*

"Nevertheless, you may have to destroy those ogres and deal with him directly."

She frowned. *They inhabit an area easily defended and that wizard and his friends have organized them. The simplest solution is to continue to send fodder at them and keep them busy until the Academy threat is dealt with. The dead are plentiful and easy to replace.*

The Dark Prophet's spies had already confirmed the size and makeup of the approaching Academy army. She had a ready plan to defeat it, but it would be more difficult if she had to waste resources dealing with this band of irritants. The size of their threat was a small one that could easily be ignored until she could turn her focus on them.

"I would agree if this bonding wizard was not with them. I do not like having one so close to the source. John tends to place his servants where they can be the greatest annoyance. If sending fodder is not enough you must use a bigger stick."

If I send my more powerful troops, I could lose resources that I need for the bigger battle to come, she said, her frustration building. *David, I could travel there and crush them easily myself if only I was not tied to this place. There are so many restrictions placed upon me here!*

The extreme power of the wraith created by Mellinda's magic meant that she had to stay within close proximity to maintain her control over it. Even with her this close to the shore, it constantly strained at its bonds. She had to descend into the black lake and touch the source directly from time to time in order to keep it from breaking free. If that happened, it would be extremely difficult for her to regain power over it again.

"Calm, Cassandra. This is why I sent my Priestess of War instead of some lesser witch. You have both the power to exact my plans and the brilliance to discover a way to do so."

The Dark Voice reached through their connection to add a shiver of pleasure to pass through her body along with his approval. She embraced the sensation. This was a rarity. Her god was much more prone to using pain as a motivation than pleasure.

Master, she pleaded. *Have you come closer to a way to heal our connection? Celos has grown even more difficult to manage.*

"I have a way," he assured her. **"However, it must be done in person. Until I receive my new body, you must persevere as you always do. Destroy the obstacles in your path. Unleash the wraith's power on the land. When the time is right, I will send someone to take over this job and you can return to my side."**

Yes, David, she said humbly. *Your will be done.*

"Contact me again when there is something to report."

The connection closed. The power of the dagger again stabbed at her mind. It took every ounce of concentration she had to place it back in the box and close the lid.

Cassandra slumped in the throne, her body drenched in sweat. Conversations with the Dark Voice were so draining. Being in the presence of that mental power . . . oh how she longed for him to regain his body so that she could stand before him again.

"Cassandra," said a soft voice. Vastyr was at her side, a crystal goblet in his hand. "I believe it is time. You thirst, do you not?"

A wave of eagerness came over her. "Yes! That would replenish me."

"Then drink." The elf lifted the goblet with his right hand and placed his left wrist over it.

Cassandra reached out with a blade of air magic, but paused at the last moment. She gave him a cautious look. "Are you certain it hasn't been too soon?"

Vastyr was a healthy elf and knew exactly what to do to provide the sustenance she needed without overstressing himself, but sometimes he grew overzealous.

Maintaining a blood slave was a very delicate balance. Drinkers that did not get enough elf magic became ravenous vampires, feeding on the blood of any magical creature they can find, never able to slake the thirst. On the other hand, drain too much blood and the elf would weaken. Their body worked quickly to replace what was lost, but eventually, an elf drained too often would wither and age. Magic could be used to speed up the elf's blood production, but blood produced this way was weaker.

One solution was to maintain a series of blood slaves. This was an expensive prospect. Compliant blood slaves were difficult to find and it was even more difficult to find two compliant blood slaves that could get along. For some reason, the compliant ones were very possessive.

Cassandra's discovery of Vastyr had been a fortunate one. She had been beholden to dwarf slavers for her drink until he had come along. His desire to please her made things all the easier.

"I am perfectly healthy, Priestess," he assured her.

She checked him with her magic all the same. As all elves did, his body glowed with the faint dark hue of earth magic. His blood levels did seem fine. She shifted to blood sight.

Blood sight was a rare gift. Most members of the blood magic races didn't even have it. It was, however, a side effect of elf drinking. She saw the deep green of his life magic. It was healthy and strong. She could not wait any longer.

Her blade of air opened a precise cut in his wrist, spilling blood into the goblet in spurts. The smell of it overwhelmed her senses and she felt the urge to place her mouth directly over the wound, but she abstained. Drinking directly was dangerous, in part, because it was difficult to know how much you had drunk.

When the goblet had filled to the precise line, she sent her energies into the wound, stitching it closed with deft strands of earth and water until it looked as if it had never been open. Cassandra took the goblet and brought it to her lips.

198

The hot liquid elixir of pure life magic entered her mouth. The flavor that coated her tongue wasn't the salty metallic tang of human blood. It was full of complex notes, almost sweet, yet slightly bitter.

Vastyr grinned as he watched her drink. Part of what made him a good slave was the fact that he enjoyed her thirst almost as much as she did.

She drained the goblet before she knew it. Warmth flooded over her. Her senses intensified. Her thought processes whirred as she thought on the problem of that bonding wizard.

Cassandra had an idea. It was a potentially expensive gamble, but the risks were slim compared to her other options. She stood and handed the goblet back to her servant. "Go. Drink. Eat. Rest. I will call for you if I need your assistance."

He said something in response, but she did not hear it. She opened the chest next to her throne and stowed away the box containing the dagger. She then moved her trophies aside, looking for two particular magical implements. She found them at the bottom, wrapped in velvet.

Cassandra took them to the center of the room and unwrapped them, placing them on the ground. Two brass orbs filled with ancient bones and bound with powerful spirits. Obedient spirits. The perfect catalysts for something monstrous.

The Priestess of War laughed. She knew just what she'd have them do.

Chapter Fifteen

"The Priestess of War? They are certain of this?" Locksher said, his eyebrow raised with a mix of interest and concern.

The assembled members of Fist's tribe were huddled around the fire in the middle of this uncommonly cold spring night. Maryanne had awakened them all after speaking with Mistress Sarine. This information was too important to wait for morning.

The gnome warrior sat on the log next to Fist with one leg draped over his knee. Ever since that encounter in the cave things between them had changed. No longer did the gnome bother with the pretense that their relationship was just a show to keep the ogresses away. She hung on him all the time. Even climbed into his bedroll with him to sleep at night.

Fist found he quite liked it. His nervousness about the situation had dissolved and he had come to realize that his feelings for her had been evolving ever since Puj's death. The way he felt about Maryanne was something he had never experienced before.

It was something kind of like the way Justan felt for Jhonate, though Fist's feelings were not as deep. Not yet. But it was also different because there wasn't any invisible wall of propriety between them keeping them apart. Although, he had to admit to himself, she was a lot more comfortable showing her affection publicly than he was.

"Yeah. Cassandra was her regular name. At least that's what Master Porthos said," Maryanne replied to Locksher with a shrug.

"I am still trying to grasp how that revelation came to be," Locksher said. Maryanne's explanation of where Master Porthos had been and how he had given Sarine this information had been very truncated. He shook his head. "But the Priestess of War?"

"Yeah," she said. "I don't understand the big surprise. She fits everything you thought she would be."

"That's true," said Fist. "She's an old priestess everyone assumed was dead. Isn't she?"

"Never heard of her," Charz said with a yawn. The scowling rock giant had been the most difficult for them to rouse. It had taken one of Squirrel's famous ear screeches to get his attention. The furry animal was hiding in his pouch at Fist's side knowing that the giant had a rock in his hand. Squirrel was pretty sure that Charz was ready to throw it as soon as he showed himself.

Fist was just glad that Squirrel was back at his side. For the last several days, Squirrel had been spending much of his time in a small cave high in the cliff wall. He was quick to talk if Fist reached out to him and watched things from behind Fist's eyes from time to time, but kept his distance. When Fist pressed him about what he was up to, the little beast would only say he was 'remembering how to be Squirrel'.

"The question we should be askin' is how do we kill this vampire the quickest," said Lyramoor. The ex-blood slave had been agitated from the moment Maryanne had identified the source of the red spirit magic. The elf was squeezing the handles of his swords so hard they could hear the creak of the leather.

"Does it really matter so much who she is?" Qenzic asked. He raised a hand defensively at the elf's responding glare. "I mean, it's good to know who we're up against, but as far as I can tell, our job hasn't changed. We've just gotta protect this place and be ready to attack when the Academy army arrives, right?"

Maryanne glanced at Fist. That was indeed the basic plan, but Fist and Maryanne were the only ones that knew about the secret weapon being brought their way. Fist didn't know what it was or how it worked yet, but once it arrived he was pretty sure their small group was going to play a much larger role than Qenzic knew.

"I think the real question we should be askin' is, 'Why am I not asleep right now?'" Charz grumbled.

"I disagree," said Locksher. "The question you should be asking yourselves is, 'Why aren't we dead already?'"

Maryanne cocked her head at the wizard, "What?"

The wizard folded his arms, that concerned look still on his face. "It amazes me just how little the five of you know. The War of the Dark Prophet was just two hundred years ago. How could you not know your history?"

Charz snorted. "I was locked up in a cage when that happened."

"I was taught my history by dwarves that kept me locked in a cage," Lyramoor added. The giant gave him an approving nod.

I was dead! said Squirrel, peeking out of his pouch.

No, Fist replied through the bond. *You weren't born yet. That's different.*

Maryanne sighed, resting her chin on her palm. "Sarine might have mentioned something about her. Big time wizardess. Got her head cracked open."

"Yeah," said Qenzic, nodding as he thought about it. "The major battles of the war were taught at the Academy. This Cassandra-uh, clogged up one of the passes, right? So that the armies of Dremaldria couldn't reach the Dark Prophet's palace?"

The wizard shook his head sadly. "I shall make this brief, since it seems that your available memory centers are in short supply. The Wizardess Cassandra was the outstanding talent of her time. She was taught by the Mage School in Khalpany, something that *our* Mage School was quite jealous of by the way. She had immense talent in earth and air magic and I suspect, though there is no proof of it in the histories that were edited after the war, a great deal of bewitching magic as well."

"You said brief, right?" Charz griped, his eyelids drooping.

Locksher didn't acknowledge the giant's remark. "Shortly after attaining the rank of wizardess, she disappeared. When Cassandra emerged again as one of the Dark Prophet's priestesses the world was put in a tizzy. The Mage Schools sent dark wizard hunters and named warriors after her. She destroyed them all and kept her battle scars as trophies. The Dark Prophet was so impressed, he made her his Priestess of War and placed her in

202

command of his armies.

"During the War of the Dark Prophet, she was the most vicious of his commanders. She never lost a battle and would often travel hundreds of miles just to destroy a wizard or wizardess she felt was a threat. In part, it was fear of her that caused the countries of the known lands to listen to the Prophet and band together.

"It finally came down to one important battlefield. The combined armies were amassed at the foot of the mountains, ready to march on the Dark Prophet's palace. Only Cassandra's army stood in the way. She was well-defended, having used her magic to turn the mountains themselves into fortifications. The battle that ensued lasted months." He looked around at them. "Do you begin to understand? The collective might of three Mage Schools and the best warriors of the Academy against one wizardess and a handful of the Dark Prophets other priestesses."

"We got it," Maryanne said, nodding slowly, her interest piqued. "So how'd she get beat?"

He shrugged. "That is actually the least interesting part of the story. It was a fluke, really. There was an unadvised and costly attack. Nevertheless, a handful of named wizards were able to get past the defenses and attack her directly."

Locksher raised a finger. "A lone dwarf somehow made it past all of the defenses and approached her while she was distracted in magical battle. He struck her down with one blow. Split her head and knocked her off of the highest cliff face."

"Split her head?" said Fist. "And she survived?"

The wizard shrugged. "I can only tell you what the histories say, at least the ones I've read, and they seem to agree. Head split open. Actually, I believe you may know the dwarf who did it. If we survive this, you could ask him some time. Lenui Firegobbler, I believe his name is. He was at the Mage School during the recent war."

"Lenny?" said Fist in surprise. He thought back to the dreams he was constantly having. In them, Lenny was always there to lift him out of the mud on his way to march to battle with everyone else. And according to Maryanne, he was on his way here with that secret weapon.

"Oh yeah," said the gnome. "Bill did mention that in passing."

Charz laughed. "No way. I kicked that braggart's arse many times and drank him under the table just as many. He was always goin' on and on about his accomplishments. Never once did he mention that."

Now that Fist thought about it, he did remember the other dwarves calling Lenny a hero. Lenny had always seemed embarrassed about that. "I don't think he likes to talk about it."

Qenzic ignored their discussion, focusing on Locksher. "So I guess your point is, this Priestess of War is a big deal and we should take her seriously."

"A big deal?" Locksher barked out a laugh. It was so uncharacteristic of him that everyone paused to stare. "She could kill us all in an instant!"

The five of them gave each other dubious looks.

"I think you should give us more credit," Charz replied. "I, for one, am pretty hard to kill."

"You think so simply. This would not be a fist fight! She wouldn't just throw lightning bolts or fireballs that we could defend against. She is the most powerful earth wizardess of her time!" He stood and gestured all around them. "We are surround by sheer cliffs on all sides. She could collapse them on top of us! She could cause them to close together and squish us like plump ants! We could do nothing to stop her!"

His outburst had been loud enough that ogres at camp fires some distance away were staring at them. Locksher noticed this and cleared his throat before sitting down. "All she would have to do is come in person."

There was silence around the campsite as everyone absorbed this statement.

"Whelp! Sounds like we're screwed," said Charz. The giant laid back onto the dirt and put his hands behind his head. "I'm gonna sleep while I can."

"Ooh!" said Rufus, who had been silent thus far. The rogue horse was usually content just watching the others and monitoring Fist's responses to what was said. "Why she not?"

"That's a good question, Rufus," Fist said and pointed a finger at Locksher. "That's the question you asked us at the very beginning. If this priestess could destroy us so easily just by coming in person, why hasn't she killed us already?"

Qenzic's head perked up. "That's right. Why keep sending countless troops for us to slaughter? Why not save them for her attack on Dremaldria? It's a waste of resources."

"Yeah," said Lyramoor. "Vampires are usually more head on."

"I doubt very much she has let herself become a full vampire," said Locksher, his expression pensive. "But other than that, you are all correct. One could suggest that she just hasn't seen us as a threat, but I don't know if that matters. Threat or not, we are at the very least a thorn in her side. And if her past history has taught us anything, she is quite hands-on. That leaves only one possible answer."

"She can't," said Maryanne.

Locksher clapped his hands together and stood enthusiastically, gesturing to the rest of them. "Indeed! Something has kept her from coming after us. Now think. What could it be?"

She has a broken leg? Squirrel wondered

"Ooh!" said Rufus, nodding his head in agreement.

"Bet she can't go too far from her source of blood," Lyramoor said, his face still tense with anger.

"Not a bad line of thinking," said Locksher, unaware that it was the elf's only line of thinking at the moment. "As an elf drinker, she would need to quench her thirst often to avoid descending into madness. However, our camp is not that great a distance from the Black Lake. Going a day or two would likely not be long enough. Besides, she could always carry some with her in a flask or something."

Fist thought hard. Something the wizard had said pricked his brain. "Maybe it is the distance . . . we might be only a day's journey from the lake, but it can't be easy to control something as big as Mellinda's evil. And distance matters with spirit magic."

"Very good!" said Locksher and Fist wondered if the wizard had just learned something from him, or if he already figured it out on his own and was just using this as a teaching moment. "Yes, I saw the immensity of that magic up close! I would imagine it is very difficult to control. So much so, that she has to reinforce her spirit magic with blood magic in order to do so."

"So we're safe for now," Qenzic said.

"Until that next attack comes," Charz said. It had been quiet for several days and everyone assumed that the next one would be quite a bit more difficult than the last.

The academy graduate shrugged. "We'll deal with that attack when it happens, but what I'm saying is that the big difficulty is going to be on the day the Academy arrives. While she's focused on them, we're supposed to charge in from this side, which is sound tactics, but what's to keep her from just squishing everyone?"

"A legitimate concern," said Locksher and the wizard glanced Maryanne's way. "I assume the High Council is aware of this development?"

"Sarine should be telling them now," Maryanne said.

"She didn't have much problem killin' wizards before," Charz reminded them.

"Yeah, but they didn't have Mistress Sherl," Fist said. "She's the best dark wizard hunter the School ever had."

"Too bad she's not coming," said Maryanne bitterly. "She's stuck back at the Mage School with the rest of the council. Valtrek wouldn't let any one of 'em go with the army. He actually kept several of the best wizards home. He said they already lost too many teachers in the last war."

Lyramoor scowled. "Why did the Bowl pick him?"

"I dunno," Maryanne pouted. "He's way too cautious."

"Maybe he knows something we don't," Fist suggested. "You know. Like maybe he has a secret plan?"

She gave him a warning frown. "That's another thing about him. He's worried about secrets above all else."

"Now-now. Second guessing the new Head Wizard will get us nowhere," Locksher said. He cleared his throat. "Heaven knows

Valtrek has a tendency to overthink things that has got him into trouble in the past. But, burned bridges aside, he has a clever mind. Undoubtedly, he feels that the wizards on their way to us will be sufficient." He nodded, then frowned as he considered what he had just said. "You wouldn't happen to have a list of who he sent, would you?"

The group did not get back to sleep until late and Fist's sleep was troubled. His dream was even more bizarre than before.

It began with Lenny's strong hands grasping his shoulder and pulling him from the muck. The dwarf's face was as battered as if he had been in a bar brawl and a tiny naked old man was sitting on his shoulder.

"Get up, young ogre," he said in a voice that wasn't his own. "There is a battle afoot!"

Fist watched him leave in confusion. Where had that come from?

"Why weren't you listening?" said Maryanne. The gnome was standing next to him, untouched by mud. Only this time she wasn't wearing her armor. She wasn't wearing a stitch. "I told you not to land on your face. Tuck your legs under you and roll!"

Standing on her shoulder was Squirrel, only he had no fur. His transformation was complete. Covered in scales, his fingers and toes tipped with black claws, he held a sword into the air. Electricity sparked around the tiny weapon and Squirrel exulted, letting out a battle cry. "Deeeaaathclaaaaawww!"

"Uh oh, Fist," said Rufus' staccato voice and Fist realized that the rogue horse was standing on his other side. Rufus pointed with one long arm. "Big snake."

Fist looked down. Instead of the multitude of tiny snakes, this time it was an enormous one. It was already attached to his torso, it enormous jaws stretched so wide that they covered him from shoulders to waist. It's fangs had to be extremely long. He imagined that they had pierced all the way through him.

"Hurry!" said Maryanne and the gnome warrior began running towards the black lake with all the others. "Hurry or we're all gonna die!"

"Ooh! Hurry Fist!" Rufus agreed and ran off after them.

In the distance, Fist could hear a terrible rumble. Lightning strikes were lancing out of the sky. Fires were raging.

"I have to hurry," he repeated and looked back down at the head of the giant snake that was attached to him. Only, it was just a head. It's neck now ended in a stump. It's eyes were milky, it's scales dry and wrinkled, and it stank of rot.

He tried to pull it off of him but it wouldn't budge. "Stupid dream."

He tried to run after everyone else. He had to try to save them. Only his arms and legs would barely move. He was just too slow.

"Too slow," he said as destruction rained down on his friends. "Too slow . . ."

"Too slow for what?" Maryanne asked. She patted his face. "Hey, wake up, big guy."

Up! Up! Squirrel agreed excitedly.

Fist squinted at the sight of the early morning sky. Maryanne was crouched beside him, already dressed. Squirrel stood on her shoulder. "You let me sleep?"

"I would've kept letting you sleep, only Lyramoor thinks a fight's coming our way," she said.

A fight! Squirrel agreed. He was wearing one of the vests that Darlan had made for him, this one in brown leather. His eagerness reminded Fist of the dream he had just woken from and he didn't like the comparison.

"I don't hear the drums," Fist remarked.

"Well, we haven't actually seen any dead approaching yet," she admitted. "But Lyramoor, you know the way he is, couldn't sleep last night so he went on a long scouting trip alone."

Fist got up and started to get dressed for battle. "What did he find?"

She helped him strap on his breastplate. "He saw

approaching shadows. Also claims he felt a rumbling under his feet and 'smelled a foul wind'."

"That is good enough for me. Lyramoor has good instincts," Fist said.

He stepped over to pick up his shield and noticed that his pack had been knocked over on its side. The water flap had fallen open and some of his belongings had spilled out. He bent to put them away and his eyes fell on a thin book. On the cover, written in Justan's precise handwriting was the title, *Fist's Book of Words*.

Fist picked it up, smiling slightly. He had lapsed in his daily ritual. He opened it, flipping through the pages with his thick fingers until he found the leaf that he had used as a bookmark. Had it really been that long since he had opened it?

Puj had given the leaf to him. It was just a regular fernwillow leaf, but the ogress had called it "big healing magic". He pushed away the feeling of sadness that welled within him and scanned down the page, looking for the first word he had not done yet.

"Indomitable," he said.

"Huh?" Maryanne said, looking over his shoulder.

"It means, impossible to defeat," he said with a nod. Fist shut the book. "Let's be 'indomitable' today."

He placed the book back into the bag just as the horn sounded from the clifftop above. The drums started beating. The tribe was called to action.

Fight! said Squirrel eagerly, leaping to Fist's shoulder.

Fist didn't quite like his bonded's tone, *You don't fight*.

Squirrel sighed, *I am Squirrel. I do Squirrel things*.

That's right, Fist said with a nod.

The ogre defenders waited at the pass' entrance just as eager for the battle as Squirrel. The throwers on the slopes above the pass watched as the enemy army came closer. At first glance, the ranks looked to be the same mix of dead goblinoids that they had come to expect. Only, they did not march down the center of the pass like usual.

The enemy stopped just before the choke point where the defenders' traps had been reset. The ogres began to feel a rumbling at their feet. Something big was approaching, pushing its way through the rear of the dead's ranks. It was bulky and lumbering.

"What the hell is that?" Maryanne asked.

"I don't know," said Fist. They were perched on a ledge thirty feet above the ogre's defenses.

As they watched, the bulky thing shouldered aside a rotting giant and approached the first trap. It was hard to make out the details of the beast from this distance. It was blocky and at least twice as tall as any of the goblinoids surrounding it. Fist thought it had a sort of brownish color to it, but there was a strange variation in its skin tone. It seemed much like the variations in the color of the strata in a cliff face.

"A rock giant?" Maryanne asked.

Ooh! Like Charz? Rufus asked through the bond. The rogue horse was even higher above the defenses, atop the cliff side.

"I didn't think there are any other giants like Charz," Fist replied. Besides, Charz just looked like a giant whose skin happened to be made out of rock. This thing looked as if it had been roughly chiseled right out of the mountainside. "We'll see how it handles our trap."

The opposing army had no way of knowing this, but there had been an addition made to the pit traps. In the bottom of the pits, along with the sharpened stakes, was now a small rock charged with Locksher's magic. The wizard had learned from the results of his last attempt and had reduced the amount of power in each rock. It wouldn't blow the entire mountainside apart, but if the creatures should try to fill the pits in again, the explosion released would do a great deal of damage.

The giant stopped just before the trap as if knowing exactly where it was, despite the excellent work that had been done to cover it up. It stood there for a short time, not moving. Then it reached its arm into the cliff wall.

This wasn't like the diggers, who had torn into the rock with their claws. This thing just pushed its hand into the rock as if it were malleable. The overlooking slopes began to shudder. Rocks began to tumble down the slopes and fall into the pass, breaking through the carefully composed latticework that hid the pits from view.

Several of the throwers that were perched above the pass lost their footing. Two of them tumbled down and into the pits. A series of explosions ripped through the pass as Locksher's rocks were triggered. If any enemies would have been standing nearby they would have been shredded by the shrapnel. Instead, the explosions only added to the landslide as more rocks, accompanied by a cloud of dirt, fell into the pass.

Maryanne fired an arrow. The giant was just barely within her range, but the arrow soared true. It skipped off of his head ineffectively. "Okay, Fist. Your turn."

Fist was already working on his spell, sending flows of air and earth both below the thing and into the sky above. A lightning bolt split the sky with a crack, striking the giant head on. All of the dead surrounding it fell silently, steam rising from their bodies. The giant didn't budge. Rock continued to tumble down the slope.

"*Rufus!*" Fist shouted both aloud and through the bond.

"Ooh!" shouted the rogue horse in reply. He had grown several times his normal size and carried a small boulder in the crook of his arm. Rufus stuck his tongue out the side of his mouth as he judged the distance. Nodding, he started to spin.

Rocks continued to tumble into the pass, filling the pits, but also clogging the pathway. Finally, the giant pulled its arm out of the rock. The tremor stopped and the stony giant began to step forward.

Rufus' boulder struck it dead center of the chest with a loud crack. The boulder shattered into several large chunks. The giant fell backwards, crushing the bodies of several of the smaller dead around it.

"Did he hurt it?" Maryanne asked. "Did he kill it?" she asked even more hopefully.

The giant lay still for nearly a full minute and then it climbed back to its feet. As far as Fist could tell, there were a couple of cracks in its chest, but evidently that wasn't enough to slow this beast down.

This one's hard to kill, Squirrel observed.

"Throw another one!" Fist shouted.

Rufus picked up another rock from the pile next to him and focused in on the giant.

The stone beast stepped into the pass once again. Rocks were strewn in uneven piles. Some were knee-high. The giant began kicking the piles over, shoving them to the side with his blocky feet to create a clear path for the dead shuffling behind him.

Rufus' next rock struck the giant's shoulder with a loud crack. This time the giant staggered, but did not fall. A small cluster of cracks in its shoulder was the only sign of damage. It continued forward.

"Maryanne, go get Wizard Locksher," Fist said. "He may be able to tell us what this is."

"Right," she said and darted off, heading for the narrow trail that led down to the camp.

Another one, Rufus, Fist sent. *This time aim for the head.*

Okay, Rufus replied.

Fist switched to mage sight. The giant below shone a deep and hungry black. He frowned. What was this? A magical construct of some sort?

Rufus' next boulder hurtled in towards its head, but this time the giant was prepared. It raised an arm and the boulder struck it with a resounding chunky thud. This time the boulder did not shatter, but rebounded and fell. Once again, the only damage was a series of cracks.

Were the blows doing any lasting damage? Fist wondered. Was there any flesh within this thing or was it solid rock all the way through? It continued to make its way through the pass, clearing space as it went, drawing nearer to the entrance where the ogres waited. Would they stand a chance against it?

"Ooh! More!" said Rufus in his huffing staccato voice, his long arm pointing.

Another large shape was entering the pass. It was about the same size and shape as the first one, but this giant was a solid brown. Fist's mage sight showed him that it glowed the same shade of black as the first one.

Throw a rock at that one, Fist instructed, hoping that there would somehow be a different effect.

Ooh! Okay! The rogue horse replied through the bond.

Not good, Squirrel observed, eating a nut calmly on Fist's shoulder.

"No kidding," Fist replied.

The rocky giant was now in range of the ogre throwers. A series of rocks much smaller than the ones Rufus had been throwing began pelting the thing to a much lesser effect. It ignored the projectiles and kept moving forward. Qenzic saw the problem and ordered the throwers to focus on the goblinoids that packed the narrow confines of the pass behind it.

"Ooh!" cried Rufus, pushing his body to the limits with a another nearly back wrenching throw. The boulder hurtled through the air towards the rocky giant's browner brother.

The rock struck the thing just under the chin with a dull thud. Pieces of the giant thing's brown flesh struck the surrounding walls with a patter. The boulder stayed there, embedded.

The thing reached up with hands that Fist could now see were much better formed than its rocky counterpart and grasped the boulder. It plucked the rock from its soft brown flesh and threw it to the side, exposing the gaping crater that the boulder had left behind.

It didn't bleed. It didn't act as if wounded. It just started forward again and Fist's jaw dropped as he watched the crater fill itself back in.

"Oh! How unfortunate," said Locksher, breathing heavily as he arrived on the ledge, Maryanne at his side. He was staring down at the rocky giant that had just reached the entrance of the pass. "A rock golem."

Chapter Sixteen

"Ohh," said Fist, beginning to understand what they were up against.

He had seen Justan's memories of the enormous plant golem that had torn through the grounds of the Mage School, killing students and teachers and destroying the school's ancient clock tower. It too had been able to take severe damage without being stopped. Its rampage had only ended after Justan had shot it with a magical arrow enhanced by the power of his Jharro bow.

"There's another one coming up the rear of the pass!" Maryanne noticed, seeing the dark brown golem's approach for the first time.

"A clay golem," Fist surmised from the way it had reacted to Rufus' attack. It had almost completely repaired the damage the boulder had caused and was continuing towards them.

"Unfortunate," Locksher said again softly, his mind churning. "Clay golems are a lesser threat, but formidable all the same."

As they spoke, the rock golem stepped out of the pass and approached the ogres' defenses. Crag's clubbers charged towards it.

Maryanne swallowed. "So how do we kill 'em?"

The wizard let out a nervous laugh. "It's-it's-it's very difficult. Uh, magic can sometimes do it. Enough brute force . . . but these were undoubtedly made by Cassandra, so I imagine they are incredibly tough."

As if to underscore his point, another of Rufus' boulders

streaked in, this one striking the rock golem directly in the head. The boulder shattered and the golem merely shook its head. The ogres arrived and began beating at its solid body, their clubs having very little effect. It swung an arm, sending several of them sprawling.

"Master Locksher, do you think you could magic up one of Maryanne's arrows?" Fist asked. "Her bow isn't strung with a dragon hair string like Justan's was, but maybe that could work?"

The wizard blinked. "I see what you're thinking. I could definitely do so, though I am not exactly sure that it would have the desired effect. The golem Sir Edge shot at the Mage School was not made of such stern stuff."

Maryanne pulled out one of her arrows that was not already charged with electric magic and handed it to the wizard. "Get creative."

"Alright," he said, frowning at the arrow in his hand. "It may take me some time to make this effective, though."

The golem swung an arm in a massive punch, sending ogres sprawling and caving in the head of one of them who had been unlucky enough to absorb the full impact of its fist. It continued up the hill past the ogre's defenses, absorbing every impact sent against it. Behind the golem, the infested dead were streaming out of the pass.

Charz shouted at the rest of the ogres to get back. Crag smartly agreed, instructing the ogres to attack the infested instead. The ogres followed the commands of their chief and soon only the rock giant stood in the path of the golem, his magic trident in hand.

"I've got to get down there," said Fist.

Me too, said Squirrel. The furry creature bounded from Fist's shoulder and started skittering agilely down the sheer cliff face.

"No!" Fist cried out and shouted through the bond. *Get back here! You can't do anything to help with that! You are not Deathclaw!*

I will help! Squirrel insisted. *I will help like Squirrel*!

Letting out a curse, Fist hurried down the trail, looking for a section of the cliff that wasn't too steep to slide down. *Squirrel watches. Squirrel plays jokes! Squirrel doesn't fight*!

Ooh, ooh! Agreed Rufus through the bond, just as worried about Squirrel as Fist was. The rogue horse climbed down the cliff face towards them.

Not any more, Squirrel said with determination. *I fight! I learned how*.

No you didn't, Fist insisted. *You watched me fight. I'm an ogre*!

You'll see, Squirrel promised.

You'll get squished! Fist came to a point in the trail where the cliff side seemed to slope away just gently enough. He jumped off the trail, sliding down towards the ground by the seat of his pants. It was a jagged, rocky stretch. His pants tore and his legs were scraped up, but Fist didn't care. He struck the ground hard and stumbled forward, pulling his mace from its harness. *Squirrel*!

Charz knew exactly what this thing was. He had fought a golem once before well over a century ago while he was still a gladiator in the Royal Arena in Khalpany. At that point in his involuntary career, he had been undefeated for ninety years straight.

The crowd had grown tired of his success. Where he had once been their favorite, they now saw him as a villain. The Unbeatable Charz was booed in every match. Attendance sagged.

The overseers felt that something needed to be done. Charz needed to be defeated so that a new champion could rise. So they hired a wizard to create a construct. A rock golem.

The golem Charz had fought that day hadn't been as large as this one. It had been about his same height, while this one was a good foot and a half taller. But it had been carved a bit better, given a strong, proud face. This one was rough-hewn, with coal-like stone for eyes, a square bulge for a nose. It's mouth was fierce though, it's jaw fixed in a scream of rage.

Killing it wouldn't be easy. Somewhere in this thing was a core of magic that held it together. Break that and the thing would collapse. Of course, the Priestess of War wouldn't have put it somewhere easy to get to. The other wizard sure hadn't. That fight had lasted for hours and in the end, he had gotten lucky, shattering just the right chunk of rock to kill it. Oh how the arena fans had hated that.

Charz smiled at the memory. This was going to be fun.

He backed up, letting the golem come towards him, luring it into an open area where he would have room to fight it. He could have his fun while the ogres fought the dead. The ogres stayed back, giving it a wide berth and the thing came right at him. It knew who the biggest and most powerful threat was. Charz found the right spot and stopped, letting it come.

Mog rushed in from the golem's side. The blue-skinned netherhulk swung his huge stalagmite club in a vicious overhand blow. The golem reached one arm up defensively and caught the blow on the forearm.

The stalagmite, a weapon that had crushed countless infested dead, broke in half. The rock golem's forearm broke too. A section sheared off, leaving the golem without a left hand, but also leaving a jagged point behind.

"Blast it, Mog!" Charz roared. "This is my fight!"

"My club!" Mog lamented, looking at the stubby remains of his once useful weapon. Thus occupied, he did not react fast enough when the golem swung his undamaged arm in a counter punch. Its rough-hewn fist caught the netherhulk in the side of the face, sending teeth and acidic saliva flying.

Squirrel came to the bottom of the cliff face determined to fight and irritated that Fist did not believe in him. Maybe he wasn't Deathclaw, but he was strong too. Fist would see.

Squirrel! Stay back! Fist shouted again through the bond.

No! Normally, Squirrel would have just closed the bond and ignored him. Only this time he needed the bond to stay open.

His head darted around, sniffing as he looked for the best target. The ogre clubbers were crowded amongst a large group of the dead. The fighting was intense, perhaps not the best place for him to be scurrying around.

Finally, a good opportunity presented itself. One of the dead, an infested gorc, peeled away from the press and made its way up the hill towards the ogre camp. No one else had spotted it yet.

Excited, Squirrel ran towards it. As he did so, he reached deep into his bond with Fist and searched for strands of the ogre's elemental magic. In Squirrel's mind, it was as if the ogre had a huge cheek pouch full of the stuff.

Squirrel had long been fascinated with Fist's elemental talents. He didn't have the intelligence to comprehend all of the ogre's lessons at the Mage School, and Darlan's lectures seemed mostly nonsensical to him, but he had always been excited by the results. He liked to watch Fist prepare his spells and one in particular had seemed fairly simple.

Squirrel leapt up onto the gorc's leg and scampered up its body. As he did so, he pulled strands of gold and black magic through the bond and wrapped them hastily around his furry body. He had practiced this countless times over the last several days and knew what to do.

The dead gorc was slow to react to Squirrel's presence. It continued its shuffling progress towards the ogre camp. The larvae inside it had scarcely noticed the furry creature's climb until it reached the back of the gorc's neck. Then Squirrel began to vibrate.

His little body shuddered, rubbing the strands of magic against each other until there was a sharp zap! Electricity shot through the gorc's body, bursting each of the larva in a puff of steam. The gorc collapsed.

See, Fist! Squirrel leapt from the rotting body before it hit the ground. He pulled more threads of gold and black magic through the bond and decided on his next target. *I can fight too!*

Fist stumbled in surprise as he saw the gorc go down. Had Squirrel really just done what he thought he saw? *Squirrel? How did you-*?

Zap!

Another dead goblinoid collapsed. Squirrel leapt from its back, his little thoughts filled with glee. *I watched you. Now I fight like Squirrel*!

Now Fist understood. Squirrel had visited his dream and saw himself with that electric sword. Then he had tried to figure out a way to duplicate it. This explained what he had been doing while he had been going off and hiding and, more importantly, why Fist's magic had seemed to drain so quickly over the last several days.

What Fist didn't understand was how that was possible. It seemed backwards. He could pull energy from Rufus, but he was supposed to be able to. He was the bonding wizard. Did this mean Rufus could start pulling magic from him too? For that matter, could he reach through the bond and use Justan's frost magic?

The avalanche of possibilities threatened to give him a headache. He pushed those thoughts aside. There were far more important things to worry about at the moment. Not far from him, Charz and Mog were tussling with that rock golem.

He pulled more energy from Rufus to replace the magic Squirrel was taking. *Just, be careful*! He warned, knowing that there was nothing he would be able to do to dissuade the little beast. *Everybody is bigger than you.*

Zap! An infested ogre collapsed.

Squirrel leapt from its body. *I know that!* He ran towards another dead goblinoid who had wandered away from the clubbers. He leapt onto its torso, his little body vibrating. *But I am faster.*

Zap!

Letting out a groan of anxiety, Fist headed towards the battle with the rock golem. He wasn't the only one. Rufus ran up right next to him. Qenzic and Lyramoor were already there pacing close to the fight, looking for a way to help.

"Ooh!" said Rufus, then he sent, *Looks hard.*

Fist had to agree with him. Mog's face was swollen and bloodied, while Charz' chest was covered in a multitude of bleeding cracks where the golem's punches had landed. Meanwhile that stone golem was tough.

It had received some gouges from Charz's trident, but the cracks that the golem had received from Rufus' thrown boulders had healed themselves. Its only lasting damage of note seemed to be the one forearm that had broken, but in Fist's mind, the jagged piece of rock that remained attached to its elbow looked like a dangerous weapon unto itself.

Charz reared back, barely dodging another swing of the golem's rocky fist. Mog jumped it from behind, wrapping his huge arms around its body and grabbing its arms, trying to immobilize it. The netherhulk was just about the same height and bulk as the golem and, though he had to visibly strain, he was able to give Charz a clear opening.

"Thanks, Mog!" Charz growled and thrust his trident dead center.

The magic of the trident allowed it to pierce magically reinforced armor and also slow healing. These attributes made it ideal for piercing the solid body of the golem. All three prongs pierced into the rock, burying themselves up to the fork.

Grinning in triumph, he tried to remove the weapon, but it had become stuck. Charz growled and put a foot on its chest, trying to pull it free, but it remained embedded. Roaring, he let go and threw a heavy punch into its face, busting it's blocky nose to powder.

"Fist!" shouted Maryanne over the tumult and Fist glanced back to the ledge to see her still standing by Locksher who was fiercely working spells on that arrow. She pointed down at the entrance to the pass.

The clay golem had just emerged. Seeing it up close, Fist could tell that it was the same size as the rock golem, only the carving of it had been far more detailed. It's color was the same uniform brown throughout, but its body had been shaped into the image of the Dark Prophet. He recognized it from tapestries he had seen at the Mage School. That same proud jaw and commanding brow, down to the robes it wore.

Its gaze was fixed on the ledge where Locksher and

Maryanne stood. It moved towards them, shoving aside any ogres or infested in its way. Several of the clubbers, including Crag himself rushed over and began bashing at its legs. The clubs hit with meaty slaps, but the only damage done was small dents that rapidly repaired themselves.

Fist realized that this golem required a different technique than the other. "Qenzic and Lyramoor! I think that one's going for Locksher. Cut pieces out of it. See if you can disable its legs."

The two swordsmen nodded and ran for the golem.

"Rufus," he said. "Go to the ledge. If it can't be stopped, carry Locksher and Maryanne to safety."

"Ooh!" *Okay*! Rufus replied and ran for the cliff face.

Fist removed his shield from his back and grabbed his mace, then moved in to help against the rock golem. The two giants were barely holding their own.

The netherhulk growled as he put all of his strength into holding the thing back. Charz had given up on retrieving his trident and continued to throw punches. Every blow chipped away at the golem's face, but the rock-like skin on the giant's hands was cracked and bleeding.

Fist rushed in, knowing that the source of the golem's power was likely somewhere in its chest or torso, but also knowing that the most dangerous thing about it was its mobility. He swung low with the bashing side of his mace, going for its knee.

The mace struck with a loud ping, chipping chunks of rock away from the joint. Something seemed to change within the golem and it acted out in rage.

Its arms still pinned, it lifted its leg and kicked out. Fist moved his shield into place just in time to catch the blow, but the force of it still sent the ogre sprawling.

It ignored another heavy punch by Charz and lifted its leg again, stomping down. It's heavy foot crushed into Mog's foot, shattering his toes and causing the netherhulk's grasp to weaken. The golem then jerked its arms down, dislocating one of Mog's shoulders and swung around, throwing the netherhulk to the ground.

Squirrel leapt atop a pile of goblinoid corpses and took a brief moment to rest. Fighting was hard work. He pulled a seed from within his cheek pouch and began to shell it while he watched Qenzic and Lyramoor fight the clay golem.

The two agile swordsmen were doing a good bit of damage with their swords, carving off chunks of soft clay with precise strikes, yet Squirrel wasn't sure exactly how much they had hurt it. Pieces of the golem littered the slope around it, but it seemed more irritated than worried. As it stepped on the pieces that had been cut from its body they were absorbed back into its flesh. Its real goal seemed to be reaching the cliff face below the place where Locksher and Maryanne stood. It swung its fists at its attackers more to keep them at a distance than to do any real damage.

Squirrel wondered how much a blow from this thing would hurt anyway. It seemed to have such tender flesh without any real bone to back it up. He received the answer to that question a moment later when Fist's father Crag came in too close with an emboldened attempt to bash in one of its legs.

The golem twisted and caught the ogre with the full force of an uppercut. There was a meaty thud and the ogre chieftain was sent flying. Squirrel watched in awe as Crag soared up over the little beast's head and crashed into one of the defensive walls before collapsing senselessly.

The clay golem stomped closer to the cliff and the two Academy swordsmen worked more quickly. They fought in concert, focusing on the same leg joint. Each one would dart in to slice when the way seemed clear and leap back when the Golem attacked.

It was working. Bigger and bigger chunks were cut away until, with a mighty cry, Qenzic's sabre cut through. The golem swung off balance, but refused to fall. It attempted to place its stump back on the lower part of its leg that the swordsman had cut free, but Qenzic grasped the severed piece and dragged it away.

Its face contorting in a silent roar, it began to shrink slightly as it attempted to regrow its leg.

"Ooh! You!" cried Rufus. The rogue horse had climbed up

to the ledge next to Locksher and had a large rock in his hand. He threw at the golem's remaining leg.

The rock slammed into the golem's thigh with a splat. The golem teetered onto its not yet fully-formed replacement leg and fell to the ground.

Qenzic and Lyramoor pounced, cutting on the fallen monster, trying to get at the core of magic that held it together. Qenzic focused on the head, hewing into it with great swipes of his father's magical sabre. Lyramoor stabbed into the golem's chest repeatedly with his twin falchions.

The golem squirmed, trying to reform its limbs so that it could stand again.

Lyramoor, thinking he had felt something hard deep within its chest, let out a cry and thrust in deeply with his right sword. Again there was something hard that his sword had just barely glanced off of. The elf warrior withdrew his sword to thrust again just as the golem's hand clenched closed around his leg.

Lyramoor cried out and tried to hack at the hand gripping him, but the golem changed its tactics. Instead of trying to regain its former shape, it pulled the elf in and began forming its bulk around him, trying to encase him.

Qenzic grabbed his friend's arm and tried to cut him free. He peeled back long slices of clay, but they just kept forming back together. Lyramoor was pulled further inside. The clay golem swung a half-formed arm, batting Qenzic away, and began to roll its large body back towards the pass.

Squirrel shook his little head. His new ability to shock was going to be of no help here. He looked for another target and saw that a few infested were still stumbling free from the ogre clubbers. Pulling more of Fist's magic from the bond he skittered towards one of them and jumped onto its torso.

Zap!

The rock golem raised its arms into the air and opened the jagged remains of its mouth in a silent roar of challenge, Charz' trident still protruding from its torso impotently.

Charz lay on the ground several yards away, having been temporarily knocked unconscious. His jaw and nose were broken, his body covered in slowly healing cracks. Mog was a short distance behind the golem on his hands and knees as he spat out another tooth. The golem's fist still sizzled where his saliva was eating into it.

Fist winced as he sat up, once again thankful for the skilled workmanship of Bettie who had made his shield for him. The stout piece of iron-reinforced wood had absorbed three tremendous blows from the golem without a splinter.

He sighed and came to one knee. He took a quick glance towards the pass and saw that the clay golem had collapsed down into a ball. Good for Lyramoor and Qenzic.

He returned his attention to the rock golem. Evidently, direct attack wasn't working against this thing. Fist sent threads of water and earth magic into the ground underneath the golem and began to break the rock apart, mixing it with a liquid sludge. Hopefully the thing would continue to stand there for just a few seconds longer until he could collapse the ground beneath it. If he could bog it down and trap it, they would have a better chance.

Mog pushed up from his knees, managing to stand despite his crushed foot. He began limping away from the golem. "'Nuff of this!"

Charz stirred, shaking his head as he regained consciousness. His eyes took in the triumphant golem and his fleeing friend. He struggled to his knees. "Hey! Mog! Where you goin'?"

"I'm hurt. I'm done," the netherhulk replied with a dismissive wave and continued to limp away, headed towards the Big Cave.

The rock golem saw Mog's attempt at escape and started towards him, stepping away from the section of rock Fist was working his magic on. Fist scowled and came to his feet, knowing that he needed to rush to the netherhulk's aid.

He wasn't fast enough.

Mog heard its approach and turned to face the rock golem just as it thrust out with its left arm. The jagged shard stump that remained of its forearm pierced his chest. Mog clutched its arm in shock. Grimacing, he spat an acidic wad into the golem's shattered face.

Fist swung his mace in an overhand strike that connected with the side of the golem's head. Half of its rocky skull sheared away and fell to the ground. The golem let Mog slide off of the end of its arm and turned to look at Fist with its one remaining eye. It didn't seem hurt by the blow or by the acid that was dissolving the remnants of its face. It seemed to be laughing.

I was too slow, Fist thought, his mind in shock.

"Mog!" Charz cried and rushed towards them, his face a rictus of rage.

Move out the way! came Rufus' voice through the bond.

Understanding, Fist turned and leapt at Charz, knocking the rock giant to the ground as Maryanne finally released her magicked arrow.

The arrow pierced the air with a hiss, its head a molten red, its shaft glowing white hot. It penetrated deep into the golem's back before collapsing, its molten mass melting the rock of the golem's torso as it continued on through.

The front of the golem's chest exploded outward in a shower of molten rock, spattering the ground next to Fist's legs. The remnants of the arrow continued to burn and the golem collapsed, slowly melting.

The heat of its destruction was so intense that Fist had to get up and walk some distance away to avoid being scalded. Charz ran around the burning thing and reached Mog's side. He grabbed the netherhulk's arm and dragged him away from the heat.

"Fist!" the giant shouted.

Swallowing, Fist ran over to joined him and sent his energies into the netherhulk's body. It didn't take long. His hands fell slowly. "I'm sorry, Charz. It tore his heart open."

"Blast it!" the giant shouted and let out a pained roar. "Mog's dead and look at me." He slammed his fist against his chest. "Look at me!"

Most of the giant's wounds were already healed. His jaw

was whole. His nose was straightening itself while Fist watched.

"It's not your fault you heal," Fist said numbly.

Charz growled and stormed over to the golem's still burning remains, walking closer than anyone else could have dared. The ground beneath it had turned molten, a trail of red rock flowing down the hill, only blackening around the edges.

The giant bent and picked up something red hot from the ground beside it. It was the handle of his trident. Or what remained of it. The prongs were gone completely. The end of the handle drooped sadly and the giant's shoulders slumped. "My weapon, too?"

The dead are leaving, Squirrel sent. He was somewhere near the entrance to the pass. The little beast was bursting with pride. *I scared them away.*

Fist looked over at the pass and saw that the infested were streaming away. The clay golem was gone as well, which meant that it had either fled with the rest of the army or Qenzic and Lyramoor had destroyed it.

Fist sighed. He needed to have a long talk with Squirrel but this wasn't the time. *I'm glad, Squirrel. You did good.*

Rufus trotted over to them, Locksher and Maryanne on his back. "Oooh," the rogue horse said.

Locksher took in the scene of the destruction and saw the angry look on Charz' face. The wizard grimaced. "I overdid it again, didn't I? I, uh . . . Weaponizing items is not exactly my forte."

Charz's trousers had begun to smoke and blacken from the heat. He scowled before tossing the handle into the rest of the burning pile and stepping away. He patted at his pants, his rocky skin steaming in the cool air as he walked towards Locksher.

"You owe me a weapon." He pointed back to the white hot pile. "If you can make me one that does that, we're even."

"I . . . don't know how useful that would be," Locksher said, taking the giant literally.

Fist, Squirrel said again. Fist could sense that he was standing on the shoulder of an unconscious ogre. *Peoples are hurt down here. Crag is sleeping.*

"We've got injuries," Fist said and trotted back down to the entrance of the pass to check on the ogres that had been caught in the golems' attack.

He found the tribe members hard at work, the burners doing their duty clearing the dead as usual. Ogress healers were already there, looking over the wounded. The situation was grim. There were seven dead and many more badly hurt. Fist approached the cluster of them around their fallen chieftain.

The ogresses were crouched beside Crag, putting poultices of leaves on his head. Fist pushed his way through them and sent magic into his father's body. His skull was fractured. Signs of a concussion. He also had cracked ribs and a multitude of bruises.

Fist set to work. When he was done with his father, he stayed to heal any others whose injuries were serious. Squirrel climbed to his shoulder and watched him work silently.

When Fist returned to his friends, he found them standing close together, not far from the remains of the golem, now mostly cool. Locksher was turning a piece of blackened rock over in his hands, but he was looking at Qenzic.

Fist trotted up to them. "Crag almost didn't make it. His skull was fractured, but I was able to heal him up. Rub, though . . . when I got there it was already too late," Fist said sadly.

Rub was Old Falog's son and one of the ogres that had been with the group when they traveled from the Mage School. He had been nowhere near as crafty as his father, but he had a good smile and as rough as he was, Fist knew he had seen some kindness in him.

Fist shook his head and spoke to Locksher. "Come, Master. There are a lot more ogres that need healing."

Locksher hesitated and Maryanne grasped Fist's arm, giving him a concerned look.

"It's Lyramoor," she said.

"What?" Fist asked.

"He's gone," said Qenzic softly. The warrior was looking down at a pendant in his hand. "That clay golem took him. It swallowed him up. I tried to stop it, but it rolled into the pass and there were just too many of those infested in the way."

"Swallowed? Then he's . . ." Fist placed a hand on the man's shoulder. "I'm sorry."

"He's not dead, though," Qenzic said, looking up at him. "That thing swallowed him up, but it didn't kill him." He lifted the pendant, showing it to Fist. It was a quartz crystal, surrounded by a frame of silver wire. "It's a life stone. My father had it and Lyramoor gave it to me just in case something like this should ever happen. He told me that if he should ever die, the crystal will shatter."

Locksher looked at the pendant and nodded. "So . . . The fact that he lives means that the Priestess of War has taken him prisoner. She'll torture him to discover everything she can. Soon enough, she'll know our weaknesses and our plans."

Fist swallowed, feeling horrible for Lyramoor, but also grateful that the elf hadn't known everything. Maybe Valtrek's demand for secrecy wasn't quite so crazy as it had seemed.

"Then what are we waiting for? We'll rescue him!" Maryanne declared. "If we leave right away, we might be able to reach the thing before it gets back to the Black Lake."

"Let's go," said Charz, his jaw fixed in determination. "I'm ready to tussle with that thing. I'd like to see it try and swallow me."

"That is a very risky plan," Locksher cautioned, his face lined with worry. "You wish to rush into the heart of the enemy army for this rescue attempt?"

"They're just fodder," Charz harrumphed.

"Fighting the dead isn't so easy when surrounded on all sides," Locksher reminded them. "You should also consider that this is what she wants. There could be a trap just waiting for us to flounce into it. You could run into Cassandra herself. She might be tied to the Black Lake, but we don't know how far that limitation extends. She could be anywhere between here and there."

"What are you saying?" Fist said, dumbfounded. "We just sit? He is our friend. We can't just leave him to be tortured in the hands of a vampire!"

"Ooh! Ooh!" Rufus agreed. "I take you!"

"No!" said Qenzic. The warrior was gripping the pendant tightly. "Locksher's right. We can't go after him."

"Why not?" Maryanne said.

"Lyramoor's not like the rest of us. He has prepared for this day ever since my father rescued him. If there's a way to escape, he'll find it."

"You're sayin' we don't even try?" Charz said.

"He made me promise that if he should ever be captured, I wouldn't go after him," Qenzic said. "He told me that if I was there, he might not be able to do the things necessary to escape. He meant it, too. But even if he can't escape, she'll never get a word out of him."

"That's just bluster!" Charz said. "The elf was always spoutin' tough talk like that, but it doesn't mean we have to listen."

Qenzic shook his head. "You don't know Lyramoor like I do." He shivered and looked down at the pendant again. "You have no idea the lengths he has gone to prepare for this situation. Heaven help the Priestess of War if she thinks she can hold him."

Chapter Seventeen

Justan looked around the imposing walls of the large room again. They were made up of a dark gray mist and the room was lit by a constant barrage of lightning flashes. At first glance, it seemed as if he was sitting in the middle of a cloud during a thunderstorm.

Only, that wasn't quite true. The dry heat in the room suggested that the mist surrounding him was smoke rather than cloud. There was also an almost sulfuric smell to the air, like there was an odious fire burning somewhere far below them. It also helped that he knew that this place was Theodore's mental creation. The imp's magical ability with fire and air didn't bring a thunderstorm to mind.

"Thanks again for agreeing to do this, Sir Edge," Willum said. The young Academy graduate was sitting across the table from Justan, his cards clutched tightly in his left hand.

"Sure. I have to admit I was curious to see what Theodore's world was like," Justan replied. Besides, the journey to bonding wizard Stolz's home had been a long and uneventful one and Jhonate had been in a mood the whole time. This seemed like a pleasant enough distraction.

Xedrion had decided that it was time to call Stolz back to Roo-Tan'lan. The looming threat of the Troll Mother and this new race of trollkin meant that someone with an intimate knowledge of their foe was sorely needed. Jhonate had been in charge of putting the mission together and since her father wouldn't approve of her taking Justan alone, she had also chosen Willum, Poz, and Qurl.

Everything had seemed fine until Vannya had been added

to the group. Justan wasn't sure how the mage had convinced Jhonate to let her come along, but one thing that was certainly evident was that it had been a mistake. Vannya and Jhonate had never gotten along.

Justan had hoped that the budding relationship between Vannya and Willum would help. After all, there was no reason for the two women to be rivals any longer. Unfortunately, Jhonate focused in on Vannya's new romance, watching over the mage and warrior like a hawk. She had not been happy with Justan when he had suggested that she not try to hold them to her own cultural standards of propriety.

Justan looked down at the remaining cards in his hand. At least the card game was going well. He was confident he could make his bid. Hopefully, Willum's cards were as strong. They were far ahead of their opponents, but unlike the game of Elements, Unity was a team game and this was the first time Justan had played with the warrior.

Justan threw a card into the center of the table. "I think this place is impressive, Theodore. You have put a lot of detail into it."

"*Ho! This is but a staging area*," Theodore replied, chewing his lip as he tossed out a card of his own. He was dressed in an odd parody of the Roo-Tan warrior style, with a hide breastplate that bulged out to make room for his ample belly. His sparse hair was pulled to the side and woven into a single braid interlaced with a sickly yellow ribbon. "*There is so much more I can do when I put focus into it. Right, Willy?*"

"It can get detailed, yeah," Willum said with a sigh. "Wait until you've sat through one of his puppet plays."

"*Ho-Ho! Yes! You must! I make them riveting. Absolutely riveting!*"

"I'll think about that," Justan said, noting the wide-eyed shake of Willum's head. "The method of getting here is a little awkward, though."

Theodore had explained that in order for the two humans to enter his world together, they must be in close physical proximity. Thus their bodies were currently lying inside Willum's tent side-by-side, each of them with a hand on the handle of the axe. Jhonate and Vannya had found the arrangement quite amusing. Especially Vannya, who had wondered if this was the way two strong male warriors "held hands".

Justan eyed the imp suspiciously. "Was that part exactly necessary, though? Or was it just another of your attempts at amusing yourself?"

"*Ho! I never 'attempt' to amuse myself, Sir Edge,*" Theodore replied, arching a thin eyebrow. "*I either succeed and therefore enjoy myself immensely, or I die a ridiculously slow death caused by boredom. Ho-ho! If I had truly wanted to amuse myself, I would have suggested that the two of you had to be nude in order for the connection to work.*"

Justan couldn't help but chuckle at the ridiculous nature of the idea.

Willum just shook his head. "We would never have agreed to that."

The imp inclined his head. "*Yes, Willy. Which is why I didn't 'attempt' it. Ho! In fact, I would be currently dying that slow death I mentioned if not for the delightful company of my partner, here.*"

"*Delightful company, am I?*" asked Artemus dully, throwing his card onto the table. His card was too low to win the trick, but he didn't seem to care. He just pushed the pile in front of Justan.

The old wizard hadn't particularly wanted to join the game this night. In the beginning, Theodore hadn't been too keen on the idea either, but Justan had insisted, making Artemus' attendance one of the qualifications of the game.

Justan had hoped that this game would distract the wizard. Artemus had grown despondent ever since Fist had told them that Porthos, Sarine's second husband was still alive. Justan had assured him that the old master was in no shape to be a rival for Sarine's heart, but Artemus had responded that the status of being alive certainly gave the wizard a leg up in the race.

The imp grinned, exposing his yellowed teeth. "*Oh yes. Ho! Master Artemus, you are a fantastic Unity player. Much better than the imbeciles my own mind conjures.*" He jerked his thumb towards Willum. "*Or Willy here.*"

"I'm not going to disagree," Willum said with a smile. "But Sir Edge and I are destroying you."

"*So you are,*" said Artemus, glancing at the score sheet. "*But that can happen when one hasn't played a game for two hundred years.*"

"Ho*! Good point, frost wizard,*" said the imp. "*But we haven't lost yet. There is still time to turn this game around.*"

Justan kept an eye on his great grandfather. The old wizard seemed to be keeping control of himself. None of the Scralag's aspects were taking over his image yet, but he worried that if Artemus grew too depressed he might just stop fighting the elemental.

He tried to think of a way to get Artemus more involved. "Theodore, I am starting to be suspicious. How can Willum and I be certain that you don't know what's on our cards?"

"*Maybe because you're winning?*" The imp's eyes narrowed, his lips pursed together. "*Ho! I find the insinuation insulting. I never stoop to cheating! What point is there in playing a game when the rules are not adhered to?*"

"I wasn't referring to your scruples or lack thereof," Justan replied. "I'm just talking about the logistics of this game. We are here in your world. The cards in our hands were created by your mind. How do you determine what order the cards are going to appear in? Are the faces of the cards determined when the deck appears or after they are dealt? No matter how it's done, you must know what's on them."

"*Ho-ho!*" scoffed the imp. "*True. I could know if I wished. But what fun would there be in that? The answer, Sir Edge, is that I choose not to know.*"

Justan snorted. "Is that even possible, Artemus?"

"*It can be done,*" Artemus said. "*I have known great wizards who spend so much time alone that they have developed a way to compartmentalize their thoughts, allowing them to play both sides of a chess game and remain intrigued.*"

"*I've done that before, too,*" said the imp. "*Ho! But I stopped because I kept being distracted by how good looking my opponent was!"*

Artemus managed a half smile as he addressed the skeptical look on Justan's face. *"It seems a strange concept, I know. But the strategy can work. Both of the wizards I knew who used this technique were grand champions of the game."*

"Sure!" Justan said drily. "If you only play against yourself, you're always the grand champion,"

"And most likely crazy," Willum added with a laugh. "Splitting your mind in two?"

Both bound spirits gave him slightly offended looks. Artemus' eyes flashed momentarily black.

Willum shrank back from the wizard's gaze. "Uh, I wasn't talking about you, Master Artemus. I meant in general. You know . . . a wizard playing both sides?" He swallowed, his voice growing softer. "Because, uh . . . how would you know which one of you . . . was the real . . . loser?"

"Ho-Ho! Good job, Willy," said Theodore with a roll of his eyes. *"If you back out of the conversation slowly enough maybe no one will notice."*

"Sorry," Willum replied sheepishly. "Still, whatever your techniques for building the game, Theodore, this night you are going to lose. I believe this will set you!"

He threw down his last card which happened to be the high universal card. This meant that Theodore and Artemus didn't make their bid. Their points had fallen into the negative. Willum and Justan were now just one hand away from victory.

"You know what that means, imp?" Willum said. He looked to Justan. "Theodore and I have a wager going on the outcome of tonight's game."

"Oh?" Justan asked. Willum's wagers with the imp often ended up in Willum having to do some ridiculous stunt for Theodore's amusement. Last time, he had been forced to drink a whole bottle of banana wine at dinner. The poor warrior had spent the evening vomiting into the canal afterwards. "So what happens when we win?"

Willum folded his arms and leaned back into his chair with a smile. "Theodore has to change the walls of this room from smoke into bouquets of pink flowers for a week."

"Ooh. Good one," Justan said approvingly.

"*It would actually be a nice change*," Artemus agreed. "*I have been wondering, Theodore, why do you keep this place so dreary?*"

"*I'm bound here with air and fire*," the imp replied. "*I find it comforting.*"

"*But certainly you could make it more cheery*," the ice wizard suggested. "*Some flames. A warm breeze?*"

"*Ho! And the icy mazes of your world are better?*" Theodore pulled in the cards with a grumble and began to shuffle the deck. His thin lips twisted in irritation, but something occurred to him and his lips slowly unfurled into a grin. "*Ho! I have a question for you, Sir Edge. You and your betrothed have been together for some time. Yes?*"

Justan gave him a cautious frown, not liking where this was headed. "We have been betrothed for a year. But we knew each other sometime before that."

"*Good-good. Because I was wondering if you could give poor Willy some advice*," the imp replied.

"Theodore," Willum warned.

The imp sent an amused sneer Willum's way. "*You see, Willy and Mage Vannya have been spending more and more time together lately and there is quite a bit of friction between the two of them. Sometimes when he's helping her with her experiments, she brushes up against him and there are so many sparks, I fear a fire may start.*"

"I mean it," Willum warned.

"*In Willum's pants*," Theodore continued.

"I don't need to hear this," Justan said with a sigh. "And Willum I hope the best for the two of you. I think it would be great if things worked out."

"*Ho-ho! I don't think that's in doubt*," Theodore replied. "*The truth is, I'm worried about poor Willy's virtue.*"

"Stop," Willum said. "It's not funny."

"*I was wondering, Sir Edge, what's your secret? I've seen*

the way you and Jhonate bin Leeths are around each other. How have you kept your woman's libido at bay so long? Can you give Willy some tips?"

Justan's eyes widened.

Artemus stood. *"That will be enough, imp. I believe you owe both of these young men an apology!"*

"Apologize? Ho-ho! These are things Willy should know. The way that mage keeps throwing herself at him, things could happen any day now." The imp placed both hands on his chest. *"And when that happens, guess who's going to have to be around to witness it."*

"Not if I throw you in a creek first," Willum replied through gritted teeth.

Justan pushed up out of his chair. "Well, that will be enough for us tonight. Artemus?"

The ice wizard gestured and a frost-covered doorway rose from the smoky floor. The door opened and an icy breeze blew into the room. Beyond it a corridor of cool cloud stretched into the distance.

"Ho-ho! Must you go so soon? I was asking for Willy's sake," the imp claimed. *"Maybe you could ask Miss Jhonate what works and let him know?*

"You know why he's doing this, don't you?" Willum asked.

"Oh, I know exactly why," Justan replied. "And I am sorry, Willum, but I am leaving anyway, because I refuse to put up with it."

The imp put on a look of mock sadness and Justan shook his head.

"Think of this, Theodore. You don't have many friends in this world. Why alienate the ones you do have? If you wish us to return, I will expect a full apology." He paused in the doorway and looked back. "Also, to be sure that you are sincere, I'll expect a favor or two."

When the door had shut behind Justan, the doorway faded from existence. The imp shrugged and leaned back in his chair, placing his hands behind his head and plopping his bare feet up onto the table.

"*And that is how you avoid a loss, Willy,*" Theodore said cheekily.

Justan left Willum's tent and stepped into a dark and cloud filled night. A warm wind was blowing, thick with moisture. He sighed. More time had passed than he thought. There had still been some daylight when he had entered the imp's world with Willum.

Hello! Rain is coming, Gwyrtha said cheerfully, padding up to him and nudging him with her toothy snout.

Justan scratched behind her horse-like ears. "Yes. I can smell it."

He glanced over at the tent that Jhonate and Vannya were sharing for the journey. It was dark inside and he did not hear voices. Justan frowned. No one was sitting at the fireside either. Evidently, the warriors had also gone to sleep already.

He walked to his own tent, but did not yet feel tired. He knew Jhonate would want to rise early so that they would reach Stolz' home before noon the following day, but the idea of sleep did not tempt him. Besides, Fist hadn't contacted him yet and Justan wanted to know if there had been an update as to Lyramoor's capture.

If you are not yet ready to sleep, why did you not stay with Willum? Deathclaw asked. The Raptoid was currently on watch, perched high in a magnolia tree. *Your 'game' with his imp did not go well?*

It went about as well as I hoped, Justan replied. *Actually, I would say that Theodore was a gentleman for far longer than I expected.*

If that is what you expected, why go? Artemus asked with curiosity.

Justan shrugged. *Everyone deserves a chance. Besides, Willum is a friend and his relationship with that imp seems to be one that will be around awhile.*

If that is the case, why did you leave? Deathclaw said. *Were the things the imp said to you so upsetting?*

Justan smirked. So the raptoid had already known the answer to his question before he asked it. Deathclaw was always listening more closely than he let on.

I am not so thin skinned as that. Though he had to admit to himself that the imp's unexpected personal attack had pushed his buttons a bit. *The thing is, Theodore needs to learn. He and Willum do not have the advantages that we do through the bond. It's not so easy for Willum to teach him humanity. Therefore, the imp will need to learn from trial and error. If he was to get away with all his antics he would see no need to change.*

You never change, Justan. You always try to make others become more human, the raptoid observed.

I've never tried to make anyone human. Humanity is full of flaws. It's about helping people become better, Justan said.

And what makes you so certain that the way you would have people do things is better? Deathclaw pressed.

Justan thought about that question for a moment. Was he being arrogant in assuming that his way of thinking was better than anyone else's? *I just go by what I feel is right. Do you think that the way I go about it is wrong?*

Deathclaw was silent as he considered his response. *I do not know. But I do think it is what makes you an effective pack leader.*

Justan blinked. *Did you just give me a compliment? Why, thank you, Deathclaw. That means a lot coming from you.*

Justan had just about decided it was best to go to bed anyway when the rain began to fall. He heard it before it came, a dull roar coming in from the east, but he didn't have time to enter his tent. As seemed standard in Malaroo when the rain fell, it fell hard. He was soaked through almost instantly. Justan's shoulders slumped.

I have an idea of something you might do, Artemus offered.

Will it somehow make me dry so I don't soak my bedroll trying to get inside my tent? he moped.

Perhaps not, my boy, Artemus replied. *But you may find it useful. I have been giving some thought to your current breakthroughs with your understanding of how your swords' magic works.*

Okay, Justan said, wondering where the wizard was going with this.

Well, as we were in the imp's realm I was pondering the different ways in which he and I have used our abilities to affect the nature of the worlds we inhabit, Artemus said, and Justan was pleased to hear him sounding suddenly like a Mage School teacher at a lectern rather than a despondent old man. *It occurred to me that as much as you have been focusing on the powers of your left sword, you have spent little time thinking on the ways you could use your right sword.*

I suppose that's because it has always seemed pretty simple. Rage stores the feelings that Peace absorbs and stores them as energy. Justan paused to wipe the water out of his eyes. The rain really was coming down hard. *Is this idea of yours something I can do inside the tent?*

No. Actually, I think this deluge may prove most beneficial to this experiment, the wizard said to Justan's disappointment. *You see, what Rage is doing with those emotions is converting them to pure energy much like the energy you withdraw from Gwyrtha.*

Justan suddenly became excited by the concept. *Do you mean to say that I could pull energy from the sword in the same way I pull it from her?*

I-I did not, but . . . well, actually perhaps you could at that. I did not think of that application. Good for you, my boy, Artemus said appreciatively. *No, the thing that occurred to me was that while Peace is a sword whose use involves spirit magic, Rage's ability is elemental based. The explosion that is released when the sword expends the energy it has stored is a pure burst of air magic.*

Huh, said Justan. *I didn't think about it that way.*

Nor had I until earlier while in the imp's domain. Several things pricked my mind. One of them was when I noticed that the makeup of his world was much more stable than the world I inhabit within your scar.

It is? Justan asked.

Yes. You see, it takes a constant stream of power, almost the entirety of both of our magical talents, to create the domain in which I reside as well as to keep the elemental from escaping. The magic you use for defensive purposes or to heal your bonded comes from Gwyrtha's energy.

You're kidding, Justan said. *How have I not noticed that?*

I didn't notice, Gwyrtha offered.

Like your sword Rage, your body automatically converts her energy into elemental magic that you can use. Unfortunately when we bonded, you didn't have Gwyrtha. So when I set up my spell, the only thing I allowed it to let through was defensive magic. If not for the interference of my rather hastily concocted spell, her energy would give you all the magic you need to use your spells offensively.

Is there a way to reverse that? Justan wondered. *Redo the spell in a more efficient manner?*

I'm afraid not, Artemus said with a mental wince. *As far as I can tell, that is. It would require undoing the spell altogether and quite frankly since I have been removed from the place of my demise, I do not know that I would remain tethered to this world long enough to cast a more efficient version. I am still giving it some thought, though. The more time I am spending awake while the elemental slumbers, the more my faculties seem to be returning.*

I see, Justan said.

However, what I have discovered may very well be the next best thing, the ice wizard said with an attempt at enthusiasm. *You see, I considered the similarities between the way you convert Gwyrtha's energies and the way Rage converts emotion and an idea occurred to me. What if you could enter your bond with Rage and change the elemental aspect of the energy it converts?*

Justan squinted. *You mean I could make it do something different than an explosion of air?*

Exactly, my boy! The explosion of air is quite effective in most cases, but have there not been times where your intention might not be to simply cause the largest amount of damage possible? With enough practice, you could use the sword to emit a halo of frost or perhaps simply light a fire. These are things that are not currently possible to you without offensive magic.

Really? Justan said, a smile spreading on his face as he warmed up to the idea. *But wouldn't the spell that keeps you in my scar hamper that use of magic as well?*

That is one beautiful thing about it! Since you are expending the sword's charged energy instead of bringing it into your body first, it works around my spell.

"And we already know it will work because it makes explosions now!" Justan said aloud, then shut his mouth, not wanting to wake the others.

Ah, wizard, said Deathclaw to Artemus. *Finally I see a sound contribution you make to the pack. I can understand why Justan does not simply wish to do away with you.*

Uh, thank you, Deathclaw, Artemus said. *I think.*

No longer at all worried about the rain, Justan stepped a short distance away from the camp, his mind full of possible applications for this new way of using Rage's power. He drew his swords and, though he now had the ability to halt his left sword's magic, he let Peace drain all his emotions and discomfort away. His mind cleared, allowing him to focus on the task at hand. He held Rage out in front of him.

Alright, so how should I go about this? Justan wondered.

It should work much like the way I used to use my bond with my dagger. You just won't be bringing your own magic through. Artemus had shown Justan many such memories while helping him manipulate his bond with Peace. *Reach through your bond with the sword and focus on the magic it has stored up.*

Justan did as he suggested, closing his eyes and sending a tendril of thought through the bond. Then, similarly to the way he looked into the bodies of his bonded, he looked into the makeup of the sword.

He could see it now, a swollen mass of pure energy contained within the sword as if it were a full bladder. He could feel that Rage yearned to release it. Justan followed the flow of magic through to the trigger point, to the place where Rage was able to convert that energy into an explosion of air and release it through the blade.

He focused in closer and, to his surprise, there was a sort of mechanism in place. The best way he could visualize it was like a series of four crystals whose colors represented the different elements. Right now, the air crystal was the only one in use.

He opened his eyes back up to the deluge of rain. He had a better understanding of the sword's process now. "Okay, what should I try first?"

Because of the rain, I felt a halo of ice would be a good simple spell to use, Artemus suggested. *This should give us a visual idea of how well it works*.

That's not such a simple spell, Justan replied. Using a pure mix of two complimentary elements like air and water was actually quite difficult. It also didn't help that Justan had never been able to practice offensive spells before.

Difficult for most wizards, but not for us, Artemus assured him. *Remember, you were born with this mix of power. The important thing is that it is a simple equation for the sword to implement. Equal amounts of air and water released at the same time. Try to focus the power through the tip of the blade if you can*.

Justan took a deep breath and focused. As he had learned to do with Peace, he sent a mental image of what he wanted Rage to do. He would have it hold back a bit, just using a third of the power it had stored. The sword's answer was eager acceptance.

You realize I'm not going to be able to see anything in this darkness, Justan said.

You'll be able to see what you need to see, Artemus assured him. *You'll primarily be using your mage sight*.

Justan nodded. Focusing further, he slowed the world around him until he could feel each individual raindrop hit his skin and hear each pat. To his mage sight, the world had a very slight blue tone.

"Here we go," he said and triggered the release.

The resulting spell was larger than he expected. A wave of frost shot from the tip of the sword in a conical shape, instantly freezing every drop of ice in its wake. It continued for thirty yards in front of him before fizzling out.

For one brief moment it was as if he saw through a window into the middle of a raging blizzard. Then the moment ended and the ice fell to the ground, quickly melting in the warm falling rain.

"It worked!" Justan said aloud and would have laughed if not for Peace's power. He shut off the emotional drain of the sword so he could enjoy his success.

Impressive, Deathclaw sent from a spot in the treetops not far from him.

It got cold real quick, Gwyrtha agreed. *But now it's not.*

Wonderful, my boy! Artemus said.

What should we try next? Justan wondered.

Perhaps more of the same, the ice wizard suggested. *Spells are best learned by repetition.*

Justan was eager to try everything he could think of, but the wizard had a point. In many ways, working magic was like training sword forms. It was best to build upon experience.

"Were you trying to usse that power on me, Ssir Edge?" asked a raspy voice to Justan's right.

Justan swung around, pointing his sword in the direction of the voice, chills running up his spine. "Talon?"

"My mussk sshould have made me impossible to detect," Talon replied, her voice so soft it was hard to hear over the rain.

Gwyrtha let out a low growl and ran over to Justan, standing between him and the raptoid. *I kill her?*

Wait-wait. Don't attack yet, Justan sent. *Wait to see if she makes a move.*

Finally, he saw her. To his mage sight, the faint droplets of blue were disrupted by her cloaked shape. He prepared his sword to act again. Perhaps that freeze spell would disable her long enough for him to stab her with Peace and discover her true intentions.

Deathclaw leapt to the ground not far from them and darted over. His sword drawn and full of the power that came to the blade at night. "Did you come here to fight, sister?"

Justan had similar thoughts. Was she here in revenge for

the mental pain he had inflicted upon her at their last meeting? He had hoped the understanding that had come between them at their last meeting would have changed her. But they had been interrupted before he could discover just how much of their shared experience had helped. "Why are you here, Talon?"

There was a crash in the bushes behind Talon's dark form as Durza tripped forward in her soaked dress. "We is here, 'cuz the Master sended us!"

"Master?" said Deathclaw suspiciously.

"Matthew sent you?" Justan asked. That mysterious prophet was the man who most recently had borne that title in Talon's memories.

"Yes! Yes! The Stranger man," Durza agreed.

Talon hissed. "He sendss uss to bring you to him. He wishess to talk."

Justan lowered his sword slowly.

Deathclaw approached his sister with a questioning chirp. He leaned in close to her cowl cautiously, his tongue flickering out of his mouth as he breathed in deeply to taste the air around her. "You smell different. Are you still broken?"

She chirped back at him and pulled back her cowl, letting the rain fall directly on her scaled head. "I feel . . . thingss. Thingss hurt that I do not like."

"Are you still broken?" Deathclaw repeated with a hiss.

Her shoulders trembled. She reached out towards him. He backed away and raised his sword between them, but she stepped slowly towards him and at the last moment, he directed the tip of the blade away from her heart. It scored her side, tearing her cloak and igniting the wound with a light that flared in the night, exposing the sorrow in her eyes.

Talon fell forward, wrapping her arms around her brother. "I am ssorry, Deathclaw. Ssooo ssorry!"

Deathclaw's body went rigid and he held his sword out over the barb of her tail, just in case this was a deception. Justan felt a confusing mix of emotions coming through the bond. What was this change? Was she more broken than ever?

"Don't worry 'bout her," Durza said, patting Justan's arm. "Talon's like this sometimes now, but not as much though. The Master says she's gettin' better. He thinks you doned a good job."

Justan wasn't so sure. Talon had gone from seeing human emotions as something alien, a curiosity to be torn apart and played with, to being overwhelmed by the understanding he had shown her at their last meeting. Sure she seemed repentant now, but considering all the horrors she had committed in the past, he wondered if it was possible for her to be reformed.

"So, you come with us now?" Durza asked.

Justan could smell the gorc's intense perfume despite the downpour. Why hadn't Deathclaw and Gwyrtha been able to sense her? Talon had mentioned something about a musk.

"We already have something to do," Justan said suspiciously. "Your master will have to wait."

"Noo. You must come now. It is big big important!" she pleaded.

"Yess," said Talon, regaining control of herself. She let go of Deathclaw and pulled the cowl back over her head, paying no mind to the shallow wound in her side that now glowed with small coals. If not for the drenching rain, her cloak would have caught fire. "You musst not delay. Timing iss important."

Justan frowned. Matthew was one of the prophets, a servant of the Creator. As such, it would normally be important that his requests be given priority.

However, the first time Justan had seen him, John had told Matthew he was under condemnation. His capture by Aloysius and his army seemed to be proof of that. Then there was his strange appearance at the treaty talks. According to Xedrion, he had led the gnome warlord safely away, leaving the rest of them to fight for themselves.

This is a strange gray area, Artemus agreed. *Follow your instincts. The Bowl chose you because it trusted you to make the right decisions.*

Great, Justan responded. He addressed Talon. "Is Matthew still a prisoner of Aloysius?"

Neither of them replied right away.

"Just cooooome," Durza begged. "You will see."

"He will have to wait," Justan decided. "We must first see Stolz."

"Stulls?" Durza asked. "You mean the man that makes those ugly fish that the weirdies like to eat?"

Deathclaw cocked his head. "He does make those strange fish that eat troll flesh."

"He is a nice man. He feeded us sometimes," Durza replied. "We camed from that way." She shook her head sadly. "He was not there. It stinked like the smell of the monster that lives under the swamps."

When the group arrived at the edge of the marshes that next morning, they discovered that Durza was right.

Stolz's home was empty and there were conflicting signs as to whether he had left of his own will. The house was a mess, something that Jhonate assured Justan was common, but there was an uneaten plate of food on his table that was covered in maggots. This suggested not only that he had been gone for some time, but that he hadn't known he wouldn't be returning.

Outside the house, next to the open marshes, were the vats where he had kept his fish. They had been left overturned and empty. It was as if the old man had given up his plans to purify the swamp and had just set the fish free. There had been quite a disagreement as to what this meant.

"I think he got eated," Durza said sadly, looking out over the marsh pond in front of his house. "The monster that lives under the swamps has comed all the way out here. It wants to eat us right now."

"What do you mean?" Vannya asked, approaching the gorc with her notepad in hand. She had been fascinated by the idea of a goblinoid with bewitching magic. "Do you have a way to sense it?"

Durza eyed her warily. "I doesn't know you."

"Oh, I'm Vannya," the mage said, holding out her hand. "I

like your dress."

Durza frowned, looking down sadly at the state of the garment. The gorc's dress had once been a light blue but was now a tattered brown. "It was pretty one time."

"Would you like me to clean it up for you?" Vannya asked.

Durza smiled, but took a cautious step back. "I can't take it off now. Don't gotta 'nother one," she said, then whispered, "That'd make me noood."

"You won't need to. Watch," Vannya said and reached out to touch the top of the gorc's matted wig.

A shimmer of air magic floated down the gorc's body and all dirt and gunk fell away from her, sliding into a circular pile around her feet. The filthy wig on her head was still just as matted, but it was now its original brilliant blond, while her ragged dress was a soft blue again.

Durza's eyes widened. "You dood that with wizardy magic!"

"That's right. I'm a mage," Vannya replied. "Can you now tell me what you were talking about before?"

"Talon! Look!" Durza bellowed and ran across the bank, leaving Vannya with a scowl. "My dress is pretty again now!"

Talon and Deathclaw were standing apart from everyone else. Deathclaw had his sword at the ready, on guard in case Talon should change and become her old self again. The two of them spoke occasionally, sometime letting out hesitant chirps. Justan could feel that Deathclaw was unhinged about the situation. He had been communicating with his sister all morning and still wasn't sure of her sanity.

Durza came up to them to exclaim over the restored beauty of her dress and Vannya followed her, determined to get answers. Justan stood by Jhonate and watched their interaction with an uneasy feeling in his stomach. He still wasn't sure what he should do.

"What is your plan, younger sister?" Qurl asked Jhonate, reminding her that he was still irritated that she had been given command over the mission above him. "Do we wait for Stolz to return?"

Jhonate frowned. "I am not certain that is a good idea. Look out at the water, Qurl. What do you see?"

He shrugged. "It is like the rest of the swamp."

"It wasn't this way the last time I was here," Jhonate replied. "His fish had cleaned the area of slime. The water was brown instead of green. Now slime clings to the reeds along the bank's edge and the air smells of trolls. I think the gorc is right. The behemoth has made its way under these waters."

Me too, said Gwyrtha. *This place smells like that big thing.*

"Gwyrtha agrees," Justan told them. "Waiting here is probably a bad idea. It could attack at any moment."

"Then why has it not?" Jhonate wondered. "What is it that makes the behemoth decide when to attack? Stolz lived here on the borders of the swamp for decades. If it did attack him, why now?"

Justan rubbed his chin. That was a good question. What was the motivation of this Troll Mother?

She is a troll behemoth, said Artemus. *Perhaps her motivations are just those of a troll. Devour and devour. It is very possible that the whole reason she has been changing her habits of late has been Mellinda's doing. That explains its uncharacteristic attack at the treaty signing.*

It could be, Justan said, though he wasn't so sure.

"We really should have brought Tarah Woodblade with us," Willum suggested. "She would have been able to tell us what Stolz was thinking before he disappeared and if the thing did attack him she might have been able to tell us what its reasons were."

Jhonate nodded. "Then that is what we must do. We will return to Roo-Tan'lan swiftly and bring her back with us. Everyone! Do not touch anything!"

Justan thought back to the day of the Troll Mother's attack. He had sliced parts of the behemoth with Peace and destroyed parts of her with Rage. Never did he receive any feeling or emotion from the flesh he was cutting. He doubted that Tarah would be able to glean anything about the behemoth's thoughts either.

He frowned as he made a decision. He knew who might

have answers.

"Hey!" Vannya ran up to them, smiling and dragging Durza by the hand. "You should hear this. Tell them, Durza. Tell them what you can do."

The gorc's eyes darted around at each of them. "I has witchy witch magic."

"And?" Vannya said with a nudge. "Tell them why the 'monster' isn't attacking us right now."

"I telled it we ain't here," Durza replied.

"You spoke to the behemoth?" Jhonate asked, suddenly interested.

Durza wrinkled her nose. "Huh?"

"I don't think she meant she actually had a conversation with it," Justan explained. "She has bewitching magic. Not bonding magic. Durza, how did you tell it we aren't here?"

"Uh. I just used my witchy stuff and I telled it we ain't nothin'" Durza replied. She waved her hands out in front of her. "We's just air."

Qurl put a hand to his forehead. "It has to be some variation of the magic Roo-Dan witches use to try and sneak by our patrols. Can you imagine if we had known this before? Our witches could have saved so many lives."

Jhonate's back straightened. "Very well. We are taking her with us. She can teach our witches how to do this spell."

"Sorry, No!" Durza said with a shake of her head. "I gots to go back to Master!"

Jhonate's jaw clenched and Justan knew that she was about to put her foot down. At the same time, he saw that Talon had heard the gorc's exclamation. She was ready to leave Deathclaw's side and head straight for them. If he didn't do something fast, there was about to be a confrontation.

He cleared his throat. "Durza is right. She can't go to Roo-Tan'lan."

Jhonate gave him a sideways glance. "Why not?"

Justan thought quickly. "Durza, who taught you how to use your magic to hide from the troll behemoth?"

"My Master," she replied.

He nodded. "Jhonate, I am going with Talon and Durza to speak with the Stranger. I have a feeling he has the answers to many of our questions. If you were to try and take Durza back with you, he might not be very understanding. She is his servant."

Jhonate pursed her lips, searching him with her eyes. Her voice came to him through his Jharro ring. *Why are you doing this?*

It is the only way, he replied, grateful she was communicating this way instead of arguing in front of the others. *Matthew will know more about the situation. I could come back with valuable information that will help your people in the war.*

It could be a trap, she reminded him. *The last time he was seen, he was helping the enemy.*

I know. They had already had that particular conversation earlier that morning. *But Talon is certain that he had a good reason for doing so. We are dealing with one of the prophets, remember?*

While they were talking, Poz returned from inspecting behind the house. He walked up to the group and saw everyone watching Justan and Jhonate. "Hey, there was nothing for me to find back there, uh . . . what are you two doing? Staring contest?"

Jhonate raised a palm in front of the Academy graduate's face.

"They are talking through that Jharro ring," Qurl explained, folding his arms.

"Oh," he said embarrassedly. "Sorry."

Then I am coming with you, Jhonate decided.

Justan shook his head slightly. *You can't. Talon said that he requested me and my bonded only. Besides, you are the Protector's daughter. If Aloysius is there, you can't be seen as negotiating with the enemy behind his back. I, however, am just a dry foot.*

Her eyes narrowed. *Father may be furious with you.*

He sometimes starts out that way, but he always sees reason, Justan said. After a second thought, he qualified that statement. *Usually. One more thing, I don't think it's a good idea for you to return here with or without Tarah Woodblade. You can see what Xedrion wants to do, but if Durza wasn't with us that behemoth very well might be trying to swallow us now.*

Frowning, Jhonate nodded and said aloud to the group, "We will leave the gorc with Sir Edge and his bonded. The rest of us will return and report to my father what we found here. Maybe we can take what Durza told us and see if our witches can figure out how to reproduce it."

Begrudgingly, she sent, *It is a good thing I love you.*

And I you, Justan replied.

Chapter Eighteen

. . . A buzzing sound filled the air. Palky couldn't move. He was frozen there, on his hands and knees in the dark. He could breathe, but that was it. Blast it, not again! He'd been so careful. What had he done? What kind of trap had he tripped?

"Hoo-wee! We got us somethin' boys!" shouted a rough voice.

It was still completely dark inside the cave, but Palky heard the distant stomping of heavy feet. A light flared somewhere behind him. To his surprise, he was staring right at a large hairy leg that was tipped with an enormous set of claws.

"Whoa ho ho!" the rough voice laughed. "What the hell's he doin' here? Donjon, go get yer daddy. Tell him that Palky's escaped again and that he durn near got himself et!"

Palky recognized that voice now. It was Whian Dill, one of the meanest of the dwarves that owned him. His heart hammered in his chest. Palky knew that whatever happened to him next wasn't going to be pleasant.

"Yes, boss!" said the younger dwarf and Palky heard him stomp away.

Whian walked up behind Palky, the light in the cave growing brighter with each step. The dwarf launched a kick into Palky's buttocks, causing him to pitch forward onto his face. Without any way to break his fall, he smacked his nose onto a rock right next to that fearsome hairy paw.

"Yer a gall-ram idjit, Palky! I know we raised you to be stupid, but this has got to be yer worst escape attempt yet!" The dwarf grasped Palky by the back of his ragged shirt and yanked him up into the air.

The thick dwarf was able to lift him easily. Palky was light for an elf his age. Though he was fifteen years old, he only weighed a slim hundred pounds. Self-imposed starvation was one of his few ways to rebel.

The collar of his shirt digging into his throat, Palky found himself face-to-face with a fearsome visage. It was an enormous beast with thick sloping horns and fangs that protruded from the side of its mouth. As blood dripped from his nose, Palky wished the thing had eaten him.

"Dunno how you got outta yer cage, but only you would be dumb enough to run yerself right into the cave of an oxbear! If we hadn't've been settin' traps fer the thing ourselves, youd've been dinner!" Whian mocked.

The dwarf threw Palky over his wide shoulder like a bony sack of flour with legs and trotted to the cave mouth. Palky's mind worked hard on his current problem, trying to come up with a way out. Unfortunately, the dwarves' paralyzing spells were just too effective. He could wait for the moment that the spell lapsed and then try and make a run for it. Only, all of the dwarves carried those spell rods in their holsters. He'd just find himself frozen again.

Whian grunted out a laugh as he waited for more dwarves to arrive. "You just wait, Palky. This time Blayne ain't gonna take it easy on you."

Palky would have shivered if he'd had the ability. This would be the tenth time he'd been caught in the act of escaping and each time the punishment had been more severe. There was only one time he had gotten farther. Two years ago he had spent ten glorious days out in the forests of Razbeck before they had found him.

That was the time Blayne had decided it wasn't worth keeping Palky pretty anymore. He was far too aggressive for them to sell him as a toy. Besides, elf skin had its own marketplace and they could carve that off a piece at a time. They had spells that would make it grow back, even if it did leave scars.

"If I was a bettin' type, and I am," Whian said as more of

his companions arrived. "I'd say that there's one insistent wizard that's finally gonna get himself that elf ear tip he's been askin' fer."

Whian tossed his glowtorch to one of the four dwarf smugglers that had come up the trail from camp. They were tough, stone-hearted dwarves with handlebar mustache's and wide brimmed hats. Well, except for one.

"How'd he get outta his cage?" wondered Lenui Firegobbler nervously. The dwarf, still young enough that he hadn't grown into his mustache, had only come into the camp with his cousin Donjon a week ago. He'd been the one who'd left the thick wire in Palky's food that had allowed him to pick his lock.

"Don't got no durn idea," Whian said. "But we'll let yer Uncle Blayne worry 'bout that. Here, take him back down and don't friggin' drop him! Idjit's so frail, he likely to break his neck."

"Yes, Boss," Lenui said and laid the elf over his own shoulder.

Whian shouted at the others. "Right! The rest of us'll go get us that oxbear that's frozen inside. It's gonna take us all to haul the thing down to the cages."

Lenui trotted down the slope towards the dwarf camp below. "Dag-gum it, Palky! Blayne'll have my arse fer dinner if he finds out I helped you! Don't you be blabbin'."

Lenui's voice was worried, but he had nothing to worry about. There was no way Palky was blabbing that little secret. If he was lucky, he'd be able to convince the young dwarf to do it again.

"Gonna talk to my momma 'bout this," the young dwarf muttered. "Ain't right. Animals're one thing. But this . . ? Listen, elf. I'll try one more time, but only after Blayne's calmed himself down."

Palky tried to take comfort in that despite the terrible punishment that was about to happen . . .

. . . In the slave markets of the orc city of Khulbath blood slavery was forbidden. Yet those who knew how to look could find it. A hidden corner of the markets where only the darkest and most perverse dared tread.

Now a slave of over two hundred years, Palky was stretched out on display, spread-eagled and immobilized, his arms and legs chained to the wall behind him. His sellers kept him there for one hour each night, naked accept for a gag in his mouth that kept him from shouting obscenities at prospective buyers. His current owners had found it difficult to sell him, not because of his scars or the missing tip of his right ear. It was the unending hatred in his eyes.

One night, a buyer approached and asked for a closer look. He was a tall man with an intense face, his body hidden beneath a gray cloak. The sellers allowed it, but only because interest had been so low.

"What is this slave's name?" he asked them.

"Palky," one seller, an orc who wore a patch over one eye, replied.

The man nodded slowly and walked up close to the elf, inspecting him in the manner of someone well versed in the slave trade. As he did so, he leaned in close. His eyes were kind. "Your name is not Palky. You are Lyramoor of the Pruball Elves. You were stolen long ago, but your people never forgot you. This is your last night as a slave."

With that, Sabre Vlad turned away. He waved a dismissive hand at the sellers. "This one is too damaged for my uses . . ."

He took one step past the disappointed orc. Then in one smooth motion, he drew his sabre and spun, hacking the orc completely in two. Several other nearby sellers cried out in alarm, rousing the guards, but it didn't matter. Vlad was soon joined by other Academy warriors and the members of the Khalpany royal guard that had hired them for this raid.

It was a bloodbath. Some few crafty smugglers got away, but most of them were either cut down or captured by the guards. The black market was shut down. No doubt another one would replace it soon enough, but for this night Khalpany's king could claim a victory.

Palky watched the slavers fall with fevered eyes. He exulted. His moment of freedom was finally at hand, but Sabre Vlad's promise of reuniting the elf with people he didn't remember held no appeal to Palky. What he wanted was this. He wanted to fight . . .

Lyramoor's mind briefly returned to the present. Disoriented, immobilized, and unable to see, he strained and struggled against the soft, but unyielding mass of the clay that surrounded him. Panicking, he hyperventilated, sucking air madly through the tiny hole the golem had left open to his mouth. The clay golem continued on, half rolling, half waddling as it made its slow way through the mountain passes.

Finally, with his body tired, Lyramoor's crazed mind drifted away again. His thoughts flitted back and forth through more of the past horrible memories he'd repressed. There were many. Taken from his people at the age of five, he'd spent near two centuries enslaved. Not all of it had been as awful as that first dwarf camp or that last slave market but some of it had been worse.

In the time he'd spent as a slave, he'd been passed from owner to owner and smuggler to smuggler, all with the same purpose; keeping him alive to harvest his blood magic. In the decades since Sabre Vlad had helped him gain his freedom, his nights were often filled by horrible dreams where he was still a slave. He greeted the rise of each new morning with the same firm thought.

Never again . . .

Cassandra rolled the large stone door to the side and let the misshapen form of the clay golem hobble inside. The magical construct was only half its original size and fit easily into the empty entryway. It was filthy with rocks, twigs, dirt, and other rubbish stuck to it.

She sent a wave of air magic over the thing, causing the

debris to clatter to the floor around it. "Vastyr! Come clean this mess!"

The pampered slave walked over with a sigh and a broom. "Oh, it's back."

"It is," she replied as she urged the golem to make its way through the open doorway.

She had not been pleased with the results of that most recent battle with the ogre tribe. Her golems were powerful creations and should have done much more damage to the tribe. Nevertheless, her plan had worked. The stone golem was to crush and destroy the enemy, creating confusion so that the clay golem could capture its target for her interrogation. There had been a short list. The only question was which target did the golem retrieve? She hadn't been able to tell.

Her connection with the wraith beneath the black lake allowed her control over each and every single larvae it commanded. Unfortunately, despite her centuries of experience in controlling inferior creatures, the Priestess of War did not have the immense mental capacity that the Troll Queen had once commanded. There was no way she could keep track of them all at once.

In addition, their abilities to sense their surroundings were very basic. Though she was able to see some things from the eyes of the dead that the larvae inhabited, it turned out that the dead had horrible eyesight. This was why she had sent her hounds on the previous attack. Perhaps she should have done so again, despite having so few left.

Cassandra guided it to the rear of the great room where her implements of torture were kept. This was going to be fun. Raj rose from his place in front of the fire and paced next to the ponderous golem, sniffing at it as it made its way. A low growl issued from his throat.

"Do you know who it is?" she asked the striped lupero, scratching its head.

Vastyr returned from the entryway and leaned the broom against the wall before retrieving the glass of wine he had left on the fireplace mantle. He took a sip as he watched the clay golem roll up to the wall next to Cassandra's workbench.

Swirling his glass, the elf asked in mild curiosity, "Does it have the wizard?"

"I do not believe so," Cassandra replied. The clay golem had made its capture just before the powerful magical strike that had destroyed the rock golem. That meant it was likely one of the other defenders of the ogre camp.

"What have you brought me? Hmm?" She caressed the outside of the clay golem's structure.

Not the rock giant or the rogue horse. They were too large for the golem's current size. Perhaps the ogre mage or the gnome archer. She hoped it was the gnome archer. Cassandra had always enjoyed the challenge of breaking the mind of a gnome and the warriors were easy to command once they were broken. She would have it firing against its own companions soon enough.

She stretched out her hand and the golem pressed up against the wall, spreading itself out so that the outline of its captive began to show. It was in a fetal position. Too small for the ogre or gnome. So one of the two warriors. Indeed, it still held a sword in one hand.

Cassandra splayed her fingers and pushed out with her palm. The golem responded, the clay contracting as it forced its captive to move. The prisoner was turned to face her, its legs and arms splayed. She swiped her hand to the side and the clay around the captive's face peeled to the side.

"Ah, so it's you," Cassandra said as a scarred and wild-eyed face was revealed. The captive let out the scream of a caged beast, then took deep breaths, his eyes darting around the room.

Raj growled. This was the half-elf that had murdered so many of its pack mates. Cassandra shushed the animal.

"Ugh," Vastyr said dismissively, taking another sip from his wine. "A half-elf. And he's ugly."

"I don't agree," she said, gazing with interest at the ear that was missing its upper half, the chunk out of his left nostril, and the puckered scar that in some ways mirrored her own, stretching from just under his right eye to his upper lip. "He is beautiful. Battle has proven him."

Cassandra switched to mage sight. The half-elf went blurry, making her unable to see anything within him. His sword, though, glowed a dull blue. Interesting. She switched to spirit sight. An earring on his intact ear glowed white and there was something else at his waist. Something distorted by the golem's flesh.

"Who are you?" she wondered.

"I am the one who will kill you," he replied, his lip curled with hatred. "Vampire."

"Me?" she said, her good eye widening slightly in surprise.

"I can see it in you, that elf blood!" he snarled. "It's coursing through your veins. Feeding you. You disgust me."

"Silence!" shouted Vastyr, storming forward. The servant slapped the half-elf across the face. "Don't you dare mock her, you weevil!"

Cassandra grasped Vastyr's robes, jerking him back from the prisoner. "Fool! Remember your place!"

The elf looked down. "Sorry, Priestess. I could not bear to hear this ugly thing speak to you like tha-."

"Enough! Sit. Calm yourself!" she ordered. Obediently, the elf moved to the front of her throne and sat on the rug in front of it, his wineglass held tightly in his lap.

"Yeah, plaything!" said the prisoner, his voice filled with venom. "I see what you are too! An obedient cow. Sit there, content to obey the owner that's eating you alive." Vastyr did not respond and the half elf sneered. "That's right. Chew your cud, you lickspittle!"

Cassandra approached the vociferous prisoner. She was unused to being yelled at, but his insults did not provoke her. They perked her interest. His attitude told her so much about him.

"Can you really see the elf blood in my veins?" she asked softly, leaning in to look at him closer. "Do you have the gift of blood sight? That's rare, even among elves. Is it a remnant of the elven side of your heritage?"

Realizing he had given too much away with his outburst, he clamped his mouth shut. A smile curled the edges of her lips.

259

"Perhaps you are a crusader? One that frees slaves? But if that's the case, what are you doing here in these mountains with a base tribe of ogres?" Sensing what was coming, Cassandra brought up a screen of air just in time to catch the glob of spittle that he spat at her face. She snorted, letting the saliva fall to the floor. "Do you know who I am? Why I'm here?"

He said nothing, simply glaring at her with seething hatred.

"Yes. You know something," she decided.

A suspicion hit her. She made a line with her finger and the clay parted down the center, exposing his torso. He wore scalemail over a light chainmail shirt. A leather weapon sash filled with throwing knives crossed his chest. The armor wasn't magical, but its appearance was quite familiar.

"You are from the Dremaldrian Battle Academy," she decided. "A scout? Here to provide information to the approaching army?"

He said nothing, spitting impotently again. She reached out with blades of air magic and cut the sash from him. The scalemail followed, as did the chain and the undershirt he wore beneath it.

Her breath caught at the sheer number of scars that crisscrossed his body. They exceeded even hers. Even more interestingly, she recognized the nature of many of them.

"No," she said in fascination and her vision switched to blood sight. His body pulsed with life and she knew the truth instantly. "You are no half-elf."

Vastyr stood and looked closer, his eyes widening in sudden understanding. "This is one of the unwilling!"

"Yes. An escaped blood slave, once owned by dwarf smugglers by the look of it," Cassandra said. "How fascinating. To go from that to being trained by the Battle Academy? What a difficult life you must have led."

She ran a fingernail across several of his scars. "Oh, they harvested your skin for potions didn't they? Then instead of healing you with magic, they just sewed you up? Unusual. They must have done that as a punishment. Were you a naughty slave?"

The ex-slave said nothing, but grinned at her wolfishly.

"I'd say you were a repeat escapee. Otherwise this wouldn't have happened." She ran her hand across his chest stopping on a pitted scar where his nipple should have been. "How exotic. And I see you're missing the tip of one ear. I know of a wizard that requests these kinds of parts, but the dwarves usually decline. They don't like to leave their livestock maimed."

The grin remained frozen on his face, but she could tell she had stricken a nerve. This explained his fervor towards Vastyr.

"These other scars, though." Cassandra fingered several thin lines that appeared over the locations of vital organs in his body. "I have many of these types of scars myself. The results of surgeries. And done with practiced hands. Do they mark the locations of magical baubles that you have had implanted? Hmm. Is that why I cannot see inside of you with my mage sight?"

He growled and her grin widened. "My, what a fascinating morsel you are. And to think I was disappointed when you arrived. You are going to tell me so much."

"You ain't learning anything from me!" he vowed. "There ain't a pain you can give me that I ain't felt before a hundred blasted times over. If the dwarves couldn't make me, neither can you! Even your spirit magic won't work on me. It don't matter how strong you are."

"You seem confident," she replied and felt him out with her bewitching magic. Strange. He seemed impenetrable. "So you have baubles for that too. How odd, considering the ban on spirit magic the last two hundred years."

"You think that ban mattered to the dwarf smugglers or the dark wizards that kept me in their dungeons? No, I protected myself from everything," he declared. "Not even your maggots work. My protection keeps your evil magic out. The minute they try to dig into my skin, they can't hear it anymore. They just become regular bugs again. I already tried it out just to make sure."

She didn't let her disappointment show. If he was correct about the nature of his protection, then that was true. Piercing his soul wouldn't matter if the wraith couldn't command the larvae within him. No matter. She could always try throwing him in the lake later. Perhaps the combined attacks of thousands of larvae would be more than his petty defenses could handle.

Besides, that was just one angle. "And what would stop me from simply removing the baubles you so eagerly had implanted?"

"Because when I had 'em put those 'baubles' inside me, I had 'em put 'em in such a way, that it'd kill me if somebody tried to get 'em out." The elf laughed. "But go ahead. I'd rather die than spend this time with you anyway."

Vastyr snorted. "He lies. No one would be that determined. No matter how unwilling!"

"Two hundred years a slave," he said, spitting again, this time in Vastyr's direction. To the servant's disgust, it landed on the hem of his pants. The ex-slave licked his lips. "Never again."

His determination was indeed formidable. Cassandra shook her head. She was confident that she could use her magic to reverse any process that a surgeon could have done. Unfortunately, extracting the devices inside him would be quite difficult if she couldn't decipher where they were in the first place. She had nothing but those scars to guide her and there were so many . . . How clever of him.

"Not all of your baubles are hidden," she said. Her spirit magic showed them clearly. "This one for instance."

Cassandra lashed out with a blade of air and the hoop earring in his pointed ear fell to the floor, cut in half. The magic in the earring fluttered and dissipated, the spirit of the animal bound to it freed. Blood dripped from the slice in his earlobe, running down his shoulder.

The ex-slave slumped in relief. "Thank you! I was worried about that one. Now my friends will think I'm dead. None of 'em will try to come and rescue me." His wolfish grin returned. "And that means I have you all to myself. As soon as I get outta this thing, you're dead."

Cassandra gritted her teeth as she realized that she had indeed played into his hands. To make matters more complicated, the blood dripping from his ear was making her mouth water. She wondered how this driven elf would feel about becoming her blood slave? Perhaps that was why he was provoking her. Maybe he would rather die.

Briefly, she considered it. Having a second slave would be useful. She wouldn't have to worry about over bleeding Vastyr anymore. The unwilling were difficult to deal with, but at least Vastyr wouldn't see him as a rival for her favor.

Sensing Cassandra's hunger, Vastyr came over with a towel to wipe the blood from the ex-slave's chest. He pulled a vial of coagulant from his pocket and rubbed the prisoner's ear with it, stopping the bleeding.

While Vastyr worked, she composed herself.

"There is another bauble. An orb." She stepped closer to her captive and pressed her finger right over the spot where her spirit sight told her it lay. She watched his eyes for a reaction. "If I were to destroy that?"

His grin broadened. "That's the one I really want you to break. Please do it. Kill us all!"

It was likely a bluff, which meant that the orb was quite important after all. Then again, it appeared that she had already done his will by destroying that earring. Cassandra changed her focus away from the mysteries in his body.

"It doesn't matter. The reason I had you brought to me in the first place was for information."

He snorted with confidence. "I already told you I ain't tellin' you nothin'."

"Fool! You are so eager to find ways to defy me that you can't stop yourself from revealing your secrets," Cassandra said with a laugh. "From your attitude I can now safely assume that the Academy and Mage School both know everything that you and your wizard friend have discovered. This means that they know that the wraith's magic is under the Dark Prophet's control. Likely, they also think they know its weakness."

She leaned forward, wanting to see the despair in his eyes. "They know very little. That army of theirs? Three thousand strong? I have that many and more from my own personal army camped in the vast caverns around us. And that doesn't even count the dead and infested, of which there are thousands more.

"As for the paltry number of wizards that the Mage School's new Head Wizard allowed to join the army?" She snorted. "He definitely didn't know who I was when he sent them out. I am the Priestess of War, High Priestess of the Dark Prophet himself! Two hundred years ago I stood alone against the wizards of the entire known lands and watched them tremble. This will be a bloodbath."

The elf's defiance began to deflate. Cassandra smiled as she saw it. His eyes lowered and his face fell, but only briefly.

The ex-slave let out an amused grunt and his eyes met hers again. "Yeah, you were the queen bee back then. But a single dwarf struck you down, didn't he? A lone dwarf with a blacksmith's hammer! Tell me, is that big scar of yours the result of his crackin' your head open, you white-eyed, slag-faced, blood-suckin', dog-mother?"

A snarl rippled her scarred features and she lashed out at him with her elemental magic. She didn't need to see into his body to know how to hurt him. He screamed, his muscles cramping as searing pain rippled through his body.

"Yes!" Vastyr said, the eager grin on his face echoing his look when she drank his blood. "Kill that unwilling monster!"

The Priestess of War didn't let it go that far. She stopped, leaving the ex-slave to slump, his muscles twitching. She let out a slow breath.

"No. Not yet. There is still more he has to tell." She licked her blackened lips and clutched the prisoner's face with one hand, bringing his eyes back up to hers. "You knew who I was before I told you."

He coughed, drool hanging from his lips. Then he laughed. "I got to you, didn't I? You didn't know the Hero of Thunder Gap was a friend of mine!" The ex-slave looked up at her again. His face was red, one of his eyes marred by a burst blood vessel. "Yeah, we know who you are and that army of three thousand you know about? They ain't scared. You're the one who don't know what you're up against."

Cassandra pondered the connotations of that statement. So there was likely another force. One that David's spies had not discovered yet.

She shrugged. It was time to accelerate things then. At their current pace, the Academy army would reach the base of the mountains in two days. Luckily, the weather was in her favor. An early spring heat wave was coming.

Cassandra sent a command out to the wraith under the lake.

"It sounds like I have time to discover the rest of what you know," she said putting together another spell. This one was more complex. Just as painful, but less likely to kill him. "Let's start with your name."

Outside of the building, Lyramoor's screams could not be heard. Even if the sounds of his agony had been able to pierce the thick stone walls, they would have been overwhelmed by the horrendous buzzing that filled the air.

There had been a shifting in the lake's writhing depths. Cracks had appeared all over the surface as thousands upon thousands of larvae pupated. The air became black with flies.

Chapter Nineteen

A cloud of flies poured from the mountain passes, blanketing the villages of the frontier in a miasma of anger and sorrow. In its adult form, the wraithflies were less efficient at transmitting the Black Lake's rage than the larvae. But that mattered little when dozens of them coated every surface. There was no escaping the magic.

The Academy army had been prepared for this eventuality. The Mage School had very few wizards with any spirit magic at this point, but they had sent along a handful of students with bewitching talents. Mistress Sarine had taught them how to make simple charms with bewitching magic that could help keep the negative effects of the flies at bay. The students had spent the entire journey so far making them and every leader in the army wore them.

Nevertheless, the swarm was greater than expected. Flies blanketed the army and antagonized every unprotected soldier. The wizards were able to destroy large numbers of them with various spells and wards, but that was only partially effective.

The flies laid eggs everywhere they went. The army's wagons of stores were protected by magical barriers, but the rations carried by individual soldiers along with the horses they rode on were vulnerable. Inevitably, signs of infestation began to be exhibited by the men. The army was slowed as fights broke out.

This is where Alfred's presence within the army proved invaluable. Through messages relayed from Wizard Beehn, the gnome warrior and bonding wizard had been able to teach the wizards how to treat anyone infested with larvae without damaging them severely. Those wearing bewitching charms were tasked with isolating anyone showing symptoms and the wizards were kept busy delivering shock treatments.

Despite the setbacks and low morale the army persevered, pressing forward up the mountain slopes and towards the passes where the true battle would take place.

The Thunder People's territory was overwhelmed.

Fist and Locksher had begun to worry when they first sensed that the weather was unseasonably warm. The wizard had already set wards over the tribe's stores, but they were completely unprepared for what happened next.

The scouts heard it first. A fierce buzzing unlike any they had ever known. The alarm was raised. The defenses were set.

The swarm came through the pass like the dark clouds in Fist's dreams. Panic set in immediately as ogres ran covered in flies that diffused anger to their susceptible minds. To Fist's spirit sight it was as if the sky was black with the dark threads connecting the swarm to the wraith beneath the lake. He could feel their anger battering against the protection of the bond.

Fist called for the defenders to fall back. He set up a crackling field of electricity to cover their retreat. Thousands of flies fell crackling and burning to the ground, but thousands more flew around or over it. He leapt onto Rufus's back, sending vibrating strands of air and earth all around them as he rode among the ogres, urging them back towards the camp.

The flies beat them there. The ogre encampment became an open brawl. The ogres battled each other, regardless of gender or previous tribal affiliations. The Black Lake's directive was clear. Fight. Hate. Consume.

The Big Cave became their refuge. Locksher set up an intense sparkling ward across the entrance. As the ogres ran inside, the flies on their bodies were electrocuted. It was a painful process, as the electrical energies passed through the ogres' bodies as well.

The moment they breached the magical wall, their wits returned to them. Ogres collapsed to the ground, weeping, their fists and mouths covered with the blood of their friends. Their fellow tribesmen grabbed onto them and pulled them further inside so that others could pass through.

Locksher, Maryanne, and Qenzic stayed inside the cave, treating injuries and helping Crag and Old Falog in directing the ogres where to go to best utilize the space. The cave had once been large enough for the entire tribe to enter easily, often sleeping close to each other during the coldest of winter nights. That was no longer the case. Their numbers had tripled since the war.

Fist and his bonded stayed outside in the swarm, helping Charz to break up fights and herd the raging ogres through the magical barrier. It wasn't an easy task. Fist had to constantly pull energy from Rufus so that he could keep a constant stream of electrical shocks going to move the fighters forward.

The rock giant, his bond making him immune to the flies effects, dragged the ogres bodily. Often he would simply punch ogres unconscious and throw them through. He had the most difficulty at the womens' caves, where many of the ogresses had fled deep inside and had to be carried out.

Rufus followed the giant's lead and worked in concert with Squirrel. Squirrel would zap the enraged ogres and Rufus, grown three times his normal size, would shove them through. The four of them worked throughout the afternoon, saving everyone they could. When they finally came in, exhausted as the sun was setting, the situation was grim.

Too many ogres had been lost. Not so many had died in the fighting, but a great many had run screaming into the mountains where they couldn't be found. Others had simply run off the cliff's edge at the rear of the territory. All said, two in ten were lost.

Fist walked out of the swarm and through the knee-high pile of dead flies in front of the wards to find the Big Cave crammed full of anxious and mourning ogres. Crag had found ways to make more room, sending the women into the old giant spider den that Mog had claimed as his home. The smaller ogres and children were told to climb up to places in the upper reaches of the cave that hadn't been in use since the goblins controlled the place.

Despite Crag's efforts, there wasn't enough room for

everyone to lay down. But when Fist made his way to the rocky outcropping where his friends sat, the ogres made room for him to collapse. Squirrel, just as exhausted, crawled into his pouch to sleep.

Noting the lack of room in the cave, Rufus shrunk himself down to the size of a large dog and promptly fell asleep at their feet. Fist thought the fierce rogue horse looked quite different in this small form. It was as if it brought out more of his true nature. He looked innocent. Gentle, even.

Maryanne scooted over so that Fist could rest his head on her lap. She ran her hand through his hair. "Things look pretty grim right now."

"I dreamt this. The cloud of flies," Fist said, thinking of the image of Crag bruised and bloodied, fighting the storm. "But I didn't imagine how bad it would be."

"What do we do now?" Qenzic asked. The Academy Graduate was holding Lyramoor's pendant in his hand. The quartz crystal had shattered the day before and he felt a deep amount of guilt over rejecting any attempt at rescue.

Locksher reached out and patted the warrior's shoulder. Keeping up the electrical field was a drain on the wizard's magic, but Locksher had once again showed his remarkable ingenuity. He had charged some rocks with earth and air magic and was using them to feed the field, leaving the drain on his powers to a trickle. If his power became too low, he could show Fist how to add to the rocks charge and keep things going.

"For now, I'd say we wait and hope that this is the worst of it. In the meantime, I shall try to devise a more efficient method of dispersing these flies," the wizard said. "We just have to hold out two more days. Then the army will arrive and the real battle will begin."

"Maybe we'll get some good news before then," Maryanne said, also watching Qenzic. He wasn't the only one who was taking Lyramoor's loss hard. Charz had gone into a rage when the warrior had told him. She looked down at Fist, stroking the tender-hearted ogre's cheek.

"I just watched Drog run off the cliff," Fist said softly.

"Remember Drog?"

"Yeah," she said. He was a tall ogre, formally of the fire tribe. He had traveled with them all the way from the Mage School. "I'm sorry. Drog was a good ogre."

"I didn't know him very well, but . . . I didn't find Burl," he realized. He sat up and yelled out to the rest of the cave. "Has anyone see Burl?"

There was a sea of sullen heads shaking.

"No, Big Fist!" shouted Old Falog. "He did not come in!"

"What're you so worried about him for?" Qenzic asked, his voice tinged with despair. "You never liked him."

"Maybe not, but he is my brother," Fist replied. Burl had been with the Dark Prophet's army during the war and had returned with a chainmail shirt and an ogre-sized sword for his efforts. It had taken some time for Fist to trust him, but lately he had begun to realize that Burl had the qualities in him that could make for a decent leader once Crag had gone.

"I had him helping me when the swarm first came," Fist said. He stood. "I need to try and find him."

Maryanne grabbed his arm. "You're exhausted. You've been using your magic all day. You need to sleep."

"Clear the damned way!" shouted a loud voice.

The wards flashed brightly as Charz pushed into the cave, dead flies falling in a cascade around him. Burl was lying over his shoulder. Charz laid him on the ground and when he stood, Fist realized that Burl's longsword was sticking out of the giant's chest.

"He had it bad," Charz said, wincing, blood running from his lips. "Couldn't knock him out easily. I had to bust him up good."

Fist pushed his way to the giant. He crouched next to Burl's unconscious form. Charz hadn't been joking. Burl's face was one solid bruise. He had to pull more energy from Rufus's depleted stores so that he could work on healing him.

Maryanne approached, looking at the sword sticking out of the giant. "We should get that sword out of you."

Charz grasped the blade and attempted to pull, but the

sword barely moved. He grimaced. "Blasted body's healed itself around the thing. Here. Feelin' kinda weak. You give it a tug. You got better leverage than me."

"Alright," the gnome said. She gripped the sword's handle and lifted one long leg, putting her foot next to the wound. "Ready?"

"I wasn't talking to you, Maryanne," Charz said with a wince. "Put your leg down. Crag's standin' right behind you."

"I will get it, skinny women," Crag agreed.

She gave Charz a deep scowl.

The giant noticed the look. "Don't bother gettin' mad at me. This really hurts! It ain't my fault you're a-."

Maryanne jumped up, placed her feet on either side of the wound, and pulled, gripping the sword handle with both hands. The giant grunted in pain as the sword budged a little, then caught again. She strained and it finally slid out with an accompanying rush of blood.

"There! Don't you ever imply I can't handle something just 'cause I'm a woman or so help me, I'll shove this thing right back in!" she snapped. Her eyebrows rose as she noticed that the last full third of the massive sword was slick with blood. "Wow, this was in there deep. What was it? Stopped up against your spine?"

Charz's eyes rolled up into his head and he fell backwards. The electric wards rippled and flashed as he lay there with his head halfway outside the cave. His arms and legs twitched. Several ogres hurriedly grabbed him. Grimacing as the electricity shocked them too, they pulled his heavy body inside. His mouth lay open, his eyelids fluttering.

"I think he was gonna say, it wasn't his fault 'you're a gnome'," Fist said, looking up from Burl's now much less swollen face.

"He does have a point, Maryanne," Locksher agreed. "Please understand, if I wanted someone filled with arrows, I would go to you first above anyone else I know. But when it comes to pulling swords out of rocks? I'd go with an ogre."

The gnome pursed her lips, but finally nodded. She looked down at the fallen giant. "Fine. I'll accept that Crag is physically

271

stronger than me. Okay? Uh . . . he's still out." She nudged Fist with her foot. "He's gonna be okay, right?"

Fist turned away from his brother to get a better look at the giant. Blood was still pouring from the wound, though just at a trickle. Fist knelt next to him and sent his magic into his chest. "Charz will heal up from pretty much anything, but-. Ooh, I guess that sword was really close to his heart."

Maryanne's hand flew to her mouth. "Oh!"

Fist looked closer just to make sure. "But . . . the artery's healed up now. Everything's closing on its own like normal. I think he fell asleep, actually."

She smacked him upside the head. "Don't scare me like that!"

"Sorry," he said.

"What we do now?" shouted Momma Zung from the rear of the cave.

"When we can go out?" asked another ogre.

Fist stood and turned to face them. "We'll wait until morning and see if the flies are still as bad. Then we'll decide what to do next. I'm sure we'll be fine."

The ogres nodded, grumbling in appreciation at Fist for speaking up.

"I think so too!" said Crag, raising his fist into the air. "The evil tried to kill the Thunder People today, but it did not! In two more mornings we will kill it with the armies of Fist's tribe!"

The ogres erupted into roars of agreement. There was much exulting and clapping of backs. It would only be later as they tried to sleep that they would remember the sorrow of friends lost.

Fist left them to their rejoicing and returned to the shelf where Locksher and Qenzic sat. Once again, he lay back. Exhaustion rolling over him. "So tired."

Maryanne, who had returned with him, looked down at Rufus laying there on his back snoring with his rear legs sticking up in the air. She clasped her hands together. "Aww, he looks cute when he's small like that. It makes me want to cuddle him. Fist, you should make him sleep small like that every night."

"I hate to ruin your mood," Qenzic interjected, his expression still as dour as it had been earlier. "But what if the Priestess of War decides to send another attack against us in the morning? Stuck in here, we'd have no warning until they were upon us. How would we mount a defense crammed in here?"

"I agree that we are in a difficult situation," Locksher agreed. "If we had known what would happen ahead of time. We could have been much better prepared."

"Yeah? Well, we weren't," Qenzic replied.

"Rufus and I will get up just before the sun and go to scout the pass. If something comes we will hurry back and warn you," Fist promised with a yawn. Maryanne scooted back up next to him and he laid his head back on her lap. His eyes began to droop.

"And if the flies are just as thick? What good does it do us if we can't leave the cave. Are we supposed to wait in here while you bonded try to go out there and fight alone?" Qenzic pressed.

"I will think on it," Locksher replied. "There are several spells I could enact to help us to perhaps weaponize the field that protects us. In fact, I . . ."

The wizard's words floated away in a jumble as Fist drifted off to sleep. He didn't dream this night. Neither did he notice when Justan tried to contact him from the swamps of Malaroo.

The modified wards were active all night, killing all flies who tried to enter the cave. They even served a secondary purpose as late that evening, several of the tribespeople who had not made it back to the cave early on, came running at them. The ogres, infested with larvae, their minds filled with bloodlust, rushed into the cave only to be electrified clean by the field.

They fell to the ground twitching and were brought over to Locksher who made sure that they would survive. Ten ogres returned to the Thunder People that way and the tribe took this as a sign that the gods of the mountain were on their side.

Locksher woke Fist early. The wizard was surprisingly perky for one that had gone so long without sleep while continually using his power. Rufus, quick to recover as usual, returned to his regular size and walked with Fist to the cave entrance. They left Squirrel behind. The little beast wouldn't be able to tell the others much, but if there was an emergency that needed their attention, he could let them know.

The cave floor was covered with piles of dead flies, their dried husks blown in by the occasional gusts of wind from outside. Fist and the rogue horse endured the painful zap of the wards and pushed through another pile of flies, this one nearly waist high.

The sky was just beginning to turn blue with the sun's approach. There weren't many live flies in the air at the moment. Though it would heat up later that day, the chill morning air had caused them to go aground. The rocky shelf of the Thunder People's camp was black with them.

Briefly, Fist considered casting a few lightning spells to wipe as many out as he could, but decided against it. He had a task at hand. Why start the day tiring himself out with spells that would hardly make a dent in the fly population when he didn't yet know what lay ahead?

Rufus took a deep breath. "Ooh! Smells bad."

Fist didn't agree. The fresh air was a great improvement over the smell of hundreds of dirty ogres crammed into one cave. Nevertheless, he knew what the rogue horse referred to. The various camp sites had been discarded, many of them with meat in some state of being cooked or prepared. There was now an underlying smell of rot in the air as the flies had spent the day feasting and laying eggs.

He climbed onto Rufus' back and the rogue horse took him up the trails and pathways that led to the clifftops. They rode out to the edge and though the ground was gray with flies, he could see no enemies marching down the pass.

Fist was momentarily relieved, but as they rode further eastward along the clifftop he saw something strange in the distance. The terrain seemed different. "What do you see, Rufus?"

The rogue horse, whose senses were more refined than his, also noticed the change. "Ooh. Its higher out there."

"Higher?" Fist prodded the rogue horse further along.

They reached the far edge of the cliffs and when they still couldn't make out the change, he had Rufus climb down the sheer cliff to the slope so that they could get closer. After an hour's ride through rough terrain that most creatures would find impassable, Rufus climbed to a high shelf and Fist saw exactly what had happened.

"Uh oh," Rufus said.

Uh oh, Squirrel echoed from behind Fist's eyes.

Fist returned to a very worried group of friends who had feared the worst when he did not return right away. Maryanne was furious. The gnome demanded to know why he had not woken her to come along with him and it took Fist several minutes to calm her down so that he could tell them what he had found.

"She has blocked us off," Fist said.

"What are you saying?" Locksher asked.

He took a deep breath. "The passes were empty. I saw no dead or infected. Just flies."

"That sounds like a good thing," said Qenzic cautiously.

"But she has cut off our route of attack," Fist said. "She has raised tall sheer walls blocking every pass and clifftop between us and the lake."

"Making sure that we cannot help the Academy army on the day of the attack," Locksher finished.

Qenzic let out a low sigh. "Leaving us to the flies. She can just ignore us now. Sooner or later we'll be overwhelmed."

Fist hoped the flies wouldn't be a problem if they could survive just a day or two longer until Lenny arrived with Master Porthos. The old witch would surely be able to keep them at bay. Surely. If only he were allowed tell the rest of his friends about it.

"There has to be a way!" Maryanne did not like the idea of being kept out of the fight. She began to pace back and forth nervously. With as little room as there was around them, this looked more than a little awkward. "But-but . . . Oh! What if we were able to reopen the old trails? You know, the ones that Locksher destroyed with his rocks?"

"You mean with the whole mountainside fallen across them?" Qenzic scoffed.

"It's hard to be sure," Fist said, scratching his head. "I couldn't see the far side from where Rufus and I were, but it wouldn't make sense for the priestess to be so thorough cutting us off from this direction while leaving those other ways open."

There was a stretch of silence as the friends brooded before Locksher finally spoke.

"I don't know that the situation is quite so grim as it seems," the wizard said cheerfully.

Qenzic sent Locksher a scowl. "What were you smoking in that pipe last night?"

The wizard ignored him. "Maryanne is right. We should attempt to clear a way through those side trails. At the very least, it will be the method the Priestess of War should least expect."

"Alright," Fist said. It would be a longer journey, adding several hours to the journey, perhaps a day if they had to take the longest route. "But the way may be blocked even then."

"Cassandra is underestimating us," Locksher declared. He grasped Qenzic's shoulder to get the warrior's attention. "A wall of rock in our path? The fact that she used this particular method to block us off means that she got very little out of Lyramoor."

Qenzic's look quickly changed from dour to interested. "I know he wouldn't talk, but why do you say that?"

"Because Fist and I happen to be quite good at earth magic. If Lyramoor had told her our true talents and abilities, she would have chosen a much more effective method. All we have to do is burrow a hole through the walls. The methods for doing that are quite simple."

"Good on Lyramoor," Charz said with a nod. The rock giant had woken from his slumber fully recovered from his wound the day before. He and Burl had been laughing about it just before Fist arrived.

Fist frowned. "Maybe, but if she was watching through the eyes of those lupolds we fought, she would know that I have earth magic."

"But you are an ogre," he said. "Most wizards see ogres with powers as a ridiculous aberration. Hardly a threat. Likely she thinks you are my pet."

"Hey!" said Maryanne, sticking up for Fist.

"He's got a point," Charz said.

Fist wasn't offended, knowing quite well how the wizards at the Mage School saw his powers. "It might not be that simple. We could travel all the way there and find that she made those walls in such a way that our magic can't tunnel through."

Locksher waved that concern away. "There is always a way. Especially if she doesn't know where we'll be coming from."

"You're forgetting about the flies," Qenzic reminded them. "Come on! We're stuck in a blasted cave! What does it matter how fancy your spells are if we can't leave?"

"I have been giving that some thought as well," Locksher said. "I have thought of a way we could possibly-."

"Wait! Wait!" said Maryanne, shushing them, her eyes wide. A smile suddenly split her face and she smacked Fist's arm. "Ha! They're here! They're here!"

"What are you talking about?" Charz wondered.

Fist's brow rose as it dawned on him what she was talking about. "Now? But-."

"Last night, I was so tired that I fell asleep right after talking to Sarine," she said. "Bill was so worried about us that they traveled through the night. He was just now close enough to be able to reach me. They are close by. Their path is just blocked by that landslide!"

Fist laughed. That was fantastic news. He hadn't expected Lenny and Old Bill to arrive for another day, just before it was time for the attack. He frowned. "Wait, did you warn them about the flies?"

"Bill says we won't have to worry about the flies anymore!" she said.

"You two have me completely lost," Charz said. "Bill's here? How?"

Locksher let out an uncharacteristic curse. He shook a finger at them. "This is Valtrek's doing isn't it? Him and his secrets! Oh, I should have known. You two have been sharing too many mysterious looks these last few weeks. I had marked them off as being explained by your love affair, but now it makes much more sense."

"I think you've all gone crazy," Qenzic said.

"There's another force coming, isn't there?" Locksher said, his pointing finger turning into a fist that he shook at Fist and Maryanne. "Waiting just on the other side of those closed pathways. I knew you were much too insistent on diverting resources to opening them up!"

"It's not a big force," Fist said. "Just a small group that Head Wizard Valtrek sent up apart from the army." He lowered his voice just above a whisper. "They have a secret weapon with them that's supposed to help us in the fight."

Locksher's anger faded somewhat. "What kind of secret weapon?"

"We don't know!" Maryanne said happily. "Valtrek told Sarine and Bill not to tell me in case I was captured and tortured to give away all our strategies!"

"Like Lyramoor was," Qenzic said, his voice hollow of emotion.

Charz let out a laugh. "Well, I ain't gonna be down at this point. That jerk Valtrek's plan's worked so far."

"Also, they have Master Porthos with them," Fist said trying to keep things enthusiastic. "So the flies shouldn't be a problem anymore."

"Really?" the graduate said. "You knew that this whole time and said nothing?"

"I-I didn't expect them to be here for another day," Fist said. "Besides, I wasn't sure if he would be able to help or not."

"Well, let's find out!" Maryanne said and began pushing her way through the press of ogres to the cave's entrance. The way was packed with ogres peering outside. There was a rumble of confusion.

The gnome stumbled through the painful wards and let out a laugh as she looked at the camp around her. "Come on! Everyone! Come out and see!"

Her friends followed her out and hesitantly, a few ogres

braved the wards to join them. The flies were gone. There were little dead husks littering the ground like flakes of pepper, but there wasn't a live fly to be seen.

"It worked! Master Porthos used his magic to make them leave!" she said.

Locksher released the spell creating the electric wards and the Thunder People spilled out into the open. There were cries of triumph and celebration. Crag praised the gods and Fist for finding a way to rescue them.

Fist and his friends traveled to the point of the landslide. Together, Fist and Locksher began using their magic to clear a path through the rock, carving a passage wide enough and flat enough that the wagons would be able to drive through. It wasn't quick work and at times it was easier to borrow the brawn of the ogre tribe, with Charz' and Rufus' help, to move stubborn boulders.

It took all morning, but by the time the sun was at its zenith, Fist made the last push. He cut out a block of rock and lowered it into the ground. Two merchant wagons came into view. Standing in front of them, grins on their faces, were Lenny and Old Bill.

Maryanne rushed over to Bill and Fist ran alongside her.

He lifted Lenny into a tight hug. "Lenny! I'm so glad to see you!"

Lenny wheezed out a laugh and patted him on the back. "Okay, you big blasted ogre! Set me down already!"

Fist set him onto the ground. "I'm sorry about missing your wedding."

"Darlan told me all about what happened," Lenny said, smacking Fist's arm. "Don't you worry. Even Bettie got over it. I-." He turned his head to look at the little animal that dropped down onto his shoulder. "Hey there, little guy. No, Squirrel. I don't want a nut right now."

"Wee?" Rufus said in his huffing voice. The rogue horse trotted up to them, his broad mouth stretching into a toothy grin. He leaned close to the dwarf, his nostrils flaring as he sniffed the air around him.

"Holee turds with wings," Lenny said, his eyes wide with

shock. "Monkeyface?"

"You know each other?" Fist said in surprise.

"Wee!" The rogue horse tackled the dwarf. They rolled across the rocky ground, both of them bursting out with laughter.

Locksher walked past them and approached Bill, a stern look on his face. "Okay, Bill. Give it up. What is this secret weapon?"

Chapter Twenty

Fist grinned as he watched Rufus wrestle with Lenny. The ogre had been looking forward to this reunion ever since Rufus had showed him his memory of the dwarf. What a marvelous turn of events to learn that Lenny had been the one to turn the rogue horse over to the Prophet after centuries spent in smugglers' hands.

"Alright. Alright! Enough, dag-blast it! Lemme get some air!" Lenny said. Reluctantly the rogue horse backed off of him. Lenny climbed to his feet and began dusting himself off. "Yer almost as bad as Gwyrtha! What's goin' on here, Fist? What the hell's Monkeyface doin' all the way up here?"

"Ooh! Roo-Fuss!" Rufus corrected.

"What?" Lenny said.

"He's trying to tell you that his name is really Rufus," Fist explained. "He doesn't like being called Monkeyface."

Rufus let out an irritated snort. "No!"

Lenny raised his hands defensively. "Okay. Shoot. Rufus it is. That's a fine name fer a rogue . . . wait a dag-gum minute! You two are bonded together, ain't you?"

"Yes. It happened over a month ago." Fist told Lenny about how he had run into Rufus fighting a dragon on the shores of the black lake.

The dwarf shook his head in amazement. "I'll be pickled. To think that John held Monkeyf-." He nodded to the rogue horse. "Rufus aside all this time just to give him to you. I tell you it makes this dwarf's heart dag-gum proud I had somethin' to do with it."

They heard an exclamation of dismay and turned to see

Qenzic talking to the three Academy guards at the second wagon. Fist immediately recognized them from the war. He knew Swen fairly well, but the other two were only acquaintances.

Lenny sighed and scratched his head. "I suppose I'd better go over and give Qenzic my condolences about old Lyramoor. Blast it, that was like a punch to my belly when Bill told me. I wanted to tell the other Academy folks about it right away, but Bill said it had to be secret 'till we got here. Blasted secrets!"

"I didn't know you knew Lyramoor all that well," Fist said

"Yeah. Back when he was a slave. Tried to help him a couple times but . . . hell I was a young fool back then. When I saw him again at the Mage School durin' the war, he durn near tried to cut me in pieces. But we had us a good talk about it and . . ." the dwarf's voice trailed off.

"I'm sorry, Lenny," Fist said. "He was my friend too."

"Ooh! Me too," Rufus agreed.

And me, said Squirrel sadly.

The dwarf nodded and rubbed a hand over his face. "I tell you, it seems like my past's been comin' back to haunt me lately."

Rufus followed Lenny as the dwarf went over to talk with the Academy guards at the second wagon. Fist and Squirrel joined Maryanne and Old Bill, who was still arguing with Locksher.

"I've already told you I can't reveal that yet, Wizard Locksher," said Bill. The old dwarf stood with arms folded, his expression firm. "Not it's dimensions. Not the type of magic it uses or even if it uses magic at all! Not until just before the battle starts. Those are the orders."

Locksher frowned. "This secretiveness has become rather ridiculous at this point, don't you think?"

"I don't disagree with you, son. I have found it bothersome on many occasions during this journey." Bill shrugged. "Nevertheless, Valtrek's plan seems to have served us well, from what I've heard."

Locksher's hands clenched. "Ohh, I wish I were a dwarf. I'd tell him where to-. Ah, you're a dwarf. You send a message to Mistress Sarine and have her tell him right where he can shove his plan!"

A chuckle escaped the old dwarf's lips. "I can't say as I expected to hear that from you, Wizard Lo-."

"And make sure that it is a vulgar term for rectum!" Locksher added.

"Oh, let me!" Maryanne volunteered. "I can tell her what to say."

They were interrupted by a creaking sound as the door to the wagon next to them slowly opened. A young-looking man with blond hair hopped out, then pulled a stair out from under the cart. He reached back in and helped out the oldest-looking human Fist had ever seen.

His face was pale and wrinkled and sagging and covered with age spots. A tuft of wispy hair topped his head. He wore a gray wizard's robe and made very careful movements as he stepped gingerly onto the step and then again onto the ground. As he did so, Fist saw that the man's arm was thin as a bone.

"I suppose I should introduce you," said Bill. He walked over to the old man. "This is Master Porthos and his apprentice, Bryon."

"I'll let you guess which is which," said the young man cheerfully.

Fist's eyebrows rose. This was Mistress Sarine's second husband? Perhaps Artemus would feel much less intimidated by the man once he saw this particular image of him.

Charz grunted. "Wait if that's Master Porthos, how're we supposed to-? I mean, is he okay? No offense, but you look-."

"Barely alive, Mr. Rock Giant," the ancient man said, one corner of his wrinkled lips raised in amusement. "I'm on my feet right now thanks to elf olives and an overabundant dose of blessing magic, but I'm one odd heartbeat away from going stone cold."

The rock giant chuckled. "I like your attitude, old man. But if that's the case, Why're you here?"

"Because you need me," Porthos replied. "If I weren't here, you would still be besieged by those flies."

"Good point," Charz admitted.

"And if I don't survive for another few days, you will have a very difficult time surviving an attack against the Priestess of War," the old man added. "Speaking of that, you should know that it's important we leave right away."

"Right now?" Fist asked. "But why?"

"Because the Priestess' intention was for her swarm to blanket this place and I have driven them off. Now, as far as I can tell, she is distracted for the moment, but if she turns her focus back on this place it will become immediately evident to her that something is wrong. We should begin our march now and let her swarm return."

"But the army is not supposed to attack for another two days," Bill said. "What are we supposed to do until then? Camp on her doorstep? That would spoil the surprise for certain."

"It is likely that will not be a problem," Locksher said, raising a calming hand. "You see, we just learned that the Priestess of War has raised a high rock wall all around the Black Lake to keep us away."

Bill frowned in confusion. "I don't see how that helps us. That just sounds like an additional problem."

"Not at all," the wizard replied. "Cassandra built that wall so that she could fight the incoming army without worrying about us attacking her flank. Unfortunately for her, it blocks her sight as well as ours. We can camp quite nicely outside her wall and she won't know we're there."

"What if she has some beast posted to look out for us?" Maryanne asked.

"I should be able to stop any creature from reporting our presence," Master Porthos said.

"Precisely," Locksher shrugged. "While she thinks we are still in our cave, immobilized by her swarm, Fist and I shall burrow a whole through her wall and we can unleash Valtrek's secret weapon on her."

Bill nodded thoughtfully. "That's actually not a bad plan at that."

Fist raised his hand. "Uh, Master Locksher, won't she be able to see that we're not in the Thunder People camp? Through the flies eyes?"

"I believe I can answer that," Porthos replied. "She can't see a thing with those blasted insects. Believe me, I've tried looking through the eye of a fly before and its terribly confusing. They see multiple images at once and not very clearly. It's a miracle they don't all just fly into the sea and kill themselves. Anyway, I'm certain that all she can tell is if the flies are in a certain area."

"Then we need to let 'em back in before she notices," Charz agreed.

Locksher looked at Fist expectantly.

Fist blinked. "Oh. I guess I'll tell the Thunder People it's time to go."

They worked as quickly as they could to mobilize the ogres. Crag was insistent that the women and children should stay behind, but there was no way to keep them safe from the flies if they stayed. The argument was short, but intense.

Ultimately, it was decided that they would bring the women and children with them up close to the new wall, but no farther. Master Porthos wouldn't be following the rest of them inside anyway. The old man and his apprentice would stay behind with the women and children, while the ogre men went forward. Old Bill would carry Porthos' naming dagger with him. The wizard would protect the army with his magic from afar.

They set out on a route that forked off of the road that Fist and Locksher had opened back up. It was a long and winding path, and it would take them much longer to get to their destination, but time was something they now had. It also helped that the path was relatively flat and wide enough that wagons were able to pass through.

They stopped on a wide rock shelf as the sun began to set. While the camp was being set up, Old Bill approached Fist and pulled him aside.

"Fist, while we have a few moments of privacy, I thought it would be a good time to talk to you about Maryanne," the dwarf said.

Fist glanced to the other side of the camp where Maryanne was talking with Charz and the Academy guards. "Okay."

"First of all, I would like to apologize for her for putting you in this delicate situation," Bill said.

Uh oh, said Squirrel who was sitting on his shoulder. He pulled a seed out of his cheek pocket and began shelling it.

Fist frowned in agreement with Squirrel. The way Bill had broached the subject made him nervous. "What situation?"

He let out an uncomfortable chuckle. "It has come to our attention that your relationship with her has developed further than any of us expected."

Fist blinked. "Who expected?"

"Sarine and Sherl and I. Kyrkon prefers to stay away from the discussion," Bill said.

Maryanne won't like this, Squirrel thought.

Fist had the sudden surety that all of them should have stayed out of the discussion. He folded his arms. "What do you want to discuss?"

"It's actually more of a warning," Bill said. "You see, Maryanne has a tendency to develop crushes on musclebound men. It's a common issue among young gnomes, but with Maryanne, these relationships tend to . . . end badly."

"Mistress Sarine mentioned this before," Fist said. In fact he had been worried a time or two when he'd seen her admiring the physique of some other ogre. "But she said that things had always ended up fine."

"Yes, but Maryanne has never taken it this far before and that is where we are concerned. You see, with each of those other men she had crushes on, she lost interest as soon as they returned her affection. Inevitably, she'd cast them off as soon as someone else caught her eye."

That's the way of things, Squirrel agreed matter-of-factly.

Fist's eyes narrowed at both of their assessments. "I don't like the way you're talking about her. You and Sarine are bonded with Maryanne. You should know her better. And what does

Darlan have to do with this?"

Bill looked taken aback. "You misunderstand me. Well, Sherl is concerned that you'll end up heartbroken and unable to focus on your studies. But Sarine and I are concerned for Maryanne. You were quite against her coming on the journey with you and she has never before felt this-."

"Bill!" came Maryanne's voice from across the camp.

Squirrel chittered out a laugh and pulled out another seed. *Here she comes.*

The dwarf's face went pale and he looked up at Fist with pleading eyes. "Don't you dare tell her what I said."

The gnome warrior stormed over to them, her fists clenched. The sunset reflected in her eyes, making them glow as red as her hair. "Blast you, Bill! I have half a mind to shoot you right through that goiter you call an Adam's apple!"

Bill put his hand up under his thick beard to feel at his throat. "It's not a goiter."

"I can't believe you. Or Sarine! Warning him away from me?" she raged.

"That's not it at all," Bill protested. "You didn't hear the whole thing I was trying to say."

"Really?" she said, hands on hips. "Then why don't you go ahead and tell me through the bond so I'll know if you're lying."

Squirrel watched their exchange with great interest, knowing that the discussion was all internal.

Bill sighed and gave Maryanne a dull look. She folded her arms and nodded, her eyes fixed on him. After a moment, Bill rolled his eyes. Her mouth dropped in outrage. He gave her a long suffering glance. She stomped her foot. He scowled back at her. She pursed her lips, her eyes wide. Finally, he threw up his hands.

"Fine! I'll stay out of it. But you know it's only because we care," Bill said, then gave Fist a helpless glance before walking away.

"That makes me so mad," Maryanne said, watching him leave. "It was mostly Wizardess Sherl, you know. Sarine let it slip that we were together and she got all worried. She thought that I seduced you and you wanted nothing to do with me! Blasted woman got it into Sarine's head that you would drop me as soon as you could." She sighed. "That old lady was worried about me."

They don't know you, Squirrel said.

Fist frowned, looking down. "It's true that I wasn't happy about you coming up here."

What? said Squirrel. *Don't say that*!

Maryanne turned to look at him and Fist's eyes rose to meet hers. There was worry in her dark eyes. He licked his lips.

"I was a normal ogre once. Like everyone here," he said.

No you weren't, Squirrel chided.

Shh! "Ever since bonding with Justan, I realized that I didn't want the same things I used to want. The way my people treated their women bothered me. And the way the women treated the men didn't seem right either.

"But the way humans do things. It's different. Not always better, but it usually is." He bit his lip as he tried to put together the next part. "I was confused when you came. I didn't know what I wanted from a woman yet. Then with Puj . . . I didn't feel the things I thought I should feel for her so I didn't always treat her good."

You tried, Squirrel said.

Fist ignored him. "But you, Maryanne, you were always straightforward with me. You tried to understand me. Yes, you pushed me and prodded me. But what Darlan told Sarine was wrong. I would never have kissed you if I didn't like you. And I never would've . . ."

"I know," she said and placed a hand against his cheek. "Now you listen, Fist. Because there's something I want to say to you."

"Just a minute," Fist said. He looked at the animal on his shoulder. *Squirrel, go away*.

Squirrel froze, a half shelled seed between his teeth. *But I'll be quiet*.

"Go," he said aloud.

Giving him a sulky snort, the furry creature scrambled

down his body and off through the camp to Rufus who was sitting at a nearby fire watching Lenny make stew.

Fist nodded and closed the bond so that he couldn't listen in. He focused his attention back on Maryanne. "Sorry."

"I don't remember much about my life before I was bonded to Sarine. I was trainin' at a small gnome sanctuary in Khalpany and let's just say, I had little thought for anything else but my bow. But then, kinda like you I guess, my eyes were opened. I had bigger thoughts and . . . baser thoughts.

"It's true I fell for a lot of males." She squeezed his arm. "The stronger the better. Sarine and Bill were probably right to assume I'd lose interest in you too. But they didn't know what I was looking for. I didn't know what I was looking for either.

"But . . . you're wrong about the way you treated Puj. You were never unfair. And you always tried to do right by her. Watching that? And the way you were when we hunted down those ogres that killed her. That's when I knew how I really felt about you."

Fist nodded. "I think that's when I started to-."

She put a finger against his lips. "Let me finish.

"The reason I always seemed so flighty-. Well, I probably was flighty. I didn't have much in the way of brains at first. But the reason I never stuck with anyone is that every other man, gnome or dwarf or whatever that I ever liked ended up being nothing but a big walking piece of garbage."

Fist smiled. "So I'm not garbage?"

"No. You are the biggest, sweetest, most wonderful person I know. And . . ." her cheeks reddened. "I love you, Fist. That's why I won't run away from you."

Fist's grin widened even further. "I've been wanting to say the same thing to you for a while now!"

Maryanne raised her eyebrows expectantly. "Then say it."

"I love you," he said and kissed her.

Chapter Twenty One

The next day's travel was a bit more difficult than the first. They had to stop several times for Fist to widen the gap between rocks so that the wagons could pass. Whenever the road was too steep for the horses, the ogres cheerfully got behind the wagons and pushed.

This was an adventure for the tribe. The men were going off to war and for once, the women were able to join them. At least part way.

They stopped that night at a wide cavern complex that had formerly belonged to the Rock People. They had been driven out by the infested, but the place was currently empty, the Priestess of War having called all her monsters back behind her wall.

The next day was to be the day of the battle. The ogres worked hard clearing out the caverns of the refuse left behind by the dead. It began to rain, but they slept comfortably in caves that ogres were meant to sleep in. The next day, the men set out before the sunrise. The women and children stayed behind along with the first wagon and Master Porthos.

The rest of their army marched for two hours down the mountain path before the wall came into view. The wall was sheer, nearly impossible for anyone save perhaps Rufus to climb. It towered above them, newly created, its color striations different from the rest of the mountainside around it. They came to the point where the path ended at the base of the wall and Bill halted the wagon.

"This is as close as we're gonna get," the dwarf said.

Charz looked out to the southeast. "I can sense Alfred out there with the rest of the army. That ridge is in the way so we can't see 'em, but they ain't far."

"The Black Lake is only maybe a mile from here," Fist said and Crag and the other ogres agreed.

"Now we wait for the right time," Locksher said.

They stood there for perhaps an hour, the atmosphere tense as Charz gave regular updates on the Academy army's progress. Finally, the army was in front of the pass, the putrid smell of the Black Lake hitting their noses. Bill decided it was time. He hurried over to the second wagon and approached the rear door.

Fist gathered around with Locksher and Maryanne and the others to await the unveiling of Valtrek's secret weapon. There had been a lot of conjecture. Charz thought that it was some kind of magic canon pulled from the Mage School's siege equipment.

Locksher's thought was that it was a device similar to the Crysalisk that Ewzad Vriil had used during the war. He and Professor Beehn had been working on something that could project a field to deflect magical attack. Perhaps he had gotten it working while Locksher was gone.

Fist had chosen not to speculate. The idea of this secret weapon had become too large to him and he didn't want to second guess it. Whatever it was, surely it was the key to their victory.

Bill grabbed the handle and paused to look back at them. "Just so you know, it's probably not what you're expecting."

"Open it up already, dag-blast it!" Lenny barked.

He pulled the door open and out from the dark interior poured a white mist. The mist had an almost sweet almost spicy fragrance that tickled at Fist's memory. Where had he smelled that smell before?

"Whew!" Mistress Sarine appeared in the doorway, wincing slightly at the sunlight. She waved a hand at the mist swirling around her face. "Goodness, Dear. You took your time. I've been standing there waiting for a solid minute!"

"Sorry, Begazzi," Bill said, reaching out a hand to help her down. Kyrkon jumped out from the mist behind her and held his hand out too.

Fist's jaw fell slightly open. That was it?

What? said Squirrel, in a similar state of shock.

"Ooh?" said Rufus. *An old lady and a elf?*

Then, walking out behind them, came Professor Beehn, followed by Wizard Spence, Wizard Windle, and Head Wizard Valtrek.

"That's nearly the entire High Council!" said Wizard Locksher in surprise.

"Except for Master Barthas," Valtrek replied, shaking the mist out of his robes. "I had to leave one of us behind in case we all died in this attack."

"You were in there the whole time?" Charz said wide-eyed.

Beehn snorted. "No, Charz. You know I've been back at the School. We came out through the mirror."

Fist placed a hand on his forehead. Now it made sense. They had used the mirror that Valtrek had with him on Justan's first journey to the Mage School.

"Where is Mistress Sherl?" he asked.

"Indeed, where is Sherl?" Sarine asked, looking around. "I swear she was right behind us."

"Oh. She said she forgot something," said Faldon the Fierce, exiting the wagon. Justan's father was dressed for war, wearing a full shirt of chainmail, the handle of his massive sword sticking up over his back. "She said she'd be right back."

Behind Faldon came many of the most dangerous fighters in the Academy, including Hugh the Shadow and Stout Harley and a slew of other graduates.

"I don't understand," said Locksher. "I thought the matching mirror was out of the country."

"I received it back from the Kingdom of Benador a few days before Beehn headed over to the Academy in his wind wagon. The timing was fortunate. Otherwise, we wouldn't have been able to transfer it to the wagons before Bill and Lenui left," Valtrek said.

Sarine snorted. "Is that why you delayed the decision to leave for so long?"

"It was a factor," the Head Wizard admitted. "I had a

backup plan, but fortunately it worked out."

As more Academy soldiers continued to spill out of the wagon Locksher cocked his head. "I didn't think your mirror could handle so many travelers."

Valtrek walked over to him. "I have been boosting its magic, working to expand the number. Right now the mirror can handle perhaps up to a hundred before it becomes unstable. The only issue is that the same number of people have to return or the pathway stays open."

"That is quite a gamble," Locksher said.

Valtrek shrugged. "If we should lose some of our number, I am sure that there will be wizards or soldiers in the army below that need a swifter way home than by foot."

"But . . . What if we should lose?" Charz asked. "Wouldn't we be leaving an open portal right back to the Mage School?"

"I will be waiting on the other side myself. If anyone unapproved should attempt it, the mirror will be broken," Valtrek replied. A smile appeared on his face. "But let's not hope for that."

"So you're not going to be fighting with us, Head Wizard?" Fist asked.

Valtrek clasped his hands together. "Battle has never been my specialty. Once I see that everyone has come through safely, I will wait here for the results."

The warriors finished their mass exodus from the wagon, sixty in all, every one of them elite. They were followed shortly by a stream of more wizards. Fist recognized most of them. Many were part time teachers of his.

Locksher's eyebrows rose suddenly. "I just had a fantastic idea! There is something I must retrieve from my rooms. Do I have time?"

Valtrek nodded. "Wizardess Sherl isn't here yet. So if you hurry."

Sighing at the thought of all the stairs that awaited him, Locksher rushed inside.

He was gone for some time. The wizards approached the wall Cassandra had raised and debated the most efficient way to bore through it, while avoiding the possibility of alerting the enemy to their presence. Faldon and the Academy Council members took Fist and Crag aside to discuss the best ways to implement the ogres into an attack formation.

Fist spent the entire time with chills running down his back. This was it. The battle he had been dreaming about for months was finally going to happen. So much of his dream made sense now. Academy warriors and Mage School wizards were now intermixed with ogres and ready to go to war.

He began to worry about the snakes. Was he really going to be bitten? If it happened would it be just one big one like in the last dream he'd had or many small ones like he'd dreamed before?

I hope none, Rufus said, attempting to be helpful.

Me too, Fist agreed. *Maybe the snakes were a . . . metaphor*? Yes, he was pretty sure that was the word. It had been in his book of words several months back. But what would snakes be a metaphor for? Perhaps they represented his need to be faster.

He perked up. Or maybe that part of the dream had already come true. He'd had that feeling when he hadn't been fast enough to stop Mog from being killed by the golem. It was a horrible thought, but maybe that part was over.

Or maybe you still get bit by snakes, Squirrel offered from within his pouch at Fist's side.

"What are you frowning so deeply about?" Maryanne asked. The gnome had been over by the wagon speaking with Sarine. Their discussion had seemed surprisingly calm. Maryanne had even hugged the old woman.

"I was just thinking about my dream," Fist said.

"Oh, the spirit dream you keep having?" She raised her hands ominously and said, "Don't forget to 'bend your knees and roll with the fall'. Right?"

Fist sighed. "Yes. That's the dream."

She threw her arm around his shoulder. "That just means it's gonna be a pretty small fall, doesn't it? Nothing to worry about. If the fall was gonna be too high it would just be like . . . 'squish'."

"Snakes," Rufus reminded her.

"Ohh," the gnome said, nodding in understanding. "That part. Well, that doesn't mean necessarily that you're gonna get bit. It could just be a . . ." She snapped her fingers. "What's it called? When it's not actually real, but a symbol for something else?"

"Why are you in such a good mood?" Fist asked.

She squeezed his shoulders. "Because it's here! Now's the time. No more thinkin' about the day. We're livin' the day! We get to fight and I really hope I get the chance to put an arrow right between that witch's black lips. Pin her tongue to the back of her mouth for Lyramoor. I think he'd like that."

Fist couldn't help but smile. "Maybe."

A new swirl of mist rolled out of the wagon door. "Fist?"

Darlan strode out of the wagon, hopping down to the ground. She was wearing thick robes of red and black with flame-like runes emblazoned all over them. These were battle robes; the robes of a war wizard. Her eyes immediately found Fist.

She beckoned him towards her. "Fist! Hurry. Come here!"

Fist started towards her just as Charz cried out.

"It's starting!" the giant said excitedly. "Alfred says it's starting!"

Just then, the earth began to vibrate. Tremors rumbled under their feet. Dirt was shaken from the wall above them, falling in a haze. Loose rocks began to tumble down the mountainside.

There was a tremendous amount of earth magic being used right then. Fist could feel it in his teeth. It wasn't being sent towards them, but somewhere to the south, near where the Academy army was approaching.

"Are you sure just one wizardess is doing that?" said one of the wizards in frightened amazement.

"Fist! Now! We don't have much time," Darlan insisted.

Fist walked up to her. "What do you need, Mistress?"

"I need you to come back to the Mage School with me," she said. "Don't worry. We'll return quickly."

"Sherl, there's no time for that," Valtrek said. "The battle has begun. The signal was given."

"Then get started," she said. "We'll catch up. You don't need me quite yet."

"But Darlan!" said Faldon, his hands raised in frustration. "Fist is one of our commanders."

"Use Qenzic," Maryanne suggested. "The ogres will listen to him."

"We'll try to return before they finish tunneling through the wall," Darlan said. She grabbed Fist's hand and began pulling him towards the wagon.

Fist looked back at Maryanne and shrugged apologetically. She gave him a worried nod in return. He was beginning to realize that another part of his dream was coming true. Everyone was going to be streaming ahead past him. He was going to miss the start of the fight.

As they reached the wagon's step, the mist swirled again and out ran Locksher, breathing heavily. He was carrying a bulky bag slung over his shoulder.

"Excuse me." The wizard hopped down and stumbled, nearly losing his feet. "Lenui Firegobbler! I need your assistance! You too, Rufus!"

Darlan pulled him up the steps and Fist called out through the bond, *Be safe, Rufus!*

Ooh-! the rogue horse replied just as the wizardess yanked Fist through the mirror at the wagon's rear wall.

Fist found himself standing in a shimmering tunnel. The floor glowed a soft blue and had a spongy feel to it. More of that fragrant mist bubbled up around his feet. The walls and the ceiling, however, were partially transparent letting him see out into an inky blackness only occasionally pierced by spots of light.

"Wait! Squirrel!" Fist said in a panic. "I didn't tell him I was going."

Darlan glanced back at him. "He's standing on your shoulder. Now come on."

Fist turned his head to see Squirrel standing next to him, wearing that leather vest he liked so much. *When did you get there?*

Squirrel shrugged. *I was here the whole time.*

"What is this place?" Fist wondered.

"A corridor through the world of dreams," Darlan replied dismissively. "It's best not to think about it. You're safe as long as you don't try to push your way out."

Fist swallowed and tried not to get too close to any of the walls.

The journey was brief. Darlan quickly reached what looked like a solid wall of blue light that blocked their way. She walked into it and pulled Fist and Squirrel along with her.

Fist stepped out of a mirror identical to the one in the wagon. They were now in the middle of a stark gray room, windowless and bare, lit only by a few glowing orbs. Darlan let go of his hand and walked towards the room's lone door.

Fist realized where they were. "This is the Magic Testing Center."

"It was the safest place to put the mirror in case we lose this fight and get invaded," she replied, opening the door.

He followed her into the hallway where Master Barthas and several Academy guards were standing by. Darlan rushed right by them without saying so much as hello. Fist jogged behind her. "Where are we going?"

His shield and mace made such a clatter on his back that she misheard what he said. "Because I made a mistake!"

Fist wanted to ask her what she meant, but Darlan burst through the front door and out into the school grounds. Fist was suddenly struck by the fact that he was running across the vibrant trimmed grass of the school. The sky was bright. The air was warm. Vibrant trees were planted in orderly rows along the pathways. The Rune tower dwarfed it all, rising to impossible heights overhead.

It was such a dreamlike experience. It seemed like ages since he had last been here and yet everything was as he had left it. He frowned as a thought occurred to him. *Squirrel am I dreaming?*

Maybe, Squirrel replied, having similar thoughts. He reached out and patted Fist's face just to be sure. *No. You're real.*

Darlan headed straight for the Rune Tower. She jogged by an elderly wizard who gave her a cheeky grin.

"Still in a hurry, Sherl?"

"Shut up, Perkins!" she snapped and Fist just caught a glimpse of his startled eyes before he had run past him too.

They headed across the bridge and inside the tower. The hallway was crowded by students coming in and out of the library. Oh how Fist missed that library. They neared the door and Fist thought he could just make out the lanky form of Vincent the librarian standing behind the desk in the center of the floor.

"Hi, Fist!" said a few students. Feeling completely out of place wearing his full armor and weaponry, he waved back at them.

"I didn't know you were back," said a student he didn't know all that well, but shared a class with.

"He's not stopping to talk to any of you!" Darlan yelled. "So step aside!"

The hallway parted as if she had cast a spell. They rushed through a door at the end of the hallway and into a wide staircase. They began to climb.

"Twice on these stairs," she grumbled. "You may have to carry me on the way back down again. Ugh, and then I have that priestess to fight. Damn me and my stupid stubborn ways!"

"What are you talking about, Mistress?" Fist asked, grateful that the steps in this particular stairwell weren't as narrow as many in the Rune Tower. "You said something about a mistake?"

"Yes! I admit it. I made many mistakes in my life, Fist," she said bitterly. "Wasted so many years of my life putting things off. Do you know how long Faldon waited for me to finally quit this job and agree to marry him?"

"Uh, no," he replied.

"Fifty years!" she said breathlessly. "We'd go on missions together. I'd see him in Reneul around testing time. I knew how we felt about each other. I even started sending him elf food to keep him young for me so that I could join him when I was done here.

"Do you know how much life we could have lived

together? How many children we could have had?"

"In fifty years?" he said. His legs were really burning now. How far up were they going? "A lot?"

"Yes! Well, I'm not sure exactly how many. Elf magic slows everything down. Maybe six? I don't know that I wanted six, but the point is, I wasted all that time! Justan is an only child all because I waited until I was 164 years old to get pregnant."

Fist didn't know how to respond to that. "Did you tell Justan this?"

Darlan let out a groan, stopping at a wide and ornate door. "Damn it, Fist! My fat mouth! He doesn't know exactly, but he guesses. You're going to tell him aren't you?"

"So that means you're . . . "

"Don't do the math!" she said, but saw in his eyes that he already had. "Fine! Yes. I'm 184 blasted years old! And this is one of those days I'm feeling it too."

Humans are old, Squirrel observed.

"You're beautiful," Fist said honestly. "I don't exactly understand the way human women age, but you look like you could have many more children if you wanted to."

Darlan sighed, cocking her head at him. "You really are sweet, Fist. And I am so sorry I got all tied in a knot over your relationship with Maryanne. It was none of my business and I'm sorry. I just see you and I get all these motherly feelings and I just kept thinking how young you were and how experienced that gnome is and I-I forgot my place."

"It's okay, Mistress," Fist said.

"Sarine told me how angry Maryanne was about my interference and I don't blame her." She shook her head. "I felt bad about it and I realized that I was expecting you to do what I did. Wait for this. Wait for that-." She paused. "I'm talking in circles, aren't I?"

"Um . . . Aren't we in a hurry?" he asked.

Darlan stomped her foot. "Yes! Dammit! Come on! And don't you dare tell Justan how much I've been swearing!" She pushed open the heavy ornate door behind her and held out her left hand. Fist reached out to grasp it and stopped, his eyes widening. "Your hand!"

Darlan looked at the naming rune on her palm and blinked for a second. "Right. Sorry. That just happened. I forgot to mention it."

"Just today?" Fist said.

"Mistress Dianne." She held up her hand so that he could see the rune clearly. "It had been weighing on me for weeks. The Bowl wanted to name me. I knew it. I've been putting it off. I was standing there by that blasted mirror with everyone else, fretting about it and then I decided not to wait anymore." She let out a short laugh. "I haven't even told Faldon yet. You're the only one who knows."

"It's close to your other name," he said and tried it out. "Mistress Dianne."

"Yeah," she said, looking at her palm again. "Too close really. It might just confuse people."

Fist looked down the hallway. He knew that hallway. He had just never been there through this entrance before. "That's the way to the Hall of Majesty."

Ooh! said Squirrel excitedly.

"Yes, Fist," Darlan replied. "It was strange. When I was walking towards the Bowl, my mind was full of anxieties and varied thoughts. But while I was standing there with my dagger in the Bowl, my new name fresh off my lips . . . your face is what came into my mind. I knew right then that I needed to drag you up here because when you were raised to apprentice I didn't let you go.

"Why, you may wonder? Because of propriety and stupid rules I'm against? That's what I told you back then and it's partly true, but mainly it was because I was scared. I didn't want to get that close to the Bowl because I knew it wanted me."

Fist grinned. "So I'm going now?"

"Yes! Yes. That's why we're here. Now get inside because this door is blasted heavy and my arm hurts from holding it open this long!"

Fist entered the hallway with its statues and paintings of named wizards and warriors of time gone by and felt an electric thrill. The last time he had been here it was just after the Academy had exploded and he had seen Tolivar named. Was that going to happen to him? Maybe it wouldn't.

It suddenly occurred to Fist that maybe the Bowl wouldn't want him and he would have wasted everyone's time. His friends could be fighting right now. Maybe dying. Was this worth it?

Yes, said Squirrel confidently. *It will choose you. You are Fist.*

Darlan led him into the ornate waiting room at the end of the hallway, but did not stop. She opened the next set of doors and they stepped into the Hall of Majesty. It was huge and open and glimmering with unending tiers of crystal chandeliers hanging from the unseen ceiling high above. And there, standing alone, was the Bowl of Souls on a pedestal of marble.

His eyes were drawn to it. The Bowl was wide and golden. Plain, yet finely detailed. Fist's heart began to thump in his chest.

He didn't remember making the steps, but suddenly he was standing before it. A quiet chanting started somewhere in the corner of his mind. His heart beat louder. Without knowing it, he pulled his mace off of the harness on his back and lowered its spiked head into the waters of the bowl.

Uh, Fist? said Squirrel worriedly.

The chanting grew louder. So did his heartbeat. He gritted his teeth as both sounds grew. The chanting and beating built until there was this pressure in his chest pushing up towards his throat. It wanted out. It hurt to hold it in.

His mouth opened and a strange series of words poured from his lips as if it wasn't him speaking, but someone else. He raised his mace back out of the water, his voice increasing in loudness until he was speaking louder than he believed possible. Suddenly, his arms fell, thrusting his mace back into the waters of the bowl.

A burst of energy erupted from the bowl, surrounding him in a shroud of brilliance. The chanting stopped. The foreign words were gone from his mind. In their place only one word was left. It burned so brightly within him that there was nothing he could do, but shout it to the heavens.

"Fist!"

His name echoed through the immensity of the room, punctuated by the tingling of countless crystal shards in the chandeliers above.

"What?" said Darlan incredulously. "No fair! You get to keep your name? I wanted to keep my name!"

Fist pulled his mace out of the water and saw the rune, wide and intricately detailed, halfway up the handle. Trembling, he looked at the back of his right hand. Nothing. He opened his left hand. There, covering his entire palm, was a rune that matched the one on his mace.

"It happened," he said numbly.

Like I said, Squirrel reminded him.

"Well," Darlan said, putting her right hand on his shoulder and holding her left out next to his. "Look at us. The Mage School just got itself two named War Wizards."

Chapter Twenty Two

Justan's journey to meet with the Stranger took a long and often miserable two days. Most of it was through shallow marsh lands and portions of that were thick with troll slime.

He rode most of the way on Gwyrtha's back with Durza sitting behind him. He had learned to loathe that perfume she wore. He didn't know where she was keeping it or when she found the time to put it on, but to his enhanced senses it was thick and overly flowery. It gave him a headache and he would have demanded she walk if she weren't so incredibly useful.

The gorc's bewitching magic not only kept them safe from the behemoth beneath them, it also kept away mindless trolls and a bevy of other dangerous and poisonous creatures that called this place home. At night, she would lure in dinner and Justan quickly learned that if he was nice and complimented her, he could request the creature he wanted.

Deathclaw stayed at Talon's side, determined to discover just how much Justan's magic had healed her. He found many of her behaviors slightly disturbing, like when she would break down into sudden fits of sobbing as they walked. But other times, he was encouraged.

She was able to carry on conversations with him, often in a mix of common speech and the chirping language of the raptoids. To Justan's dismay, this discussion often had something to do with some aspect of Justan's life. Talon remembered many things from the memories Justan had forced upon her and Deathclaw knew most of it from his own delving through the bond. With the different paths their lives had taken since being changed by Ewzad Vriil, this puzzling over Justan's human faults was one of the few things they still had in common.

On the afternoon of the second day, Durza assured Justan that they were coming close to their destination; a place she called the "Village of the Weirdies." Shortly before their arrival, Deathclaw contacted Justan through the bond.

I have had some time to speak with Talon and still I am unsure about something.

Is that so? Justan asked. *What is it?*

She is . . . not broken in the way she used to be anymore, but I am not certain that this changes anything.

What do you mean? Justan wondered.

Talon did so many things that I have come to see as . . . evil.

Justan's eyebrows rose. This was the first time he had heard Deathclaw refer to that term. The raptoid understood the logical reasons for avoiding evil acts, but he had always struggled with the human definition of right and wrong. *Yes. That is absolutely true.*

She was very bad, Gwyrtha agreed.

Deathclaw was silent for a moment as he chose his next words. *Before you changed her, I believed that it was my duty to destroy her. To end her evil in this world.*

Justan wasn't so certain that he was fully responsible for changing her, but that wasn't Deathclaw's point. *And now?*

I am not sure that my duty has changed.

Really? Justan replied. *Do you feel like she would do those evil things again?*

It is hard to say. At the moment, no. But even if she were never to hurt people again, it would not erase the things she has done. The people she tortured. The innocents she slaughtered? They will remain dead.

Justan nodded. *I think I understand your dilemma. This is the question of proper punishment. Should she suffer as her victims suffered?*

Yes! Gwyrtha decided, memories of Talon's misdeeds ruminating in her head. *She killed Coal.*

She did do that, Justan said sadly. *And that cannot be changed.*

Deathclaw cocked his head. *You speak as if you agree, but your thoughts feel as though you disagree.*

Durza, who was sitting behind Justan, suddenly jerked his shirt. "Stop! Stop Gertha! I gotta pee!"

Gwyrtha stopped so that the gorc could splash down into the ankle-deep water and crouch behind some marsh rushes. While they waited, Justan tried to answer Deathclaw's question fairly.

It's a complex issue. One that has been argued throughout our history. Let me ask you a question. If you were to kill Talon right now, in punishment for all her evil acts, would that erase the things she had done. Will those she killed return?

No, said Gwyrtha.

Some believe that the punishment should follow the crime. Those that murder should receive death, Justan said. *Others believe that by killing those who murder, we become murderers ourselves.*

"Okay, I'm done peein'," Durza said, sloshing back over to Justan. He sighed as he reached down to help her back up, knowing that she had just peed in the same water that was now dripping off of her feet and down Gwyrtha's side.

They continued on and Deathclaw's thoughts were filled with irritation. *Why do you tell me what these 'others' believe? And what does this have to do with Talon's evils?*

I told you those things because I want you to fully understand both sides of the issue you are asking me about, Justan replied. *What do you think is the correct way?*

I am not the human. If I knew the answer I would not be asking you, Deathclaw grumped. *Stop asking me questions and tell me what you think I should do!*

Deathclaw's frustration reminded Justan of the way he had felt when his mother would try to teach him philosophical concepts. His thoughts soured. He was sounding like his mother.

Alright, Deathclaw. This is what I think. I believe that we should do what is necessary to stop evil from happening. We should not hesitate to kill an attacker if it will save a friend. We should not hesitate to hurt someone if that keeps them from hurting others.

As for punishment after the fact? It depends on the situation. Will the punishment save others in the future? Then yes. If it is just for our own selfish desire for vengeance, then I feel it is wrong.

You are right, Justan, Gwyrtha said. *You are good.*

Hmm, said Deathclaw. *I understand your thoughts on this. But when it comes to Talon I still do not know which is the right answer.*

Neither do I, Justan replied. *However, I did learn something that may help. When Talon first met the Prophet, she asked him to kill her and he refused. He helped her to combat the evil feelings inside her and sent her to Matthew. When she met Matthew, she asked him to kill her and he refused. If those two men, who know more about the possible future than we do, were not certain enough to kill her, how can we be?*

Deathclaw grew silent as he digested what had been said. *I will continue to watch her,* he decided.

Not long after that, they arrived at a short slope that took them onto dry land. The area was bordered by wide trees with massive roots that dipped into the water and in between the trees were well trodden trails.

It was at this point that Durza called out for them to stop, saying happily, "Master is comin'!"

"Finally," Justan sighed. He looked around, noting a distinct lack of troll trails. How could that be when they were so far into the Troll Swamp? It was the first time he had seen a dry patch that wasn't crisscrossed with the stuff. It had been particularly annoying when trying to find a place to sleep for the night.

"There you are!" said a cheerful voice.

Walking between two of the large trees was Matthew. Like John, he was a man of average height with an average face that faded from memory when one wasn't looking directly at him. Unlike the haggard and sickly man Justan had seen in Talon's memories, he looked quite healthy. The robe he wore was a fine one and he held a lit pipe in his left hand.

Durza pranced over to him with a beaming smile and he patted the top of her head. "You did a very good job, Durza. Thank you."

"You still have that sword in your back, I see," Justan said. The handle of the weapon was sticking up at an angle over the Stranger's left shoulder. It looked as if it were simply sheathed on his back, but Justan knew the blade was sheathed in the man's skin.

"Hello to you too, Sir Edge," Matthew replied, his smile fading only slightly. "And you have a rogue horse I see. This one looks familiar to me. Gwyrtha, isn't it? It is nice to see you again. That bond is good for you, I think. You seem much brighter than the last time we met."

Hello, Matthew, she said neutrally and he nodded as if he had heard her.

When did you meet him? Justan sent.

With John, she said, her memories flickering back to times that the Prophet had ridden her into Malaroo. *He isn't always this nice.*

"Talon," the Stranger said. She approached him slowly and he pushed back the cowl that covered her frightening face. He cupped her cheek with one hand and nodded. "Better. Remember what I told you. A bit at a time."

"Yes, Master," she said with tearful eyes and pulled the cowl back over her head.

"And you must be her brother." He approached Deathclaw and held out his hand. The raptoid cocked his head in curiosity, but shook it. "Ah, you are much further along than she is. It is good to see a dragon that has chosen to expand his mind. Tell me. Have you yet decided Talon's fate?"

"I have . . . not," Deathclaw replied.

Matthew nodded sagely. "I am sure you will make the right decision." He paused and raised an eyebrow. "My, that sword that you wear across your back. Is that . . . Star?"

"Yes," said the raptoid uneasily, removing his hand from the man's. "You know it?"

"I do," he said. "Would you mind if I looked at it?"

Deathclaw looked at Justan and Justan gave him a shrug, unsure what this was about. His eyes wary, Deathclaw drew the sword and held it out flat across his palms.

Matthew placed his pipe firmly in the corner of his mouth and let out a thoughtful grunt as he took the sword from the raptoid. "I haven't seen this sword in centuries. How strangely fortuitous that it should appear here now in your hands. I wonder if John had something to do with that."

"I would doubt that," Deathclaw said. "I took it from one of Ewzad Vriil's servants I killed. I kept it to help me kill Talon."

Justan glanced at Deathclaw's sister to gauge her reaction. She stood silently, her hood casting a shadow over her features. If this information was at all disturbing to Talon, she did not show it.

Matthew nodded. "Yes, well Star has been passed around many times by people who did not know its intended use." He held it back out to Deathclaw. "It seems to have taken quite well to you. Do you know its intended use?"

Deathclaw took the weapon back from him and slid it into its sheath. "Star likes to kill trolls. It burns hotter when used for that purpose." His brow furrowed slightly. "It . . . hates these swamps."

"I imagine it would," he said. Matthew turned to Justan and Justan wondered if he had chosen to speak to everyone else first so that he would be disarmed by the man's newfound charm. "Well, Sir Edge. You look like a man full of questions."

"And you look like a man who has turned over a new leaf," Justan said. "Is that real or is it due to the sword in your back?"

The Stranger sighed, but his smile didn't lessen this time. "I would say that the answer is yes to both those questions."

"That's a cryptic answer," Justan replied. "People who use those are usually trying to cover a lie."

"No lies. I believe I have changed and part of it is because of this sword in my back. Let's just say that I required a lesson in humility." Matthew studied Justan's reaction and took a draw on his pipe. "Tell me. What do you think this sword is?"

"From the runes on its hilt, I'd say it was a spirit magic weapon, though I knew that from my spirit sight before I saw the hilt. Also, Tolynn mentioned it when talking about your appearance at the treaty talks," Justan replied. "The prevailing rumor is that the sword is piercing your spirit, allowing the gnome warlord to control you. The demons in his army believe that. Is that true?"

"It is no longer true," Matthew said. "I am bound by promises made, but not by the powers of this weapon. Right now the sword is just a symbol. A symbol that Warlord Aloysius does not yet fully trust me."

"I can't say as I blame him. I am partially tempted to stab you with my own sword to find out for sure." This was true, but something told Justan that was an incredibly bad idea.

"If I remember right, the last time we met, you were the one being straightforward and I was the one being standoffish." Matthew laughed. "Enough already! If you're trying to impress me, it isn't necessary. I have been impressed with you from the moment John brought you into my home."

"I'm not attempting to impress you," Justan replied, though once the words left his lips, he realized that wasn't quite true. "I am trying to figure you out."

"I'm kind of complicated," the Stranger said. "I've been around a long time."

Justan gritted his teeth, refusing to be charmed. "Yes, but the real question is, has your condemnation been lifted?"

Matthew sighed and held out his hand. "You were named by the Bowl of Souls. You are a bonding wizard. The Creator has placed his favor on you. Grasp my hand and tell me what you believe."

Frowning slightly, Justan reached out and took the man's hand. A tingling warmth flooded up his arm. It was the same feeling he had felt in the presence of the Bowl. He was immediately overcome by the assurance that this man had his Master's approval.

Justan let out a breath that he didn't even know he'd been holding. "I believe you."

Matthew smiled and patted his arm. "My power isn't fully back yet. It's a process. I am not the man John is. I never was. But I am trying my best."

"Alright," said Justan. "So why did you ask me to come here?"

The man let go of his hand and leaned back, taking a draw on his pipe. As he spoke, fragrant smoke floated into the air like tendrils. "I brought you here because I need your help convincing Warlord Aloysius and Xedrion bin Leeths to save the Known Lands."

Justan stared at Matthew long and hard. "Saving the Known Lands is an important task. Still, I'm not so sure I grasp your premise."

"Walk with me," the Stranger said, "And I will explain on the way."

Matthew led Justan down a well-trodden path through the trees, Deathclaw and Gwyrtha following with Talon and Durza close behind.

"As you know, Sir Edge, before my recent rousting, I had my head in the sand for a very long time. During that time I let several situations around me develop to the point that they have gone out of control. One of them is this situation with the Troll Mother."

Justan frowned, not liking the sound of that. Just how much had the Stranger's laziness affected the world? "She is one of your responsibilities?"

"Directly? No. Trolls are not a species under my supervision. I'm not sure they qualify as a species at all. They are more like a malignancy, a disease left over from Mellinda's evil plans centuries ago. However, I did take a responsibility upon myself that is directly related to her creation."

They rounded a large tree and a wide open clearing came into view. Taking up this area was an odd village. The buildings were very basic in construction; tall round shacks whose walls were made of logs and long poles that were held together with a mix of mud and swamp grasses. Walking amongst the shacks were tall, muscular creatures who looked vaguely troll-like. They were naked, but sexless, with bushy black hair atop their heads and a slight greenish tint to their skin.

"Thulls," Deathclaw said, sending Justan an image of the beast that Stolz had been bonded to.

"Yes, that's right," Mathew said, pausing for a moment for Justan to take the village in. "The thulls were once a populous people, living very basic and wild lives in the swamps. That is, until the Roo people began domesticating them and using them as slave labor."

"And they are the race Mellinda created the trolls from," Justan said, remembering the story. As he watched the thulls move by, he noticed that a few of them walked with small children at their side.

"Correct," Matthew replied. "She found it amusing to use the Roo's own slaves against them. One unfortunate side effect of the horrible magic she used to make her stolen thulls into trolls was that it removed their souls."

"Nice rhyme, Master!" Durza enthused.

"That was unintentional, but thank you," Matthew said with a sigh. He started walking forward again, leading them towards the village.

"When the Roo people fled their swamps to escape Mellinda's armies, they left the thulls behind to fight for themselves. As you know, trolls will attack anything, but for some reason they seem to instinctually see the thulls as having the souls that they are missing. They have an odd habit of banding together in large groups to attack thull settlements. As a result, the species was almost entirely wiped out. Only this one village remains."

As they walked between the shacks, many of the large thulls approached them. The gentle giants reached their clawed hands out towards them, but did not touch them. Matthew reached his hand out towards them as well.

"This is their way of greeting. By showing them our claws openly, they see we are no threat," he explained.

Justan held his hands out towards them, as did Deathclaw.

Gwyrtha bared her teeth. They bared their own sharp teeth back at her in a friendly manner.

"What does this have to do with your responsibility?" Justan asked.

Matthew again puffed on his pipe. "When I first came to the swamps looking for a dwelling far from the races under my charge and their constant need for guidance." He sighed. "I came upon this village. They had been beset for days, fighting the vile trolls. Most of them had fallen. I knew, watching the battle that if I did not act, I would witness the end of the species."

"So you saved them," Deathclaw said.

"It was probably the last order of my Master that I obeyed for a long time," Matthew replied. "I drove the trolls away and then I left the thulls a gift."

He stopped at the center of the village where there was a structure different from the others. It had a roof held up by poles at the four corners, but no walls. Inside was a small shrine surrounded by offerings of dead frogs and fishes. In the center on top of a brightly colored rock, was a white orb.

Justan could feel the power radiating from it and when he switched to spirit sight, it glowed like a beacon. "This is what keeps the trolls away?"

"It is now. I had a less powerful version in the beginning, but that is where my involvement in this mess began."

Justan frowned. "Protecting this place made you responsible for the Troll Mother?"

Matthew let out a sad chuckle. "Over the years that I lived here I continued to notice a change in the Troll Mother's behavior. She seemed more and more aggressive. It was becoming harder to keep the trolls out and there were a few times when she swallowed someone from the village itself.

"So one day I paid a visit to KhanzaRoo itself and used my influence to calm her directly. It was then that I met the very first of those people that now call themselves trollkin. It was an odd thing. Mostly troll except for around the face. He called himself, 'The First'. Those were the only words he seemed to know at the time."

"How long ago was that?" Justan asked.

Matthew waved a hand absently. "A few centuries and as far as I knew, he was the only one. An aberration. A hiccup where the Troll Mother swallowed a morsel and instead of killing it and feeding on it, changed it and spat it back out with at least part of its soul intact."

"Has this been going on that long?" Justan asked.

"No," Matthew said. "There wasn't another for some time. My calming of the Troll Mother may have had something to do with that. She made far fewer trolls which meant less hassle. The village was kept safe with little maintenance. I was satisfied. But then again, I am becoming increasingly unsettled by the possibility that my calming of the Troll Mother changed her in some way. Part of me wonders if she used that time to think. Perhaps the presence of that first creature encouraged her.

"She eventually stopped making new trolls all together. It was a few short years ago that I saw a second aberration. This one was different. Half troll, half animal, it was wild and mindless. It killed three thulls before they killed it. More came. I increased the power of protection as much as I could even though I was under condemnation. Then John sent Talon and Durza to me. Durza's gift is a blessing. She could do what I couldn't at the time and keep both the Troll Mother and the trollkin away."

Matthew nodded towards the shrine. "That orb is another gift from John. I was able to make it strong enough to duplicate Durza's job so that she did not have to spend as much time at the village."

Justan found it difficult to comprehend what Matthew was saying. "You're telling me that you knew this was going on? You might even have had something to do with causing it? And still you said nothing? All those villages swallowed up while Xedrion tried to discover the problem and you could have just told him?"

The Stranger sighed. "I am not proud of my behavior, Sir Edge. Yes, I ignored it because I did not consider the Roo-Tan under my realm of responsibility."

"And because it would have meant you leaving your house again," Justan surmised.

"And sheer laziness, yes." He spread his arms wide. "Cast your stones and they will hit me because I am guilty of all those things. However, I am trying to rectify that."

Justan folded his arms. "And this is where you need my help."

Matthew went to take another pull on his pipe and was disappointed that it had run dry. He tapped the pipe against the heel of his boot to knock out the ashes and began filling it again from a pouch in his pocket.

"I am sure you are aware of the current dilemma. On one side, we have the Roo-Tan, strong and with the support of elven magic, but suddenly lacking in manpower. On another side, the newly-titled Mer-Dan Collective, the product of years of scheming by Warlord Aloysius."

"So he is behind their creation," Justan said.

Matthew nodded. He reached out a finger and touched the tobacco. How he lit it, Justan was not sure because he didn't see anything with his mage sight. Matthew took a few puffs.

"He was in constant contact with the merpeople in Pearl Cove. How they were able to convince the Roo-Dan to band together, I'm not quite sure. But it was all part of his perhaps poorly conceived plan to pull Malaroo under the banner of his Third Great Alberri empire.

"At any rate, the Mer-Dan Collective still has much greater numbers than the Roo-Tan, as well as a tactical genius the world has not seen since the Time of the Warlords. What they are lacking is cohesiveness. Their people are scared. Shaken by the disaster at the treaty talks."

Justan shook his head. "And you want me to help that monster? After all he's done. That 'disaster' was his fault!"

"Warlord Aloysius is not quite the monster you think. Yes, he's misguided. But his intentions have always been for what he sees as the better good of the people. Though the treaty disaster happened in part because he invited Mellinda and her trollkin, he did so with the intent to destroy them. The Troll Mother's attack caught him by surprise just as much as everyone else."

"I don't doubt that he was surprised," Justan allowed. "But

I do doubt the purity of his intentions."

"You are right to do so," Matthew said. "Be that as it may, I still ask for your help. Like him or not, these two nations need to work together or they will be overrun."

Justan scowled. "When I go back to Roo-Tan'lan, I'll tell the Protector what you said. Maybe it will be enough to convince him to meet with your gnome warlord again."

"I am afraid that will not be good enough," Matthew said.

"It may have to be. I cannot force the Protector to do anything. Nor do I want to try." Justan said.

Matthew gave him a firm look. "As my condemnation has been lifted, I have seen several paths this could take. The only one where these two leaders work together is if you take a direct part."

Justan threw up his hands. "What does that even mean?"

"Follow me," Matthew said. He turned and continued through the village. "Meet Warlord Aloysius and take measure of him yourself. Then decide."

Justan didn't like the sound of that. He felt like he was being manipulated. Nevertheless, he did as the Stranger asked.

You despise this gnome, Deathclaw sent, following closely behind him.

He has done vile things. He killed Esmine in an attempt to make a weapon to control people's minds. He started a war in his own country just to get rid of his rivals. When I told Matthew I thought he was a monster, I meant it.

Does he deserve death? Deathclaw asked.

Justan hesitated to answer. *That depends on different factors.*

You have an opportunity, Deathclaw suggested. *You are going to meet this gnome.*

I am not an assassin, Justan replied.

I am, Deathclaw replied. *You decide. If you feel that his death will save others in the future, I will kill him for you.*

I don't think you were listening very closely when we talked earlier, Justan said.

Behind a stand of wide trees, just outside of the village

proper a large tent had been erected. A series of smaller tents surrounded it. Justan saw guards from the Roo-Dan, merpeople, and imp races.

"You brought part of his army to this village under your protection?" Justan asked incredulously.

"It is neutral ground, Sir Edge. Belonging to no side in this conflict," Matthew said. "They have no more reason to harm the thulls than you do. The thulls have no resources worth conquering."

Still frowning, Justan followed Matthew to the tent. The guards let Matthew in, but were nervous at the sight of Deathclaw and Gwyrtha.

"They are my bonded," Justan said to Matthew. "They come with me or I leave right now."

A man appeared at the tent opening wearing a white robe with a red sash. He ordered the guards to let Justan and his bonded inside.

It was a wide tent separated into multiple rooms by canvas walls. In the main room was a single high backed chair where Warlord Aloysius sat. The gnome was dressed in black chainmail that glowed with elemental protection and there was a circlet on his brow that let off a white shimmer.

"Warlord Aloysius," said Matthew. "May I introduce Sir Edge, twice named at the Bowl of Souls and bonding wizard. With him are Deathclaw, the brother of my servant Talon, and the rogue horse Gwyrtha."

"What an impressive visitor," the gnome said. He rose from his chair and looked Justan up and down. "I must say, there are few souls in this world who could boast of more impressive titles than yours. And at such a young age."

This was the first time Justan had seen the gnome up close. There was a definite presence to him unlike any gnome he had met. Perhaps the closest was Alfred. The warlord was handsome and despite the arrogance that poured from his very pores, he had charm.

Justan refused to let those attributes affect him. "Yet none of those titles were ones I sought."

The gnome raised an eyebrow. "That is a bit of an aggressive reaction to praise freely given. I take it that you arrive before me with preconceived notions?"

"I know many things about you," Justan said.

"I see. You have heard of past acts of mine that, no doubt, sound atrocious without context. You likely have the same source as the Protector," he said.

"Firsthand accounts," Justan said. "And from friends. People who I trust."

Aloysius nodded. "I see I have quite the barrier to overcome. Perhaps if I gave my side to the tale?"

"I'm not sure I would believe anything you said," Justan said and frowned, realizing the truth of that statement as it left his mouth. He nodded to himself. "In fact, there is nothing you can say that would convince me you were in the right."

Tell me if you wish it done, Deathclaw said.

Justan's thoughts continued to churn. *Stay your hand for now.*

Aloysius turned to Matthew. "Then what was the point of this exercise, Stranger? You drag me all this way in the hopes that this person can help and now he refuses to even listen?"

"He's not done speaking," Matthew replied.

"Tell me, Warlord," said Justan. "What is your true goal?"

Aloysius swung around to face him. "To protect this world in the battle that is yet to come."

Justan nodded. "In order to reach that goal, are you willing to make a sacrifice?"

"I have already sacrificed much to get where I am," he asked suspiciously. "What do you ask of me?"

"Matthew wants me to help you get Xedrion back to the treaty table," Justan replied. "The only way I would be able to do that is if I trusted you implicitly."

"You've already said that you refuse to believe anything I say," Aloysius replied.

"This won't be about words," Justan said and he drew his left sword. Peace attempted to take his emotions, but Justan refused. This was not a time for detached thought.

The steward with the red sash leapt in front of the gnome. "Make one more move and you die."

"Put down your weapon, Oliver," Aloysius said with a frown. He cocked his head at Justan. "What is this about, Sir Edge? Assassination would not seem your style."

"My sword works in a way very similar to yours," Justan explained. He flipped the sword around and pointed the tip at the ground. so that the dagger-like point that protruded below the handle was facing up. "Except that instead of taking the will of the person pierced by its blade, it creates a bond."

"I see," Aloysius said curiously, approaching Justan and bending to look over the blade with fascination. "How fascinating. I am quite an expert when it comes to different types of weaponry. Your sword is exquisite. A master smith created this. The design . . . unique. But the runes tell the true story here."

He straightened. "I believe I understand what you want. I allow you to pierce my flesh with this blade. You then plunder my mind and discover my motivations, perhaps my foulest secrets will be exposed?"

"Openness," Justan said. "The bond created will go both ways if I allow it. You do this and we will understand each other on a level that only a bonding wizard and his bonded can understand. And yes, if there are foul secrets I will find them. If I see what Matthew sees in you, I will help you. I will take you to Xedrion and tell him with absolute certainty that he should listen."

"And if you should not agree with the Stranger?" Aloysius asked. "If you should find that I am the abomination that your friend, Tarah Woodblade thinks me to be?"

"Then it is likely that my bonded and I will attempt to kill you," Justan replied.

"And succeed," Deathclaw added.

Matthew frowned. "Sir Edge, I believe you are taking this a bit too far."

"Openness," Justan repeated, his eyes not leaving the gnome. "Are you willing to show me that you aren't a monster?"

"You ask a great deal," the gnome said with narrowed eyes.

"You know who I am," Justan replied. "Those titles Matthew told you should say a good deal about me. One thing he forgot to mention is that I am also a bearer of Jharro wood. I promised my allegiance to the grove."

"Very well," Aloysius decided. "What do you wish me to do?"

"You can't be serious, Scholar!" said the red-sashed steward.

"Oliver, you forget yourself!" Aloysius snapped. "I am no mere scholar for you to baby! I look at this man and what I see is someone with the type of power I should not fear!"

"Hold out your hand," Justan said.

The gnome did so. Justan slowed the world around him. Then he grabbed the warlord's hand and shoved it onto the dagger end of his sword.

Instantly, the gnome's thoughts poured into his mind. Aloysius was shocked at the lack of pain. He was also quite nervous about the thought of having Justan in his mind.

Good, Justan thought. He dove into the gnome's memories.

This was different from the memories of Talon. They were deeper. He was much longer lived. They were also sharper. This was a mind that did not forget. He saw a mind that was proud and uncompromising. A mind that held logic and his main goal above all else.

Justan went deeper, skimming to the beginning. He saw Aloysius as a child, inquisitive but physical. The stewards determined that he was a warrior at first. He enjoyed swordplay, but he didn't care much for the animal they brought him. He watched its death with confusion more than sadness or guilt.

"Why did you kill this rabbit?" he asked. "Are you hungry?"

"You killed it! For refusing to learn your sword," said the steward, a red-faced man that Aloysius immediately knew disliked dealing with children.

"You killed it. I saw you," Aloysius insisted. Meanwhile

another gnome child wept in the corner over the loss of the kitten he had come to love so much. "You killed Cletus' kitten, too. Why? Are you trying to make him mean like you?"

The steward, surprised by the child's reaction, returned to the testers and told them that Aloysius did not belong with the warriors. He had a scholar's mind.

They tested the gnome child and discovered that he was beyond brilliant. He was adopted into a major house and given tutors to discover his true focus. Noting his early interest in weapons, they started him with a study of tactics. The child devoured the subject and wrote his first essay disputing the teachings of one of the great tacticians.

Aloysius moved on from subject to subject, showing brilliance in each. Nevertheless, he always found himself going back to weapons in his spare time. The stewards noticed this and were alarmed. What was wrong with this gnome?

Then one day, when he had reached his teenage years, Aloysius' stewards were taken away. They were replaced by a new group with shrewder eyes. With them was the red-faced man who had killed that rabbit in front of him as a child. He wore a red sash and handed Aloysius a new book. A history of the gnome warlords.

A new focus had been created. Aloysius now knew what he was destined to become. He studied all he could on the two previous gnome warlords. Then he studied their teacher, the ageless man known as the Stranger. He researched his methods and his decent into apathy. The more Aloysius learned about the man, the more he knew he was on his own.

This is where Aloysius' studies took a darker turn. He studied the villains. These were the types of foes he would need to defeat one day and to defeat them, he needed to understand them. He researched the tactics of the human and imp warlords. He spent a long time on the Dark Prophet.

He saw the flaws in their goals, but not always in their methods. He filed that knowledge away. He then turned his gaze on the dangers of the world. As the gnome warlord of this era, he would be needed to protect the known lands, but from what? It was unclear.

He had but one choice. Prepare for all threats. This meant he needed to accrue power.

Power was not a thing normally placed in the hands of a gnome. This was self-evident in the steward system. So he learned to work around it.

Justan pushed ahead. He saw Aloysius' stalwart desire. He saw the atrocities committed in the name of future good.

Attempts at open advancement of his goals were always shut down so Aloysius grew devious and underhanded. He became the spider behind the scenes of the gnome homeland. He forged alliances with dark wizards, always with the intention of destroying them in the end.

Justan saw Aloysius decide to start the war to cleanse his country. He saw his botched attempt at binding a rogue horse. He saw the gnome's true intentions at the day of the treaty signing.

Justan pulled back from the gnomes memories in exhaustion. *I have seen what I needed to see*, he told the gnome.

As have I, replied Aloysius, for as Justan had been looking through his memories, the gnome had been looking through Justan's.

Justan pulled the gnome's hand off of his sword, healing the wound as he went. When he was finished all that was left was the tiniest cut.

"What a remarkably fascinating experience," Aloysius said, flexing his hand, while giving Justan a curious look. "You are a surprisingly complicated individual."

Justan glared at him and turned on the Stranger. It was all he could do not to punch the ancient man in his negligent face. "This is your fault! You left him alone!"

"Yes I did," Matthew said. "I accept full responsibility. I was not listening or I would have been at his side when he was born."

"Well, you need to make up for it now!" Justan said.

Matthew nodded humbly. "That is what I am attempting."

"That was actually quite tiring." Aloysius slumped back

into his chair. "So tell me, Sir Edge. What did you find in that head of mine?"

"You're guilty of all of it! Everything I heard is true!" Justan snapped. "Even if you did those things in some misguided attempt for a better future, it does not make any of them acceptable."

Should I kill him? Deathclaw asked.

Of course not! Justan replied.

The gnome warlord nodded. "After seeing your life and learning you the way I have, I knew you would feel that way. And yet I also know you will not kill me."

"I can't," Justan said, slamming his fist into his palm. "Heaven knows you deserve it! That doesn't matter, though. You have got to change your ways, but we are going to need you."

"Very good!" Aloysius said. "So you have decided to help me?"

Justan glared at the flippant way he said that. "I will do what I can. But not for some distant future when you're 'supposed' to be the general that leads us against nebulous evil. I'm doing it because we need you now. We are going to have to work together for the safety of the Grove."

"I agree wholeheartedly," Aloysius said with a smile.

Justan's glare didn't lessen. "There is a problem, though. As things are now, Xedrion will not trust a word you say."

"Won't he? He'll now have your word." The gnome said. "Matthew's word."

"Matthew? You mean the prophet that you are trying to control with your sword?" Justan said in derision. "Xedrion has been suspicious from the moment he saw you two together on the day of the treaty." He shook his head. "Before we do anything else, you need to remove that sword from his back."

Matthew stepped forward and placed a hand on Justan's shoulder. "It is okay, Sir Edge. That is a step he will make when he is ready to release control. He-."

"Yes-yes. That is what you keep telling me," Aloysius interrupted. He looked to Justan. "But let me ask you something, my friend. You now know me better than anyone else. What are my feelings for the Stranger?"

"All your life, you learned to hate him," Justan said.

The gnome raised an eyebrow. "And now?"

"Now you fear him," Justan replied. "Because he can't be controlled."

Aloysius shook his head. "Because if I set him free, I have no guarantee that he will not abandon us again."

"You don't," Justan agreed. "But then again, maybe you do. You have already been given proof that the Creator believes he's reformed."

"For now," Aloysius said dismissively. "The Creator is too eager to forgive His servants. The Dark Prophet reformed three times before the Prophet was given permission to destroy him. I do not have that luxury."

Justan stood firm. "You're a logical thinker, but in this case, you are letting your emotions rule you."

"I am not!" the warlord scoffed.

Justan held out his sword. "Do you want to hold onto Peace and think this through again?"

Aloysius narrowed his eyes. Grimacing, he stepped over to the Stranger and grasped the handle. "Very well, Sir Edge. I see that this must be done."

"Are you certain?" Matthew asked, surprised at his quick acceptance.

"Of course not!" Aloysius said. He took a deep breath. "Before I do this, I need some assurances from you."

Matthew nodded. "Such as?"

"You must continue to leave the birth rates of the races untouched," Aloysius said.

"That goes against my recommendations," Matthew warned. "But I will keep it as you wish."

"Secondly, I want you very aware of one thing. You may have reformed yourself for now, but if you should ever return to your former ways, I will pierce you again and, if your master allows it, strike you dead!" the gnome promised.

"Aloysius," Justan said. "I'm afraid I must give you the same warning. If you should ever turn into the monstrosity that you have so nearly become, I will be forced to kill you myself."

"I will trust you to do what you feel is right, Sir Edge," Aloysius said and in one smooth motion, removed the Sword of Mastery from the Stranger's back.

Justan stumbled. A sudden tingle came over him.

What is it? Deathclaw asked, feeling the same tingling but not as strongly.

Justan realized that its source was from the bond. But how? He checked briefly and realized it was coming from his connection to Fist.

"Are you alright, Sir Edge?" Matthew asked.

"Hold on," Justan said. He closed his eyes and reached through the bond as far as he could in his distracted state. A few moments later, he had his answer. "How is that possible? Surely it's not. He's far off in the mountains right now. Or he should be."

What happened? Gwyrtha wondered.

Justan let out a short laugh. "Fist has been named."

Chapter Twenty Three

Lyramoor hung limply, anchored to the wall by the clay golem's unyielding flesh. Thick bands of it encircled his waist, feet, and arms, leaving his chest and head bare. She had stripped him down, leaving him without protection.

Days of torture had turned his mind numb. His only solace was that she hadn't broken through his protections. The magical devices implanted in his body were still there, most importantly the one that allowed him to hide from pain. This was the device in his abdomen near his lower back, the only one that she could see with her spirit sight. Thankfully, his bluff had worked and she hadn't yet dared try to remove it.

It was a brass ball containing the soul of a small dog named Tiko.

Lyramoor had first come across Tiko a year after being rescued by Sabre Vlad and his Academy unit. Lyramoor had not attempted to join the Academy right away. He was wealthy thanks to Khalpany's king, who had paid him a princely sum as compensation for being held as a blood slave in his kingdom. He was also restless, eager to enjoy his newfound freedom.

His first journey had been to the elf homeland of his birth. The Pruball elves had been generous to him, welcoming him with open arms. He had even been able to meet his parents, who were overjoyed to see him. However, after two centuries at the hands of dwarves and orcs and dark wizards, he was no longer recognizable as their child. He was no longer recognizable as an elf. He stayed less than a month before things had grown so uncomfortable for him that he left in the night.

He had traveled then, aimlessly searching for ways to

guarantee his freedom. He preferred to travel alone, untrusting of merchants and caravans. One night, while sleeping not far outside the city Gladstone he woke up to find Tiko staring back at him.

The small dog, shivering, half starved, and sickly, looked at him with trusting eyes. No one looked at Lyramoor with trusting eyes. Not back then. His look of perpetual anger had not faded from his days as a slave and the scars on his face told people that he was dangerous.

Tiko had remained his only companion for the space of two years. Lyramoor spent the time in Alberri, traveling to surgeons and wizards willing to accept his coin in order to give him the protections he sought. Sadly, the dog's illnesses were not something that food and companionship could fix.

Lyramoor had a wizard place the brass ball, bound with Tiko's soul, into his body where they would never be apart again. The place where his long ago harvested kidney had been was the perfect spot. Now, whenever in times of deep distress, whether it be the pain of torture or the trauma of the nightmares that plagued him, his mind could retreat to Tiko and the dog would comfort him.

He left Tiko now and returned to a body that was aching and trembling. He lifted his head and looked around the great room. The priestess was gone, as was her hound. He felt a vibration in the wall behind him and wondered if the battle had already started.

He had failed. Somehow, despite all his preparations, he had been unable to escape. There were metal implements hidden under his scars in several places. Picks for opening locks, small blades for cutting rope, even a throwing knife hidden in his shin. But the priestess had been too thorough.

He had no way to reach them. Even if he could his hands were now useless. She had broken his fingers. There was only one way he could help his friends now and it was something he dreaded above all else.

Lyramoor let out a bitter groan.

"Still alive, unwilling dog?" said Vastyr.

The pampered elf slave was sitting in his mistress' throne,

one knee thrown over the armrest. He held a wineglass in one hand, but the liquid inside was translucent and the color of amber, likely something stronger than wine.

Lyramoor looked over at his right hand. He winced. It was a mangled sight, his fingers bent and fixed at odd angles. Nevertheless, Cassandra had made one small mistake. It was so small she had missed it.

He thought fast. This was the first time he had been conscious while left alone with the slave. "Is that firewater?"

"If only," the elf said with a sigh. "Whiskey. Haven't had firewater in ages."

"She don't mind you gettin' drunk? Won't that mess up her blood feast?" he said with a bit more venom than intended.

Vastyr glared. "It adds to the experience, which you would know if you weren't a disgusting vagabond."

Lyramoor gritted his teeth, which hurt because Cassandra had shattered two of them. Willing elf slaves like Vaster were brought up in families with "blood drinker" hosts. They were taught from a young age that the sole point of their noble existence was to maintain their "blood drinker's" habits and save them from devolving into frenzied vampires.

They called themselves the "Willing." To Lyramoor, they were willing traitors, content to perpetuate an irredeemable evil. Pampered cattle is what they were.

He licked his lips and tried to make his voice sound understanding. "I knew that. Just not all drinkers like it. My first drinker said it gave her a headache."

"How dare you call them that!" Vastyr snapped. He leaned back in the throne and took a gulp of his liquor. "Know your place, low thing."

"You're wrong about me, Vastyr. I wasn't always one of the unwilling," Lyramoor lied. He made up a tale on the spot hoping that the slave was as simple minded as he seemed. "I was born to a willing family. Our mistress was killed. Our family went to ground, but we were grabbed up by dwarves."

"Indeed?" Vastyr's interest had been piqued. He turned in the throne and faced the captured elf. "What was this mistress' name?"

It wasn't hard to pull one out of his mind. The dwarves had often talked about prospective buyers and vampires were always being hunted down and killed. Some of the high nobles managed to keep their drinking a secret all while fostering willing slaves like they were herds of foolish goats. "Kami D'Llen."

Vastyr looked impressed. The Willing were very strange about their regard for noble drinkers. "Really? That was before my time. But I heard of this mistress of yours. I thought that her willing were well taken care of after her murder."

"We weren't the lucky ones." He looked down. "I was passed from dwarf to dwarf ever since. Taught to hate all drinkers."

"I heard they do that," Vastyr said in disgust.

"I only got one thing left to remember her by. Her mark," he said.

The elf slave frowned. Marking a willing slave with a tattoo was a bit of a taboo, but some elf "families" did it willingly. "Kami D'Llen marked you herself?"

"My mother marked me at birth. That way I'd never forget." He looked back over at his hand. "You can still see it on my wrist."

"Really?" The pampered elf stood and approached him cautiously. "On your right wrist?"

"Yeah. The dwarves tried to hide it with a scar, but you can still see it," Lyramoor said. The elf continued to approach. "It's partly covered by the clay but, agh! It hurts to move my hand but I'll try to let you see it."

"That long scar at the base of your palm?" Vastyr asked, trying not to get too close. He kept out of the captive's reach but tried to peer at the bit of the scar that moved right along Lyramoor's vein.

"Right. It's in blue ink . . ." Lyramoor sent a mental command to the tiny spirit of the deathwhisper hidden in his arm.

A needle sprang forth from the scar like a tiny dart, piercing Vastyr just in the corner of his eye. The deathwhisper was a tiny fleshy creature prized by assassins for its deadly venom. Its bound spirit had been waiting for that moment eagerly for decades, holding the poison within the needle until the right victim came along.

The pampered slave squealed, dropping his glass to break on the ground. He gingerly reached up and pulled the tiny needle out and flung it on the ground. "You monster! You filthy beast!"

His legs wobbled. He fell to the floor, cutting his face on the broken glass. He was numb by that time, unable to move. He only bled for a few seconds.

Lyramoor's laugh was grim. Next came the hard part. He sent his thoughts back to spend a few last moments with Tiko while he waited.

The Priestess of War stood at the cliff's edge, her form hidden by cunning weaves of air. It was here on this very section of the cliff that she had been struck down, caught unawares by a young dwarf with a magic hammer. It was for that reason she desired to launch her attack from this point. Let it become a place of victory instead of shame.

Cassandra smiled as she looked down at the slopes below. The Academy army with their paltry three thousand looked small from up here. She had to credit them for their perseverance.

Two solid days swarmed by wraithflies had barely slowed them down. Still, with supplies contaminated and constant fights breaking out, morale had to be low. Why not crush it completely? She had no reason to draw this out. A dejected army made for easy slaughter.

Grasping her mace in her right hand, she reached her earth magic into the cliffside below. Slowly, she raised both arms in the air. Using the mace wasn't necessary, nor was raising her arms, but there was something satisfying about doing it.

The massive walls she had risen to hide her armies lowered back into the earth. The entire mountainside rumbled with such a raw display of power. The men afoot were jolted. Horses reared in surprise and a few men fell from their backs.

Out from hidden caverns and passages to the west and east side of the Academy forces came her army of orcs and human warslaves. Directly down the center, from the northern passes that led to the Black Lake, came her army of dead and infested.

The Academy forces faced numbers twice their size and Cassandra hadn't yet released her reserves. Still, the well-trained troops behaved admirably, falling into disciplined ranks. Shieldmen and pikemen marched at the front, wizards and archers at the rear.

It was foolishness. Nevertheless, she couldn't help but add one final jolt of fear. It was an old tactic and a bit dramatic, but she was fond of the old ways. Just as the armies rushed together, Cassandra sent out another surge of elemental magic.

Streams of air magic flowed over the army below to carry her words to all of the enemy forces. Her voice was reverberating and powerful, shaking the men below to their core.

"YOU COME TO YOUR DEATH! HAIL TO THE DARK PROPHET! HIS PRIESTESS OF WAR DESTROYS ALL!"

The old tactic was effective. The Academy's front line was shaken just as the armies clashed. It buckled in several places, shieldmen were knocked down and pikemen rushed.

The downside of that spell was that it gave away her position to everyone with mage sight. Cassandra hurried away from the edge, throwing up shields of magic behind her as fireballs and lightning strikes were launched by wizards below. The clifftop was pounded and the section of rock where she had stood fell away, crashing to the slopes below. Undoubtedly many of her dead army were crushed, but they were of no concern. There were always plenty more.

As she walked briskly across the clifftop shelf towards the canyon that overlooked the Black Lake, she was joined by Raj. The striped lupero's shoulders were at the same height as her head as it walked beside her.

His smaller packmates were stationed at various points of interest around the passes below, ready to alert her if anything unexpected should occur. Two of his fellow luperos were on the ground not far from the battle, positioned so that she could keep watch and return if the situation needed her personal presence once again. That was unlikely, though.

"Raj, low!" she commanded and the long-limbed lupero crouched so that she could swing her leg over his back.

Luperos weren't often kept as riding animals. Their narrow bodies weren't well suited for saddles. An alfa lupero like Raj, however, was strong and fast and able to climb into areas that regular mounts could not reach.

"Hut!" She laid across his back, wrapping her arms and legs around his torso as he sped off. This method of riding often seemed awkward to those who had never attempted it before, but to someone with a practiced grip it was an easy and comfortable ride.

He took her down a narrow canyon ledge. She frowned momentarily as the heat and stench of the lake enveloped her. This was part of her assignment and she knew that she would need to get used to it.

David had not given her any indication as to how long she would be stationed in this place. The only thing she knew for sure was that once the world heard about the Academy's defeat in these mountains today, they would come for her again. She would be well-prepared when that day came.

They were half way down the canyon wall when the first unexpected attack happened. It was a silent assault. Something unseen.

Half of her blood magic-infused bonds with the wraith were cut free. Cassandra cried out in mental agony as the backlash of magic slammed into her soul with tremendous force. She lost her grip on Raj and slipped.

Cassandra fell, her body rebounding off the narrow ledge and tumbling towards the lake below. In a way it was a similar event to the blow that had felled her two hundred years before. Only this time, she was better prepared. Taking swift control of the situation, she reached out with her earth magic, building a barrier around her.

Before she hit the lake's surface, she was already pursuing her attacker.

Cassandra's mind dove into her remaining connection with the wraith. It's amorphous black form was already raging, sensing that its shackles had been weakened. She ignored it for the moment and looked for a possible figure retreating in the darkness. It had to be someone of great power. Few could have avoided the traps she had left here.

She saw it. A white form. To her eye, it was as an eagle soaring among the countless black strands that connected the wraith's power to the world. Only this eagle was on fire. Every strand it touched gave way immediately.

Somewhere in the physical world, flies were falling dead by the hundreds, larvae simply bursting, their tiny minds crushed by the same backlash of power that had caused Cassandra such pain. Minor losses, all considered. But the fact that it had been able to cut her connections was not to be discounted. This was a powerful enemy and experienced.

She would crush it quickly. The form she took in the void was that of a lupero, red and fearsome. Cassandra pursued the eagle, strands of mental power issuing from her body like red hairs ready to entangle her prey.

The eagle saw her approach instantly. It's moves were agile, it dodged the majority of her strands and those few that did get through, it burned away. Nevertheless, her pursuit was dogged.

Cassandra looked for the strand of light that connected the eagle to its host body. If she cut that strand, the battle was over. But she could not find it. Her clever enemy had found a way to disguise his strand.

It didn't matter. As agile as the eagle was, she was faster. As determined as he was, she was more powerful. She followed him to the outer edge of the wraith's dark world, to the farthest reaches of its pinpricks of light. Then inexplicably, he vanished.

Cassandra raged. How was that possible? There was no escape. Not unless he had entered back to his body, but she would have seen it. Had the eagle somehow disguised the window back to his mind the same way he had disguised the line of life that led to it?

She soared back down to the wraith's black mass. It was

straining at the remaining red strands binding its will. Left alone much longer, it might have been able to break free. As it was, re-binding it was a struggle. Each strand of power she lashed around it drained her considerably.

It was a good thing she was close. If the eagle had struck while Cassandra was still on the cliffs above, she might not have been able to regain control, but that was no longer a worry. Not with her body already having fallen within the lake's depths.

Once she had finished, she set a new series of traps. Their strength hampered the wraith's distance of control somewhat, but it was a necessary precaution until this attacker was caught. Finished, but wearied, she returned to her body.

She was enveloped in the lake's living sludge. Her body was protected by a shell of earth, but her mobility was greatly limited. Normally, when entering the lake, she anchored herself to the ground with an armor of rock. Her unexpected fall had left her somewhat buoyant.

Cassandra was suspended ten feet under the surface, no way to push forward physically. She had no choice but to use her elemental magic and in a very inefficient manner. She sent a powerful burst of air magic out behind her, propelling herself forward. It was slow going, the thick sludge did not like to be moved and she was constantly buffeted by the large bodies of the creatures around her.

By the time she reached the shore, both her spirit and elemental magic had been drained considerably. She shed the sludge surrounding her and Raj ran up to her. She stepped up the pathway between the dead and approached the stone door to her home.

Before walking inside, she reached out to her luperos stationed near the battle. The fight was still raging. It seemed that the early advantage she had given her forces had been overcome and at the moment neither side was gaining ground. Things were likely still well in hand, but the Academy forces were better trained than she had expected. Once she had recharged herself, she would make another appearance and end things.

She rolled aside the stone door and ordered Raj to stay

outside. "Vastyr!"

When the elf did not respond immediately, her hands clenched. He had better not have drunken himself into slumber. She needed his blood now and it was best if he was conscious to tell her when to stop.

She rolled the door shut behind herself. "Vastyr! Now. I need you."

"I don't think he's gonna be much help at this point," called Lyramoor.

Cassandra stormed into the room, half expecting to find that the scarred elf had escaped. Instead, she saw that he was still restrained to the wall. Vastyr, though, was collapsed on the floor not far from him. She could smell the slave's blood.

"Vastyr!" she said and rushed to his side. He was lying on a broken glass. He was dead. Her eyes swung up to Lyramoor.

"He wasn't being nice to me," the captive said. "So I killed him."

Her eyes widened, fury building within her. "How could you have?"

Lyramoor spat. "I have lots of experience, you disgusting, ugly, arrogant, vampire!"

A roar of primal rage built in her chest, but she held back, resisting the urge to rush up and crush him. Her anger had little to do with his petty threats or because of any great feelings she had for Vastyr. But this was the most inconvenient time to lose her source of blood. Growling, she swiped out her hand and the golem spread out, covering his entire body except his eyes, nose, and mouth.

He let out a laugh. "You think this will stop me from killing you too?"

"I will deal with you later!" she said.

Now was a crucial time. She would have to drink what she could from Vastyr's corpse. With the proper spells, she could keep what was in him from degrading, but she could not make his dead body produce more.

The captive would have to suffice as a source until she

could get a replacement, but drinking from him now would be too great a strain on his tortured body. To make matters more difficult, she couldn't heal him correctly because of those blasted devices that kept her from being able to see inside him.

She turned her attention back on Vastyr. The smell of the small amount of blood from the cuts on his face was already causing her to tremble. She lifted his arm, sent magic into his body to force his heart to pump.

Then she paused. How had the elf killed him? She inspected his body closer with her magic. His blood vessels were damaged. His brain had hemorrhaged. She dropped his arm. "Poison?"

Lyramoor swore.

"You crafty, bastard," she said, looking up at the ex-slave with new respect. "You very nearly tricked me into killing myself."

"He's still fresh," the elf said. "It's not too late."

Cassandra approached him, licking her lips. "You have just volunteered to be my new slave."

Fear entered his eyes, but he quickly pushed it aside. "You don't want me, witch! I'm sick. I have broken bones. My blood's dirty."

"That just adds to the flavor," she said. Cassandra gestured and the clay parted, exposing his neck. She could see his artery pulsing as his heart raced. Yes. This was fear. "All those years a slave and now you return to the fold."

"Just kill me. I killed your lover. Kill me!" Lyramoor demanded.

She didn't bother to dispute his assertion. "Oh, I'm not killing you. Pet."

"No! Never again. Never again!" he yelled.

Cassandra had the golem cover his mouth, tiring of his voice. She couldn't take it directly from his neck. Any healing she did would be crude and that was too crucial an area. She moved more clay aside, exposing the inside joint of his arm. This would do.

A quick slice of air opened him up nicely. She fastened her lips around the wound.

Pleasure overcame her. His blood was just as sweet as Vastyr's, possibly sweeter. And what was that other odd flavor? There was something else. Something hot?

She backed away, spitting out the current mouthful. It burned. Her lips, her tongue, her throat . . .

Cassandra tore the clay from his face. "What is this?"

He began to laugh. "I got you. I got you good!"

The burning intensified. It had entered her belly. Her eyes were tearing, her nose watering. "How?"

"Panthel root," he said weakly and she realized that he was still bleeding.

"Panthel? Impossible. Panthel root is lethal poison to elves."

"In tiny enough doses, it just hurts." He chuckled. "Twenty long years of small doses. Twenty years of feelin' like my own blood is on fire, but I got used to it. Ends up its worth it."

"But I'm not an elf," she said. Her stomach felt as if it were boiling. How much had she drank? "It doesn't hurt humans."

His eyelids began to droop. "A vampire's body changes. See, I learned this long ago. Dwarfs traffic in lots of things. They learned somethin' about Panthel root. In a vampire, it just stops their body from absorbing elf magic. Permanently."

"No," she said.

"That's right. You're no longer a vampire." He managed a smile. "Ends up I'm the cure."

Chapter Twenty Four

"Road-cloggin', field-burnin', boot-dippin', flamin' horse apples!" Lenui shouted.

The dwarf was hanging from Rufus' neck as they dangled hundreds of feet above the ground. The cliff face was sheer and their descent was slow. To make things worse, the durn rogue horse was laughing!

"Ooh! Ooh! You! Fun-ny! Wee!" Rufus huffed, his body shaking as he looked for the next hand hold.

"I'm not friggin' funny, dag-blast it! I just don't wanna die fallin' off this cliff holdin' a bag of hot rocks!"

Rufus bellowed out another laugh. "Ooh! Hot rock!"

"Eat a dog log, you snot-flicker!" Lenui shouted. "That was literal!"

Tied to Lenui's belt, dangling down behind the dwarf, was the sack that Locksher had given him. The wizard's plan had been a blasted good one if only they survived the trip.

To take his mind off of the descent, Lenny tried a different tactic than cursing. "You wanna know how I know 'bout this place, Rufus?"

"Okay," the rogue horse replied, just before reaching one long arm out and swinging over to a small ledge.

"Balls! Biscuits and gravy!" Lenui lamented. He took several deep breaths. "Okay, so me'n the boys was just a bunch of young loudmouths who didn't know what danger meant. We heard about this fight in the mountains and me with this new fancy armor I made, I wanted to test it out. So I talked the boys into comin' with me."

"Ooh. Boys?" Rufus asked. His next handhold was just out of reach so he caused his arm to lengthen, stretching a good six inches longer than usual. He grasped the bulge in the rock and they were swinging again.

Lenui clenched his eyes closed and gritted his teeth. "Young dwarfs. We was all under eighty, just grown into our britches. Couple of us had families already. But we was fierce. Eager to fight. 'Specially 'gainst this high-falootin' Dark Prophet worshipper.

"We came up and joined up with the Dremald Garrison troops. We marched'n drank'n ate good trail food. It was a grand ol' time. But when we got close to the mountains things changed. It was dark. That priestess had her old magic sendin' chills across the whole blasted army."

The more Lenui got into finally telling the story, the less the climb affected him. The events of those days, long banished from his thoughts were coming back to life for him.

"Us, though? We was dwarfs. Magic don't hit us as hard. We just laughed a little louder and that seemed to help. Soon enough the cliffs was in front of us. Most've the army was already fightin' we could hear it. You know why they called it Thunder Gap?"

"Ooh! No." Rufus said, stretching his arm out again.

Lenui managed to ignore the swinging this time. "There was this big pass surrounded by goblinoid caves that was a straight shoot all the way up to the main road to the Dark Prophet's palace. That Priestess of War had herself set up right in the middle of it. Walls set up. Buildin's outta the rock. Her army'd come in from Khalpany to keep the good folk from getting' through to kick the Dark Prophet's arse.

"They called it Thunder Gap 'cause she kept a stream of lightnin' bolts hammerin' the army day'n night. It was hell up there. Only way to survive was to have a wizard with you. Well we thought this'd be a fight to remember, but the line to get in was too friggin' long!

"Then we saw these two wizards and a handful of fighters headin' up a trail up the Cliffside and decided to follow 'em. Now

I never did learn the names of them wizards. Didn't care much at the time. Guess one of 'em could've been Porthos fer all I know."

"Ooh! Down more?" Rufus asked.

Grimacing, Lenui hazarded a look down. He could just barely see the trail and the cave entrance another twenty feet down. "Little to the right and then down a bit more."

Rufus swung over and hung above the entrance and then lengthened his arms, lowering them down. Soon his rear legs touched down. Lenui dropped to the path.

"If you'cn do that why didn't you just stretch yer durn arms down the whole friggin' way?" he grumped.

Rufus' eyes went wide and he grabbed at his shoulders. "Ooh! Ow! Hurt!"

Lenui shrugged. "Hell if I ever understand the way you things work."

The cave entrance was still a good hundred feet from the bottom of the cliff face. The narrow trail that led up to it was worn and had crumbled away in places. From where they were, they could just hear the fighting around the corner of the cliff and up a short rise.

"This trail weren't lookin' this bad back then," Lenui observed. He opened the bag Locksher had given him and pulled out a glow orb. He peered into the cave and slapped the orb to turn it on. "Now this thing stretches in a ways."

They walked inside and Lenui grabbed Buster, holding the hammer in his right hand. They made their way into the cave and continued down a passageway at the back. It was a winding corridor that widened and shrank, causing the rogue horse to have to widen and shrink with it.

"Stinks!" Rufus observed, holding his huge nostrils shut.

"What're you talkin' 'bout?" Lenui said continuing deeper. Then he rounded a corner and coughed. "Ugh! Yer right! Smells like somebody cut the feet off a hunnerd kobalds and threw 'em in here!"

"Ooh! Feet and poop!" Rufus agreed.

"Guess that makes sense," Lenui said, continuing to edge

forward. "This cave wanders 'round all the way up to the gap. That's how we snuck in past all her defenses. Well, thinkin' back now, it could've been Porthos' doin' 'cause she had a purty close watch on every way in.

"When we came out there was a big fight goin' on between that priestess and some other wizards. It was all fancy and loud and we was all excited. My boys and I, we ran right past the wizards we'd followed in and we headed up the trail, twenty dwarfs with our weapons in our hands and nothin' between our ears."

His voice lowered, the memory feeling a bit too real now that they were coming so close to the spot where it all happened.

"We fought our way past goblinoids and big dog things. Our weapons were magic and our bodies were young and we felt invincible. Then we reached the top of the cliff where the blasted lady stood and she noticed us."

His voice shook. "Boys never stood a chance. We was hit by five lightnin' bolts at once. Even dwarfs can fry. The boys fell smokin' in their boots. I fell too, but the armor saved me. I had that crab suit worked up with so many runes it would've taken ten more hits just like that."

Rufus put his hand on the dwarf's shoulder. "Wee . . ."

"Yeah, I know. Hell, the rest is old news now. That priestess turned around to take one more wizard. I stood and ran at her, Buster rarin'. I yelled somethin' I thought was smart at the time. Don't recall what it was anymore. She turned to look just as I swung. Buster hit her just under the eye.

"Anyway, the boys was dead. Folks said I was a hero. Fer what? I just wanted to show off my armor and prove my tallywhacker was longest. Got my friends kilt. Walked home by myself feelin' like the lowest dwarf ever."

They moved forward in silence around a few more bends. "I figger this cave ain't much longer. I was thinkin' it should come out somewhere right below where they say that lake . . ."

They stopped because the way ahead of them was blocked by a solid wall of blubbery black sludge. It gave off a revolting heat and just looking at it made Lenui angry. Something big and white moved inside of it, causing a chunk to slide down to the floor.

"I wanna punch somethin'," he observed. "And that ain't the feelin' I should have when lookin' at somethin' nasty like this."

"Rocks?" Rufus suggested, still plugging his nose.

"Right. This is as far as we're goin' I think," Lenui replied.

He opened the sack and pulled out a few of the fist-sized rocks. There were air runes chiseled into them and Lenui had worked with enough magicked ore that they made his skin crawl. These things were packed too tight. He wouldn't allow one of them a hundred feet from his forge.

"You reckon we should space 'em out?" he wondered.

In response, Rufus took one of the rocks and threw it into the black sludge. It disappeared into the stuff with a splat. Lenui nodded and followed suit, throwing each rock in to join the other. He could see one of them slowly sinking to the bottom.

No sooner had the last one gone in, then there was a shifting inside the sludge. That long white thing made itself known again only this time it reached out towards them. The wall of sludge began to slide their way.

"Go!" Rufus shouted and grabbed the back of Lenui's leather armor. The rogue started rushing back the way they had come, dragging the dwarf along behind him.

"I can run, dag-blast it!" Lenui complained. Then his hand was jarred against the wall and the glow orb bounced to the ground to be covered by the sludge. Knowing that white grasping tentacle was still waving towards him, Lenui changed his mind. "Pull faster! Pull faster!"

Finally the rogue horse pulled him into the cavern opening. They stopped and listened, but could no longer hear the slurp of advancing sludge. Lenui searched frantically in the bag worried that the trigger stick had been dropped along with everything else.

He held it up in his fingers, a long wooden dowel with a series of runes across it. According to Locksher, all they had to do was snap it and the rocks would blow.

"Now?" Rufus wondered.

Lenui shook his head. "No way. I got the feelin' we wanna

get way the hell away from here before this thing goes."

"Liar!" Cassandra shouted. She rushed up and grasped Lyramoor's head, digging her fingernails into his scalp. What he had said was impossible. He could not take away her blood magic!

Working out of sheer desperation, she focused all of her considerable talent into a fine point and pierced through the haze caused by the devices in his body. She forced her thoughts into his mind. He had to be lying. Or there was antidote somewhere.

Caught by surprise and weakened by loss of blood, Lyramoor could give her little resistance. What she found, did not please her. There was no cure.

No more elf magic. No more ability to stay young. No more ways to heal.

Snarling, Cassandra pushed away from him. She grasped her mace. A shriek passed her burning lips as she swung the magical weapon into his chest.

The elf's chest collapsed. The rock wall behind him caved in. The golem's magic faded. Dirt spilled into the room, covering many of her fine furs.

Defeat. No. She stumbled over to the chest next to her throne. The fire in her stomach was spreading out into her veins. She reached inside for the jade box.

Shuddering, Cassandra sat in her throne and opened the box. The pain from the elf's blood was so severe, she barely felt the dagger's compulsion. She gripped the handle. *David*!

"What is this, Cassandra?" His voice sounded distracted.

I-I've been hurt. Poisoned. My blood slave is dead.

"What is this foolishness? You are in the midst of a battle!"

My magic is low. I need your help.

"Now is not the time! I am in a battle of my own. John found a way to disrupt my plan!"

I will be unable to control the wraith, she said. *My blood*

342

magic is fading even now.

"Very well. I will give you a small portion of my energy. I cannot spare much."

The burning in Cassandra's body eased. There was still pain, but it was manageable. She felt her strength returning. She wasn't completely restored, but this was much better.

I will win, she vowed. *But my ability to use elf magic is gone.*

"There are other ways to extend life. There are other ways to heal wounds. Win your battle and return to me. The wraith has served its purpose now. Leave it to spread chaos on its own."

Yes, David. Thank you!

"Go, my Priestess of War. Conquer!"

Yes, my god!

Cassandra closed the lid to the box. There was one more thing she had grasped from the elf's mind before killing him. A single name. A familiar name.

Master Porthos.

Now she had an identity to go with the eagle she had face earlier. The human wizard had been instrumental in the battle that had felled her so long ago. It was his magic that had let the invading force get so close to her and catch her unawares. How had he lived so long?

"No matter," Cassandra said aloud. She would have him now.

The Priestess of War leaned back in her throne and closed her eyes. She had to work quickly while her control over the wraith was still active. Where was he? If Porthos was working against her, that could explain how the Academy army was able to survive the plague of flies.

She dove into her connection with the wraith and rode its senses. It made no sense trying to search through the eyes of individual infested or worse, flies with their confusing faceted eyesight. Instead, she looked at an overall view of the battle before. If a bewitching specialist was working against her it would appear as a hole in the wraith's magic, a spot where its control could not reach.

There was nothing immediately obvious. Flies blanketed the battlefield. Any spots of protection where small, nothing that would identify a witch of such power.

Her fists clenched in irritation. What else could it be? Where . . ? An idea occurred to her. What if she had misunderstood Lyramoor's weakened thoughts. What if Master Porthos wasn't with the army, but instead was with the ogres and that other annoying group?

She sent her thoughts westward to the ogre encampment and discovered that it was blanketed with flies as planned. There was one strange thing, however. She could sense very few infested ogres, a mere thirty living and another twenty dead. There should have been hundreds of them by now.

Cassandra understood now. The ogres weren't there. They must have left, but where could they have gone? The passes were covered in flies just as heavily as the encampment and they couldn't have come to help the Academy army. Her walls would have stopped that. Had they fled out of the mountains altogether?

Doggedly, she continued, looking along every pass and pathway until she found it. A wide gap where there were no flies at all. It was a good two day's travel from the ogre's camp.

Very clever. By moving them, he had avoided her finding out about his presence accidentally. Well, that tactic was about to burn him. She just needed a way into his mind. To do that, she needed to find a creature under his control.

It didn't take long. The fool was helping feed the tribe by luring in animals for them to kill. She saw the mind of a deer approaching the camp, a strand of white spirit magic attached to it.

Cassandra pounced. Using the considerable might of the wraith combined with her own prowess, she broke through his bewitching barrier and dove into the deer's mind, following its connection back to him.

What she found surprised her. This wasn't an adversary. This was a man nearly dead. That was why she hadn't been able to see the eagle's lifeline and that was why he had been able to hide the entrance to his mind in the darkness.

As powerful as his magic was, his life force was very dim. He was a wisp of a man. His heartbeat was as the flutter of a moth. His voice came to her mind.

Ah, so you found me, he said.

You're an old man, she said with revulsion.

So are you, my dear, he said, his thoughts a soft wheeze. *But a lady. I meant an old lady.*

Cassandra growled. *You're not worth my time.*

You are likely right. I think I've done just about my share of the battle, he decided. *I'm content. This is a good way to die.*

You disgust me, she said and snuffed out his life.

Feeling unsatisfied, she returned her thoughts to her own body and stood. Suddenly, she was assailed by alerts from her hounds. Intruders at her flank and they were almost upon her!

They had been trying to get through to her for some time, but the connection had been closed. That Porthos! Somehow the old man had been blocking her even here!

Cassandra ordered her hounds to attack. Then she raised the dead forces on the beach and started them marching on the invaders. She gripped her mace tightly in her hand and headed for the door. How dare the enemy take the battle to her?

Fist and Darlan rushed out of the wagon to discover that everyone but Valtrek was gone. The Head Wizard, who had been sitting on the driver's bench, turned to look at the two of them. He lifted his eyebrow. "They pierced through the wall some time ago. You will have to rush to catch up."

"Sorry," Darlan said, and showed him her palm as she ran by. "We had to get ourselves named!"

"You're-!" Valtrek stood. "Both of you?"

"Yes!" yelled Fist as he followed behind her. He waved his left hand back at the wizard. "Uh, Mistress Dianne?"

"Go on," she replied. "Use your mace and run ahead. They might need your help!"

"Okay," Fist said. He gripped his mace and felt it's familiar speed take over. He reached the wall and saw the tunnel burrowed through the base of it. He ran through, a smile on his face.

He couldn't believe he was actually named just like Justan. Well, not as a warrior, a fact that bothered him only slightly. He knew it was rare to be named as both. But if he had to choose just one, being a wizard was something to be proud of. It didn't diminish his fighting ability at all.

Ooh! Fist! Rufus sent, happy to sense his return.

Rufus! I got named!

Ooh? the rogue horse said, confused.

My name's still Fist, though. Where are you?

I'm with Wee. Climbing, the rogue horse said. And Fist got the sense that the dwarf was hanging onto his back.

Oh. Be careful, he warned.

Just then, a lightning bolt flashed somewhere not far down the path. A loud crack echoed through the air. "Squirrel?"

I'm ready, Squirrel replied, preparing to pull magic through the bond.

Fist slowed to a stop. "Not this time. This priestess is too dangerous."

I will be Squirrel, the furry creature replied and jumped from his shoulder to a rock shelf next to the trail.

"Just don't be a dead Squirrel," he said and ran on again, clutching his mace.

Another lightning bolt struck, then a series of several more. He could see the flash in the air, but the boulders lining the trail were disrupting his view. He was missing the battle. Hopefully everyone was okay.

He rounded a boulder and nearly tripped over the bodies of two ogres with their throats torn out. Not too far away, covered in sword wounds was the corpse of a lupero.

As he was bending over them, there was a muffled thud. A body arced through the air towards him. Fist watched in disturbed shock as a man in Academy armor crashed to the ground not far from him.

Fist rushed over to try and help him, but he was too late. It was someone Fist knew only slightly. The man's eyes were sightless. His breastplate, though engraved with earth magic runes, was bashed in.

Breathing deeply, he remembered what Darlan had taught him about fighting another wizard. *Shields first.* Fist pulled his shield off of his back.

He continued to run. *Have a spell prepared. Don't try to think one up on the spot.* Fist prepared one in his mind.

He rounded the corner and the slope opened up before him. The Academy warriors and ogre tribesmen were facing an army of thousands of dead and a dozen growling lupids with more still approaching from the shores of the black lake. The wizards stood behind them with spell-diffusing shields raised. Lightning bolts fell among the infested dead, dropping them ten or more at a time.

The Priestess of War stood in front of her house of stone, facing them all. She was dark and scarred, yet somehow beautiful in her shining armor and red cloak. Her mace radiated a mix of earth and water magic so terrible it warped the air around it.

As he watched, a warrior managed to round the edge of the dead horde and run towards her. Fist realized that it was Wild Dinnis, one of the Academy guards that had come up with Lenny and Bill. He was the one with Tolivar's old sword.

The priestess watched his approach with calm detachment. Her mace was clutched in her right hand while her left arm was raised, directing the magical shield over her head that absorbed or deflected the spells being hurled at her.

Fist ran around the Academy line, looking for a thin spot among the dead for his attack.

Dinnis ran at her, a roar of rage bursting from his throat. She swung her mace in an almost casual manner, handling the weapon as if it weighed mere ounces. Dinnis managed to dive to the side, barely avoiding the mace's pronged ridges.

He came up in a spin, his sword, Meredith, arcing in at her back. The priestess brought her mace back around in a swift flick. The two weapons collided.

Meredith shattered into tiny splinters. Dinnis fell back, his eyes wide, his sword hand mangled. The priestess took a single step towards him and swung her mace down, pounding the graduate into the ground.

"No," Fist said.

His word was echoed by fierce shouts along the line as the warriors redoubled their efforts. Arrows arced in from Swen and Maryanne, but the priestess' shield deflected them all.

"Hey! Witch!" shouted Charz. The giant, who had been fighting alongside a group of ogres down by the shoreline, charged up the slope pushing his way through the ineffective dead ranks. Several ogres ran at his side. "You're mine."

She watched impassively as the giant approached, then swung her left arm towards him. The round rock that stood in front of her door rolled down the hill towards him. Charz snorted and stepped aside, but the rock turned in its path and bowled him over, coming to a stop on top of him. The giant let out an impotent roar. He could not get the stone to move.

Cassandra turned back to the rest of her attackers and pointed her mace at them in a clear taunt. Her mocking voice echoed, boosted by threads of air. "Who will be next?"

Fist had finally found the best angle for his spell. He anchored one set of vibrating strands on the iron of his shield, but before he could anchor the other strands, the priestess launched a spell of her own.

A volley of air magic shards rose into the air just above her shield. The shards rose fifty feet into the air, then fragmented and shot down towards her opposing forces, each fragment becoming a needle thin blade.

The blades fell among the Academy warriors and Mage School Wizards like tiny darts. The wizards' shields caught many of them, but many more got through. Several people and ogres fell. Others were wounded, but stood.

Fist sensed that the priestess was preparing a second volley. He anchored his second set of vibrating strands of earth and air on the chainmail shirt on Dinnis' body. The priestess was standing between them.

The lightning bolt streaked horizontally, its arc covering

the distance between his shield and Dinnis' armor. A dozen dead between them dropped to the ground. Electricity crackled around the priestess' body. Fist caught a glimpse of her good eye wide in surprise.

Now was the moment. He ran at her, using the path between the dead that his strike had created, his mace boosting his speed. The lightning bolt faded, but the electricity continued to crackle around her form. She turned her head, her surprised eye watching his approach. The tattoos on the exposed flesh of her arms gave off a green glow.

Fist charged her, his mace swung back, his shield leading. She brought her mace low in an upward strike. He leapt, swinging his mace down, spiked side facing her.

Cassandra's mace connected with Fist's shield, shattering the wood into kindling. The iron that backed the shield was dented in. The bones in Fist's left arm, caught between the shield and his breastplate, should have been crushed to powder. However, that was the arm his naming rune was on.

His arm, though crushed, was not broken. The force of the blow launched him skyward up and over the priestess' head.

Fist saw everything happen as if slowed down. Pieces of his shield scattered in every direction, some of them pinging off of his forehead. He felt a great pressure in his chest. The world was falling away. He was soaring.

Then the world spun as his feet flipped up over his head and he realized he wasn't flying any more. He was falling. His feet continued their turn and the slope was rushing back up at him. He could hear Maryanne's voice in his mind, shouting instructions.

He bent his knees and absorbed the impact in a roll. The remnant of his shield flew off of his arm and his roll continued as the slope steepened. He was now in a tumble. His body was battered by the weight of his breastplate until he came to a stop face first in the muck.

Not mud. Muck. Sludge. His upper body had hit the lake.

Fist tried to move, to pull his face out of the hot goop. The wind had been knocked out of him. He was still in shock over the whole experience. It was like his dream, but this time Lenny did not arrive to lift his head. He could feel hundreds of larvae stinging him as they tried to burrow into his skin.

Straining, Fist pushed himself up. His mouth opened into a gasp. A chunk of sludge fell into his mouth. Larvae were on his tongue, burrowing into his gums.

Sorry, Fist! Squirrel said, landing on the still-clean back of his head.

Zap!

All the larvae in a ten foot radius around Fist burst into ash. The black sludge sizzled as it was eaten back from the shoreline in a circular line around him. The edges glowed red with coals.

Fist spat ashes out of his mouth. "Thank you, Squirrel!"

He rose to his feet with a groan. He hurt all over. He could barely move his left arm. He turned to look back up the slope.

The battle was going poorly. Another storm of air blades darted into the academy ranks. Several ogres and two wizards collapsed. Swen fell. Fist couldn't see Hugh the Shadow.

Then Mistress Dianne arrived. She strode down the slope towards them, winded, but resplendent in her war wizard garb.

"Heal the fallen and take cover!" Darlan commanded to the wizards still standing.

Immediately, a tumbling of fireballs fell from the sky over Cassandra's head. The priestess' shield caught most of them, but a few exploded onto the ground around her, spattering her with molten bits of rock. Once again, the runes on her arms flashed and the flames fell away, their only lasting damage being smoldering patches on her cloak.

Cassandra smirked. "A dark wizard hunter?"

Darlan continued to stride forward. She held out her hand and the rock around her began to redden and smoke. Cassandra sent a lightning bolt down at her, but it scattered in the air above her head,

A large beast emerged from behind a rock and crept towards her. With its red fur and black stripe, Fist recognized it as the alpha lupero

"Darlan!" Fist shouted.

The lupero darted towards her. Darlan turned and pointed at it and the rock that had glowed around her turned molten and rose up. The lupero tried to change course, but it was too late. The beast was covered in molten lava.

"Raj!" Cassandra screamed. A volley of air blades arced through the air towards Darlan. Boulders uprooted themselves and began rolling towards her.

Uh, Fist! warned Squirrel.

Fist turned as a large form rose slowly from the lake. As the sludge fell from it, its form was revealed. It was a giant snake, a dead thing, and the anger of the wraith burned in its cold eyes.

Fist realized he didn't have his mace with him. He backed up slowly as the thing reared back.

Shock shock shock! Squirrel reminded him.

"Right," he said, hurriedly bringing up threads of air and earth. Electricity built around him. The snake struck.

The weight of its attack bore Fist back to the ground. Electricity arced through the length of the thing, extending into the Black Lake, destroying larvae and burning sludge. The snake collapsed.

Fist lay there for a moment, not sure at first if the snake's teeth had pierced him or not. Then he remembered the breastplate he was wearing. He let out a sigh of relief. "Squirrel, are you okay?"

Yes, Squirrel said, standing on the ground not too far from him. *Hurry. Get up.*

Fist pushed the heavy weight of the thing to the side and rolled slowly to his knees. Everything hurt. He looked up the slope to see that Darlan's battle had reached near incomprehensible intensity.

Air blades shattered to sparkles above her head. Boulders that rolled towards her melted to slag before they reached her. She was standing on a pool of molten rock.

The Priestess of War deflected a constant barrage of fireballs. Her black lips were pulled back from her teeth in a snarl. Her cloak caught on fire. Finally, she let it fall from her shoulders and Fist saw that the rest of her was untouched.

He tried to climb back to his feet. Maybe he could help. He put one foot up.

Darlan gestured and her pool of lava rose up in the form of a large wave. It cascaded down the hill towards the priestess.

With a groan, Fist climbed to his feet. He took a step. Everything hurt.

Cassandra made a large sweeping gesture with both hands and an intense gust of wind blew at the wave of molten rock. It reversed its course, bubbling back up the slope towards Darlan.

The lava surged high over her head. Darlan raised her arms defensively. The wave engulfed her. The priestess let out a shout of triumph and the rock cooled instantly. A lump in the cracked blackened rock was the only sign that Darlan had been there.

"No," Fist said. He stumbled forward. "Darlan!"

The priestess opened her mouth in a laugh. Maryanne shot an arrow, intending to put it down the witch's throat. The priestess caught the arrow at the last moment.

"You again?" Cassandra snapped. She sent the arrow back at Maryanne. The gnome turned her head to dodge, but the arrow pierced her cheek, penetrating through her mouth to stick out the other side.

"Maryanne!" Fist said, his voice a panic. He tried to run, but his limbs wouldn't behave. "No-no-no."

The priestess sent another volley of air blades towards the huddled survivors.

He was too slow. They were all going to die.

"Too slow," he said numbly.

He watched Stout Harley charge the priestess. Her mace crumpled his shield as easily as it had crumpled Fist's.

"Too slow."

Rufus's voice entered his mind from somewhere far away. *No! You're not slow. You're Fist!*

He blinked, unsure what the rogue horse meant.

Squirrel explained. *Justan is Edge. You are Fist.*

Fist looked down on the ground at his feet and saw his mace. He bent and picked it up. He saw the rune on its handle and thought back to the things Justan had recently learned about his swords. A smile broadened his face. "I am Fist."

He was named now. Fist reached through his new bond with the mace. He latched onto its magic and bolstered it. Increased it.

He was no longer slow.

Harley knelt on the ground in front of the priestess, his shield arm broken, his breastplate dented. Blood streamed from his lips as he watched her fatal blow descend. It never connected.

Fist's mace struck the side of her head.

Cassandra jerked to the side, her helmet's magic absorbing most of the impact. She spun around sending her mace in a quick backhand swing. Fist stepped back and it missed by inches.

"Who are you?" she asked.

His mace connected with the side of her head again. The jade stone on her forehead cracked. She stumbled again, catching herself on the stone wall in front of her house. "But you're just an o-."

He did not want to talk. His mace rebounded off the side of her head once more, slamming it against the wall of her stone building. The jade stone shattered.

"Stop!" she shouted, swinging her mace in a vicious backhand.

Fist leaned back, letting it pass in front of his face.

"You cannot do this!" Her scarred face was twisted into a snarl. "I am the Priestess of W-!"

He struck her again and again. There was nothing she could do. He was too fast. Her runes flared less and less as her protections continued to fail. She slid to the ground.

"David . . ." she whispered through bloodied lips.

Fist's mace rained down blows. He did not stop until he was certain that there was no way she'd be able to come back.

Epilogue

It was over.

Fist let go of his mace's magic and his shoulders slumped. The euphoria that had come from discovering his newfound power faded and the pain of his injuries returned. Wincing, he turned to see several of his friends standing and staring at him.

"Maryanne!" he shouted.

To his relief, she seemed to be fine. The gnome warrior was standing there, watching him in wonder, a bloody arrow held loosely in one hand while a wizard looked at her torn cheeks.

Stout Harley wheezed as he tried to reach the latch to remove his breastplate. Fist quickly helped him. The defensive master, though perhaps suffering from a few broken ribs to go along with his shattered arm, appeared that he would survive. Fist asked two ogres to help the man over to the wizards.

Fist stumbled up the slope to the field of blackened lava where Darlan had been overwhelmed. Tears welled in his eyes. How was he going to tell Justan?

Faldon the Fierce came up next to him. The tall warrior was suffering from a few nasty gashes, but his armor seemed to have protected him from the worst of the priestess' aerial attacks. "It's okay, Fist. I think she's fine under there. She's just trapped."

"Are you sure?" Fist asked, hope rising in his chest.

Faldon sighed and walked up to the lump where she lay. "Yes. I've seen this happen once before. She was quite embarrassed by it. Trapped by her own spell."

Fist lifted his mace. "Do we dare break it up?"

"We just need to be careful," he said with a nod. "I think

she's got a protective layer around her, but she can't heat up the rock around her hot enough to melt it without burning herself."

Fist tapped the rock a few times with his mace and Faldon let out a surprised chuckle. "Is that where she was taking you?"

Fist saw that the warrior was looking at the rune on his mace. "Oh yeah. We both got named."

Faldon's eyes widened. "Darlan stood before the Bowl?"

"She said she had put it off too long," Fist said.

He reached his magic into the crust of rock and came upon the protective barrier that Faldon had been talking about. He could see why she couldn't get out. The barrier was extremely dense to keep out the heat. It would probably be brittle though. He gave it a solid whack.

The rock burst apart throwing Fist and Faldon back. Darlan stood in the midst of the broken rock, her hands clenched, her hair singed. She looked around. "Where is she?"

"Fist killed her," Faldon said, climbing quickly to his feet. "You were named today?"

"We'll talk about that in a minute." She glanced over her husband's injuries quickly and then looked to Fist who was grimacing while trying to climb to his feet. He was stuck on his knees.

Darlan reached out and placed a hand on either side of his face. "You got her, Fist? You killed the Priestess of War?"

"Yes, Mistress. I used my bond with my mace to-."

She bent down and kissed him full on the lips. To Fist's astonishment, a tingle shot through his body. His aches and pains eased. He could move his left arm again.

Darlan pulled back and smoothed back his hair. "You did a good job, Fist. Thank you for protecting everyone when I couldn't."

Fist blinked back at her, not knowing what to say.

"Hey, I thought you saved those for me," Faldon complained.

"I made a one-time exception," she replied and just to prove it, she kissed him too.

"Hey!" snapped Maryanne, storming up to them, fully healed. "What was that?"

Fist scrambled to his feet. "Oh, she-uh. She healed me."

The gnome warrior frowned and glanced back at Darlan thoughtfully. The wizardess was still kissing her husband, putting the finishing touches on his healing. Maryanne looked back at him. "Can you do that too?"

"No, but I sure could kiss you," he said, pulling her in close to him. "You scared me. When I saw you get shot, I-."

"How do you think I felt?" she retorted. "You got knocked all the way to the blasted lake!"

"I'm just glad you're okay," Fist said.

Maryanne cocked her head at him. "When you beat that witch, the way you were moving . . . How did you do that?"

"Oh," Fist said. He held up his left hand. "I got named today."

Maryanne's eyes widened in surprise. She grasped his hand, feeling the thickness of the rune and a smile curled her lips. Then she looked back into his eyes and frowned slightly. "A big named wizard. So what do I call you now? Master something?"

He smiled. "You're beautiful, you know that?"

"Well? What is it?" She looked at him expectantly. "It's not something stupid sounding is it?"

"No, it's still Fist," he assured her.

Maryanne blinked. "Is that allowed?"

"Hey you two," said Darlan. "Let's see who else needs healing."

They rushed over to the site where the wizards were gathered. Along the way, they passed a crew of ogre clubbers that were still beating at the infested dead to make sure they couldn't be a threat. Charz was helping them, having been freed from under the rock.

Expressions were grim. All told, there were twelve Academy soldiers dead, seven wizards and forty ogres. Among those who were too far gone for healing were Wild Dinnis and Wizard Windle of the High Council. Swen, Hugh the Shadow, and

Crag had been gravely wounded, but ultimately healable.

The combined Academy and Mage School army that had been battling far below had proven victorious. The moment Cassandra had died, the dead stopped working in concert, but just started attacking everyone. The Academy army had withdrawn awhile and let the goblinoids wear themselves down before charging back in to finish things up.

Two more sad discoveries soon followed. Not only did Qenzic find Lyramoor's body inside Cassandra's house, but it was discovered that Master Porthos had not made it either. His naming dagger, which Old Bill had been carrying, had cracked down the middle.

There was one last issue to deal with. They stood out on the slope overlooking the immensity of the Black Lake and wondered how best to destroy it. The important part was getting to the two moonrat eyes somewhere at the center of the thing. They needed to do it soon. They could feel the wraith's hunger and anger reaching for them even now.

Fist was about to suggest an idea when there was a sudden great thud from somewhere below them. The impact of it ran from Fist's toes up to his chest and he grew very worried. Was this some other part of the Dark Prophet's plan?

Dust began to fall from the canyon walls. There was a great creak. A two-hundred-foot wide section of the canyon's western wall fell outward. Many hundreds of tons of rock crashed into the valley beyond.

The Black Lake poured out of the enormous opening in the wall, emptying its filth and the strange twisted beasts within its depths down the mountainside in a massive slow-moving flood. The ogres let out a triumphant roar.

Locksher grunted uncomfortably. "That was a larger result than I had planned."

"Holee cat on a cracker! That coulda been us!" shouted Lenny from the cliff top high above. He and Rufus were standing not twenty yards from where the canyon wall had fallen away.

"That should make things easier," Darlan said.

"Isn't this a bad thing? Like a terrible thing?" Maryanne

said. "Didn't we just spread the evil all down the blasted mountainside?"

"It's definitely a mess," Locksher admitted. "But once we destroy the source of the wraith all of this mess will cease to be a threat. Who knows? It might even be good for the trees. Fresh decayed matter means happy vegetation."

Somehow Fist doubted it would end up that way. He couldn't imagine any type of good coming out of this evil.

The Wizards lined up on the shoreline and sent lightning bolts and streams of fire into the lakebed where the sludge still clung to the rock like a bad disease. Strangely-shaped toothy creatures and many tentacled monstrosities clung and floundered in shallow pools of the sludge that remained. The wizards burned them with lightning and fire.

They spent the rest of the day burning and cleaning before they found the spot where it had all originated. Qenzic and Faldon where very helpful here since they knew where the moonrat had been killed, but even then it was difficult to pinpoint because of how immensely the landscape had changed.

The source was a blackened spot of earth with a single hole two feet in diameter at its center.

The stench of death and the feeling of overwhelming rage was strong here. Together, Darlan and Fist reached their magic into the earth and forced the underlying rock upward, pushing the evil's source to the surface. Somewhat disappointingly, it was just as everyone had supposed. Two small orange moonrat eyes, only they has grown partially together in a goopy mass.

They let Crag have the honor. Fist's father swung his club, bursting the eyes to pulp.

Their mission finally complete, Maryanne wrapped her arm around Fist's waist and placed her head on his shoulder. "What is your plan now, Big Guy?"

"Rufus and Squirrel and I need go to Malaroo and help Justan," Fist replied. "Do you want to come with us?"

*　　*　　*

A figure awakened in a dark and wet place. The air was moist and full of the Mother's scent. He didn't know much at the moment, but he recognized that. As his eyes slowly adjusted to the dark a new kind of sight came to him.

Instead of using light as a source for his vision, he was able to see things in shades of heat. To this new way of looking, the place he sat in was full of life and movement in shades of reds and pinks and oranges.

He now saw that there were many other people in this place. Most of them were hanging upside down. Some were fully formed. Others were mutated and strange. All of them in some way were his kin. These were his people. They too belonged to the Mother.

The figure smiled. Soon enough he would get to leave this place. Then he could serve the Mother. Excited, he shouted, "Serve the Mother!"

"Serve the Mother!" was the echoed cry of hundreds, some of them still sleeping, not ready for birth.

There was a great shifting in the Mother's flesh around him. Something was happening. Eagerly, he stood.

He looked at his body, ran curious hands over it. It was a good body, he thought. And strong with well-developed muscles. His hands were wide and powerful with stout claws, good for digging, perhaps. Whatever the Mother wanted. And the King. That's right. He had a King too. That was a good thought.

There was a great shifting in the Mother's flesh again. It felt as though he were rising into the air. What a strange sensation.

Then the light changed. He switched back to using light as his source of vision. This was nice. He could see so much more detail. He could see his fellow brothers and sisters waiting with him, each with their own unique shape and shade of skin.

The Mother wanted him to leave now. Somehow he knew it. He began walking forward and many of the others, the ones fully formed, came with him. Outside of this pink place was a land of vibrant green. Lush grasses and leafy trees. Such beauty.

He stepped out of the Mother's womb and onto the banks

of a marsh lake. He had no memories of seeing a lake before, but he knew what it was called. He stood in amazement, taking in the wonders of this bright new world until one of his people grabbed his arm and moved him to stand to the side. To stand by the others newly born.

Someone important was coming. How exciting. He looked down the line to see who it could be and was somewhat disappointed to discover that it was not his king.

This was a woman. Not a woman born of the Mother, but a human woman. That was not necessarily a good thing. As this woman walked down the line of new brothers and sisters, she stopped a time or two to make an adjustment, change something about a face or an arm or something.

She had magic. He hoped she would see no need to change him. He waited patiently until it was his turn. She stopped and looked him over.

"Well-well. The Mother has been learning, hasn't she?" said the woman who was not of his people. She had thick black hair with a single blond lock in the center. "Part dwarf, I would say. How interesting." She looked closer at him. "What pretty green eyes you have. A unique feature among the trollkin."

"Thank you!" he said proudly.

"You're quite pretty, too. I just might know someone who would like to get to know you. Tell me. Do you have a name?"

"Yes," he said and it suddenly came to him. "My name is Djeri."

*   *   *

Tarah didn't make it half way through her training run before the sickness that had been plaguing her all morning overcame her. She fell to her knees in the Jharro Grove and vomited all over one of the ancient roots. She heaved a couple times, losing her breakfast of eggs and mashed bananas.

"Sorry, Old Cranky," Tarah said, apologizing to the tree.

Tolynn turned around and doubled back to see what was

delaying her. "What are you doing, girl? Talk and run. Talk and run."

"Sorry," Tarah said. "I've been feeling a little sick."

"How strange. There is usually not illness in the grove," Tolynn replied. "Of course, lately, there has been an unusually large number of pregnancies . . ." The dark-skinned elf's brow furrowed. "Tarah, stand up."

Tarah did as she asked. Tolynn cocked her head at her and nudged her limbs a time or two, then placed her ear against Tarah's chest.

The elf pulled back and shook her head. "I do not know why I did not notice this before. Tarah, did you know that you are with child?"

The Bowl of Souls series will continue in

The finale of the Jharro Grove Saga: Behemoth

In the meantime, please check out Trevor H. Cooley's latest book:

Noose Jumpers : A Mythological Western A preview chapter of which follows.

Like Trevor H. Cooley on Facebook:
https://www.facebook.com/EyeOfTheMoonrat
Follow him on Twitter @Edgewriter
Or on his website http://trevorhcooley.com/

If you wish to become a Patron and become part of the creation of this world, you can join at
https://www.patreon.com/trevorhcooley

Book reviews are always welcome!

Please spread the word. The Bowl of Souls needs your help.

The Bowl of Souls series:
THE MOONRAT SAGA
Book One: Eye of the Moonrat
Book 1.5: Hilt's Pride
Book Two: Messenger of the Dark Prophet
Book Three: Hunt of the Bandham
Book Four: The War of Stardeon
Book Five: Mother of the Moonrat

THE JHARRO GROVE SAGA
Book Six: Tarah Woodblade
Book Seven: Protector of the Grove
Book Eight: The Ogre Apprentice
Book Nine: The Troll King
Book Ten: Priestess of War
Book Eleven: Behemoth

THE DARK PROPHET SAGA
12. Sir Edge
13. Halfbreeds (2021)

The Wizard of Mysteries
1. Tallow Jones: Wizard Detective
2. Tallow Jones: Blood Trail
3. (Upcoming)

Noose Jumpers Preview

Right in Front of His Wanted Poster

An excerpt from the Tale of Tom Dunn

"There's no such thing as cheating at cards. It's all just part of the game." – William "Canada Bill" Jones' last words before being choked to death, Charity Hospital, 1880.

Now that the trains ran through Luna Gorda, the town boasted of no less than four hotels. The Cloverleaf Hotel was the oldest and smallest of them. It was a narrow two story building consisting of three small guest rooms and a bath upstairs and a common area and kitchen downstairs. Established in the early days of the settlement, the Cloverleaf Hotel had long been owned by the O'Malley family. Proprietorship had been passed down through two generations until, at the time of this tale, it was owned and operated by Miss Joline O'Malley.

The small, but cozy parlor of the hotel was filled by a modest bar and two tables, one of which was occupied by four men playing a game of cards. This meant that the small bar needed to be tended and, this early in the day, that meant that the responsibility fell to Joline herself.

She sat glumly behind the bar reading a dime novel, only looking up occasionally to shoot irritated glares at the men when they asked for something. Most of those glares fell upon Tom Dunn. The nerve of him, calling a game together in her parlor in the middle of the day. If she'd had the ability, her eyes would have burned a hole right through the back of his head. She had better things to do than wait on him. On top of that, he expected her to keep her mouth shut about his reputation. If the three men he was playing with hadn't been guests at her hotel, she would have kicked him out.

Tom, who had his back to her, was wearing a new hat he had bought just the day before. It was a wide-brimmed Stetson in the 'gambler style' and he had pinned a tilted red star to the side of it. His jacket was lying across the back of the chair behind him and the striped blue shirt he wore had the sleeves rolled up so that the men he played with couldn't suspect him of hiding cards.

Tom grinned as he dealt out the latest hand of cards. "Joline! A round of whiskey for my friends here! I'm buying!"

If the other men at his table were pleased by his generosity, they didn't show it. All he got was a general grunt from the three of them. After all, he had won the last three hands and at this point he was buying them drinks with their own money.

Joline slammed her book down on the bar top. Grumbling, she poured four shots of whiskey into tumblers and carried them out to the table.

She started with Albert Swen, a railroad employee that was staying at the hotel while waiting for his next assignment to roll into town. He was a hard, but mild-faced man with a thick chin strap of a beard.

He nodded at her as she placed the glass in front of him, but addressed the man sitting at the table to his right. "So you live in Puerta Muerte, huh?"

"Yep," said Jorge with a drunken smirk as he cast away the cards he didn't want. Jorge was a squat Hispanic man who had the rough demeanor of someone who knew how to handle himself in a fight. He had come in town to visit his mistress on his day off and things hadn't gone well. Jorge already had a tall bottle of cheap wine open in front of him and barely noticed when Joline gave him the whiskey. "Gimme three."

"Puerta Muerte? That's about twenty miles from here," said Denny Dodge, a traveling salesman passing through town. Unlike the other two of Tom's players, he was dressed all neat and tidy, his mustache oiled and shaped into neat curls on the ends. "In

Texas, right?"

Jorge nodded. "Yep. Five miles east of the border."

Joline served Tom last. He was a handsome man and his mixed Anglo and Mexican heritage showed in his tanned skin and thick black hair. He was grinning cockily as he looked at the cards in his hand. He barely looked up at her when she placed the glass in front of him.

"Thanks, darlin'," he said in an offhand manner and she realized that he hadn't drank the first glass she had given him. It was still full.

Joline wanted to smack his narrow mustache right off of his lips. She settled for leaning in close to his ear. "You and I are gonna have us a little talk when this is over."

If Tom heard the menace in her tone, he didn't show it. He spoke to Jorge. "I hear Puerta Muerte's a dangerous place. Folks say it's full of bandits."

Jorge chuckled. "Well, that ain't wrong. But it's safe enough if you got the Sheriff on your side."

Joline turned to storm back to the bar and wasn't aware that she had walked right through the specter of the fifth man at the table. She did, however, feel the pinch that the apparition left on her behind. She lurched and gritted her teeth, but resisted the urge to break a glass over Tom's head. She resolved to spit in his next glass instead.

Jorge tossed some coins into the small pile in the center of the table. "I'll call."

Albert shrugged. "Two pair." He laid his cards down to show a pair of tens and jacks.

"Blast!" said Denny, throwing his cards down.

"Three of a kind," Jorge said with a grin, showing off the three nines in his hand. He reached for the pile of assorted coins.

"Wait," said Tom. He laid his cards down to show three kings and two jacks. "Full house."

Jorge's smile fell. "Aw hell. Again?"

"Best luck I had in months," said Tom.

Denny picked up the cards and Tom pulled in the coins.

The specter disappeared from behind Jorge and reappeared next to Tom. The strong smell of cloves rolled past Tom's nostrils. It always smelled like cloves when the Kid appeared.

The specter looked to be somewhere in his teens, but Tom wasn't sure how old he really was. All he knew was that the Kid was slight of frame and had a youthful face. He wore a pistol on each hip just like Tom did and a Mexican sombrero hung on his back, held there by a cord around his neck.

The specter leaned in close to Tom's ear. "Boooored!"

Tom winced slightly but he didn't reply to the loud outburst, knowing that the other players at the table hadn't registered the disturbance. The Kid was like an impish ghost that only Tom could see or hear. An annoying, but sometimes useful ghost.

The Kid flounced into an empty chair, sitting in it sideways with one leg over the armrest. "What're we doing here, Tommy?"

Denny finished shuffling the cards and started to deal, but Tom stuck out his hand. "Cut?"

Denny plopped the cards down and Tom cut them. As he did so, he expertly palmed a card. Denny started dealing again.

The Kid snorted. "Cheating for small stakes? You ain't gonna make your name that way. Come on. There's bigger fish elsewhere in town."

Tom cleared his throat. "So Jorge, I hear they got some good games going down in Puerta Muerte but I never dared try heading down there. How does a man get the Sheriff 'on his side' as you say?"

"What're you talking about, Tommy boy?" the Kid asked. "You hate that sheriff."

Denny nodded in interest. "Yeah, how do you get in with the man? I been looking for a new place to sell my wares."

The specter, with a bored look, gestured at Denny and the cards spilled clumsily out of the dealer's hands. Denny swore and picked them back up to reshuffle them before he could continue dealing.

Jorge put down his emptied whiskey tumbler and grinned at

being the center of conversation. His voice was slightly slurred. "Well, it ain't easy. I'm okay 'cause I work for him. Other than that . . . well, you ain't heard it from me, but you gotta grease the right palms if you know what I mean."

Tom pretended innocence. "Grease palms? Sounds unsanitary."

The Kid laughed sarcastically, then gave Tom a deadpan look. "Seriously, I'm gonna cause all kinds of havoc if you don't get out of here soon."

"Gimme two," said Albert the railroad employee, oblivious to the Kid's threats. He discarded two cards and picked up his replacements as he replied to Tom. "He means you got to pay the Sheriff for protection. I heard about that. It's a shame, but he ain't the only sheriff around with that policy."

"Oh," said Tom, discarding two cards of his own. He looked to Jorge. "Is it expensive?"

Jorge hiccupped. "Depends if he likes you." He leaned towards Denny. "I wouldn't go there if I were you, salesman. The Sheriff don't like ballyhoo men."

Albert tossed in two quarters. "Raise you fifty. So what do you do for the Sheriff that keeps you safe, Jorge?"

Jorge took a drink directly from the bottle in front of him and wiped his mouth before saying proudly, "I work at the bank in town."

Tom shot a meaningful glance to the Kid and scoffed. "A bank? In a town full of outlaws? Who'd dare put their money in there?"

"Hey! I keep it safe!" Jorge said with a frown. "'Sides, no one's even tried to rob it since the Sheriff started putting his own money in there. No one would dare."

The Kid was now leaning forward with interest.

"The Sheriff puts his own money in?" Tom's eyebrows furrowed in disbelief. "I heard he sends it out of town."

Jorge shook his head. "No way. I seen it myself. He has his own safe in the vault that no one else can use. Makes the deposits hisself." Jorge paused, blinking suddenly as if realizing he had said too much. "But you didn't hear that from me."

A smug look briefly crossed Tom's face and he winked at The Kid. "No worries. It's none of my business anyhow."

"Now you're talkin'," said the Kid with a chuckle.

Jorge looked blearily down at his cards and scowled, then tossed them on the table. "I'm done, boys. Gotta try and see the missus one last time before I head back to town. Got a shift tomorrow."

He picked up his bottle, which now had about a third left in it, and planted it against his lips. He tilted his head way back. The Kid, a mischievous look on his face, reached out and made a squeezing motion with his hand.

The remaining wine in the bottle sprayed out into Jorge's mouth and down the front of his shirt. The man coughed and sputtered, looking at the bottle like it was possessed. The other three men stared at him for a moment, then laughed.

Jorge looked back at them as if trying to decide whether or not to get angry. Finally, he chuckled and stood from his chair. He shook his head as he wiped off what liquid he could. "Well that caps it. I'm off."

The bank guard grabbed what remaining money he had off of the table and walked out toward the front door, muttering to himself.

"The rest of you still in?" Tom asked.

"Yeah," Albert said, scratching his head.

"Me too," said Denny. He chewed his lip while looking at his cards. "I don't get what he was saying. If Puerta Muerte's full of outlaws, why would they be so scared of a lawman? You'd think they'd just shoot him."

"Some have tried," Tom said and tossed in another quarter. "I'll raise you two bits."

Denny tossed in a quarter of his own. "And?"

"Ain't you heard?" Albert said. The railroad man's eyes went wide and his voice took on a mysterious tone. "They say he can't be hit by bullets."

Tom snorted. "Yeah, I heard that, too. Bunch of hogwash if

you ask me."

"I don't know," said the Kid. The specter turned in his chair and propped his feet up on the table, placing his hands behind his head. "Come on, Tommy. You seen stranger things."

Denny seemed just as dubious as Tom. "Seems to me they just haven't found the right shooter." The salesman sighed. "I call. What y'all got?"

Albert laid down his cards. "Two pair. Aces high."

Tom grinned and dropped his cards on the table. "Three kings."

"No way!" said Denny, scowling as he threw down his cards. "Five hands in a row you had three kings. No one's that lucky."

Tom pulled the pile of coins towards him. "You're right. I'd best stop now."

"Just a minute," said Albert with a frown. "That's my drinking money. I want a chance to win it back."

Tom gave them both an apologetic smile. "Sorry, a good gambler knows when his luck is out and that's my last gasp. I'm calling it a day. Maybe we can play again another time."

"Finally!" the Kid groaned and disappeared in an aromatic cloud of clove.

The two remaining men grumbled as Tom stood. He pulled on his coat and gathered his winnings into a leather pouch, then stopped by the bar to pay his tab. "Joline, your service was dag-gum remarkable. As usual."

He smiled back at the scowl she gave him and dropped a few extra dollars and change on the bar. With a tip of his hat, he turned and walked out the door.

Tom stepped out onto the hotel's front porch and winced at the sunlight. It was a beautiful day; clear and hot. The old main street was sparsely populated with people going about their business, mostly locals. He could hear the hammering of nails from two streets over. New buildings were still being built.

Tom's grin widened. He loved the new Luna Gorda. It had once been a dreary place in his mind; a slow-paced town where the locals got nowhere, but the train's coming had brought new life to the place. He envisioned that one day it could be as big as Mesilla or Santa Fe.

Part of him itched to head over to the new street and peruse the shops again, perhaps spend some of that money he had just made. Unfortunately, his business was in the old section of town. He started walking down the street towards the saloon, nodding to folks along the way.

Tom stopped in front of the jailhouse as something caught his eye. He turned and looked at the bulletin board covered in wanted posters. A giggle escaped his lips and he moved closer, jumping up the two steps to the porch. Amid the jumble of bounty promises were the three members of his gang.

Luke's poster read, *Luke Bassett, of the Red Star Gang. Wanted for Robbery and Public Disturbance. Reward, $150.* The artist's rendering was a decent one, highly detailed, though the person who had drawn it obviously was working only from eyewitness accounts. They had drawn a surprisingly accurate depiction of Luke's intense eyes, but most of his face was obscured by a bandana marked with a tilted star.

Sandy's poster wasn't quite as well done. The artist had drawn him with a full beard and his hair looked darker than the dusty brown it really was. His bounty was a bit higher than Luke's for some reason at $175.

Tom's grin fell away as he saw his own wanted poster. The artist had drawn Tom with an overwide nose, his eyes slightly crossed, and there was a stupid grin on his face. His bounty was also lower than the others, which he found insulting. But the thing that bothered him the most was the way they had written his name. It read, *Tomas Jefferson Dunn, of the Red Star Gang. Wanted for Robbery. Bounty $125.*

Tom drew back, his face twisted with disgust. He caught the smell of cloves as the Kid appeared next to him. The specter pointed at the wanted poster and let out a guffaw.

"They still ain't changed it, huh? You never have told me how that happened. What was it? Marshals get your name wrong? Or was your daddy just a bad speller?"

Tom frowned. It was actually worse. His father had wanted to name him after one of the founding fathers, but his mother had wanted to name him Tomas after his grandfather. "Shut up, Kid."

"Hey!" said a child's voice and Tom looked down to see that just a few feet away was a young boy with a piece of coal in his hand. He was using it to draw on the walkway.

Tom put on a smile. "Sorry. What's your name?"

The child's eyes narrowed suspiciously. "Neddy."

"Hi, Neddy. Mind if I borrow that piece of coal?" Tom asked. "Just for one second." He snatched it from Neddy's hand before the child had time to decide. "I'll give it back. I promise."

His jaw set, Tom took the piece of coal and began working on the poster.

In the parlor of the Cloverleaf Hotel, Albert and Denny were still sitting at the table looking unhappy.

"I just know my luck was about to turn around," Albert was saying. Surely there was a way he could make the money back. "Denny, you going anywhere soon?"

The salesman put down his drink and shrugged. "My train don't come in for a few hours yet. Why?"

Albert turned towards the bar. "Hey, Miss Joline. There anyone else staying here that we can call down to play a game?"

Joline put her dime novel down and gave him a dull look. "Nope. You two are the only ones here for the day."

"Aw hell," Albert moped.

Joline frowned. Why wouldn't the men just leave already? As long as they were sitting in the common room drinking, she had to stay. She made a decision.

Joline shook her head exaggeratedly. "I really can't believe you boys actually went and played a game with Tom Dunn in the first place."

"What do you mean?" Albert said, suddenly suspicious. "He famous or something?"

Joline didn't bother to suppress her smile. "Famous for

cheating, maybe." Both men stood and she added, "He couldn't have gone far."

Tom stood back and nodded in satisfaction at the changes he had made to the poster. The smile on his face in the poster no longer looked quite so goofy and he had given it a proper mustache. More importantly, he had blackened out some of the letters and it now read, *Tom Dunn, of the Red Star Gang. Wanted for Robbery. Bounty $725.00.*

"Sad," said the Kid in amusement.

"I think it's a definite improvement," Tom replied.

He tossed the piece of coal back to the child just as the door to the inn burst open. Albert and Denny spilled out, wincing as their eyes adjusted to the sun. Tom quickly turned to head across the street, but it was too late. The two men started towards him.

"Hey!" shouted Albert. "You stop there, Tom Dunn!"

"Yeah, you . . . scoundrel!" echoed Denny. The other people in the street turned to look.

The Kid chuckled. "Gee, I wonder what gave you away?"

Tom sighed. "Joline, I'd bet. She still hasn't forgiven me for kissing her sister."

"Well, you gonna fight it out in front of the jail?" the Kid asked, gesturing at Tom's wanted poster.

"Uh, no," Tom replied and walked towards the two men, wearing a disarming smile. He met them in front of the general store. "What is it, gentlemen?" He started patting his pockets. "Did I forget something back there?"

"We want our money back, sir!" Denny harrumphed.

Tom blinked innocently. "And why would I do that?"

Albert pointed a stiff finger. "You were cheating!"

"Woah now," Tom said, feigning shock. "Hey, that's a slanderous charge. Why'd you think that?"

"We know!" Denny insisted.

"That's right," Albert agreed. "Pay up. No one gets three

kings five hands in a row."

The Kid appeared atop a horse tethered in front of the store. He sat atop the horse's rump cross-legged, and sucked at his teeth. "Sloppy."

Tom placed his hands on his hips not far from his two pistols, "That was just blind luck, sirs. Do you have any proof of this?"

Albert, eying the guns, drew his own pistol and pointed it at Tom. "The hell with proof, cheater! Give us our money and we'll be on our way."

"Put the gun down, Albert," Tom said. He left his expression unfazed, but he was surprised by this aggressive behavior from the railroad man. "You ain't gonna shoot. Sheriff Dale's office is just over there and he is a personal friend."

"Oh ain't I?" Albert's lips pulled back from his teeth and he pulled back the hammer with a click. "I ain't about to let a thief cheat me and get away with it."

Denny licked his lips. The salesman had seen enough gunfights in his travels and had no desire to be caught in the middle of one. The other onlookers had similar thoughts and began entering buildings or heading for alleyways where they could watch from safety.

Looking uncomfortable, Denny said, "Just give the winnings over, Dunn. Then we'll let you go like nothing happened."

"Well, I protest! I take great offense at being called a cheater," Tom said. "Still, I suppose I have no choice . . ."

Tom reached into the pocket of his jacket and pulled out the pouch of coins. Albert held out his free hand, but Tom tossed the pouch at the man's gun. Albert turned and fumbled with the pouch, finally catching it in the crook of his arm. By that time, Tom had already run up to him.

He started with a punch to Albert's nose, which rocked the man's head back. Tom then grabbed the man's wrist and twisted, wrenching the gun from his fingers. He breathed a sigh of relief that it didn't go off.

Albert punched him in the ribs with his free hand and Tom

swung an elbow into the side of the man's face. This knocked the railroad man back far enough that Tom was able to get his foot up. Tom's front kick caught the railroad man in the stomach and sent him stumbling backwards.

Tom let the purse fall and cracked the railroad man's gun open. He shook the bullets onto the ground, then tossed the gun to the side and took a step back. "Now I want you two to stop and think for just a dag-gum moment-!"

Denny surprised him with a flying tackle from behind that took Tom to the ground. Tom's hat flew off and he ended up with a mouthful of dirt. He twisted, trying to shake the man off.

Tom sputtered, spitting mud. "Damnit, Denny! Get off me!"

The salesman was no brawler, but he held on tight and he was behind Tom in such a position that it was hard for Tom to get any leverage. They tussled for a while until Tom was finally able to flip over so that he was on top of the man.

Tom pried at the man's fingers, twisting them until, with a yelp of pain, the salesman finally let go. Tom rolled to his feet and when Denny tried to sit up, Tom lashed out with a right hook. The salesman fell to his back; out cold.

"Stop right there!" said Albert. The railroad man was down on one knee and was clutching his pistol, having used the time of Denny's distraction to retrieve and load it.

"Great." Tom grimaced, spitting again. He was now covered in fine dirt that had adhered to his sweat. His hair was sticking up in all directions. "I'm sure I look ridiculous."

Albert stood. "Now pick that purse back up and this time you walk over and hand it to me." He cocked the hammer and glared. His split lip and bloodied nose made him look all the more furious. "And don't you think I won't shoot."

What Albert didn't know was that he was now standing directly behind the horse that Tom's ghostly companion was perched on. Just as Tom was about to retrieve the purse, the Kid cried out and smacked the horse across the rump.

Tom was the only one who saw what had happened, but the horse definitely felt it. The poor beast felt a sting like twenty horseflies biting at once. It let out a scream and kicked out with both rear hooves, catching Albert right in the lower back.

The kick sent the unfortunate railroad man up on his toes. He let out a shocked cry and his finger convulsed around the trigger. The gun went off, causing the spectators to gasp. Luckily, the force of the kick had knocked Albert's aim high and the bullet shot harmlessly into the air.

Tom took the opportunity to step forward deliver an uppercut that knocked the man out. As Albert hit the dirt, Tom dusted himself off and picked up his pouch of winnings.

He looked up at the Kid. "I'm surprised you interfered like that."

The Kid shrugged. "The horse did it."

They were interrupted by the sound of the door of the Sheriff's Office slamming open. "Tomas Jefferson Dun!" shouted Sheriff Jim Dale.

Tom rolled his eyes at the way the Sheriff had pronounced his name, putting so much emphasis on the Mexican way of saying it. He turned. "It's just Tom! You know that, Dale."

Dale stood in the open doorway of his office with a shotgun in his hands. He was a middle-aged man with a thick mustache and the confident demeanor that came from his years of experience training under the retired Sheriff Paul. He stormed toward Tom, his deputy following closely behind him with a rifle at the ready.

"What the hell're you doing starting a fight right outside my door?" Dale asked, his voice flabbergasted. "Right in front of your wanted poster, even?"

"I didn't start no fight," Tom insisted. He pointed at the fallen forms of Albert and Denny. "I was being robbed! That man drew on me and that man tried to help him."

Sheriff Dale chuckled. "They were robbing you? Right. What'd you do? Cheat them at cards?"

Tom frowned. "I cheated nobody, Dale. It was just a friendly game."

"I saw it, Uncle Dale, sir!" said the boy that Tom had taken the coal from earlier. "Those men did start the fight."

Dale glanced at the child, then gazed down the street at all the onlookers that had come out from their cover. He raised his voice. "Anyone see anything different?" There were a few noncommittal head shakes, but no one spoke up. He turned back to face Tom. "I should arrest you right now."

"What for?" Tom protested. "I didn't shoot nobody. I didn't rob nobody. You can't even get me for being drunk in the streets." He took a few steps toward the Sheriff and opened his mouth. "Here! Smell my breath."

The Sheriff raised a disgusted hand and called out to his deputy. "Ted, go get the Doc. These men need seein' to."

Tom feigned offense. "Ain't you going to ask me if I want you to arrest these men?"

"There's only two reasons I don't haul you in right now," Dale said, raising two fingers. "First, your momma makes the best pie in town and I know she won't forgive me. Second, your tiny bounty ain't worth my time."

"Two reasons?" Tom said. "I'm impressed, Sheriff. I didn't know you could count that high." At Dale's enraged scowl, he raised his hands and added, "Just a joke. I wasn't gonna ask you to haul them in. I think they've learned their lesson."

Dale spat. "Get out of my sight, Tom. Next time you make a ruckus in my town I will arrest you. And that's a promise."

"Understood," Tom replied. He walked over and picked up his new hat. He smacked the dust off of it, frowning at the way it clung to the felt.

"And that goes for your friends too," Dale added. "You tell 'em I said it!"

Tom raised a hand in acknowledgement and headed across the street and into Hank's Saloon.

Thank you for reading the preview.

Please join us for status updates and fun.

Like us on Facebook at the Trevor H. Cooley page:
https://www.facebook.com/EyeOfTheMoonrat

Follow on Twitter @Edgewriter

Or on our website http://trevorhcooley.com/

Please spread the word. The Bowl of Souls needs your help.